Praise for

Going Through the Notions

"A quaint little village, quirky characters, and a crafty
killer—I loved it!"

—Laura Childs, *New York Times* bestselling author of
Sweet Tea Revenge

"Cate Price's *Going Through the Notions* has everything I
read cozy mysteries for—a terrific setting, a smart plot, and
well-rounded, clever characters. Lucky us—it's the first in
an all-new series (Deadly Notions)—and I can't wait for the
next one! Cate Price is a natural-born storyteller."

—Mariah Stewart, *New York Times* bestselling author of
The Long Way Home

"A fun and fast-paced debut filled with eccentric characters,
quirky humor, and small-town drama."

—Ali Brandon, national bestselling author of
A Novel Way to Die

Going Through the Notions

Cate Price

BERKLEY PRIME CRIME, NEW YORK

THE BERKLEY PUBLISHING GROUP
Published by the Penguin Group
Penguin Group (USA)
375 Hudson Street, New York, New York 10014, USA

USA | Canada | UK | Ireland | Australia | New Zealand | India | South Africa | China

Penguin Books Ltd., Registered Offices: 80 Strand, London WC2R 0RL, England
For more information about the Penguin Group, visit penguin.com.

GOING THROUGH THE NOTIONS

A Berkley Prime Crime Book / published by arrangement with the author

Berkley Prime Crime Books are published by The Berkley Publishing Group.
BERKLEY® PRIME CRIME and the PRIME CRIME logo are trademarks of
Penguin Group (USA).

For information, address: The Berkley Publishing Group,
a division of Penguin Group (USA).
375 Hudson Street, New York, New York 10014.

ISBN: 978-0-425-25879-8

PUBLISHING HISTORY
Berkley Prime Crime mass-market edition / September 2013

PRINTED IN THE UNITED STATES OF AMERICA

10 9 8 7 6 5 4 3 2 1

Cover illustration by Ben Perini.
Cover logo *Pin* copyright © Roman Sotola and *Floral Pattern* © LDesign.
Cover design by Diana Kolsky.
Interior text design by Laura K. Corless.

ALWAYS LEARNING   PEARSON

For Jackie

Acknowledgments

This book is dedicated to the two great "Jackies" in my life.

The first is my funny, wonderful daughter, Jackie Buden, who always cheers me on, not just in writing, but in all things. The second is my lovely editor, Jackie Cantor, who provided the guidelines for the Deadly Notions Mysteries. What a gift you are to a first-time author with your intoxicating enthusiasm for my work and your gentle, clever guidance. I feel so very lucky.

Thank you to my original agent at BookEnds, LLC, Lauren Ruth, who pulled me out of the slush pile, and now to the fabulous Jessica Alvarez for your warm professionalism.

Terri Brisbin and Mariah Stewart gave invaluable advice on the publishing business in the beginning and I will be forever grateful. For reading the first book in this series and providing such great quotes, a massive thank-you to Ali Brandon, Laura Childs, and again, Mariah Stewart.

There are so many friends in the Valley Forge Romance Writers who have helped me with my writing over the years. I can't name you all, but thank you from the bottom of my heart. Special thanks in regard to this particular book go to Adele Downs, Carla Kempert, and Ann LaBar Russek.

To Debra Lew Harder, wise critique partner and treasured friend, thank you for everything.

For insights into the life of a teacher, gratitude to Gina Danna, Ashlyn Macnamara, Melissa Macfie, Carla Kempert, and Carla's mom, Darlene. I'd also like to give a shout-out to another writing group that is very dear to my heart—the Lalalas!

For unwavering support and belief in me, even as I sometimes doubted myself, mega thanks to Jay DiSanto, Patti Mazzola, Maria McCouch, Owen Pritchard, and Debi Wargo. Guys, the drinks are on me.

And finally, to the person who first instilled in me a love of reading, and introduced me to so many of my all-time favorite authors—thanks, Mum.

Chapter One

In my twenties, I fell madly in love with an electric blue pair of Manolo Blahniks in Bloomingdale's front window. In my thirties, I lusted after bare-chested runners with washboard stomachs and golden biceps sweating in Central Park. In my forties, all I really yearned for was a day off with a good book.

Now in my late fifties, I've finally discovered my true passion in life. It's for my store, a haven of all kinds of sewing notions and antiques named Sometimes a Great Notion. What can I say? I've always had a thing for Paul Newman, too.

My heart was currently thumping in anticipation of acquiring an antique dollhouse I'd spotted in the pre-bidding walk-through prior to the auction in Sheepville tonight. My dear husband, Joe, the recipient of some of that aforementioned lust over the years, was driving in his usual careful, and in my opinion, rather pedantic manner.

"Step on it, Joe, or we'll never get there!"

"Easy, Daisy. We'll make it in plenty of time."

I leaned out of the window of our Subaru station wagon

into the balmy June evening air, willing the last mile of
country road to pass by as quickly as possible.

Not only had the dollhouse caught my eye, but there was a
beautiful Singer Featherweight up for bid, a small vintage sewing machine prized by quilters. Either one would look wonderful in the window of the shop. There were plenty of other
treasures to be had, too—tins of Bakelite buttons, several boxes
of musty, but restorable tablecloths, glass doorknobs salvaged
from century-old buildings, and some wooden darning eggs.

Gravel crunched under the car's tires as we pulled into
the parking lot at twenty minutes to seven. Plenty of time
to register and get my bidder's number before the evening's
events started. As usual, Joe was right.

Angus Backstead, the auctioneer, and his wife lived in a
pristine white stucco three-story farmhouse across from the
auction building. A Pennsylvania Dutch hex sign featuring
a circle of blue and red flowers and sheaves of wheat adorned
the front of the house. Baskets of overflowing pink and white
impatiens hanging on the powder blue painted porch swung
gently in the breeze.

A good crowd had already gathered. It would be a hum-
dinger of an auction tonight.

I loved the auction. It was almost like going to the
theater—the drama, the tragedy, and sometimes the comedy,
like when Sally McIntire forgot she left her red string bikini
underwear in the drawer of a nightstand she'd consigned,
and the winning bidder, inspecting his purchase, held it aloft
for everyone to see.

I hopped out of the car before it had barely stopped moving. I spotted my good friend, Martha Bristol, as well as
several of the other regulars. Various pieces of farm equipment, miscellaneous furniture, and box lots sat on the tar-
mac, ready to be auctioned off first before we went inside.

But what were all the police cars doing here?

The door to the low-slung building opened, and I gasped
as I saw Angus being led out in handcuffs. His face,

normally ruddy from a lifetime of outdoor labor and his beloved Irish whiskey, was deathly pale. He spotted Joe and me standing at the edge of the crowd.

"I didn't do it!" he cried as a policeman maneuvered him into a car. A little too forcefully, as Angus banged his snowy white head on the top of the door frame.

"Hey! Be careful with him," I shouted. The door slammed shut as Angus cried out to us one last time. "Help me, Daisy!"

But it was too late. The cruiser was already pulling away.

Joe laid a steadying hand on my arm. It was always that way between us. Joe, calm and solid as a rock, and me, impulsive and quick to react.

"What the hell's going on?" I demanded as Martha sailed up to us. She was an imposing sight in a purple, green, and yellow floral summer dress, belted tightly under her large bosom. Her long legs looked even longer in strappy yellow sandals, and her glorious mane of red hair was bundled up into a precarious knot. Kind of like a vintage Barbie on steroids. Martha was my age, but she wasn't leaving her youth behind without a fight.

"Jimmy Kratz was found bludgeoned to death in the barn behind his house this morning," she announced.

"What?"

Jimmy was one of the auction regulars, too. He owned a company called CleanUp and CloseOut. When people needed their basements cleaned out, or even a whole house, they called Jimmy. Some of it was pure trash, some of it he used himself, and some of the scrap metal he took to the local salvage yard. And some of the better stuff he sold at auction and scratched out a living that way.

"Well, why on earth do they think Angus had anything to do with it?" I asked.

"Jimmy stole a collection of fancy fountain pens that were due to be sold tonight. They're saying they were worth tens of thousands of dollars."

"Yeah, nowt like the usual rubbish." Cyril Mackey, the

English curmudgeon who ran the salvage yard, sidled up alongside us. He nodded to Joe, but ignored Martha and me. As usual, he wore a flat cap and a tweed jacket that had seen better days. He was a Yorkshireman of indeterminate age and background, and as tough as the heather clinging to the moors in a bitter gale blowing off the Pennines.

Martha sniffed at the sight of Cyril. "Apparently the physical evidence points to Angus as the culprit. His fingerprints are all over the murder weapon—a heavy barn beam."

"They were drinking together in the pub last night," Cyril continued, addressing Joe. "You know how Angus likes to shoot his bloody mouth off. Everyone heard him crowing about those damn pens. He were right proud of the fact that he had summat decent to sell for once."

Joe nodded at him. "Go on."

"He had one beer and one whiskey too many, so Jimmy took his keys and drove him home. The keys to the auction house were also on that key ring, which is how the coppers think Jimmy managed to pinch the stuff."

Martha glared at Cyril. "As I was *saying*, in the morning, Angus must have noticed the pens were missing. He realized Jimmy had the keys and went over to his house. There was some sort of argument, and he hit him with the beam."

"Angus couldn't have lifted something like that," I said. "He's in his early sixties, for God's sake. Joe, how much do you think a barn beam would weigh?"

"Not sure. Probably well over a hundred pounds. Maybe one-fifty."

"You ever see him haul some of this merchandise around?" Cyril spat a stream of tobacco juice onto the parking lot, perilously close to Martha's yellow sandals. "Steamer trunks, mahogany furniture, boxes of books? The man's still as strong as an ox."

"Oh my God, here comes poor Betty." Martha grabbed my arm as we saw Angus's wife being helped out of the auction building.

Betty had recently had hip surgery, and was still walking with a slow, painful gait. While Martha stayed behind as roving reporter on the scene, Joe and I brought Betty over to the house. Joe rummaged around in the kitchen and made tea while I got her settled in an armchair in the living room, propped up with some cushions.

"He didn't do it, Daisy. No matter what they're saying." Betty murmured her thanks as Joe gave her a cup of tea.

"Of course he didn't." I sat down on a faded cotton love seat with a cabbage rose design.

"Angus was too drunk for me and Jimmy to get him indoors, so we left him in the glider out on the porch. The big oaf was snoring like to wake the dead. I heard him come in later this morning and take a shower. My neighbor took me shopping, but I didn't see him or speak to him before I left. I was still too mad."

Shopping to calm down. I could appreciate that. Retail therapy always worked for me.

"So where are these pens? Do the police have them?"

"No, they're gone. The police searched Jimmy's place, the barn, the auction building. They even went through everything in the house, too. *Everything.* It was so embarrassing."

A tear trickled down her wrinkled cheek. Joe handed her a box of tissues from the coffee table.

Angus and Betty had befriended us when we first bought a house in Millbury, a neighboring village about five miles away. Betty and I made a joke of the fact that while she was named Betty Backstead by marriage, I'd never quite been able to call myself Daisy Daly. I'd kept my maiden name of Buchanan. And yes, in case you're wondering, my sainted mother was a huge F. Scott Fitzgerald fan.

"You know how Angus carries on when he's been drinking," she said. "He talks your ear off. Anyone in that pub could have had the idea to steal them. I'm not even sure Jimmy did it."

"But what does Angus say?"

"He can't remember anything past leaving the bar. He can't remember how he got home." She took a sip of tea. "It's the drinking, Daisy. It's been getting bad lately. He has blackouts. Loses whole chunks of time. I've begged him to get help, but he wouldn't listen. And now this . . ."

She blew her nose again. "He forgets things all the time. He even forgets where he's going. I do the driving now or we'd end up in Pittsburgh."

Twenty minutes later, after straightening up the house, Joe and I took our leave of Betty. I promised to stop by the next day.

Joe and I were both silent as we pulled out of the lot and back onto Sheepville Pike. I stared out of the car window at the rolling road, flanked by trees and fields on either side. We passed the riding stable, The Paddocks, with its white corrugated metal buildings, horse trailers, and red barn with grassy bank leading up to the main door. A split rail wooden fence stretched the length of the property, and a red cart wheel was propped up at the entrance.

Past fields filled with bright green rows of ripening cornstalks, the Wet Hen pottery studio, and the Christmas tree farm. Past grand old homes faced with fieldstone, and tall Victorians with arched windows and narrow porch columns.

But I never could stay quiet for long.

"This whole thing doesn't make sense, Joe. I can see that Angus would be mad at Jimmy for stealing the pens, but why kill him? Why not just take the pens and go on home?"

"Well, maybe he didn't mean to kill him," Joe said as he turned onto River Road. "Maybe he hit him in a rage, and hit him a bit too hard. Angus doesn't know his own strength sometimes."

"And what would Jimmy do with a bunch of fountain pens?"

"Sell them?"

"Yeah, but that's not the kind of circles Jimmy moves in," I said. "If you were looking to buy a Harley-Davidson motorcycle engine or a box of washing machine parts, he's your man. This is way out of his league. Or was, I should say."

Trees seemed to meet above us in a loosely woven canopy that dappled the road with fading sunlight. Once in a while I caught a glimpse of the canal and the Delaware River beyond. Near a low stone bridge down on Grist Mill Road, a sign advertised the 4-H Fair coming in August.

Joe took a right to head into our tiny village of Millbury, Pennsylvania, a pretty cluster of nineteenth-century shops and homes that time had almost forgotten.

"And if they were that valuable, why not put them up for auction in Philadelphia instead? Maybe Jimmy was stealing them for someone else."

Joe let me ramble on with my musings until we arrived home, a Greek Revival–style house right on Main Street.

"I tell you what, Joe. I know Angus is innocent, and I'm going to do whatever it takes to prove it."

The next morning, Betty called, crying. Angus had been denied bail, apparently because of his confused mental state and the potential to be a danger to others, as well as himself.

I'd been looking forward all week to a day off with Joe. Perhaps we'd take a trip out to the Amish country for more quilts for the store, or sip a Bloody Mary at a lazy brunch at the Bridgewater Inn. But this was more important. I kissed Joe good-bye, hopped in the Subaru, and headed for Sheepville.

I couldn't help the usual flush of pride at seeing Sometimes a Great Notion as I drove past. I'd be changing the front window display tomorrow as I did every Monday to keep things fresh. There were new treasures from an estate sale that I couldn't wait to unpack.

My store was situated in what used to be a Victorian home right on Main Street. It was painted a dark sage, with

beetroot and cream accentuating the windows, spindles, and
gingerbread trim. A black porch with obsolete gaslights
hanging overhead was accessible from either end by three
steps. Next to the front door sat an iron cauldron filled with
pink geraniums and lime green leafy coleus.

Past the bicycle shop and Sweet Mabel's, the ice cream
parlor. Both stores did a nice trade from bicyclists using the
canal towpath alongside the river. Many of the storefronts
were empty now, however, because of the difficult local
economy. The video store had closed, as well as the jeweler's
and a real estate office. A few of us remained, and we supported one another as much as we could.

Our quaint village didn't have a real supermarket, only
a historic post office with a convenience store attached. Or
even a real restaurant for that matter. There was the Last
Stop Diner, housed in an old trolley car, but it closed at
3 p.m. Residents had to go to Sheepville for the bank, library,
hardware and liquor stores, and any major shopping.

I headed up Grist Mill and turned right onto River Road.
Trees lush with summer growth blocked the view of homes
that were visible through bare branches in winter. Here and
there was a hint of a venerable stone mansion, or a gorgeous
Queen Anne, proudly decked out in its authentic historic
colors. At some points the road, canal, and river ran close
together, and sometimes the twisting two-lane road with its
rusted metal barrier veered away. Yellow traffic signs for
DEER CROSSING, SLIPPERY WINTER CONDITIONS, and SHARP
CURVES flashed by in quick succession.

When I pulled up in front of the Backsteads', Betty was
waiting for me on the porch. She sat stiffly at attention,
holding her pocketbook on her lap with both hands. I helped
her into my car, and we made the thirty-minute drive south
on Sheepville Pike to the County Correctional Facility.

The lobby officer checked to see if we were both on the
approved visiting list. Thank God Angus had the presence
of mind to add me, too. We were asked to show some photo

identification, and I registered my car's year, make, model, and license number. Visitors weren't allowed to bring any valuables in, only identification and keys, so I went back outside and locked our pocketbooks in the trunk of the car. Betty and I were searched with drug detection equipment and asked to remove our shoes. By the end of this process, I could feel her trembling next to me as we sat and waited to be called.

Finally they brought us to a cramped room filled with round plastic tables and chairs. We were instructed that we could embrace Angus at the beginning and end, but apart from that, no physical contact was allowed. If we left our seats for any reason, the visit would be terminated.

A few minutes later, Angus shuffled in. His white hair was sticking up in places, and he still looked unnaturally pale. The jovial mountain of a man I cherished suddenly looked much older, and more than a little bewildered.

Betty clung to him, sobbing, and he patted her back awkwardly.

"Hush now, Betty. Don't carry on so."

He looked over his wife's head at me. "Hullo, Brat."

"Hi, Angus." I summoned up a smile.

He always used to tease me that I was a fancy city girl because I'd lived in New York for most of my life. That I'd be afraid of some good old country dirt when we jumped into his truck and went off on our picking adventures together.

I just laughed. Heck, I'd taught in the city's public school system, had been assigned to a teaching position in Harlem in the early days, and even stared down the barrel of a gun once. Dust, cobwebs, or even a spider or two wouldn't be enough to put me off.

Angus and I found we were kindred spirits, bonded in the thrill of the hunt, as we chased down hidden treasures hoarded away in the barns, attics, closets, and basements of Eastern Pennsylvania. Joe, who preferred to stay home and putter in the garden or tinker with an old car, teased me that I had a new boyfriend. But the truth was Angus had become the protective big brother I'd never had.

Finally the guard motioned that the Backsteads needed to break apart, and we sat down on the hard seats.

"How are you doing, Angus?" I asked.

"Well, I'm stuck here in the slammer, but apart from that, I'm okay." He smiled ruefully. "I do have a hell of a head-ache, though."

I wanted to say, it's probably from the gallon of whiskey you poured down your throat, but I didn't. He must have drunk an awful lot to still be in bad shape this morning, some thirty-six hours later.

He leaned forward, eyes intent on me.

"I didn't do it, Daisy. I didn't kill Jimmy."

"I know you didn't. But what the heck happened on Friday night?"

"I don't remember. I mean, I was there at the pub with him, knocking back a few, and next thing I knew, I woke up on our porch, feeling like the rear end of a camel. But the rest is a little fuzzy."

It was hard to hear above the people at neighboring tables, all talking at once. The echoes of myriad conversations bounced around the confines of the crowded room.

Angus winced as he grabbed the seat to pull his chair closer.

"What's the matter with your hands?"

He turned his massive palms up to me and I gasped. They were chock-full of splinters, some deeply embedded, and turning his work-roughened skin an angry red.

Chapter Two

✱

"How did they get like this, Angus?" I asked, my heart racing.

He peered closer at his hands. "Damned if I know. I can't see a thing without my reading glasses. They hurt like the devil, though."

His faded blue eyes brightened. "Daisy, you should have seen those pens. They were beautiful. Really something else."

Suddenly he started his familiar rapid-fire auctioneer chant. Loudly.

"One, one thousand, one, now two, two thousand, will you give me two, over in the corner, do I hear ten, ten thousand, yes, I have ten, now do I have—"

"Angus!" I fought back a moment of panic. What the hell was the matter with him? People were staring at us, some of them chuckling softly.

"Listen to me. Did you pick up a barn beam at Jimmy's?" I held my breath while he frowned, staring off into space for what seemed like at least two minutes, and then his expression finally cleared.

"Well, yes, it was right in the doorway of the barn. I didn't want anyone to trip over it."

In spite of the dire situation, I had to smile. Even dead drunk, Angus was still thinking of the safety of others.

"Ah, *now* it's coming back to me," he said. "We stopped at his place before we came home. Went out to the barn for one last nightcap. Like I needed another one. Jimmy keeps a fridge full of beer out there."

"Did you go back to Jimmy's again the next morning when you noticed the pens missing?"

"No! I didn't even realize they were stolen until the cops showed up. I assumed they were still locked up the way I left them on Friday. Right, Betty?"

Betty bit her lip, but didn't answer.

"What?"

"Well, you have been a bit forgetful lately, Angus."

"I am not, damn it. I—" He slapped a hand on the plastic table, and quickly sucked in a breath, wincing again.

I stood up and addressed the guard at the doorway. "Excuse me, please. This man needs medical attention." When required, I could still turn on my schoolteacher voice. If it worked on a room full of hormone-driven teenagers, it should work like a charm on one bored rural cop. "Immediately, if not sooner."

The man nodded, unimpressed. "We'll take care of it after the visit. Now sit down, ma'am, or I'll have to ask you to leave."

I glared at him. One of the desirable qualities in a teacher that I unfortunately lacked was an adequate supply of patience.

"Ma'am? Sit down."

I'd have to watch myself or I'd be stuck in the clink with Angus.

I gritted my teeth and sat back down on the plastic seat

with a thump. "Take us through yesterday morning, Angus," I said. "Everything you did."

"Well, when I woke up on the porch, I went in the house and took a shower. Betty had gone shopping, so I fed the cat and read the paper. Then I didn't feel so good, so I lay down again. I think I must have missed the pre-auction walk-through."

Betty nodded in weary agreement.

"Next thing I knew, the cops were banging on the door."

The lights flickered too soon, signaling the end of the half hour, and we had to leave. I promised to drive Betty back again on Wednesday, the next permitted visiting day for his section of the prison.

Betty was silent until we got back in the car.

"I don't want to go back to that place ever again, Daisy."

"What do you mean? What about Angus?"

"You'll still visit him, won't you?" She stared at me with pleading eyes. "It's just too awful. I can't bear it."

I blew out a breath as I started the engine. Betty's defeatist attitude was not going to help her husband one iota. But I needed to keep in mind she was older than me and still frail from her recent surgery. "He's going to be okay, Betty. He'll be home before you know it, getting under your feet and annoying you like always."

That brought a small smile.

I cranked down the window as we passed the lavender farm, and I breathed in deeply, hoping the sweet, yet spicy scent would help relax the tightness in my neck. Long purple rows stretched up from the side of the road toward the little stone shop where they sold soaps, lotions, and dried bunches of the pungent herb.

Angus and I used to crack each other up as we drove through the countryside on our travels. He'd say, "How come you're called Daisy, but you don't wear any Daisy Dukes?"

"Ha, ha, *well done*, Angus. Or should that be medium rare, Burger Boy?"

He'd tease me about getting my fancy clothes messed up as we clambered over piles of junk or walked through muddy fields at an outdoor flea market. I ignored him, concentrating on looking for diamonds in the rough, although I had relaxed my wardrobe somewhat over the past year. While he treated his wife in the most old-fashioned way, acting as the man of the house, oddly enough he expected me to hold my own and not act "like a girl" at all. Sink or swim was his mantra as he mentored me in the fine art of haggling for the best deals.

Now I was addicted to auctions, flea markets, and yard sales. It seemed as though my car braked automatically when it saw the signs. I'd even been known to pick up stuff off the side of the road. It was amazing what people threw out. One man's trash is another's treasure, as they say.

Betty and I were quiet for a few moments until suddenly I thought of something.

"Hey, Betty, if Jimmy drove Angus home on Friday night, isn't your truck still at the pub?"

"No, Jimmy drove it here, and then he walked the rest of the way home."

"That's strange. You'd think he wouldn't be in good enough shape to walk that far."

"He said he needed to clear his head. One of his friends had given him a ride to the pub in the first place."

"But Jimmy still kept the keys, though, right?"

Betty shrugged. "I suppose he held on to them so Angus wouldn't be tempted to drive."

"And to get into the auction building." I gasped. "Wait a minute. I know why he walked. If he took the truck, you would have heard when he drove off. This way, he could double back and make a silent getaway afterwards with the loot." I felt a rising sense of excitement. "And if Jimmy still had the keys, Angus *couldn't* have driven back to his place the next morning."

She shook her head. "There's a spare set hanging in the kitchen."

"Oh." Deflated, I fell silent, too.

We passed the turnoff to Burning Barn Road, which led to an artists' colony where a semifamous watercolor painter taught classes. On either side of us, fields of crops bordered with split rail fences stretched as far as they could until dense forests barred their progress. With some of these rural towns, there was no way to get there from here other than to go the long way around.

Betty and I had lunch together in Sheepville, and then I brought her home. She gave me Angus's eyeglasses and a couple more things he'd requested. I promised I'd call her after I saw him again.

I made a stop at the town's supermarket to pick up some essentials. In the winter I stocked up on multiples of paper towels, laundry detergent, toilet paper, and yes, several bottles of wine, like a crazed domesticated squirrel. River Road wasn't much fun in deep snow and treacherous black ice. During the summer, Joe and I enjoyed a bounty of vegetables from our garden. There was a farm stand close by, and I only needed to make the trip once a week.

About half a mile down Sheepville Pike, I passed Jimmy's place. I wasn't quite sure where he lived, but I recognized the battered gray Chevy pickup truck with the magnetic signs on its sides for CleanUp and CloseOut.

A long gravel driveway led up to a white Colonial farmhouse, with its adjacent barn and henhouses. It was set a good distance back from the road, surrounded by open pasture, with one large oak tree in front. Dust kicked up around my car as I turned in, sincerely hoping that Jimmy's wife didn't shoot strangers on sight.

The bed of his truck was still stuffed with all kinds of junk—broken kitchen chairs, stained mattresses, and cardboard boxes. The bumper was splattered with stickers such as I LOVE MY COUNTRY, BUT FEAR MY GOVERNMENT, and GUT SALMON? A wooden dresser caught my eye until I got closer and saw that the legs were broken off, and there was an ugly gash in the side.

Jimmy's house was the same way. From the road it looked all right, but up close it was pretty dilapidated. The white stucco over stone was missing in places, and green asphalt shingles were peeling up where the angles of roof met. A wide porch around the front of the house held some webbed deck chairs and a lumpy harvest gold and green brocade couch.

Jimmy's wife appeared as I pulled up next to the barn and got out of the car. Her body was that of a skinny sixteen-year-old, and her hair was light brown and baby fine. She wore a faded summer shift, and her feet were bare in the dust.

"Hi, Reenie."

Her real name was Noreen, but everyone called her Reenie.

"What are you doing here, Mrs. Buchanan?"

Two small children with grubby faces ran up and clung to her side. They wore the same wary look as their mother.

"Please. Call me Daisy. I—um—stopped to see how you were doing. I'm so sorry about Jimmy."

"Yeah, thanks."

There was an awkward silence.

"Well, I have to finish the afternoon milking," Reenie said.

"I don't mean to intrude. I just thought that—"

"You can come with me if you'd like to visit."

"Okay."

I followed her into the barn, which was in the same sad state of disrepair as the house. I glanced around quickly, but there was no sign of blood on the ground, for which I was truly thankful.

She washed her hands and sat down next to a black and white Holstein, which was standing on a concrete slab in the milking parlor. From another bucket of water, she washed and dried the udder carefully. She set a stainless steel pail underneath the cow, and bumped her fist gently against it. I guessed she was imitating the action of a calf coming to suckle against its mother.

"Do *you* think Angus did it, Reenie?" I asked quietly.

She shrugged. "Who knows? Men can do some pretty bad things when they're drunk and angry."

Reenie seemed to relax as she warmed to her task, taking the teats in both hands from opposite corners of the udder, producing a thin squirt, and working in a sure rhythm until the flow became more constant. The cow stood placidly chewing on grain, surveying me with calm brown eyes. I didn't think I'd have been so content to have someone pulling on my nipples like that.

"It doesn't hurt them," she said as if reading my mind. "If she wasn't milked, she'd be swollen and sore. They actually come up to the barn themselves at milking time."

I stood near the head of the cow, not at its bony rear end. I might be a city girl, but I knew enough to stay out of range of a swift kick.

"Jimmy and Angus came out here for a nightcap," Reenie said. "I'd had enough of waiting up for him by that time, so I went to bed. How they ever made it to Angus's house, I don't know. They were stumbling drunk. Jimmy must have slept in the barn when he came home. He often did that when he tied one on."

Her skin was almost translucent, and faintly mottled. She wasn't much older than my daughter, but her face had aged beyond her time, and her teeth were tobacco-stained. The only parts of Reenie that looked strong were her thickly veined forearms and hands.

"Did Angus come back here the next day?" I asked. "Were they arguing? Did you see anything at all?"

Her eyes shifted away from me, and back down at the bucket. "I had the air-conditioning on. That window unit is real noisy so I didn't hear a thing. Only thing I seen was

Jimmy lying on the ground in the morning when I came out to milk the cows." Her hand fisted against her mouth as she squeezed her eyes shut.

I wanted to hug her, but dealing with Reenie was like approaching a fawn in the forest. I sensed that there was something she was hiding, something she could tell me, if only I could muster my meager supply of patience.

I glanced at the barn beam sitting near the doorway of the barn. A pile of them was stacked against the wall. I wandered over to take a closer look.

"Jimmy was planning on fixing some of the rotted parts of the roof," Reenie said.

I bent down and tried to lift the end of one, but could barely budge it an inch. "He must have been pretty strong."

"No one knows that better than me. Who's going to fix this place now?" She stared up at the ceiling in despair. Sunlight slanted through the gaps in the wooden wall, and dust motes danced in the air around her head.

"Angus was going to help with the repairs. He and Jimmy moved the wood in here."

I drew in a deep breath. "So Angus's fingerprints are probably on every single beam in this place?"

She nodded.

"Did you tell the police that?"

"They didn't ask."

I stifled a heavy sigh. And why hadn't Angus thought to tell me that himself? Yes, his fingerprints would still be on the "murder weapon," but it painted a much better picture that he'd handled all the beams anyway while helping Jimmy with the construction.

Reenie wiped her brow with the back of her hand. "I don't know how I'll pay the mortgage. Jimmy didn't have any life insurance. I make a little money from selling the milk and fresh eggs from the chickens, but it's not enough to live on."

My heart went out to her. She had no money, her husband was a drunk, and now he was dead, leaving her with two young children to care for on her own. I decided right then and there that I'd find a way to help.

She stood up and carefully placed the pail of milk to one side. She washed and dried the cow's udder again and let her out of the stanchion and back into the field.

I didn't want to outstay my welcome, plus I had groceries sitting in the car. It didn't feel too hot outside today, but I didn't want to push my luck.

"Well, I'd better get going."

"Hold on, Daisy. I have something for you."

She dashed over to the henhouse and came back a minute later with a wooden basket full of brown speckled eggs.

"Oh, that's very nice of you, Reenie, but I couldn't take these. Or at least let me pay you for them."

She held up a hand.

"You're the only person in this whole freaking town who's bothered to stop by and see how I'm doing. You're a real nice lady. Not like the rest of those snobs."

I swallowed a prickle of guilt. My motive for coming wasn't so pure. Yes, I wanted to make sure she was okay, but I was also on the lookout for any clues that could help me clear Angus.

I saw her gaze flicker to the bags stashed in the backseat of the station wagon.

"Look, I'm going to visit Betty again tomorrow," I said. "Can I pick you up something—is there anything you need?"

She shook her head. "You don't have to do that."

I opened my car door. The children appeared again as if by magic and peered at me from behind their mother, clutching at her thin dress.

Reenie ran her hand through her hair, making it stick up like tufts of thistledown.

"Actually, yeah, now that I think about it, I could use a carton of Marlboros and a six of Coors Light."

I hoped I managed to keep my expression neutral. "Okay. Anything else? Anything for the kids?"

"Nah, they're fine."

As I pulled out of the driveway, my mind was already making a list for them anyway—some coloring books, crayons, games, and some fresh fruit and cereal.

The car hit a pothole and I groaned, hoping I hadn't messed up the alignment.

I thought of how handy Joe was at our house, and for the umpteenth time in my life, of how lucky I was. Sometimes he didn't say much, but his calm and reassuring presence was enough. I treasured him as carefully as any precious antique, which, he would laughingly say, he *was* one now.

The pale blue sky over the deserted country road was streaked with gray clouds tinged with pink, as if they were lit from above with a rose-colored spotlight. Like one of those Renaissance paintings with angels dancing in the heavens.

On the outer edge of the village of Millbury, I drove by the dead-end road leading to Cyril Mackey's salvage yard with its eclectic collection of rusty garden gates, birdbaths, old Coca-Cola machines, and bicycles in various states of disrepair. A sign on the building in the back that was his office and also supposedly his home said, KEEP OUT. I thought it might be worthwhile to stop and chat with Cyril the next time he was open.

A few minutes later, I pulled up in front of our lovingly restored 1842 Greek Revival home with black shutters flanking its many windows. Six fluted Doric columns supported the triangular-shaped pedimented gable, and provided a grand porch that spanned the width of the house.

In the front yard, masses of yellow coreopsis, pink phlox, Jacob's ladder, and purple Russian sage grew in glorious profusion behind a classic white picket fence.

We'd purchased the house almost thirty years ago for a vacation getaway. It had been a stretch at the time, but I was careful with our budget. We worked on it every chance we got, and rented it out for about ten years. When Joe, sick of the rat race, convinced me to take early retirement from teaching last year, we were able to pay off what was left of the mortgage.

It seemed as soon as one thing was fixed, though, something else broke. Like playing a never-ending game of Whac-A-Mole with a house. Greek Revivals were notorious for roofing problems because of the low pitch of the roof, and Joe always had some kind of project going on.

I grabbed as many bags of groceries as I could carry, opened the front door, and headed into the wide central hall. I sniffed the air appreciatively. One benefit of no restaurant in town, apart from the diner, was that Joe had become an excellent cook, and spoiled me with a gourmet meal every night.

The house was light and airy because of its twelve-foot-high ceilings and the six-over-six double-hung windows, some of them tall enough to literally step through onto the porch. I hurried past the living room with its grand proportions and original millwork, the dining room with its iron-fronted fireplace, and the double parlor divided by pocket doors.

In the cherry-paneled library was the old steamer trunk that we used as a coffee table. Joe and I had gone to the auction one night, and on impulse I placed a bid. The metal trunk turned out to be stuffed with all sorts of beads, fabrics, hand-embroidered bed and table linens, and sewing notions. It was the inspiration for the store.

I found Joe in the kitchen, which was the only part of the house we hadn't renovated yet.

"Hello, my hero. Smells amazing in here. What are you making?"

Joe took the bags, set them down on the scarred butcher block table, and enfolded me in his big arms. I allowed myself a few moments to breathe, enjoying the feel of his body against mine before I peered over his shoulder.

"Oh, boy, crab cakes. My favorite."

"Together with a salad of greens and herbs tossed with a champagne vinaigrette and a saffron rice pilaf. Will that please the lady?"

"Most definitely." I grinned at him.

He still looked good. To me anyway. Of course, his hair had turned gray a few years ago, he was a little thicker around the middle, and he had his share of physical ailments, but he'd always been a well-built guy. Not bad for sixty-three. Reluctantly, I let go of him as he moved over to the stove to turn the heat down under the pan.

Joe went out to the car for the rest of the groceries, while I stocked the refrigerator and put the dry goods in the walk-in pantry. The delicate perfume of roses on the trellis drifted in through the kitchen window.

It was such a lovely evening that we decided to eat outside. Joe carried our dinner plates, and I brought a bottle of wine and two glasses.

On the flagstone patio, mismatched wicker chairs painted a pastel green sat around a long iron table. Six-inch pots of basil, thyme, and oregano formed a fragrant centerpiece, and wisteria clambering above us on the pergola provided a welcome shade. Orange nasturtiums spilled over the sides of a fluted stone urn in one corner.

I took a bite of my crab cake, murmuring with pleasure at the crisp crust and succulent perfectly seasoned crabmeat. Joe poured the wine, and I filled him in on the day's events as we ate.

"Poor Angus. I keep thinking about him sitting in that jail all alone. Betty was so traumatized she says she's not going back. I guess the visitations will be up to me now."

"He's been a good friend to us, Daisy. Remember the winter when the pipes burst?"

It was only a few years into our home ownership in Millbury. We were in New York, living paycheck to paycheck, and the renters had called in a panic. It was right before the end of the school term, I was knee-deep in grading papers, and Joe couldn't take time away from some critical negotiations as representative for the electricians' union. Joe and I had panicked a little ourselves. How would we handle things long distance, and how would we carry both mortgages if the renters decided to pull up stakes and move out?

Angus was a powerhouse. He'd coordinated everything, even done a lot of the cleanup himself, and saved our home, plus our rental income. He'd also helped Joe with numerous other projects over the years. He always refused to take any monetary compensation, saying the only gift he ever needed was our friendship.

"Does Angus have a good lawyer?" Joe asked as he drizzled vinaigrette dressing over his salad greens.

I watched a fat bumblebee suckle on a yellow hibiscus. "Betty said they're using Warren Zeigler. He's been their family lawyer forever."

"He probably needs a good criminal attorney. I could make some calls if you like." Joe's dark eyes regarded me steadily.

I stared at him, my throat suddenly tight. Even though I had just visited Angus in prison, a surreal experience to say the least, somehow this brought it home to me that the situation *was* real. Desperately real. It wasn't some temporary misunderstanding. Angus wasn't getting out of prison tomorrow or the next day. Heck, it was even possible he could be tried and convicted of a crime he didn't commit.

"I'll talk to Betty. But Joe, I'm really worried about him, regardless. He seems so confused. It's like he was falling apart in front of my eyes."

"Well, he did take a good conk on his head getting into that police car."

"Oh, God, you're right, I'd forgotten about that. But Betty seems to think it's been going on for a while."

"Then I hope it's nothing serious."

I thought of my boisterous linebacker-sized friend, always full of funny stories, with an encyclopedic knowledge of collectibles. Was all that lively intelligence to be lost to a devastating disease that would turn his brain to nothing more than a mass of useless spongy tissue?

Early on Monday morning, before I opened the store, I headed over to the police station in Sheepville. I told the desk sergeant on duty at reception that I'd like to see the detective in charge of the investigation.

"You would, would you?"

"Yes, please."

"You in, Frank?" The sergeant turned to a heavyset man in short shirtsleeves sitting at a desk behind him who was eating thick slabs of French toast, smothered in maple syrup, out of a Styrofoam container.

"Sure." The detective pointed his plastic fork at me. "I know who you are. That lady from the sewing store, right?"

"Yes. I'm Daisy Buchanan. And you are?"

"Detective Ramsbottom," he said, without bothering to get up. He stuffed a piece of sausage into his mouth.

"Your pal Angus isn't doing himself any favors, you know." His speech was muffled. "He can't remember much. His mind seems to have blanked out about whacking Jimmy, too."

I blew out a breath, feeling my blood pressure rocket. "Maybe he's confused because of the bang to his head on the cruiser door. Maybe someone could argue a case for *police brutality*."

He actually had the nerve to roll his eyes at me, and then he smiled, as if trying to be kind. "I know he's your friend, but I also know he done it."

"He did it."

"What?"

"Sorry, I don't mean that *Angus* did it. I mean that you used improper grammar." Hey, I couldn't help it. I was a schoolteacher for most of my life. Old habits die hard.

He licked his fingers one by one, then wiped them on his pants and ambled over to me.

I thanked God for small mercies when he didn't offer to shake my hand.

"Look, Detective, I only stopped in because I wanted to let you know that Angus was helping Jimmy repair the barn. His fingerprints were on every single beam in that place. I'm also positive he didn't go back to Jimmy's the next morning. You have Angus Backstead locked up in jail, and meanwhile the real killer is running around somewhere scot-free."

The detective's wide smile faded. "And I'll let *you* know that your pal Angus is a drunk, has a vicious temper, and it's not the first time he's been in trouble with the law. The investigation is continuing, but *I'm* positive that we have our man. Now if you'll excuse me, I have work to do . . ."

I restrained myself from asking if that included scarfing down more breakfast treats, and made a dignified exit. Time was running short and I raced back to Millbury to open Sometimes a Great Notion. The sky darkened with burgeoning gray clouds. A thunderstorm was threatened on the weather forecast, but I hoped it wouldn't keep the customers away.

Not only had Angus helped with getting the store off the ground by giving me auction merchandise at cost, but he'd worked with Joe to fix the nineteenth-century storefront to accommodate present-day customers. Two big glass display windows jutted out onto the porch—a new addition to the original house.

The main shop was situated in what used to be the front parlor and living room, but the walls had been opened up between to make one space. I used the dining room as an office and prep area, and there was a kitchen and powder room in the back.

I walked in, turned on the stereo, and soon the sounds of 1940s jazz music wafted through the air.

An antique Mennonite star quilt hung on one wall with handwrought iron clamps, and on the facing wall were black and white photographs of Main Street from a hundred years ago, when the road was nothing but dirt. Actually, Millbury didn't look a whole lot different today.

The huge ten-drawer seed counter, manufactured by the Walker Bin Company, was one of my most prized possessions. It had glass-fronted loading bins that pulled down and housed spools of unused French ribbons from the 1920s, a stack of Simplicity and McCall sewing patterns, piles of braided trim, and a collection of tortoiseshell hair combs.

I breathed in the faint familiar scent of lavender and furniture polish as I wandered through the store, gently arranging things.

A Welsh dresser stood with its drawers partially open, displaying vintage fabric remnants, unfinished quilt tops, and dresser scarves. In the center of the room, a collection of wooden crates stacked together were laden with other great finds, including a bolt of Irish linen dress fabric, still with the original label, a feed sack patchwork coverlet, and hand-embroidered place mats and napkins. I ran my fingers through a sea of glass beads in a lithographed tin doily keeper, and hoped these rescued treasures would go to a good home.

I'd barely set the coffeepot on to brew when Martha breezed through the front door, carrying a tray of her famous baked goodies.

"Good God, that doll gives me a funny turn every time I come in," she said, as she always did, referring to my salvaged mannequin in the corner.

"It's not a doll, it's a mannequin," I responded, as I always did.

I'd named her Alice, and she was decked out for the season in a Christian Dior pink brocade dress and jacket, looking a little like Jackie O, with white gloves and an antique parasol on her arm.

Martha set the tray down on top of the counter. "Crème

Brûlée Cheesecake Squares. They're quite delicious, if I do say so myself."

Today, Martha's buttercup yellow linen dress stretched tightly across her bosom, which was fine, because her décolletage still looked pretty good. The problem was it stretched across the rest of her, too.

With her bright red hair, orange lipstick, and crimson fingernails, she looked as though you could stand in front of her and warm your hands on a cold winter's day. The sight of her never failed to cheer me up.

My store had somehow become the hub for news, gossip, a good cup of coffee, and tasty treats. Martha claimed not to gossip, but she was actually my chief source of information. She was also a talented baker, and brought her creations into the store so she wouldn't be tempted to eat them at home. She'd become a widow a few years ago. Some said, rather unkindly, that poor Teddy Bristol had dug his grave with his knife and fork.

The doorbell chimed, and Eleanor Reid stepped lightly into the store. Eleanor was one of my fellow store owners along Main Street. She ran a business called A Stitch Back in Time, where she restored vintage wedding gowns.

"Did you hear the news that Angus was arrested?" she asked us.

"News? News?" Martha placed her hands on her ample hips. "Where have you *been*, woman? That's ancient history by now!"

Eleanor had a wiry flat-chested body, and from a distance she could be mistaken for a little old man. She wore her white hair cropped short, had sharp features, and wore black pants and a black shirt, regardless of the weather or season. For a business that dealt in romance, she was the unlikeliest purveyor, but she was an expert seamstress, and often a customer for my antique buttons, ribbon, and lace.

I told them about my visit with the uncooperative detective.

Martha popped one of the cheesecake squares into her mouth. "Well, that doesn't surprise me. Frank Ramsbottom and Angus Backstead don't get along. They're bitter enemies, in fact, so I'm sure he'll be content to go with the easy solution of pinning the murder charge on our favorite auctioneer."

"Really? Bitter enemies?" I poured three mugs of coffee. "I can't believe someone as friendly and generous as Angus could have any enemies at all."

"Oh, yes. I remember when Angus got in a nasty fight when he was younger. He nearly beat the other guy to a pulp before the fight was stopped. That's probably how come the police already had his fingerprints on file. Right, Eleanor?"

Eleanor shook her head. "I didn't hang around with your crowd. You were in the cheerleader and jock contingent. I was one of the geeks, remember?"

"Oh, this wasn't in high school, although he got in plenty of fights back then, too. This was when Angus must have been in his forties."

I had no idea about Angus's violent side until now. I'd certainly never seen any evidence of it.

"Daisy, it doesn't look good," Martha said, lowering her voice. "Angus was the last person to see Jimmy alive, and his fingerprints are all over the murder weapon. According to Ramsbottom, his big footprints are everywhere in and around that barn. And other than Jimmy's and Reenie's, his are the only strange footprints there."

I bit my lip. Angus did have unusually large feet, and he always wore the same scruffy work boots.

"Betty has to special order his shoes on-line," Eleanor said. "Or rather, she asks me to do it for her, and she pays me when they come in." She wiggled her eyebrows. "You know what they say. Big hands. Big feet. Big—"

The doorbell rang again. Saved by the bell.

Chris Paxson came in, carrying his own mug. He was

the cute thirty-something-year-old guy who owned the bicycle shop.

I gave him coffee, he politely declined Martha's offer of one of her treats, and he wandered over to the back of the store where I'd hung a former post office sign that said MAIL, except I'd crossed it out and written MALE. Underneath sat a rectangular wooden toolbox that Joe filled with small treasures. Everything cost five dollars. Keep it simple for the men, he'd advised me.

The odd thing was that little box did a roaring business all by itself. Men who were hanging around while their wives shopped often poked through it. It was also an excuse for the single men in town to visit. After all, this was where the women congregated.

Currently it held things like an old silver belt buckle, a bag of vintage marbles, a pocket watch, a Victorian glass paperweight that looked like an eyeball, and sharpening stones for a straight razor. Chris selected a neat camping knife and fork combo set, and pulled a five-dollar bill out of his tight biker's shorts.

"Well, I'd better get going. Thanks for the coffee, ladies."

"Anytime," Martha said.

We all watched him leave, his lean athlete's body a welcome sight on a gloomy morning.

"I want to take that boy home and give him a large bowl of pasta," Martha declared. "He's too damn skinny."

"What are you talking about?" Eleanor shook her head in disgust. "Look at that ass. He's perfect."

"Eleanor!" I exclaimed. "You're old enough to be his mother."

"Thank you very much for pointing that out, Daisy, but I'm not dead yet. I can still window-shop, can't I?"

I smiled as I went to put on another pot of coffee. Joe sometimes jokingly called the three of us "The Coven," which might be a bit unfair, but it was true that women over fifty did possess a certain indisputable power.

I grabbed one of the cheesecake squares while the going was good. Creamy luscious cheesecake filling, a crunchy, buttery graham cracker crust, and toasted toffee crumble topping made me moan in delight. "Oh, Martha, these are evil!"

More of the local ladies drifted in, including Debby Millerton, the librarian from Sheepville. All the talk was of the murder. This was the most exciting thing to happen in Millbury since the pastor's wife had run off with a *female* parishioner.

Some actual customers arrived next, so I put Martha in charge of hospitality. The two clients wanted a closer look at the sewing station in the shape of a miniature rocking chair displayed in the front window. I turned it around to show them how the spools of colored threads sat on the little armrests, and the front had a pullout drawer for notions, with top slots for several pairs of scissors.

They asked me more about the store, so I explained that the idea was to offer "new" old stock. Vintage, but untouched. I gestured to the unopened packages of Lucky needles, flawless wax flowers for ladies' hats still in their paper wrappers, and snaps, hooks, and fasteners on their original cards.

As the granddaughter of a milliner, and as a former teacher, I loved educating clients who might have a mild interest in sewing or antiques, and watch it turn into a real passion. The more people knew, the more enthusiastic they became.

Dimly I heard Martha across the room repeating my words. "Vintage and untouched? Heck, that sounds like me. I haven't had sex in so long, I'm practically a virgin again."

Eleanor snickered, and I hurriedly kept talking to distract my customers. Sometimes it was a good thing that my store was such a haven for gossip and camaraderie, making the store appear busy and alive, and sometimes it was a bit of a liability.

The ladies decided to purchase the sewing station, so I

moved it out of the front window and set it near the register. They said they would look around some more, so I busied myself with filling the space in the window with a 1930s Beech-Nut Gum display case, a silk sample swatch book, and some pristine tatted linen hankies.

All the while I kept half an ear open for the gossip behind me. When the discussion turned back to Angus, I was shocked to hear a note of resentment in the voices of the locals. To hear how jealous people were of the Backsteads, who still operated a thriving business in spite of the downturn in the economy.

The depressed economic conditions had also helped me obtain a rock-bottom rent for my store space when I first opened, I thought, with a soupçon of guilt.

I'd built a successful business myself by word of mouth, and now sold not only to crafters, but to collectors, interior designers, antiques dealers, and treasure hunters, some of whom came from hundreds of miles away. Like Eleanor's, mine was a destination shop. Our little village of Millbury was too far off the beaten track for the casual tourist. Although unlike me, Eleanor only opened her store when she damn well felt like it.

Once the customers and the other women had departed, I mentioned to Martha, Debby, and Eleanor that I thought I might stop and visit Cyril Mackey at his junkyard. I had a feeling that if anyone could come up with some information about the night of the murder, it might be Cyril.

Martha choked on her third cheesecake square.

"Why do you want to see that disgusting old fart? The man needs a haircut, a shower, and some clean clothes, and that's just for starters. Last time I saw him in town, I offered to pay for a trip to the barber."

I winced. "And what did he say to that?"

She sniffed. "Nothing I can repeat in polite company." Noting the almost empty plate, she addressed Eleanor. "How many of those have you eaten?"

Eleanor shrugged. "Not sure. Five, maybe six. More?"

"How the hell do you stay so skinny?"

"Not sure. I eat like a pig. That is, when I remember."

"See, Daisy, this is the kind of comment from her that drives me *insane*. How can someone just *forget* to eat?"

The doorbell chimed again, and I ran a hand through my hair. It was turning out to be a busy day.

On the doorstep stood a gorgeous young woman, long blond hair trailing across her shoulders. She wore a filmy gauze top and a full-length silk skirt, with a colorful Indian scarf tied expertly around her neck.

She flung her arms wide. "Hi, Mom. Surprise!"

Chapter Three

❋

"**S**arah! What on earth are you doing here?" I rushed over and hugged my daughter, and even managed to kiss her on the cheek before she strode into the store.

"Oh, you know. I'm sort of between films right now, so I thought I'd come home and chill for a while."

Debby clasped her hands together. "Films! How exciting!" She was always going to the Ritz, an art house cinema in the Old City district of Philadelphia that featured independent and foreign films and documentaries.

"Wow, it's always like a party in this place. Look at these." Sarah took the last of the cheesecake squares and smiled at Martha. "Awesome."

"Thank you, darling. Glad there was at least *one* left for you," Martha said with an arch look at Eleanor.

Eleanor was a former costume designer, and had worked on some of the same movie sets as Sarah. After one of her visits home, Sarah had told her about Millbury, and intrigued, Eleanor came to check it out. She saw the empty storefront across the street from me and that was it.

"Sarah, do you remember that last shoot from hell we did together? With Robert Malone, the crazed director on the Western debacle? I still have nightmares about that one."

"He was a complete maniac. Overcoked and overbudget."

"The man decided he needed two hundred extras at the last minute, all of them in period costume. I wanted to strangle him with a length of rickrack trim."

Sarah laughed. "So I take it you don't miss the movie business, E?"

"Not one bit, thank you very much. There's not enough gin in the world to make it bearable. Besides, I've finally found my true niche in life. Just like your mother."

"Oh, yeah. How's biz with the dusty old sewing things, Mom?"

"Pretty good," I answered. "Although I clean every item before it's displayed, Sarah. I honestly don't think they're *that* dusty . . ."

I was drowned out by my group of friends as they peppered her with questions about her exciting career. She had Joe's easy charm and ability to get along with anyone. I saw their expressions of delight as she turned her attention from one to the next. Like a beautiful butterfly landing on a flower beside you. You held your breath because you didn't want it to fly away.

I felt like I'd been holding my breath around Sarah for most of her life.

I saw her gaze flick over to me and she smiled, but I hoped it wouldn't turn out to be a "Mom Improvement Weekend." I'd intended to color my hair yesterday, but other events took precedence and I prayed my roots weren't showing.

I was wearing my usual outfit of a faded denim jacket, white T-shirt, and what she would disparagingly call "mom jeans," my old boot-cut Levi's. Hey, they were comfortable, and while I lugged boxes around and was on my feet all day, comfort was my main concern. My only jewelry consisted of the simple gold hoops Joe had given me when we opened the store.

"I must admit I do miss the breakfast burritos on set," Eleanor said. "They were the best! How was your latest shoot?"

"The only good part about that movie was that I got to practice my fight-scene techniques. The stand-in was sick one day, so I filled in. All the stuff they taught us in film school finally paid off."

Debby groaned as she looked at her watch. "I'm running late for my shift at the library, but I *have* to hear more insider tales of the film industry. Can we go to lunch soon? Please?"

"Sure," Sarah said. "I'll be around for a few days."

Debby reluctantly said good-bye, and rushed off.

"Well, we must be going, too," Eleanor announced. "We have to attend the monthly meeting of the Historical Society." Eleanor was the president, and Martha was the secretary, in charge of taking the minutes at the meetings.

"Don't you mean the *Hysterical* Society?" asked Martha. She winked at us as she followed Eleanor out the front door.

Sarah laughed. "Those two never change, do they, Mom?"

"No." I grinned at her. "And I hope they never do."

She wandered over to the store's computer. "How's the website coming along?"

"Great, thanks to you."

She'd set me up with a site, and I knew enough to be dangerous. At least to fill orders that came in over the Internet and answer questions on certain merchandise. I'd even toyed with the idea of starting a blog, but I wasn't quite there yet.

"Come on now, Sarah. What's the matter?" As much as I knew she loved us, my daughter thought Millbury was insufferably dull. There had to be some pressing reason why she was here.

I narrowed my eyes at her. Sarah changed boyfriends

every six months whether she needed to or not. Actually it seemed to coincide with the conclusion of each new film.

"How's—um . . ." I struggled to remember the latest one's name.

"Oh *God*. Please don't mention Peter to me. I never want to see, hear, or speak to him ever again."

"Okay."

"Jeez, Mom, he had the nerve to break up with me at the wrap party. At the *wrap party*. With *me*."

"But why?"

"I *said* I didn't want to talk about it."

"Okay."

Apparently for once the tables had turned, and Sarah was the victim of the latest breakup. She'd come home to lick her wounds. I sighed inwardly. Sarah with a broken heart was a wealth of additional drama that I really didn't need right now.

Sometimes I wished she had more of Joe's sweetness and maybe more of my tact. It was typical of her lack of thought-fulness that she would show up with no notice, but no matter. I adored her nonetheless.

A couple of hours later, she'd checked the website thoroughly, made some updates, and she sighed, too, obviously bored to death. The familiar anxiety rose up inside my chest as I worried about how to keep her happy and entertained.

"Do you want to sort some buttons for me?"

"Mom! I'm not a little kid anymore."

But she followed me into the former dining room. The maple two-piece dovetailed workbench had a recessed portion in the middle for sorting and separating items. I poured out a bag of buttons I'd picked up at the last auction—a mix of wood, bone, Czech glass, jet, metal, silver, pewter, and mother-of-pearl. She slumped into a chair and began sorting them in a desultory fashion.

When I'd rearranged the front window display three times, and I hadn't had a customer in over an hour, I decided my nerves couldn't take it anymore.

"Sarah, I'm going to close early today, but I have to run a couple of errands before I go home. I'm sure you're anxious to see Dad."

"Oh, I already stopped to see Daddy on the way here."

I squashed an irrational stab of jealousy. "Well, do you want to come with me, then?"

"Why not?" She sighed again. "There's nothing else to do."

I counted to ten, and then counted to ten again for good measure. I took the six-pack of beer and some other items out of the fridge and prepared my unorthodox care basket. Sarah raised a languid eyebrow, but didn't comment. It was as if the energy had completely drained from her body.

A few minutes later, though, as we bumped over the potholes on the Kratzes' driveway, she perked up. "Wow. Look at this place, Mom. It's about as far from Manhattan as you could get, right?"

"Hey, you wanted a change of scene. Be careful what you wish for."

We grinned at each other. Sarah slung her ever-present camera around her neck, and I hefted the basket out of the backseat.

I found Reenie in the kitchen, boiling milk on the stove. A collection of glass jugs stood on the counter next to her. The room was dark and cool because the window over the sink was almost completely covered by the creeping vine growing up the outside of the house.

Reenie unpacked the basket eagerly, grabbing the beer first, and stashing a pack of cigarettes in the pocket of her apron. Apples, bananas, yogurt, and granola bars didn't seem to hold as much interest, and she held up a package of peanut butter crackers with a look of dismay.

"Peanut butter! Oh, Daisy, we can't have these in the house. Jimmy's allergic—or well—he was. I guess it don't matter no more . . ." Her voice trailed off as her eyes filled with tears.

The two children crept in from the living room. The girl

looked to be about six years old, and the little boy was a couple of years younger.

"You must be starting first grade soon, right?" I said to the girl, smiling at her. "Are you excited?" The child looked at me blankly. Reenie made no comment.

The younger one sniffed, his nose running. Reenie pinched the mucus from under his nose, and wiped it on her apron.

Sarah made a small choking sound. "Would you excuse me? I—um—need to get some air."

"Want to go see our chickens?" asked the boy.

"Sure," Sarah answered, in that same slightly jaded tone she used with me. She strode outside, and the kids followed, gazing up at her as if she were some kind of movie star.

Reenie turned the burner off on the stove and cracked open a cold beer.

"You want one, Daisy?"

I didn't really, but maybe if we shared a drink together, she would talk. I'd gotten the feeling last time that there was something she wanted to tell me.

"Okay, thanks."

Reenie handed me a bottle and then lit a cigarette with trembling fingers.

I took a tiny sip of my beer and waited.

She started speaking slowly, as if picking her words. "I think I know why Jimmy died. He had some kind of deal going on with this company that was hired to sell stuff from people's estates." She took a long drag on her cigarette. "I don't really know much about it. To me, it was just another one of Jimmy's crazy get-rich-quick schemes." She laughed without humor and gestured to the kitchen around her. "You can see how well *they* worked."

The Formica table with its fake gray marble surface was chipped, and the brown and white speckled linoleum floor was missing a few tiles. There were no cabinets, only make-shift open shelves. The fridge looked like something Jimmy had salvaged at one time because it was too small for the space it sat in, and the range had to be at least twenty years old.

The whole place needed gutting.

"But how was Jimmy involved?"

Reenie tipped the beer bottle up and took another swallow. It was already half empty.

"This company would send valuable things out from the city to a country auction like Sheepville, where they'd sell for a much lower price. They'd hire a local to go and bid on the items. He'd hand the merchandise back to them afterwards, and they'd sell the stuff for a much higher price somewhere else down the road."

"Do you know the name of the company?"

She shook her head. "Nope. Don't think Jimmy knew either. He was only ever contacted by this one guy, who said they'd be in touch after the auction."

"So he planned to bid on a collection of very expensive fountain pens, with his own money, risking thousands of dollars for someone he never met and had no idea how to contact?" My voice rose as I finished the question. I didn't know Jimmy that well, but he didn't sound too bright to me.

"Oh no, they said they'd give him the money to bid with—the night before. He was supposed to get paid a flat fee for doing the job. Seemed like he was getting nervous about the whole thing, though. He'd be on the phone and then hang up whenever I came in the room."

Reenie picked at the label on her beer bottle. "Maybe he got cold feet. Or he got greedy and decided to do a double cross. Maybe Jimmy realized how much they were really worth from talking with Angus, and somehow these people figured out he was going to screw them."

"Did you tell the police any of this?"

"No. I got no faith in the cops to take care of things. I'm still not sure what Jimmy was up to. Or if it was even illegal."

"But you could save Angus!"

"I don't want to get in trouble. Who would look after the

kids if I was locked up?" She started crying again. "I'm afraid of the police. What if they thought *I* had something to do with it? I can't prove I didn't. I'm Jimmy's wife after all."

I bit my lip. I didn't want to push too hard. I had to keep the lines of communication open if I was going to help Angus. But hey, I was an expert at treading on eggshells, thanks to Sarah.

"Reenie, it's okay. I'll try to figure things out. At some point we may need to talk to the police . . ." I held up a hand as she started to protest. *Quiet in the classroom.* "But let me see what I can come up with first."

She wiped a hand across her eyes, and stubbed out her second cigarette.

"Look, why don't you go take a nice shower?" I suggested. "Sarah and I will watch the kids. It'll make you feel better."

She started to protest and then nodded in weary agreement, and headed upstairs. I tipped the rest of my beer into the sink, and put the remaining bottles in the refrigerator, together with the fruit and yogurt. I noted with a pang how empty the shelves were, apart from some lovely big brown eggs in a blue-striped bowl.

I wandered outside and followed the sound of childish laughter to find Sarah and the kids over by the henhouse. My daughter smiled at me, the sunlight behind turning her blond hair into a hazy golden cloud.

I smiled back. "What are you doing?"

"Taking pictures of rug rats."

She held up her camera so I could see, and scrolled through shots she'd taken of the children. Swinging on a tire swing, feeding the chickens, chasing each other round the big oak tree. She'd captured their wild laughter, the sweet softness of their rosy cheeks, and also the fleeting haunted look behind their eyes.

They laughed even more when Sarah mock screamed as the rooster came toward her.

"That's Fancy Pants." The boy bent and grabbed a chicken running by and clutched it to his chest, like he was holding an overweight cat. "And this is Miss Penny." When he set it down, the chicken took off in a squawking hurry, and they both chased it, squealing, skinny arms and legs flying.

I quickly gave Sarah the CliffsNotes version of my conversation with their mother.

Sarah frowned. "Sounds kind of sketch to trust some guy out in the country that you don't know to be part of such a scheme."

"I was thinking the same thing. And I suppose it's not completely illegal, but it's not particularly ethical either."

"But if Jimmy *did* figure out what the pens were worth, it might have been a good enough reason to risk keeping them. Look at this place, Mom. It must have been tempting."

I nodded. "Good point. Of course, whoever it is was also taking a gamble that no one would outbid Jimmy. But at a Saturday night auction in Sheepville, who would have that kind of ready money? Only a specific collector who would be willing to cough up the big bucks."

Sarah shuddered as she stared at the decrepit farmhouse. "I'd be freaked out about living here on my own with a killer on the loose."

"Well, I guess there's no reason for whoever did it to stick around now."

As we shepherded the children back into the kitchen, and I was encouraging them to wash their hands and faces at the sink, Reenie came hurtling down the wooden stairs, carrying a suitcase.

"I found this in the spare bedroom. That *bastard!*"

I glanced at Sarah, and she quickly hurried the kids outside again.

"That son of a bitch was all packed and ready to leave his wife and family for some cash and a dozen old pens?" She paced through the kitchen, heaving for breath. "When

I think about what I had to put up with, Daisy. The drinking every night, spending what little money we had at the bar, and now he does this to me? How *dare* he leave me in such a mess?"

She suddenly dropped the suitcase with a crash on the floor and hung her head, her wet hair covering her face.

I had no words, so I went over and hugged her. She clung to me like a child, crying noisily, her tears soaking through my shirt.

After we left Reenie's, I made a stop to see Betty, but the house was locked up tight with no lights on. She must have gone to visit her brother.

Sarah leaned back against the car's headrest. "Can we go home now, *please?* Why are you taking care of all these people anyway, Mom?"

"It's what I do, Sarah."

"Yes, but it's not your problem."

"I promised Angus I'd do whatever I could to help."

Silence reigned in the car as we drove the few miles back to Millbury. When we walked into the house, Joe wasn't around, so we went out to the garden to find him tinkering with his latest find from Cyril's salvage yard—a rusty Schwinn Orange Krate Stingray bicycle.

A young dog bounded up to us from around the corner of the shed.

"Hey, Buddy." Sarah ruffled the dog's ears as he jumped up and planted his huge paws against her chest.

"Do you know this dog? Is he yours?" I asked faintly, surveying the exuberant yellow Lab or retriever-type mix.

"He showed up on the set one day. He didn't have a collar and no one came to claim him, so I kept him."

I exhaled slowly. Her condo in the city, which Joe and I sold her for way below market value when we moved to Millbury for good, did not allow pets. Typical of Sarah and her impulsive nature—always doing things without thinking them through.

"You shouldn't let him jump up on you like that." When the puppy came over to me, I gently pushed him back down to the ground. I only petted him when he was sitting, his tail wagging furiously.

The pup gazed up at Joe, who had obviously accepted him right away. Joe never met a man, woman, or animal he didn't like, and who didn't instantly adore him in return.

He met my exasperated gaze, as if to say, *Take a deep breath, Daisy.* "Come on inside, girls, and see what I have planned for dinner."

Sometimes over the years I'd thought that our personalities seemed better suited for the other's job. Joe was more careful and patient than me, sterling qualities in a teacher, but as head negotiator for his electricians' union, it seemed as though more of a fiery personality was required. Like mine. Joe said that he had always played good cop in negotiations. Seemed like I was stuck forever in the role of bad cop, at least where Sarah was concerned.

I sighed. The dog looked as though he needed a great deal of training, which my laid-back daughter would probably not provide.

As we ate our perfectly grilled filet mignon and succulent lobster tails, Sarah regaled us with tales of the city and a rundown of her latest film. She had graduated from NYU in the film studies program, and now worked in continuity as a script supervisor. I sipped my wine, trying to ignore the puppy's head resting on my knee and hopeful glances toward my steak.

I still missed New York. The hustle and bustle and endless hours of window-shopping. When I was younger, I'd catch a bus from the Lower East Side up to the Garment District and lose myself for the day, gazing in the dusty storefront windows, fascinated with the endless displays of French ribbons, braided trim, velvet and satin passementerie.

In fact, like Sarah, I'd been a bit bored when I first moved to Millbury. Opening the store had been my salvation. And Joe's.

"How's the condo, Sarah?" Joe asked as he speared a bite of asparagus.

"Great! You guys wouldn't recognize the place. I had it painted an eggshell white throughout and completely gutted the kitchen and powder room. The cabinets are absolutely gorgeous. Natural maple, with stainless steel appliances. I even have a wine cooler!"

Joe grinned and they clinked wineglasses.

I raised my glass a little too late. "Did you end up keeping any of the furniture?"

"No, sorry, Mom. I sold it. I needed every penny for the reconstruction and the new living room set."

I told myself not to be upset. It was her condo now after all, but it would have been nice if she was sentimental about at least one of her parents' old possessions.

After dinner, Sarah took a phone call, and when she came back to the table, she was fighting back tears.

"Sweetheart, are you okay?" I asked.

"That was Peter. Trying to tell me I should give us another chance. That I walked away from a great relationship."

I was confused. "But I thought he broke up with you."

"Only after I broke up with him first. I don't know why he doesn't get the message."

"Well, maybe you *should* give him another chance." Sarah was completely focused on her career, which was fine, but I worried that she would never let anyone in sufficiently to share her life.

Sarah exhaled. Impressive how she could convey such a large amount of irritation and disdain in one simple breath.

"I didn't come here to be lectured. God, Mom, it would be nice to get a little *understanding* or *sympathy* for a change."

Didn't I always give her that?

Our earlier rapport at Reenie's had drifted away like the evening breeze that was swaying the hanging baskets of white petunias and blue trailing lobelia out on the back porch.

Joe and Sarah went outside with the dog while I started doing the dishes. I could hear the easy murmur of their voices, but not what they were saying.

I poured another glass of wine and wondered how long she would stay.

At the store, I was in my element. I was funny, welcoming, talkative, knowledgeable—a great businesswoman dealing with top designers and wealthy collectors.

When my daughter was around, it seemed like I always said the wrong thing. A little older, a little dowdier, a little less confident.

I wished she shared my passion for my precious antique stock, and wondered how I could have given birth to a child who was so utterly different from me. I'd also wanted to raise a daughter who could stand on her own two feet and not rely on anyone to take care of her. Boy, had I achieved that goal, and then some. Sarah was fiercely independent and brutally opinionated.

Okay, well, maybe in some ways we were alike. As the old saying goes, be careful what you wish for.

Through the kitchen window I could see Joe out on the glider, talking to her. The moon above was a pale lemon slice in a lilac sky.

Dear Joe. Thirty-four years of marriage. Sure we'd had our fights. Times when I wanted to choke him, or times I'd threatened to sleep in the spare bedroom, but somehow we'd always worked it out. One of us had apologized first, and then of course, there was the lovemaking to make up.

I grinned to myself. Sarah would probably not want to believe that her parents ever had sex. But we did, even at our age. And very good sex, too, I might add.

The night was breezy and cool, and I sighed in relief

when I was finally nestled in Joe's arms in our bed. Sarah had gone to her room, and the puppy was crated in the kitchen.

Joe kissed me, and I melted into him, relaxing for the first time all day. Things were starting to get interesting when suddenly mournful howls erupted from downstairs. After a few excruciating minutes of this racket that Sarah was obviously able to sleep through, Joe got up and went downstairs to soothe the pup. I fell asleep before he came back to bed.

I left the house early the next morning. Sarah was asleep, Joe was taking care of the dog, and I had lots I wanted to do before opening the store. Number one on the list was to check on Betty, scout out the auction building, and dig up any information on those missing fountain pens.

Mist still clung in wisps to the low stone walls and rolled over the tops of the fields as I rode my bicycle toward Sheepville. It was so quiet, it was easy to think I was the only person up and alive at this hour, until I heard the rumble of a tractor in the distance. A purple, blue, and yellow checkered hot air balloon drifted over the tops of the trees, and I pedaled hard, trying to keep it in sight.

River Road was cool and peaceful, too, the musty damp of the moss and undergrowth replacing the manure smell of the fields. Steep hillsides with rock formations and dense undergrowth mixed with rhododendrons and vines towered up above me on the side farthest from the water. The incline pushed my muscles to work hard as I navigated the twists and turns, but it was a relief to feel the blood coursing through my veins, washing away some of the tension of the past few days.

The lights were on in the auction building when I rode up, so I parked the bike near the double doors, and walked inside.

"Hello? Anyone here?"

Betty came out of the office, an anxious look on her face.

"How are you, Betty? How's the hip?"

"Improving. I get a bit better each day." She hugged me. "Thanks for coming, Daisy. I just made some tea. Would you like some?"

"Tea would be great." I'd only had one cup of coffee at home, and until I got to the store, I would be running seriously low on caffeine.

I followed her into the office and she pulled another mug down from the shelf.

"I'm worried about keeping this place going until Angus gets back. There's a lot of merchandise that needs to be sold. I know how to do it, from watching him all these years, but the thing is . . ."

"What?"

"I can't see myself getting up on the stage and shouting out the numbers. I'd be scared to death." She twisted the ends of her shawl-like sweater.

"Well, let's think. Maybe you could hire someone to do it. How about Patsy?"

"From the diner?"

"Yeah. She'd get a kick out of it. She has the right personality and her voice is certainly loud enough. Plus, I'm sure she could use some extra money."

Betty brightened. "Yes. That's a good idea."

I was about to broach the subject of hiring a decent attorney, when suddenly the office door banged open with a crash.

The woman standing in the doorway was tall and thin, with black hair pulled back into a chignon that enhanced an extremely long, but elegant, neck. She wore a simple wrap dress that looked like it cost a teacher's salary for a month, and was so gaunt her hipbones showed through the silky fabric.

"Have the pens been found yet?" she demanded. "How the *hell* could you people have been so careless?"

I stepped closer to Betty. "Excuse me, but who are you?"

"She thought I wouldn't find out about her little scheme, but I did!" Her smile was triumphant. "That bimbo took great delight in telling me she was selling them, but wouldn't tell me where out of *spite*. I heard through my connections that some valuable pens were up for auction out in the boondocks. And so here I am!"

"The bimbo?" I asked, feeling as though I'd tuned in on a movie that was already halfway through.

"My father's new wife." She took a deep, shuddering breath. "Those pens belonged to my father, David Adams, an avid collector. He recently passed away. Knowing how much I wanted them, knowing how important Daddy's pens were to me, she put them up for auction. God, I hate that bitch."

Betty's mouth hung open, her tea untouched.

"I was even willing to buy them back, which is why I came all the way from New York, only to find out they had been stolen."

I held up a hand. "Excuse me, but who *are* you?"

"Fiona Adams," she snapped, impatient with the interruption.

"Well, I'm Daisy Buchanan, and this is—"

"This would never have happened at a reputable auction house like Sotheby's or Christie's. I have no idea why she would let important collectibles be sold at such a podunk place. It's not as if we're selling boxes of *National Geographic* magazines, for Christ's sake."

"Why do you think she sent them here?" My pulse accelerated. Was this the connection to the crooked estate liquidation company?

Fiona snorted. "Because she's a stupid twit."

"If she did put them up at Sotheby's or Christie's, you'd have had to pay a lot more to get them back."

"That's not the point," she snarled.

Now that I studied her more closely, I saw that the elegance was tainted by the fact that her nose was rather hooked, and her teeth stuck out a shade too much, but in spite of that, she was still strangely attractive.

And how could she be so sure that the pens were hers?

She must have been thinking along the same lines as me when she turned to Betty. "I need to see the photos," she demanded. "The full catalog description of the items."

"I'm sorry," Betty stammered. "But there aren't any. Angus must have forgotten to do it. He used to be so meticulous."

Normally auction items were cataloged, assigned a lot number, and photographed, but not this time, in yet another example of Angus's recent absentminded behavior. Or was he involved in the shady scheme, too? I shook my head. I wasn't going to let myself go down that road.

"I wasted most of Sunday trying to get some answers out of that moronic detective. And I came here again yesterday, but no one was around." Fiona Adams glared at Betty, who mumbled something about being at her brother's house for the day.

"Oh, for God's sake. I don't know how much more of this crap I can take." She pulled out a long slim cigarette and was about to light it, when I stepped forward.

"You can't smoke in here. Come outside with me, please." Not only did I not want her smoking in the building, but Betty was getting visibly upset.

I walked out without looking back, but I heard her high heels strike the concrete floor as she followed me. I had to smile at the thought of this hyper woman haranguing Detective Ramsbottom, but I'd be damned if I'd let her bully poor Betty.

"Do you have any idea how much those pens are worth?" She shook her head and let out a thin stream of smoke once we were outside. "Never mind. You couldn't possibly understand."

I gritted my teeth. Hey, I was from New York, too. And a person didn't live in the Big Apple, and teach there for years, without acquiring a little moxie.

"Look, I might not know much about fountain pens, but I do know something about antiques." I rattled off a few descriptions of choice items at the store, and their impressive retail prices. I knew I was showing off, but I had to assert some control over the situation. *Hands at your sides, class, facing front, eyes on me!*

"I suppose I see your point," she said stiffly.

"I want to find out what happened as much as you do. Then I can prove my good friend Angus didn't kill Jimmy Kratz."

"Mark my words. I'm going to find those pens, and that bitch is going to pay." She threw her spent cigarette on the ground and stalked over to a silver Mercedes-Benz Roadster slanted across a parking space.

I watched her leave, deep in thought. She was definitely a loose cannon, and there was something very odd about this whole situation.

Was she connected to this suspicious estate company that had done the dirty on Jimmy? Or had she stolen the pens herself, and was only cleverly making a fuss now to draw attention away from herself as a suspect?

Chapter Four

Betty opened the door an inch and peered outside. "Is that horrible woman gone?"

"Yes, don't worry. I'm sure we've seen the last of her." I hoped I sounded convincing enough as I picked up the cigarette butt and threw it into the trash can. "Betty, I want to talk to you about something important. About legal representation for Angus."

"Oh, we already have a lawyer. Warren Zeigler."

"Yes, but don't you think you might need a good criminal attorney instead?"

"Why? Angus is innocent."

I sucked in a breath. "I know that, Betty, but—"

"Oh, I couldn't do that to Warren. He's like family to us now." She patted my hand. "He's very good, Daisy. I trust him completely. And in the good Lord. He will take care of everything. You'll see."

I didn't want to contradict her, but I thought He might need us to step up and do our bit, too. I glanced at my watch.

"Yikes. I'd better get back. I have to grab a shower before opening the store."

I hugged Betty and pedaled back to Millbury. Damn it, I'd wanted to go see Cyril Mackey this morning as well, but I'd run out of time.

Less than an hour later, breathless and hair still damp, I'd barely opened the door to Sometimes a Great Notion when Martha waltzed in.

"Good God, that doll—"

"Martha!" I cut her off before she could launch into the usual routine. "Could you do me a huge favor? I need you to take care of something for me."

"Sure. You want me to babysit Chris Paxson for you?"

"No, but how about the store? For a few minutes. Please?"

A look of panic spread across her freckled face. "But I don't know the first thing about sewing. I can't even sew on a button, for Pete's sake. What about Eleanor? Can't you ask her?"

"She has her own store to look after." I took the plate from Martha's outstretched hands and hurried to the door.

"Wait a minute—"

"Call me on my cell if anyone comes, or if there are questions you can't answer. I'll be right back. Thanks, Martha, I owe you one!"

I ran to the house to pick up the car so I could get to Cyril's place and back as fast as possible. As I drove down Main Street, a few raindrops spattered the car's windshield. A couple of minutes later, I turned off onto the dead-end road that led to the salvage yard, where the rusted gate was propped open by a giant iron rooster. I drove in as far as I could until the jumble of wooden porch posts, church pews, painted shutters, gargoyles, and what looked like an old barber's chair blocked my way.

Cyril ambled out of the building, wearing his flat cap and tweed jacket, looking a bit like a bookie who'd fallen on hard times.

The smile on his face faded when he saw it was me who stepped out of the Subaru, and not Joe.

"What are *you* doing here?"

This guy didn't need a junkyard dog. He was meaner than a whole pack of them.

I kept my smile firmly in place. "What can I say? Guess you drew the short straw today." I knew Cyril liked Joe because Joe could never stop here without buying some rusty relic to bring home and fix.

As he continued to glower, I proffered my peace offering—the plate of Martha's famous oatmeal cherry cookies. "Look, Cyril, I just want to chat for a minute. About Angus."

"That bossy boots woman isn't with you, is she?" he asked, with a furtive glance beyond me back toward the car.

"No, I came alone," I said, feeling as though I was in some kind of low-budget gangster movie.

Raindrops were falling harder now, dotting the plastic cling wrap as Cyril took the plate from my hands. "Well, I suppose you'd best come in."

The mobile home–type building had two doors on the side of it. He walked past the first door, and opened up the second one at the back.

I followed him in and stopped stock-still. I wasn't sure what I'd been expecting, but this wide, bright kitchen definitely wasn't it. Next to the window at the end sat a white table covered by a lace tablecloth, with a vigorous Boston fern hanging in the far corner. On the table, a tea cozy snuggled around a brown ceramic teapot, and a silver rack held several pieces of toast. I'd only ever seen one before in a hotel. The fragrance of freshly toasted bread still hung in the air.

A double doorway from the white-tiled kitchen opened to a decent-sized living room. There were a few antiques. Not many, but the pieces he had were nice, like the grandfather clock in the corner and a mahogany cabinet holding some Minton bone china. A recliner covered with a crocheted brown, orange, and yellow afghan was angled in front of the television.

The place was spare, but clean and neat. That first door to the trailer must have been his office. I was right—he did live here in this place, on this deserted dead-end road, all by himself.

"Were ya born in a barn?" he barked. "Put the wood in t'hole."

"I beg your pardon?"

He gestured to the door behind me.

"Oh, right. Sorry." I turned and shut it.

"Cuppa tea?" He glared at me as he asked the question.

"Oh, no, it's okay. I don't want to put you to any trouble."

"You already did. And as I can see you aren't leaving until you get what you came for, you may as well park yerself."

"Fine." I glared back and sat down at the kitchen table. A square Limoges plate held the remains of his breakfast—some scrambled eggs and a corner of a piece of toast. He'd been working on a crossword puzzle in the newspaper.

While he busied himself getting a mug out of a kitchen cabinet, I took a surreptitious glance at the puzzle. It was mainly filled in with his wavering capital letters, except for one long twelve-letter word with a *c* as the third letter and a *t* at the end. The clue was "defies authority." I knew I drove Sarah and Joe crazy whenever we watched *Wheel of Fortune*. I could solve it with only one letter showing, or sometimes none at all.

Cyril handed me a mug and I took a sip of the tea. It was strong and sweet. "Thank you. Just the way I like it."

Not that he'd bothered to ask if I took milk and sugar.

He sat down opposite me and bit into one of Martha's cookies. "Now then, was there summat you wanted to ask me?"

"Yes." I cleared my throat, and took another mouthful of the delicious brew. "The thing is, Angus doesn't seem to be able to remember much about that night at the pub with Jimmy. You were there. I was hoping you could shed some light on the situation. I mean, were they really that drunk? Did you notice anything unusual?"

"Well, Jimmy was sloshed. As per usual." He dunked the rest of the cookie in his tea. "Angus was goin' sideways, too, but believe it or not, I've seen him worse. Although lately he don't seem to know whether it's Tuesday or Christmas, the poor bugger."

I blew out a breath. "I know. Now, were he and Jimmy getting along?"

"Aye, fair t'middlin. Jimmy was buying drinks like there was no tomorrow."

But as it turned out, there wasn't one. For him.

"Do you know who else could have wanted to murder Jimmy? Because we both know Angus didn't do it. Did he have any enemies? Was he in any kind of trouble?"

He shrugged. "Not that I know of. Although Jimmy weren't no prince, neither."

"Any strangers in the bar? Like a tall, black-haired woman?" I didn't mention the estate company yet. I wanted to be careful with the trust Reenie had placed in me.

Cyril stared out the window at the rain, which was coming down harder and making long, wet strikes against the glass.

I racked my mind for other good detective-type questions. Damn it. The police should be dealing with this cantankerous old man. I didn't know what the hell I was doing.

I finished my tea. The slogan on the outside of my mug read, NOT A POT TO PISS IN. I set it carefully down on the table.

There was silence between us for a few more moments.

Cyril glanced at me. His eyes were hazel, almost greenish in this light. I'd never noticed the color before. His gray hair straggled out from under his cap, his clothes were a mess, but his eyes were positively beautiful. Almost hypnotic.

"Ah don't remember much about math in school," he said quietly, "but if *a* equals *b*, it don't necessarily equal *c* as well. Maybe Jimmy's murder is nowt to do with Jimmy *or* the pens. Angus had some enemies, you know."

"Like who?"

"Well, the Perkins family in Sheepville, for one. A year or so ago, Angus bought their grandmother's estate as a whole house buyout."

I nodded. Angus sometimes paid a flat fee for entire estate contents, instead of taking items on consignment.

"Turns out the merchandise were worth a damn sight more when it was auctioned off individually. The two grandsons are especially brassed off."

"You mean angry?"

"Aye. And those lads were in the pub that night. They could have realized this was the perfect opportunity to get their own back."

"So you think they could have killed Jimmy to pin the murder on Angus and get their revenge? And recover their money by stealing the pens?"

Cyril shrugged. "Who knows? Jimmy was also the one that recommended they hire Angus in the first place. Kill two birds with one stone, if you catch my drift." He took another of Martha's oatmeal cookies and pointed it at me. "These sweets aren't too bad. I didn't peg you for a good cook."

"Actually I didn't make them. That bossy woman did."

Cyril raised his eyebrows a fraction and took another appreciative bite.

My cell phone beeped with a missed call. "Well, I'd better get back to the store. Thanks for your time, Cyril. And for the tea."

On the way across the lot toward my car, I noticed an interesting boot scraper made out of iron in the shape of a squirrel. I bent down to take a closer look. The rain had let up momentarily, and the rising heat was going to turn this day into a steam bath later on.

"You're going to take this withee?"

I glanced up. It wasn't really a question.

"Um, okay. How much is it?"

"Ten dollars."

I didn't dare argue. "Fine." I forked over the money and stuffed the squirrel under my arm, while also stuffing down the feeling I'd been had.

"Next time, bring some coffee."

I grinned. That sounded as close to an invitation to come back as I was ever likely to get. As I pulled out of the lot, I called to him. "It's *recalcitrant*, by the way."

"What is?" he shouted.

"Three across. On your crossword puzzle."

I checked my phone. The missed call was from Joe.

"Hi, babe," he said when I called him back. "Wondering where the car was. Thought I'd go over and see if Betty needed some manly muscle to get ready for the auction this Saturday. It's the least I can do after all Angus has done for us."

"Oh, Joe, you've read my mind. I was going to ask if you'd mind helping her with the heavy stuff. But as usual, you're one step ahead of me. What's Sarah doing today?"

"Still sleeping right now. I fed the pup and walked him, so he's all set."

"I see. Anyway, I'm dropping the car off in a couple of minutes. I just went to visit Cyril Mackey."

"Yeah? Did you have fun?"

I grunted. "Honestly, I don't know how you put up with that man."

Joe laughed. "Oh, he's okay once you get to know him. I never can leave there without taking something with me, though. I can't believe he let you off the hook so easily."

There was a short silence.

"Daisy? Did you have to buy something?"

"Look, it was very nice talking to you, Joe, but I've got to go." I hung up to the roar of my husband's laughter.

I parked the car outside our house and hurried back to the store, dodging raindrops. It didn't matter that I hadn't fully dried my hair earlier. It was wet again now anyway.

The striped pole was turning outside the barber shop across the street, and a customer was already sitting in the cracked red vinyl chair. Tony Zappata, the barber, or Tony Z as he called himself, was a transplant from South Philly. Short in stature, but a giant in personality, he embodied the nation's impression of Philadelphians. Warmhearted enough to give you the shirt off their back, but tough enough to rip it off again and slap you with it, depending on the occasion and their mood. He was also a pretty good tenor and belted out operatic arias to entertain his clientele while he worked.

Next door to Tony's, Eleanor's shop was still dark. A pair of mannequins dressed in exquisite antique wedding gowns posed together in the shadowy front window.

I entered Sometimes a Great Notion to the sound of the cash register ringing. It was an ornate brass National model from 1914, and Martha was stuffing it with five-dollar bills, looking like the Cheshire cat who'd swallowed a gallon of cream.

The store was full of men. One man was poking through the MALE box, and two others were drinking coffee and chatting.

Two more sat at a bistro table that Martha must have moved from the sewing room upstairs. They were playing Shut the Box, a vintage dice game.

Eleanor was there, too. "Have you lost your *mind*, leaving this one running the place?"

I grinned. "It looks as though she's handled everything pretty well."

She raised an eyebrow as if to say she begged to differ. "I guess Sarah wasn't around to watch the store?"

"It was easier to ask Martha." I looked into Eleanor's dark gray eyes and knew she understood.

She nodded. "So how long will Sarah be staying?"

"No idea." I set the squirrel down on the floor. Eleanor was right. It was ridiculous that I was afraid to ask my own daughter to do me a favor. "And it seems as though I can never say or do the right thing when she's around, as hard as I try."

"Maybe don't try so hard?" Eleanor laid a hand on my arm. "We all have our blind spots, Daisy. It's okay." In contrast to her mannish appearance, her hands were beautiful. Feminine and elegant, the nails painted a pale pink.

I sighed. "Sarah gets along so well with her dad, but when I talk to her, it's like my timing is always off. When all I want to do is help her find the same purpose and joy in life that I've found with this business."

Eleanor smiled. "*And* you worry too much."

"I know. It's part of my DNA. I can't help it."

I went over to hug Martha. "Thanks. Nice touch with the table, by the way."

"Hey, I know what men like." She winked at me. "Just call me large and in charge." She bustled off to ring up another purchase. The MALE box was almost empty.

Eleanor poured herself a cup of coffee and looked around. "What? No treats this morning?"

Martha sniffed from behind the cash register. "Well, I *did* make oatmeal cherry cookies, but someone gave them away."

"Relax. I have some of your shortbread in the kitchen." Before things turned violent, I hurried into the back and retrieved a tin of buttery shortbread fingers.

"So what did you find out from the evil troll down the lane?" Martha asked.

I quickly told them about the Perkins family and the estate sale where they felt they had gotten robbed.

"That's just the luck of the draw. It's not Angus's fault. They could have chosen to have a regular auction if they wanted." Martha trailed her fingers over her upswept hair, where a few red tendrils were escaping.

Eleanor plucked a biscuit from the tin. "That grandmother was an old hag. Bet they couldn't wait to get rid of her, and her stuff, too."

"That's not all," I said. "Some crazed woman called Fiona Adams showed up at the auction house this morning, claiming the pens belonged to her dead father. His new wife sent them here instead of auctioning them off in New York. The whole thing seems very strange to me."

I handed Martha a cup of coffee.

"Thank you, Daisy. The plot thickens, eh? And now I hear Vikki, the bartender over at the pub, is trying to backtrack, saying Angus wasn't *that* drunk. Probably worried about the liability. Too bad she already told everyone how smashed he was. That woman can't keep her mouth shut about anything."

Eleanor rolled her eyes at me, and I hid a smile. I loved Martha, but she couldn't keep anything to herself either. I'd learned the hard way not to tell her any deep dark secrets. Those I reserved for Eleanor.

"Look, guys, Betty is still going ahead with the auction this weekend," I said. "We have to help her out. I'm going to ask Patsy to do the bid calling, and Joe will move the heavy stuff, but we'll need someone to run the snack counter like Betty usually does, because she'll be busy overseeing and—"

"Snack counter! I call the snack counter." Martha raised an arm in the air.

"And I'll take the cold hard cash." Eleanor drained her mug. "Good coffee as always, Daisy. You know how I like my coffee. Like ah like my men. Hot, black, and strong," she murmured in her best Mae West imitation, garnering a few interested glances from the men over at the dice game.

Martha nodded toward the bistro table. "I was thinking we could put a mini television over there, volume on low, of course, so the men could watch the baseball games and—"

"Jiminy Cricket, don't make it *too* comfortable for them," Eleanor protested. "How are we supposed to gossip about the male population of this village if they're hanging around here? Besides, they have Tony Z's."

I turned off the coffee machine. "I've always wondered how Tony stays in business at ten dollars a person. I don't think he's changed his prices since 1970."

"Yes, but think about how often guys need a haircut," Eleanor pointed out. "Some of them come here every single week."

"True. And I guess he's such a character that he has a loyal clientele who make it a point to travel to see him. It's like the men's own version of Sometimes a Great Notion."

"Exactly. So they don't need to horn in on our spot."

After Martha and Eleanor left, and the men disappeared, I called Detective Ramsbottom. "A woman named Fiona Adams was at the auction house today, claiming the stolen pens belong to her."

"Yeah? That nutcase tortured me for the best part of Sunday. So what?"

"Well, have you checked out her story?"

"There were no high-heeled footprints in the mud around Jimmy's barn, if that's what you're getting at. Oh, wait. You think she whacked him to death with her diamond ring?" He laughed until he started coughing.

I wanted to smash the phone against the counter. "And another thing. Apparently the Perkinses are very angry about a sale that Angus handled for their grandmother's estate about a year ago. Jimmy was the one that recommended Angus for the job. Perhaps you should consider looking into their whereabouts on the morning of the murder?"

"You think those boys killed *someone else* to get revenge

on Backstead?" I could hear Ramsbottom eating. Perhaps a foot-long meatball hoagie with an extra large side of fries.

At the thought of French fries, my stomach grumbled.

"I don't know. Sounds like you're clutching at straws, Mrs. Daly."

"Buchanan." Even as I corrected him, I sighed. My theories sounded pretty weak to me, too, once I voiced them out loud.

Ramsbottom said he had to go, and hung up abruptly. I slammed the phone down and went in search of sustenance.

The store had a real kitchen, seeing as it was once a home, so there was no excuse not to eat healthy food. I pulled a container of Joe's homemade split pea and ham soup from the freezer and put it in the microwave, but I only had a chance to eat a few bites before the phone started ringing. One call was from an interior designer looking for vintage curtain panels for a child's room. I had several in stock, plus some antique toys to accessorize the shelving. I promised to meet her after work on Thursday evening because she couldn't come during store hours.

As soon as I had a moment to breathe, Cyril Mackey's words came back to me. *Was* there another way of looking at this whole thing? Even though the Perkins theory sounded weak, maybe he had a point.

One thing was for sure. I'd need to keep my mind, ears, and eyes open to every possibility.

I remembered one of the first jobs I had as a teacher. There was one little boy who simply could not sit still, and it was nearly impossible to get him engaged in the lessons. Until the day I sat the kids in a circle on the floor instead of at their desks. I told them the story of Paul Revere, and he was transfixed. I'll never know whether it was the change of location or the delivery, but either way I had him, and knew that was my "teaching moment." It also taught me to think outside the box and not be afraid to approach a problem from a new direction.

Sarah finally drifted in during the early afternoon.

"How's the puppy doing?" I asked.

"He's okay. I let him run around in the backyard for a while before I came over."

I made a mental note to check around the yard when I got home. I had visions of going out into the grass in my bare feet one morning and finding that she hadn't bothered to clean up after the dog.

I took a deep breath. "You know we love having you here, Sarah, but don't you have to go back to work sometime? When's the next film?"

Sarah shrugged and clicked through some messages on her cell phone. "No idea."

The condo in New York was in a full-service, door-attendant building. Even though she'd bought it from us for way below what we could have sold it for on the open market, it was still a decent-sized payment for a single woman. I knew she made good money on films, but it wasn't consistent income, and she'd just spent a fortune on remodeling and new furniture.

I swallowed and tried again. "I worry about you making your mortgage, that's all."

"Something will come along soon," she said, not looking up from the phone. "Don't *worry* so much, Mom."

I gritted my teeth. If one more person told me that I worried too much today, I'd have a stroke.

I'd seen the kids whose parents didn't pay attention, who didn't worry, and who didn't come to parent-teacher meetings. Those were the parents who left teenagers home alone when they went to their beach house on Long Island, and were surprised when the police came calling on Monday night.

Joe and Sarah were definitely peas in a pod with their laid-back attitudes to life. It was all very well to be so loosey-goosey, but it was because of my drive that we'd bought the condo, and had been able to afford her college education. Now we had this store that provided a nice income for Joe and me.

Although Joe would probably be content to live in a tent at the bottom of the yard.

I shook my head, even as I smiled. He'd still be a great cook, even on a propane camping stove.

Some customers came in looking for ribbons and trim. As I showed them around, I watched Sarah out of the corner of my eye. Occasionally she laughed, and then frowned at the phone, her fingers moving lightning fast. I wondered if she was networking or chatting with her friends. The film business was like any other business. You had to stay in the game and be seen, not sequestered away in some Bucks County backwater. Although with the way everyone was connected via the Internet these days, I supposed it didn't matter so much.

"Yo, Daisy! Wazzup?"

The boisterous yell resounded through the store as it did every day about this time. Patsy Elliott, the waitress from the Last Stop Diner, usually came in after her shift to chat before she picked up her daughter from school. Her raspy barroom voice sounded like she smoked a hundred cigarettes a day, but she didn't. It was a stark contrast to her clear skin, bright blue eyes, and dark curly hair, all glowing with good health.

Today her leggy nine-year-old daughter, Claire, was with her, hanging behind her mother, dark eyes shining. Arched eyebrows framed her huge brown eyes, and she would be a stunner when she grew up.

Claire was the one who usually helped me sort the buttons. I bent down and she gave me a tight hug. I clung back for a moment, cherishing the feel of her little arms around my neck.

Sarah glanced at us, an unreadable expression on her face.

"Patsy!" I hugged Patsy, too, for good measure. "Just the

person I wanted to see. How would you feel about bid calling the auction on Saturday night? Betty will pay you. Probably a couple of hundred bucks for a few hours' work?"

"Hell, yeah. Sounds like fun. The diner has been slow lately. I can definitely use that kind of money." Most people might have balked at being asked to do something they'd never done before, but not Patsy.

"Oops! Mommy, you swore." Claire held out her hand. "You owe me a quarter."

Patsy sighed and fished a coin out of her waitress apron. "After church I promised to give her a quarter each time I said a bad word."

Claire beamed at us. "I have two dollars and seventy-five cents so far, and it's only Tuesday."

Sarah and I laughed. To say Patsy's language was salty was an understatement. I cringed myself sometimes at her brash speech.

"At this rate, I'll be broke before the weekend. That's why the auctioneer gig will come in handy." Patsy settled her slender form into one of the bistro chairs. The diner uniform was hideous—a brown polyester dress with puffed sleeves and an orange and white checked apron—but Patsy could make a garbage bag look like designer couture.

The customers brought their ribbon lengths to the counter and I rang them up, and thanked them for visiting.

"Now, what about this chanting thing?" Patsy said after they left. "I can never understand what the hell those guys are saying." She automatically reached in her pocket and held out another quarter to Claire.

I smiled. "At first I couldn't understand what they were saying at auctions either. But Angus told me that it's really about the numbers. The rest is just filler. The main thing is to create a sense of excitement and urgency to drive the price up and keep the pace moving."

"But how do I learn how to do it?"

"Well, you can practice counting pairs of numbers like

one, one, two, two, three, three, and so on. Then try it backwards. Or count up in increments of fives or tens. Or practice tongue twisters. I'll see Angus tomorrow. I'll ask him for some pointers for you."

"Five, ten, fifteen, twenty. Twenty, fifteen, ten, five." Claire smiled at me. "One, one, two, two, three, three—"

"Jesus. Thanks a lot, Daisy." Patsy groaned. "See what I'll have to listen to for the rest of the week?"

For all that I thought I'd had it rough in New York sometimes, it was nothing compared to the life Patsy had led, but she'd survived, flourished even. It had made her somewhat hard, though, and to say that she practiced tough love with her daughter was an understatement. No candy except on special occasions, no TV during the week, and a long list of chores to complete for her pocket money.

Although perhaps I should have taken a page out of Patsy's book. As a teenager, Sarah was constantly losing things like her cell phone, but instead of making her save up her pocket money for a new one, Joe bought her a replacement. We'd paid the full ticket to put her through college so she wouldn't be encumbered by loans, but I wondered if Sarah appreciated how much Joe and I had sacrificed to give her that gift.

The door bell rang, and an elderly woman stepped into the store. She wore a black wool coat in spite of the heat, and clutched a white paper shopping bag. Thanks to gossip queen Martha, I knew Mary Willis was recently widowed, and her husband had died with no life insurance. They'd spent everything they had on his medical bills.

"I'm sorry. I don't mean to interrupt," Mary murmured, hovering at the entrance.

"Please, come in." I waved to welcome her in. "How can I help you?"

She held out the bag. "I hope I'm not wasting your time . . . but I was wondering . . . would you be interested in buying some of these?"

It looked as though there was a pile of neatly folded

linens inside. I smiled at her. "Why don't we go into the prep area, where we can take a better look?"

I switched the light on in the former dining room, and we spread them out on the maple workbench.

There was a set of white Irish linen damask dinner napkins, some place mats with beautiful embroidery and cutwork featuring flowers and butterflies with a scalloped edging, and an exquisite Madeira organdy and cotton tablecloth with twelve matching napkins.

"These are beautiful, Mary." They were all in very good condition with no tears or stains. The lacework was finely done, and I did a mental calculation of the total value.

In the background I could hear Claire still softly practicing her chant, and Patsy chatting with Sarah, occasionally barking with laughter.

"What were you thinking?" I asked. *First lesson in negotiation. See what the other party has in mind.* "How much do you want for them?"

"Fifty dollars?" she whispered as she clutched the empty bag, worry rumpling her thin features.

"For everything?" I exclaimed in shock. "Oh, no, Mary. They're worth far more than that."

The fact that the organdy tablecloth still had its matching napkins greatly enhanced the value, and I would ask about four hundred dollars retail for the set. The Irish linens alone would fetch well over a hundred dollars.

Patsy gave me an arch look from across the room, but I ignored it. Even though I was two decades older than her, I often felt as though she was the wise woman and I was the naïve one.

But one of the first lessons I'd learned from Angus was to cultivate good karma. You never wanted to hurt someone, because it could come back to bite you one day. And the people that you played fair with, well, they could suddenly remember an old treasure in the attic that they were now inclined to sell, and you just hit picker pay dirt.

"How about five hundred dollars for the lot?"

"Really?" Mary touched the edge of the tablecloth with fingers that shook. Fingers that were mottled with age spots, the knuckles swollen with arthritis.

"Yes, really. That's a fair price, Mary."

"Oh my Lord, yes, it certainly is, but I never expected . . . you know, I've never even used them. My mother-in-law gave them to me years ago. I was saving them for a special occasion."

As I counted out money from the register, I thought about how after Teddy Bristol died, Martha took her diamond earrings out of the safe and announced she planned on wearing them every day. She used her crystal and best china for every meal now, too. An image also popped into my head of Cyril Mackey eating breakfast off his Limoges plate.

Poor Mary Willis had saved her linens for so long, waiting for the special occasion that never came.

"I have more things at home. Would you like to see them?" Mary ventured, with a little more color in her face now as she carefully placed the bills in her wallet.

"Yes, sure, and anything else you think might sell. Sewing notions, children's toys, any small antiques—bring it over!"

"You know, I don't know how many times I've thought about coming in here, but I never had the nerve to. I'm glad I finally did."

I smiled. "Me, too. See you again soon."

I watched her leave, hoping that now she might be able to afford some prescriptions, or her electric bill, or some such thing.

The door had barely closed behind her before Patsy said, "Well, folks, there's a lesson in how *not* to make money."

Sarah smiled and shook her head. "Yeah, you're too soft, Mom."

"No," I murmured, "you're wrong. It's not always about the money." They chuckled, but I ignored them as I laid the linens out on display. I felt Claire's small hand slip into mine and I squeezed it tight in gratitude.

Patsy slowly unfolded her long body out of the chair. "Hey, Sarah, if you ever want to hit the town one night, let me know, and I'll ask my sister to babysit."

"By town, you mean . . ."

Patsy stared at her. "Sheepville. There's a great band at the pub on Friday nights."

I held my breath.

Sarah smiled as if it was the most exciting offer she'd ever had. "Awesome. I'd love to." Her smile encompassed me, and I thanked her with my answering grin. I knew Sheepville was not Sarah's idea of civilization, but it was all we had. Of course, there was Philadelphia, but I'd run into many people who had lived around here all their lives and never ventured into the city. It was like asking them if they'd ever traveled to Mars.

"Patsy, do you know the Perkins family?" I asked. "Sounds like they don't get along with Angus. I thought I might pay them a visit."

Patsy shook her head. "Be careful, Daisy. You don't want to mess around with that crowd. They're a bad lot."

"I heard they run a farm supply and feed store outside of Sheepville?"

"Yeah, the Perkins boys own it. Well, they're not really boys anymore—they're in their late twenties—but we've always called them that. They were a couple years behind me at school. I could tell you some stories that would curl your hair."

Patsy glanced over at Claire and arched her back.

"Ow. Come on kid, let's go practice. Five, five, ten, ten, twenty, twenty. Daisy, see you later. Sarah, I'll call you about going out."

Chapter Five

That night when we got home, Joe was putting the finishing touches to a bouillabaisse, a traditional French seafood stew full of cooked fish and vegetables. A wonderful feast, but not a cheap dish to make, by any means.

As I dropped my bag on the kitchen table and kicked off my shoes, I tried to stop adding up the cost of the ingredients in the giant cooking pot. One whole lobster, a pound of shrimp, sea bass, and some fresh mussels and littleneck clams. That must have cost a pretty penny.

Stop it, Daisy.

The yellow-haired dog sat in an ungainly stance behind Joe, one back leg straight, one sprawled out the way some puppies sit, in rapt attention at the saffron-and-fish-scented mist swirling through the kitchen.

Joe disappeared down the basement steps and came back with a bottle of 2009 Montrachet, a very nice white burgundy. We'd bought it a couple of years ago on a trip to our favorite wine shop, in Lambertville, New Jersey, just across the bridge from New Hope, Pennsylvania, and it had been gathering dust ever since.

"I thought we were saving it for a special occasion," I said beneath my breath. Sarah was engrossed in her cell phone as usual.

"It is. Our daughter came home." He set it down on the butcher block table that was well over six inches thick and pulled a corkscrew out of his pocket with a flourish.

I looked at him, in his blue-striped apron, a faint flush on his high cheekbones from the heat of the stove, and the excitement in his dark eyes, and wondered why I couldn't be as uncomplicated. *Dear Joe.*

"You know what? You're right. Let's open it!"

Sarah and I watched as he set three goblets on the table and poured an inch or so of the golden liquid into each one.

"Buddy chewed up Daddy's slippers today," Sarah said, sliding a glance at me.

Joe chuckled and handed us both a glass. "That's okay. I needed a new pair anyway." He reached down and ruffled the puppy's ears.

I stifled a pang of guilt for working so much and not paying the dog enough attention, but hey, it wasn't even my dog. And for all his laissez-faire treatment, he seemed content enough.

Joe touched his glass to mine. "You worry too much," he said, smiling.

Third person today.

I took a slug of the gorgeous wine because I didn't feel up to dying from a stroke right now.

"So. How did you come up with the name Buddy for him, Sarah?"

"Hmm, I don't know. Had to call him something, and I haven't had time to think of anything else."

I looked down at the happy-go-lucky dog, whose tail immediately starting waving when he sensed my appraisal. "He reminds me of a history professor I once knew called

Jasper Weckert. He was so exuberant, so full of life, and yes, a little annoying sometimes, but you couldn't help but like him."

"Hey, Jasper!" Joe slapped his knee.

The dog wagged his tail even harder.

Sarah nodded. "He likes it. It's cool. And a more stylin' name than Buddy anyway."

After dinner was cleared away, we played a game of Monopoly, just like the good old days, and as usual, Joe spent his money first. I bought railroads, and Sarah ended up with Park Place. She built a row of hotels on it and bankrupted her parents.

I sipped my wine and watched the candlelight dance up the exposed brick wall in the kitchen and tried to let it all go. Maybe everyone was right. Maybe I did worry too much.

I'd color my hair tomorrow night.

The next morning was Wednesday, visiting day again for Angus's section of the prison. I woke up without the alarm, got dressed in a hurry, and arrived in the parking lot of the correctional facility at a few minutes before 8 a.m.

Angus came into the room, his hands bandaged and his hair neatly combed, but his expression somber. I rushed up and hugged him. Angus gave the best hugs. Kind of like hugging a friendly bear, or a live boulder.

"How are you feeling?" I asked.

"Okay, I guess. I still have a damn headache that won't quit."

"Will they give you some aspirin?"

"Took some, but it's not helping." He frowned as he looked beyond me. "Where's Betty?"

I sighed. "She had hip surgery, don't you remember? It's still hard for her to get around. And hey, what am I— chopped liver?"

His face relaxed a little. "No, and I still can't believe you eat that stuff. It's disgusting."

I grinned. Ah, the good old New York delis. They were the best—with their smoked salmon, corned beef, pastrami, and pickled herring in sour cream. I loved it all. "I can't believe *you* eat scrapple," I countered.

Scrapple is a Pennsylvania Dutch delicacy, and I use the word lightly, that's made of a mush of pork scraps formed into a semisolid congealed loaf. It's not for the faint of heart.

"What's the status, Angus?" I asked as we sat down. "When's your preliminary hearing? Have you talked to Warren?"

Angus shrugged. "I think it's scheduled for early next week. I dunno. I'm beginning to feel like I'll never get out of here. Seems like everyone's made up their minds about me already anyway."

I made a mental note to visit Warren and see if I could get some sense out of him, if not from Angus or Betty. If I wasn't satisfied, I'd try to get another lawyer in place before the hearing.

"Angus. Look, I'm doing my best to help you, but I have to ask you a few questions."

He sighed. "We've been through this before. I told you I don't remember much about that night."

I waved a hand impatiently. "Not about the night of Jimmy's murder. Now, this might sound a little off base, but I was wondering if someone might have killed Jimmy simply to get *you* in trouble?"

He snorted, but I persevered.

"Someone with a grudge against you. Like the Perkins boys, for instance."

His cheeks reddened. "I gave that family a good deal, fair and square. They were in such an all-fired rush to get their paws on the cash, they didn't want to wait for an auction. I gave it my best guess in the time they gave me, but yes, it's true, I didn't go over everything as carefully as if I'd brought it back to the auction building and gone through it one item at a time."

He shifted his chair closer to the table, the legs scraping against the floor. "Those boys act as if they made no money that day, Daisy, but they got a good price for everything, and the old lady's house, too. They used the money to open their feed store. It's not my fault they pissed a lot of it away at the bar."

He pointed at me. "In fact, remember the stuff I gave you when you opened your shop?"

I nodded, a sinking feeling in my chest.

"A lot of it came from that buyout."

Great.

"And what about the fight that got you in trouble when you were younger? The one that got you arrested the first time?"

Angus rubbed a large hand across his face. "What is this, Daisy? The Spanish Inquisition?"

"Yeah, well, you know me when I'm on a roll. Take no prisoners. Oops, pardon the pun."

We grinned at each other, in a ghost of the old camaraderie.

His face grew serious again as he stared past me as if seeing the long-ago scene in his mind.

"It was a Saturday night. Betty and I had gone to the movies in Sheepville. We were coming out afterwards, and this guy backhanded his wife right in front of us. Smacked her straight across the face. Guess he didn't like something she said."

I sucked in a breath, memories like dark shadows hovering over my shoulder.

"I couldn't stand by and let him treat a woman like that, Daisy. I saw red. Bright, fricking fire engine red. I could hardly see, I was so mad."

"So you beat him up?"

"Hell, yeah. I beat the living crap out of him." Angus pounded one fist into the palm of the other hand, making a loud smacking noise in spite of the bandages.

I gripped the edges of my plastic seat.

"I kept hitting and hitting and hitting him, and his face was just mush at that point, but I couldn't stop. They had to pull me off of him. What was left of him."

His eyes were full of remembered fury. As I stared into those blazing eyes, I wondered how well I really knew Angus Backstead. This man, capable of uncontrolled violence, was a complete stranger.

Whether it was a hot flash or an anxiety attack, I wasn't sure, but a surge of panic swept over me, and sweat prickled across my face and down my back.

I fought the urge to jump up and get the hell out of the room.

Angus suddenly started the loud chanting thing, like he did last time.

I wiped a hand across my forehead. "Damn it, Angus, stop it!" My voice cracked, but I managed to get the words out.

The guard at the door took a step closer.

"Don't want to talk about this anymore," Angus mumbled. "It's your fault. You're getting me upset."

"It's okay," I said, both to Angus and the guard, holding up a shaking hand. "Look, we'll talk about something else, all right? Just relax. Relax."

My heart was still pounding, but I plastered a bright smile on my face.

"Hey, you'll be glad to hear Betty's going ahead with the auction this weekend. But don't worry, we've got it covered. We're all helping out."

He was still muttering, staring at his hands, lost in his own despondent world. The dear friend I knew was gone, to a place where I couldn't touch him.

Come back to me, Angus.

"Patsy has agreed to step in for you with the bid calling. Can you picture that?"

A faint smile appeared.

"I told her about the filler words and to practice counting numbers backwards and forwards, but do you have any other tips for her?"

At that, his eyes seemed to regain their focus. He took a deep breath. "The thing is, you have to move an awful lot of stuff in a short period of time, and the chant is how you keep people's attention. It's almost like singing. It's faster than normal speech. You sort of hypnotize the bidders with the rhythm, the cadence of it."

"Okay. And how do you keep track of what the bid is?"

"Every auctioneer has his own way. Palms up can mean odd numbers, palms down for an even hundred-dollar bid. Tell Patsy not to worry about trying to go too fast when she's starting out. At the end of the day, the main job of an auctioneer is to communicate. If the audience can't understand him, he's not doing a good job."

Talking about auctioneering was calming him down.

I was still uncomfortably warm, my shirt clinging to my back with perspiration, but I could feel my heartbeat slowly returning to normal.

What a mess we were. Angus and me.

Staring across the table at my friend, I realized how much I had always depended on Angus—on his enormous strength, on his boisterous devil-may-care attitude that made me feel as though we could bulldoze our way through anything.

Now he needed me, whether he knew it or not, and I would be there for him.

"Angus, what about the time we went picking in Lancaster? Remember that? When you sent me up into the rafters of that decrepit barn?"

He laughed. "Yeah. You were smaller so you could climb better than me. I gave you some good advice, right? Don't fall through!"

"Thanks a lot. I was glad I was wearing jeans and sneakers that day."

I'd clambered like a monkey up a rickety ladder into the hayloft to retrieve a box of Buddy L toy vehicles that the owner told us were up there. I still remembered the joy on Angus's face upon seeing the old toys made of pressed steel. Like a kid on Christmas morning. He also had a passion for automotive and gasoline signs, and he'd found a couple of Esso Motor Oil signs outside the barn.

I'd done well, too. I'd picked up an antique dress form that was now proudly displayed in Eleanor's shop and a box of Standard sewing machine accessories and buttons. Plus a rare Singer leather sewing machine that Joe had later painstakingly oiled and restored, and that I'd sold for a big profit to a collector.

People in the country are savers, even hoarders. In New York, with space at a premium, you had to be ruthless about what you kept, but here, where farmhouses were passed down through generations, if no one had the energy to clean out the recesses of the attic each time it changed hands, the stuff built up.

It seemed like Angus wanted to talk about the old days and our adventures in picking, so I let him ramble. How mentoring me and taking me out on the road had reignited his passion for collecting. About the mint Baldwin Tidioute bone-handled jackknife with excellent blades that was one of his favorite finds.

We were quiet for a moment, reliving our memories. Doing rock, paper, scissors when it was something we both wanted. How we'd slap each other five on the way home, flushed with success.

Angus grinned at me. "I remember dragging your lazy ass out of bed more than once and listening to all the moaning and groaning until I got you a cup of coffee."

He would insist on picking me up at 5 a.m. on auction days, saying that the early bird got the worm. He wanted to be there on the dot of preview time to have a chance to look at every item. To me, it was still the middle of the night.

I'd be struggling out of bed to the sound of Joe mumbling, "What time is it? Thought the point of being retired was that we didn't have to get up early anymore." School days had been crazy early in order to make the commute into downtown Brooklyn.

But it didn't take me long to learn to jump out of bed when the alarm went off, the adrenaline already rushing through my veins.

The lights flickered, signaling the end of the visit. As the guard motioned that we had to leave, I was almost at the door before I realized I had forgotten to ask the most important question of all.

"Wait—Angus—who was the guy? The guy that you almost beat to death?"

"Oh, didn't I tell you? Hank Ramsbottom. Detective Frank Ramsbottom's father."

Chapter Six

I stumbled out of the prison, the memory of Angus's wry, defeated expression burned into my brain. No wonder he felt as though the situation was hopeless. If the detective on your case held a major grudge against you, did you really stand much of a chance, no matter how good your attorney? In a small community like this, where the police, the judge, the DA, and other officials were so tight, it made the odds against him stacked even higher.

On the way home, I stopped for gas on the outskirts of Sheepville.

Betty's brother, George Hildebrand, owned the garage, and he came over to the car when he saw me, wiping his hands on a rag.

I told him about visiting Angus at the prison.

"How's he doing?" he asked.

"He's okay, I guess, I—"

"Oh, it's just terrible, isn't it? Terrible situation. We've had Betty over a lot lately. Don't want her to sit home brooding by herself. I go and pick her up, you know. She doesn't like to drive at night. Neither does my Annie. It's really something to get older, isn't it? Everything starts going on you. The knees, the hips, the eyes. No idea why they call it the Golden Years . . ."

George was one of those people who could talk and talk, and talk some more, whether he had an audience or not. I watched the dollar amount on the gas pump click higher and higher. I pulled the nozzle out when I couldn't stand it anymore, even though the tank wasn't completely full.

He was still carrying on, something about Angus bringing the car in for an oil change on Friday. "Don't you know he forgot to pay? Good old Angus. But that's par for the course lately."

"Wait—what did you just say?" I stared at the sticker on my windshield and its mileage reminder for the next service.

"About what? Not paying?"

"About Angus coming in for an oil change? On Friday?"

"Yes. Friday afternoon."

Before he went to the pub with Jimmy Kratz.

"Thanks, George. Thanks for your help!" I barely remembered to rip my credit card receipt off the machine before I jumped in my car and waved good-bye to a startled George.

I clicked my odometer to zero, drove to Angus's house, and turned around. I drove back to Sheepville, stopped in front of the pub, and drove back to his house again.

Exactly 2.1 miles.

I got out of the Subaru, ran over to Angus's Ford F-150 pickup, and peered through the window at the odometer and the sticker. About two miles difference between the two, which proved that he didn't drive the half mile to Jimmy's the next morning and back again.

"Yes! Daisy Buchanan, you're a genius!"

Hold on, genius. If Jimmy walked home, why couldn't Angus have walked to Jimmy's, too? That's what the police will say.

I frowned, smoothing out a patch of kicked-up gravel with the bottom of my shoe.

But why *would* Angus walk? His first instinct would be to jump in the truck and get there as fast as possible, assuming he'd found the pens missing and was pissed off at Jimmy. He'd have sobered up enough to feel like he could drive, and wouldn't be thinking about subtleties like oil change stickers.

I glanced at my watch. I still had time to visit the detective and tell him about this new discovery. Knowing what I knew now, I wasn't assured of a great reception.

The desk sergeant punched a button on his phone, and held a muttered brief conversation before gesturing to the hallway behind the reception desk. "You can go on back."

I hurried down the hall toward an open doorway at the end. Ramsbottom didn't actually have an office, more like a piece of the back room. I ran the gauntlet of the other officers glancing my way—some with casual interest, others with more pointed stares—as I picked my way through their desks to where the hefty detective sat in the far-right-hand corner.

"Well, this is a pleasure, Mrs. Daly," he said, his tone indicating the opposite. To my surprise, he wasn't sitting around stuffing his face today. Only nursing a giant plastic cup of iced coffee with a straw.

He waved for me to sit down in front of the desk as his cell phone rang. "Lemme call you back," he murmured to whoever was on the other end and slipped the phone into the holster on his belt.

I quickly explained about the oil change and how it proved that Angus never drove back to Jimmy's on Saturday morning.

Ramsbottom took a long suck of his drink. "Backstead could of walked to Jimmy Kratz's place."

"*Could* have," I said. "But why would he? Angus would have sobered up enough by then to think he could drive. He'd want to get there as fast as possible. Assuming he went there at all. Which he didn't."

Ramsbottom shook his head. "You can't know the exact route Angus Backstead would of driven that day. Sorry, ma'am, but it's not a strong enough piece of evidence."

His cell phone rang again. "Excuse me, I have to take this call."

Staggered by his politeness in actually excusing himself for the phone call, I got up and took a few steps away from the desk to give him some space, although in this open room no one had much privacy.

I wandered over to the pictures and awards on a wall that had been painted white at one time. One of the photos caught my eye. It was a thinner version of Ramsbottom—about the same age as the detective was now. A picture of a handsome man with his young son. This must be his father, Hank Ramsbottom. The man Angus had almost beaten to death.

Ramsbottom was talking so low I could hardly hear. He was leaning away from me, the love handles on his back spilling over the top of his pants and testing the limits of his pale blue cotton shirt.

During school-exam periods, I had perfected the art of appearing to be engrossed in the work on my desk, but could pick up on the rustle of a note being passed, or even feel a glance or words being mouthed between students.

I did it now as I studied the photos and listened to Ramsbottom's end of the conversation. Something about a big event going down on Saturday night. It sounded like he was making sure everyone knew to show up on time, and to keep the plans top secret. Must be a drug bust or something.

Another photo showed more clearly the young detective at his high school graduation, again with his father smiling proudly next to him.

A few moments later, I sensed Ramsbottom standing behind me.

"I know that your father was the man Angus had the fight with years ago," I said quietly, staring at the pictures.

He cleared his throat. "My dad was never quite right after that. He was what they called 'slow' back then. Today, we'd say 'brain damaged.'"

I felt queasy picturing the scene as Angus had described it. The man prone on the sidewalk, unconscious, his face a hideous bloody pulp.

"Angus Backstead couldn't remember much about *that* fight either. Said he saw red, and next thing he knew, he was being led away in handcuffs. I've read the report. It's like he blanks out about the part where he goes apeshit."

I remembered Angus talking about seeing red.

"My father's symptoms didn't show up right away." His voice was softer now. "It started with some slurred speech, occasional blackouts. Sometimes he'd just fall asleep without warning and then he'd be fine for a while. Then he started having epileptic seizures."

I turned to face him. "Did the brain damage from the fight cause the seizures?" I whispered.

He shrugged. "The doctors said it was hard to tell. Irregardless, a few years later he had an accident with a combine harvester. I seen it happen. I was twenty-three years old."

Ramsbottom looked over my shoulder, gazing at the pictures on the wall. "The starter motor stuck. He got down to fix it, but he forgot to leave the stopper out."

I swallowed. I wanted to ask him to please stop telling me the story, but my throat closed up tight.

"A seizure dropped him to the ground and that's when the machine fired up and ran over him. Took both his legs off. I managed to pull him free. My mother called the ambulance, and they were there in a matter of minutes, but there was nothing anyone could do. He died from a massive loss of blood."

Oh no. Not now. I could feel myself spiraling down to that dark place—full of pain, terror, and premature, senseless death.

As those familiar black wings flapped around my head and the walls wavered, I gripped Ramsbottom's arm.

"Jeez. Are you okay, Mrs. Daly? You're white as a ghost. Here, sit down. Put your head between your legs."

He lowered me gently to the floor, and I sat there for a minute, head between my knees, sweating and clammy, fighting the spinning of the room.

The other cops were around me now, too. One of them handed me a triangular cone of ice water and I gratefully gulped it down. "Ma'am? Are you ill?" he asked.

"I didn't eat breakfast. Must be low blood sugar or something," I mumbled.

"You want that I should get you a donut?"

I was too sick to correct his grammar. "No, thank you. I'll be fine."

A couple of minutes later, after I had sucked down more cold water, and I was okay apart from the sheen of sweat still covering my body, I accepted Ramsbottom's help as he lifted me to my feet.

I clung to him for a moment. "I'm so sorry for your loss," I managed. "I had no idea."

He nodded, his heavy-lidded eyes full of remembered grief.

For the first time I saw him as a person, someone else with a tragedy in their life. I'd dismissed him as an ignorant oaf, but now all I saw was a fatherless young man.

I stumbled over to the desk and retrieved my pocketbook from where I'd left it on the chair. Ramsbottom picked up his cup and drained the last dregs of iced coffee out of the bottom of it, the sound like water swirling out of the bottom of a bathtub.

"The man's a menace, Mrs. Daly. For all intensive purposes, my father died outside the movie theater that day.

Now you see why I could care less what happens to Angus Backstead."

"You *couldn't* care less."

He stared at me. "That's what I said."

When I got to Sometimes a Great Notion, it was well past opening time. Martha must have stopped by and left the covered plate that was sitting on the porch.

After the rain the day before, summer had returned, more determined than ever. The ninety-plus-degree humid air lay over the village like a hot, wet blanket, shutting down the supply of oxygen and making it difficult for its inhabitants to breathe. I hurried into the store, set the plate on the counter, and sank onto a stool behind the register.

"Oh my God," I whispered, still struggling to process the events of the morning. I was convinced now that Ramsbottom would do nothing to try and find other suspects. If Angus was going to be saved, it would be up to me.

But seeds of doubt were prickling through my mind— from the last person I thought could have sown them. Things weren't so cut and dried for me anymore.

Angus always talked about karma. This was karma with a vengeance.

Could the Angus Backstead I knew be the same person who, in a violent rage, had hurt someone so badly as to leave him brain damaged? Was it possible that Angus had mentally blocked out doing the same thing to Jimmy?

I squeezed my eyes shut against the insidious doubt creeping through my brain like the vines clambering over Reenie's kitchen window.

The shop was blessedly cool. A UV film on the windows blocked the severity of the sun's glare, providing filtered light to protect the fabrics. The hum of the powerful air-conditioning system Angus had installed was working full force.

Damn it, I needed coffee, but couldn't seem to find the energy to get up and make it.

I glanced at the gold rococo mirror next to the counter. A reflection of an aging woman with swollen eyes, pale skin, and a thick gray stripe down the center of her hair stared back at me.

"But who the hell cares?" I said to her. I gathered my hair up into a bun, pulling the damp strands underneath off my neck and securing it all with a rhinestone hair clip.

I lifted up the edge of aluminum foil wrapped around the plate. Blueberry scones. They looked delicious. I folded the foil down again. Even though I hadn't eaten breakfast, my appetite was gone.

It was silly, but I felt guilty for feeling sympathy for Ramsbottom, too.

Was it too far-fetched to think *he* might have killed Jimmy to frame Angus?

Well, no more far-fetched than thinking the Perkins boys did it. And Ramsbottom certainly had a better motive.

The detective wasn't in great shape, though. He looked like one of those guys who'd had the size and muscle to play high school football, but the years and weight had crept up and softened him. He certainly couldn't wield a heavy barn beam.

Wait a minute. Could Jimmy have been beaten up somewhere else, with some other kind of weapon, and brought *back* to the crime scene? To the place where Ramsbottom knew Angus's fingerprints would be all over everything?

But that still didn't solve the problem of the only footprints around the barn belonging to Angus.

Although who had said that? *Ramsbottom.*

And who'd said Jimmy had been hit with a barn beam in the first place? *Ramsbottom.*

If you were out for revenge, as a police officer, there were probably plenty of ways to mess with the evidence.

All my life, I'd been brought up to respect those in

authority. My own father had been a firefighter. It was hard to believe that an officer of the law would stoop that low.

I shivered. In spite of the heat and humidity outside, now that the damp sweat had dried on my skin, I was suddenly chilled to the bone.

I'd meant to ask Angus about the estate company that had consigned the pens, too, but after he got so upset, I didn't dare push it. Tonight I planned to go over and help Betty after work, so I'd dig around the auction building and see what information I could find.

Although how the heck would I research this company, even if I did find out who it was, without jeopardizing Reenie? Call them up and say, "Hey, how are you doing? Are you the people who were cooking up some underhanded scheme with Jimmy Kratz, and when he double-crossed you, you decided to do him in?"

Crap. I had absolutely no clue how to go about it. It was the same feeling I'd had when I questioned Cyril. I wasn't a detective, for God's sake. I was simply a former school-teacher who now owned a sewing notions store.

No one had come into Sometimes a Great Notion yet today. The brutal humidity was as effective as a blinding snowstorm in deterring shoppers. But for once I was grateful the store wasn't busy. The lack of business would give me a chance to get my act together and unpack some new merchandise.

If I could ever find the strength to get off this damn stool, that is.

Another image popped into my mind. Years ago, when he was still working construction before he devoted himself to the auction business full-time, Angus had brought home a bucket of baby blackbirds. They'd been abandoned by their mother on the construction site. He showed me the sorry little group at the bottom of the empty five-gallon paint bucket and said he planned to take them to the nature center when they opened the next day.

He'd fed the birds with a baby dropper and nursed them through the night, but when I stopped by in the morning, they had all died.

Angus was sitting there, on a wooden bench in his workshop, tears streaming down his ruddy, weather-roughened face that he didn't even bother to wipe away. Sick at the loss myself, I sat there beside him, not knowing what to say.

After some time had passed, I whispered that I didn't know what I could do to help.

"You were here and you cared," he said finally. "That's good enough for me."

How was I supposed to reconcile the man I knew, gruff, unbelievably generous, protector of the weak, to someone everyone believed to be a killer?

I squeezed my eyes shut for a moment and then hauled myself to my feet.

Come on Daisy, make the coffee. Stat. And lots of it.

Perhaps I'd pay another visit to Reenie and pressure her into telling Ramsbottom about Jimmy's deal to bid on the pens. The detective might listen to her, if not me. I knew she was scared, but so was I. For my best friend, Angus.

It seemed as though there were other more compelling suspects than the estate company anyway. Like the Perkins family. Like Ramsbottom. Like Fiona Adams.

And what about Hank Ramsbottom's wife? Was she still around? She wasn't in any of the photos on the wall. I also needed to go see Warren Zeigler, the attorney, and satisfy myself that he was doing everything possible to get Angus acquitted.

As the coffee brewed, I brought a couple of boxes down from the bedroom upstairs.

I liked to display merchandise so that it didn't look too "organized." So a buyer could still feel the same thrill of the hunt that I'd felt on our picking adventures. The idea was that you could walk around the store several times and still spot something new. I set an apothecary cabinet near the counter with an inlaid rosewood box on top. On a small table nearby, I grouped some thimbles, lithographed paper packages of hand sewing needles, and sixty-year-old German sequins.

"What do you think, Alice? Do you like it?" Over in the corner, Alice the mannequin kept her expression carefully composed.

"Wait, you don't have to say anything. You're right. Too formal." I added a whimsical note with a pincushion in the shape of a large strawberry.

I stood back to admire my tableau. Much better. Alice was often helpful like that.

I still remembered with fondness, and more than a little longing, the twenty yards of fine French satin I'd found in the trunk I'd bought at auction that fateful day a year ago.

A glorious deep blue with a peacock design. It killed me to sell it, but the profit from the sale had paid the rent for the next three months, which was a huge help for a fledgling business. I'd kept a scrap of the peacock fabric in a two-inch photo frame next to the register as a remembrance.

I had worried at first that I would have a coronary each time I made a sale, but I'd come to the way of thinking that I had these treasures only for a short while. That they were in my safekeeping until they went to a good home.

Often I wondered who had sat in the child's scarred wooden school desk, or who had labored over the tiny stitches in a needlework sampler. Out of the next box, I picked up a slim burgundy glass perfume bottle with a silver stopper, and when I held it up to my nose, I caught a faint hint of the fragrance that had once been inside. I tried to picture the woman who'd worn it; the scent a connection between us through time.

As a child, I remembered hanging on to my grandmother's every word, listening to her stories and memories of life as a milliner, soaking up as much history as I could. I was enraptured with the sewing notions used to trim hats: the ribbons, braids, glass beads, veiling, velvet and organdy flowers.

I slumped down again, the caffeine rush worn off, swallowing against a bittersweet longing for the past.

"Hey, Alice, you know I think my daughter would be hard-pressed to tell someone much about my life. And she certainly doesn't understand my connection to all these beautiful old things."

Alice, diplomatic as ever, didn't comment, but there was a wealth of understanding in those almond-shaped eyes framed by impossibly long lashes.

I blinked when Sarah walked in the door, as if thinking about her had conjured her up.

"Who were you talking to, Mom?"

I could feel the flush heating up my neck and cheeks. "Oh, um, you know, just practicing my sales pitches."

"Oh-ka-a-ay." She wrinkled her nose and looked around the store. "You need help with anything?"

She must have been utterly bored out of her mind if she was asking me for something to do. But I wasn't about to look a gift horse in the mouth.

Not that Sarah would even know what that old-fashioned phrase meant.

I walked over to the computer and pulled up a file. "Well, I've been doing some after-hours open houses, about one every couple of months, specifically for interior designers and high-end collectors. I need to send out an e-mail blast for the next one. Would you like to create the flyer?"

"Sure." Sarah skimmed through my file, which showed past events that featured French linens, quilts and samplers, or vintage jewelry, bags, and clothing.

I pointed to some of the more recent images. "See, they usually have a specific theme, and I serve cheese and wine, and of course offer a substantial discount for that evening only."

"This is actually a cool idea, Mom. I didn't know you were doing this."

Score one for old Daisy.

"What's the theme this time?" she asked.

"I have quite a lot of children's items right now. The auction this weekend will give me a chance to focus and acquire even more." I thought about the dollhouse that would be up for bid and my pulse accelerated again.

"Ah, so *that's* why you're helping Betty Backstead with the auction. I see your ulterior motive!" Sarah grinned at me.

"Brat." I grimaced and nudged her with my elbow.

I showed her some of the items in the corner of the store—a lithographed tin sand pail, an early 1900s Blue Onion toy silverware set, a Chautauqua home-schooling desk, and a 1930s heavy pressed steel toy metal stove that was green and white jadeite with an orange back panel.

She seemed to take a little more interest in the children's toys than she ever did in the sewing notions.

I smiled to myself. *There's more than one way to skin a cat.*

As I took photos of Mary Willis's table linens for the website, I glanced surreptitiously at my daughter. Her blond hair fell in a shiny golden wave over her shoulder, and she bit her full bottom lip in concentration as she worked at the computer.

I couldn't believe Sarah was still hanging around Millbury. She must be more burned out and upset than I'd realized.

As a child, she'd been fascinated with the movies, and she had a funny habit of dotting her speech with snippets of film dialogue. It was sometimes hard to tell where the movie left off, and where the real conversation began. In fact, she had named this store after the film *Sometimes a Great Notion,* starring Paul Newman, Henry Fonda, and Lee Remick.

Tears stung my eyes, but I willed them away. Sarah didn't deal with my sentimentality too well. I remembered a conversation I'd had with her when she must have been about five, and I was in my thirties.

"Why do old ladies always cut their hair so short, Mom?" she asked as she played with my long dark brown locks.

I smiled at her. "I don't know, Sarah."

"Promise me you'll never cut yours?"

"Well, I'll have to cut it sometime," I teased.

Even today I kept it shoulder length, but now I had to dye it to achieve that rich chestnut color. Coloring my hair every month was such a production. It was something, like my period, that I wouldn't mind not having to go through anymore. One of these days I'd let it go all gray. But not this week.

I sighed. Damn it, when was I going to find the time to do my hair?

"You have a lot of clients in this database."

Sarah's comment broke my reverie.

I straightened up. "Yes, the store has really hit its stride. And with interest in crafts on the upswing, it should turn a nice profit again this year."

"You seem to have lots of friends in this town, too. Are you happy here, Mom?"

"Yes, I am," I said carefully, camera hanging down, not quite sure where she was going with this.

"That's good."

I wanted to broach the subject of how to make Sarah happy, too. I opened my mouth, but before I could find the right words, the doorbell rang and our token male on the street, Chris Paxson from the bicycle shop, walked in.

After I introduced him to Sarah, I apologized for the state of the MALE box. It was sadly depleted from Martha's shift the day before.

"Actually I'm looking for a gift for my mother," he said.

Sarah hopped down from her stool. "Here, I'll show you around."

Chris followed her, transfixed. I think he'd have bought the phone book if she'd shown it to him. I was poised, ready to step in, but as I listened, it sounded like she was doing fine. Maybe she'd absorbed more knowledge about the store than she'd realized.

I peeked at the computer screen. The flyer was perfect. A collage of the photos of children's accessories for sale, superimposed over a watermarked photo of the store, featuring a Raggedy Ann in a rocking chair, who seemed to welcome guests in. The font she'd selected was an antique child's picture book style, but still easy to read. I shook my head at her innate creativity. I'd have wrestled with this all afternoon.

I looked out of the store's front display windows to see Martha trying to parallel park. She drove a white 1977 Lincoln Continental that was about half a city block long. The backseat with its opera lights in the corners was so expansive you could stretch your legs all the way straight out, and then some. I'd ridden in it once, but only once. That was enough.

The unfortunate neighbor who lived opposite her house had a mailbox that had started off normal size but, after the number of times Martha had backed straight out of her driveway and plowed it down, was now about two feet off the ground after numerous replantings. The mailman was threatening not to deliver mail to it anymore.

After several tries Martha finally left the car angled halfway up on the sidewalk.

Chris chose the inlaid rosewood sewing box, which would have been my first choice anyway. It really was a beautiful piece. I added a packet of vintage needles and a silver thimble as a treat. He chatted with Sarah while I rang up the purchase and put it into one of my signature shopping bags with its peacock blue grosgrain drawstring.

"Nice parking job," I called out as the door crashed open and a wild-eyed Martha strode in.

"Good God, that doll gives me a funny turn every time I come in, it's like a steam bath out there, where the hell were you this morning, did you get the scones?" She sucked in a long shuddering breath.

"Yes, thank you," I said meekly.

"Can you believe this horrendous humidity? I hope it improves by the weekend. That auction house isn't air-conditioned, you know. Just a few stupid ceiling fans."

Martha glared at the three of us. "I'm telling you right now, that poky little snack bar will be hotter than the inside of a pizza oven. I'll be sweating like a hooker in church."

Chris Paxson, intelligent male that he was, quickly said his farewells, and with one last longing look at Sarah, he left.

"Martha, forget about the heat for a second," I pleaded. "I have news."

I explained my brilliant theory about the oil change and the truck, and going to see the detective. "And the worst thing is, are you ready for this, the guy that Angus beat up was Ramsbottom's father."

"No!" Sarah and Martha exclaimed in unison.

"Angus is screwed, then." Martha lifted her heavy mane of red hair and stood in front of the vent blowing cold air, moaning in relief.

"This is a family store, thank you very much. Watch the language." Eleanor appeared as if by magic.

I poured Eleanor a cup of coffee. "Apparently Ramsbottom Senior hit his wife across the face when they were coming out of the movies one night. Angus saw that and just lost it. The guy was never quite right afterwards, and had a terrible accident with a combine harvester a few years later. And while it might not be fair, I think Ramsbottom blames Angus for his father's eventual death, too."

Eleanor gracefully accepted the cup with her long slender fingers. She could drink coffee all day long and sleep like a baby. "Wonder if the father beat Junior as well?"

I stared at her. "You know, I didn't think about that, but I should have. When I was teaching, I'd suspect some students had abusive parents. I'd want to help, but the odd thing was, if the police ever got involved, the kids were ready to defend the parents to the end."

"Like a weird sort of Stockholm syndrome thing?"

"I guess so."

The door bell jangled and Cyril Mackey marched into the store.

Chapter Seven

※

We stood there, frozen in place, as he came up to us.

"I brought tha plate back," he announced, thrusting it at me.

"Um, thank you." It was actually Martha's plate, but I wasn't about to correct him.

"Them treats were champion," Cyril growled, turning to her.

Martha simply nodded, hands still raised above her head holding her hair, her cheeks flushed. She had always been outspoken, and now with Teddy gone, she usually said whatever she damn well felt like saying, but this was the first time I had ever seen her rendered speechless.

"Ay, up." Cyril observed her with interest for a few moments, and then looked around, sizing up the store. "Freezing in here."

With the body-hugging Lycra wrap top Martha was wearing, it was easy to see what he was getting at.

Silence reigned as we all struggled to form a sentence.

He focused on me again. "How's Angus, then?"

"He's okay. I visited him this morning." I cleared my throat with an effort. "Um—we're going to help Betty with the auction this weekend."

Cyril nodded. "Just as well. That old biddy couldn't organize a piss-up in a brewery."

"Good God, man, there are ladies present!" Martha exploded, finally finding her voice, hands collapsing to her sides, and her hair falling down in red waves.

I fought the urge to close my eyes, but Cyril merely put up a hand as if to calm a skittish mare. "Now then, simmer down, lass."

Martha looked like an apoplectic goldfish as she opened and closed her mouth.

Cyril shrugged. "Thought you women would be nattering on in here. Always heard it were like a party or summat, but nowt much happening, far as I can see."

I hurriedly wrapped some of the shortbread in aluminum foil and pressed it into his hands.

"Much obliged." He tipped his cap at us. "Afternoon, ladies." And with that, he was gone.

There was another minute of shocked silence until Martha spoke.

"Good *God*. Who does that man think he is anyway?"

She turned on me. "And why the hell did you have to give him more treats? It's like feeding a stray cat. You know it'll be back for more."

I handed her the clean plate. "I don't know. I couldn't think of anything else to do at the time."

"I think he fancies you," Eleanor said to Martha.

Sarah burst out laughing, and after a moment, I joined in.

Martha slammed the plate down so hard it was a miracle it didn't break. "Don't mess with me today, woman. It's too stinking hot. If I wasn't so old, I'd think I was having hot flashes."

She twirled her hair up into a thick knot, grabbed a jade

hairpin from a glass jar, and stabbed the whole mass with
it. "Maybe I have a brain tumor or something. That's one of
the symptoms, you know."

"Too much self-diagnosis on the Internet is dangerous to
your health." Eleanor drained her coffee cup.

I brought over the pot for a refill and grinned at Sarah.
If laughter was good for the heart, I should live to about a
hundred and fifty after spending time with these two.

Business in the store picked up after Eleanor and Martha
left, and I was busy for the rest of the afternoon.

"Tell Daddy I'll be late," I said to Sarah as she headed
home around four o'clock. "You guys go ahead and eat dinner without me. I'm going to help Betty after work."

All down the twisting River Road, houses in a gamut of
styles rose up along one side with stone walls appearing
to catch them from sliding right down into the water. Some
were cottages cramped together, with tiny front doors no
more than a few feet from the road, and flowers spilling over
window planters. Some were exuberant Victorians painted
aqua, rose, and peach with the Stars and Stripes flying
proudly on their porches. And some were breathtaking prop-
erties with curved stone archways and pillars, mullioned
windows, Tudor markings, and garages that looked like barn
doors set into the side of the rock.

The Delaware River was sluggish in this heat, its wide
brown expanse of water dappled with patches of green. River
Road crossed over the canal, so as I headed toward
Sheepville, the river was always on my left, but sometimes
the canal was to the left, sometimes to the right. Masses of
Queen Anne's lace and goldenrod grew in unfettered aban-
don along its banks.

White onion-shaped finials on a fence overlooking the
river surrounded a blue-shingled house with a white sign
that read, HOME-AT-LAST.

Betty was busy cataloging items when I arrived, including the coveted dollhouse.

It might be a good birthday present for Claire. Her birthday wasn't until Halloween, but I knew she'd appreciate it.

"Hi, Betty. Good news! Patsy's agreed to be the auctioneer on Saturday."

Betty clapped her hands together. "Oh, that's wonderful. Now I just hope I can get ready in time."

"Hey, did you ever find out where those pens came from?"

She shook her head. "I went through everything for the police, but I couldn't find any records. They're probably filed in some strange place, but they have to be here somewhere. They'll turn up sooner or later."

I looked around the crowded office with its haphazard piles of papers covering the desk, with more stacked in the corners and on top of the filing cabinets.

Maybe later rather than sooner.

"It's strange that no one from the company has contacted me for insurance purposes. Anyway, I'm making sure all the paperwork is correct for *this* auction," she said with a firm set to her mouth.

I hid my surprise as I followed her out to the main floor. Angus had always been the one in charge. Guess meek and mild Betty was taking over now.

She gave me the job of labeling the box lots.

I checked the description next to the numbers on my list as I attached the stickers, noting items I'd like to bid on with one part of my brain, while random thoughts skittered through my head. Cataloging all the things *I* had to take care of: Trying to save Angus, run the store, plan the open house, help with the auction, not to mention the mess at home, which didn't even feel like mine anymore.

We'd dropped right back into the same old patterns as when Sarah was a teenager—leaving her breakfast dishes in the sink instead of the dishwasher, damp towels across the floor of the bathroom, shoes wherever she happened to kick them off, and clothes strewn everywhere.

Oh, and not to mention Jasper.

I felt like I had to keep an eye on him all the time because no one else did. This morning he'd chewed the cord off the vacuum cleaner while I was taking a shower.

Why did I always have to be the responsible one? My upbringing had centered on following rules and doing the right thing. At school, I was always the one to organize birthday celebrations for the other teachers. I was the one who bought the card and got everyone to sign it. I was the one who stopped at the bakery early before school to pick up the cake.

Why was it always *me*, damn it?

I slapped on another sticker. Just once, I'd like to do something wild. That's why hanging out with Angus was so much fun. He made me feel like a kid again. Sometimes we laughed so hard that my stomach literally hurt by the time I got home. Not to say that Joe and I didn't have fun. But with Angus, he was so irreverent and exuberant, it was a whole different experience—the overflowing joy of simply being alive.

Around nine o'clock, I was exhausted, and so was Betty. I told her I'd be back the next night to help her again.

"Hi, babe," Joe said as I walked into the kitchen to find him playing cards with Sarah. "We had Chinese. Want me to heat some up for you?"

"In a minute. Right now I need a hug."

Joe quickly got up and folded me into his arms. I breathed a sigh of relief and held on to him, raising my face up for his kiss.

"Aw, cut out the sappy stuff, you two," Sarah mock complained, like she did when she was a kid.

Joe and I laughed and we broke apart. He squeezed my shoulders one last time.

I saw a shadow cross Sarah's face. No doubt she was

thinking of her recent ill-fated love affair. For the hundredth time I hoped that one day she'd find the same happiness I'd found with Joe.

The next morning, the temperature was already rising when I got up and let Jasper out into the yard. It would be even hotter and more humid than yesterday, if that was possible.

I hadn't slept well, and the thought of another long day at the store and another night with Betty was overwhelming me before I'd even begun. A wave of exhaustion, no, more like a tsunami, crashed over me. I hadn't been this tired since I quit teaching. That schedule of long days and even longer nights spent grading papers and going over lesson plans was a killer. Somehow I'd done it then, but I was out of practice.

"Oh, no!" I exclaimed out loud as I brought the dog back inside. I'd forgotten about my appointment with the designer to see the children's merchandise. "I can't believe I did that."

I was usually so organized. I must be losing my mind. Suddenly I had a glimpse of how Angus must feel. A brain like a cotton ball, tired, worried, and emotionally wrung out to boot.

"What's the matter?" Sarah wandered into the kitchen.

"I'm double booked. I have an appointment to meet someone tonight, and I also promised to help Betty again."

"You look tired, Mom," she observed, head to one side.

I breathed out slowly. "Thanks." Were my wrinkles showing more than usual? God knows my gray roots were. I looked sharply at her, but I could only read concern in her eyes.

"Look, Dad and I can go and help Mrs. Backstead. Why don't you concentrate on the store?" Sarah held up her ever-present camera. "I'll take the pictures and keep it all under control."

Joe came in at that moment. "And I'll be the grunt man. You just tell me where you want things."

I hesitated a moment too long.

"Jeez, Mom. I think I can handle it," Sarah snapped. "You have no idea of what I deal with on a film set. It's *crazy*. Everything is shot out of order and it takes some heavy-duty organizational skills to keep it together. Give me some credit."

Let it go, Daisy.

I forced a smile. "Okay, I'll take you up on the offer. Thanks."

That night I met the designer, and when she mentioned she was searching for an antique christening gown, I handed her one of Eleanor's business cards. In a small town like this, the store owners had to stick together, and we often recommended one another to clients. The designer was delighted with her purchases, praising me on my eye for the unusual, and for the quality of the merchandise, and I knew I'd made another good connection.

Sometimes I wished Sarah could be a fly on the wall at those moments, and see me when I was at my best.

When I got home, Sarah and Joe were watching a movie on our new flat-screen TV in the library. Joe offered to fix me some dinner, but I had passed the hungry stage a couple of hours ago. Besides, I didn't want to disturb him. He was relaxing on the chocolate-colored leather couch, his feet up on the old steamer trunk.

I kicked my sandals off and snuggled up next to him.

"Hello, stranger," I whispered. "I feel like I never see you anymore." I wanted to ask them how things were going at the auction, but Sarah made a shushing noise, so I leaned my head on Joe's shoulder and tried to follow the story line of the film. The next thing I knew, it was two hours later, and he was carrying me off to bed.

Joe pulled me next to his large body, spooning me, and I think if I'd had the energy to turn over, we might have made love, but somehow sleep seemed more enticing.

Friday flew by, too, in a blur of appointments, phone calls, and website sales. In addition to this weekend's auction, at which I planned to do some major bidding, I would need to get to some more auctions and estate sales soon and replenish my stock, but I'd hardly had a moment to breathe.

I fretted that we'd be ready for Saturday, but when I got home that night, Joe assured me that Betty and Sarah had everything well in hand. We ordered pizza for dinner as even Joe was too tired to cook.

Finally, at 9 p.m. on Friday night, I colored my damn hair.

S aturday morning dawned bright and clear, and Joe, Sarah, and I headed over to Sheepville right after breakfast.

The auction building sat on three acres, with parking for a hundred cars, plus room for overspill onto the mowed fields surrounding the property. It was a large, low structure, clad in corrugated light gray metal. Inside the lobby was the reception desk, where customers registered, and also paid for their purchases afterward. Then came the snack bar, the office and bathrooms, and finally the main auction space with fluorescent light bars hanging overhead and several industrial-sized ceiling fans.

Rows of wooden folding seats that Angus had salvaged from a theater before demolition sat in the center of the concrete floor. In front of the bank of seats was the stage, and around the room were tables displaying merchandise. Large pieces of furniture were situated along the back wall, and artwork for sale hung on a paneled movable partition.

Some material would be sold "as is," and some items had to be cleaned, polished, and repaired before auction time. Joe also had the patience for restoration, among his other stellar qualities, and he went over to the tables to fix a few last things as I walked around with Betty and Sarah.

I knew I'd have to restrain myself from checking over what they'd done, but it all looked neat and organized.

Sarah handed me a catalog. The photos were crisp and clear and the merchandise well lit. "Betty told me something about each piece and I wrote up the descriptions."

"She's so talented and capable," Betty said, gazing at Sarah in admiration. "I couldn't have done it without her."

"Sarah, this is great." A wash of relief swept over me. "I'm impressed."

"Why do you sound so surprised?" Betty said. "She *is* your daughter after all."

I grinned at Sarah and we strolled around the room together as I made a list of items I planned to bid on. The beautiful antique dollhouse, of course, with its handmade furniture, hand-sewn linen curtains, real glass windows, and a miniature needlepoint carpet. Also the Singer Featherweight sewing machine and an old spool cabinet that read, "J & P Coats best six cord spool cotton cabinet. White, black and colors for hand and machine. Warranted 200 yards."

There was a huge amount of merchandise to be sold. Lots of nice pieces like an oak rolltop desk, a grandfather clock, a lovely set of English Regency dining chairs, an extensive collection of Depression glass, and a jelly cupboard.

We stayed through the pre-auction walk-through and then went home to relax for a couple of hours. While Sarah took a nap, I took Jasper for a walk.

He really was a good pup, already walking to heel with me. I could feel his joy in all the scents of the countryside. He sniffed at every tree and telephone pole and kept lifting his leg even though he was peed out after about two miles. I hoped he would behave while we were at the auction tonight.

A tired dog is a good dog.

Chapter Eight

❇

I could feel the buzz in the air before we even entered the auction building. With no sale last week, the crowd was full of a pent-up urge to buy.

Joe went off to find Betty while I took one last walk around. The "warm-up" lots had been moved into the loading area. Small valuable antiques, china, and jewelry were housed in locked rolling cabinets that could be wheeled up to the stage when their numbers came up.

There were plenty of familiar faces in the crowd, and it was easy to pick out the dealers. Auction halls are typically not well lit, and the pros were the ones armed with flashlights, tape measures, and magnifying glasses. They wore an intense expression as they cruised up and down the rows, making bets with each other about how high a price various items would bring. One man bear-crawled underneath a dresser in front of me, and I had to step over his boots, which stuck out into the aisle. Sometimes parts were "married together," such as a highboy with a chest on top, and you had to make sure they were an original set.

Old men outweighed the women about two to one, many in plaid shirts and jeans, and several with long tobacco-stained beards. The old men, I mean. Well, for the most part.

"Better than the junk they usually have," said one as he picked up a brass Westinghouse fan.

"Yup. Saw a fan like that sell at auction in Hatfield last week for three hundred dollars." His friend smoothed down the edges of his mustache. "All depends on condition."

They nodded sagely at each other. *Condition* was the magic word.

Some people just came for the entertainment every Saturday. They didn't even register for a bidder number. I passed a husband saying to his wife, "There's lots of stuff here this time, honey. You should be able to find yourself something *else* we don't need!"

To the far right was an area with metal basement-type shelving holding the box lots. Typically the cardboard boxes contained miscellaneous items such as books, Christmas decorations, tools, kitchen utensils, and whatever else was too small or inexpensive to auction off individually. A bidder bought the whole thing for a few dollars.

Tablecloths and napkins, Victorian lithographed picture blocks, glass doorknobs, and vintage buttons were added to my list. *Ah, vintage buttons.* To me, they were like jewelry now. I'd become fascinated with how many different kinds there were. My mouth watered as I spotted butterscotch Bakelite, enameled metal, and some unusual ivory "spaghetti" extruded knot varieties.

Real jewelry was good, too, because it didn't take up much space, and was sometimes a purchase that loosened up a buyer for something else in the store. Besides, I needed to dress up Alice.

Usually I focused on a certain type of item. At flea markets, it required tunnel vision to let the sewing notions jump out at me. Tonight, however, a set of French Majolica green oyster dishes caught my eye. I figured I had the poetic license to put certain pieces in my store that weren't strictly sewing-related. Everything sold in the end.

My heart jumped as I recognized the tall figure of Fiona Adams striding through the crowd. What the heck was she doing here? Was she planning to make trouble? I braced myself as she came nearer, but she stalked right past, with no sign of recognition on her face.

I stared after her. I don't know why it irritated me so much that the obnoxious Ms. Adams had passed over me like another piece of furniture up for bid. I didn't want to talk to her anyway.

I've often been told I have a nice face. People say I remind them of their sister's best friend, or their neighbor. More often than not, though, they never remember meeting me in the first place. Nice equaled forgettable, it seemed.

I thought of Martha, or Sarah, or even Eleanor. No one could forget them.

Especially not Martha. I wondered what she'd be wearing tonight. Probably be a bit over the top as usual, but somehow she pulled it off.

Back in the day, I'd been the best-dressed teacher on the Lower East Side, fulfilling my shopping addiction on a limited budget by zeroing in on all the designer fashion sales. But the suits and dresses were long gone, and today I was invisible in a comfortable top and jeans.

Crap.

Joe caught up to me. He said he was planning on bidding on a cigar cutter from the 1880s, a piece of Trench art from World War II, a set of wooden golf clubs, and a vintage U.S. Army suitcase. I raised an eyebrow at the expensive-sounding list. He grinned at me like a guilty little boy. I had to keep an eye on Joe at auction. It was so easy to get seduced by the challenge of outbidding someone else, and he invariably got caught up in the excitement and forgot about his budget.

Cyril Mackey made his way down the aisle toward us.

"Hi, there," Joe said.

"Hey up, me old cock."

"How are you, Cyril?" I asked.

"Champion. But tha makes a better door than a winder."

"Excuse me?"

"I think he wants you to get out of the way." Joe slid an arm around my shoulder and pulled me closer as Cyril nudged past to inspect a set of vintage beer steins.

I rolled my eyes at Joe and we kept walking.

"That old man looks like he belongs in a garbage dump," a woman near us cackled to her friend, and they both snickered as they pointed at Cyril. "I wonder what color that nasty jacket was originally."

I glanced back to where Cyril, wearing his usual tweed jacket of some indeterminate shade of green, or perhaps it was brown, had his hands clasped behind his back as he inspected the mugs. He must have heard them, but he made no sign of it.

Like an island unto himself.

From the way he was standing, I wondered whether he had been in the military at one time.

It struck me that none of us really knew anything about him. What had brought him to Millbury in the first place? Did he have any family? I felt a pang that we'd never bothered to find out.

The ceiling fans turning high above us weren't doing much to cool down the place, and flushed with heat from being in the middle of so many bodies, I suddenly craved some cool air.

"Joe, I'm going to go and check on Martha and Patsy."

He nodded. "I'll save us some seats."

I squeezed my way toward the hallway. The usual snack counter fare was hot dogs, hamburgers, popcorn, donuts, and pretzels, but tonight Martha had added her own barbecued pulled pork sandwiches and homemade strawberry ice cream.

She was wearing an orange, pink, and teal baby doll top, white Capri pants, and gold sandals. Even though her hair was piled high, her face was still rosy from the heat, and her neck and breasts glistened with moisture as she made the pork sandwiches as fast as she could for the growing line of customers.

I figured discretion was the better part of valor. I'd talk to her later.

Claire was in her element running the popcorn and soda machines, and there were so many fans going inside the tiny snack bar that she was also kept busy placing heavy objects on the piles of paper napkins so they didn't blow away.

I gratefully accepted an ice cold cup of Diet Coke, put fifty cents in the tip jar, and glanced at my watch. Fifteen minutes to go. I'd better check on Patsy.

I found her in the office, pacing up and down its twelve-foot length.

"How's it going?"

"Oh, damn it, Daisy. I don't know why I ever let you talk me into this." Patsy automatically handed me a quarter, but I gently set it on the desk and grabbed her hands to stop the nervous motion.

"Hey, come on, you're going to be great." I'd never seen her so rattled.

She gestured toward the window that looked out over the main gallery. "Look at all those freaking people! And all this stuff has to be sold *tonight*?"

"Yes. But it's okay. That's what the chant is for—to keep things moving quickly."

It was critical that the auction was not waiting on the auctioneer. And there *was* an awful lot of stuff to move out the door. She'd need to be really fast.

I didn't tell her that, though.

At school, I used to help out with theater productions and I always told the kids they'd be great, no matter what. I knew that once they were onstage, they'd settle down and, heck, even enjoy it.

"Just take it easy at first. No one expects you to be as experienced as Angus. And most of the people out there you know anyway."

"Yeah?" She peered through the window again. "I've been practicing on the diner regulars all week."

"I've got some last-minute tips for you." Instinctively I knew that for her to focus on absorbing new information would suck up some of the anxiety. "If Betty tells you 'one money' on something, it means the bidding is for so much apiece, but it's a set that stays together. For instance, for a set of six chairs, it's easier for the bidders to think about a bid of one hundred dollars per chair, knowing it will be multiplied by six at the end."

Patsy nodded. "Got it."

Betty poked her head in the door. "It's showtime, folks."

Patsy sucked in a breath and threw back her shoulders.

"Go get 'em, tiger," I said. "And don't forget to watch for my bidder number."

I found Joe near the front, sat on the seat he'd saved for me, and felt the familiar tingle of anticipation. Like the curtain rising on opening night. I took a quick look around me and wondered which of these seemingly innocuous people would be my nemesis in a bidding war for the dollhouse. Would I emerge victorious?

I caught a glimpse of Fiona Adams in the back, gingerly swiping at one of the chairs with a lace handkerchief before she sat down. The first time I'd met her, she wore nothing but black. This time she was in a winter white designer suit that was striking against her dark hair, but who the heck wore an outfit like that to a country auction?

Betty sat at a desk next to the podium with a laptop open

in front of her. She'd be keeping track of the bidder numbers and sale prices.

First up were the box lots to warm up the crowd. A collection of Pabst Blue Ribbon paraphernalia was number one.

"Would you give five dollars to start this box?" Patsy's voice sounded strong and clear, so maybe it was only me who heard the slight waver in its tone.

One of the old men with long beards waggled his bidder card.

"And ten, do I hear ten?"

Patsy pointed to a man at the back of the room, who nodded imperceptibly.

"Fifteen now?"

No movement. "How about twelve, do I have twelve dollars?"

The second man nodded again.

"Twelve, twelve, now fifteen, do I have fifteen?"

The first old man shook his head.

"Fifteen anywhere? Sold! For twelve dollars to bidder number 202!" She crashed the hammer down on the podium.

I caught her eye and gave her a thumbs-up sign.

The rest of the boxes went along the same tack—a box of car collector magazines, Barbie dolls, books, tools, and kitchen items. I scored with a winning bid of eight dollars for a box of costume jewelry, and five dollars for a box of old postcards and some wooden darning eggs.

Next up were what were called "smalls." Not surprisingly, small things like a Spode cake server, a jewelry box, some Royal Copenhagen plates, and Fiesta Ware.

One of the regular auction helpers carried a tray across the floor in front of the stage for everyone to take another look. Waiting in the wings was Sarah with the next item to keep the merchandise moving. As soon as the previous piece was sold to the highest bidder, another one came up onstage.

The excitement was building. You could feel it in the

room, like the rising pressure in the air when a storm was coming.

Patsy was warming up, too.

"Start me at five and *go*!" she yelled, pointing to a punched tin lantern. "Five, I have five, now seven anywhere?"

An old man in front of me raised his handkerchief a millimeter.

I hoped Patsy would spot him, but she already had. Being a waitress, Patsy was used to scanning the crowd to pick up signals—whether someone was ready for another cup of coffee or looking for their check. Sometimes she was a one-man show down at the diner, especially in the early morning if another waitress was late or hungover.

"Seven, seven, now ten, will you give me ten?"

It was amazing how many different ways there were to bid. One guy slid his eyeglasses down his nose a fraction, one raised his eyebrows, another waved his bidder card, someone else nodded, and someone called out "yes."

Right now, she was pacing, yelling, "Will you go ten-dollar bid? You want it, Tommy Allebach? Yeah? You *got* it, baby!"

I smiled to myself. I knew she'd have the right personality for this. She was popular in town, confident, sharp, and could think on her feet. She was having fun now with the people in the crowd. Angus had been good at that, too—a gentle mixture of teasing, pushing, and prodding to drive the bidding with the dealers and regular customers.

She pointed to the Waterford bowl that Sarah carried. "Tommy, I think you should take this one. How about fifty? Don't be cheap now!" She waved her hammer back and forth between two bidders.

"Fifty, now fifty, now seventy-five, thank you, how about eighty, eighty? I sold it at seventy-five! Bidder number 43, you are a lucky man!"

Now that she had her sea legs, she blazed through the smalls and was on to the bigger items, her cheeks flushed, and her patter smoother and more rapid fire. A smoking stand was first, a pair of end tables, then the grandfather clock, which sold for a good price, a train set, and now the set of wooden golf clubs, which sparked a huge bidding war. Once the bids started going above three hundred dollars, I kicked Joe gently in the ankle, but it was like calling a dog that was chasing a cat and had lost the ability to hear its owner. Finally it got too rich even for his blood, and the set eventually sold for well over five hundred. If Betty was giving Patsy a percentage of the commission, she was in the money tonight.

Next up was a vintage Sew-O-Matic child's toy sewing machine in the original box. I snapped to attention. You had to be on point to get what you wanted.

"Come on, folks, don't pass it up, do I hear ten?"

I waved my card. There was a short skirmish between me and another woman at the end of the next row, until I bid twenty-five dollars and she backed out.

"Going to let it go for twenty-five," Patsy called. "Here we go, *sold* to bidder 21!"

She grinned at me as she brought the hammer down with a satisfying crash.

Twenty-five dollars was a good deal. I'd ask at least seventy-five for it in the store. I gripped my bidder number. The thrill of a winning bid was a high like no other.

The items came faster and faster now, and my wins were piling up. A Hepplewhite blanket chest sponge-painted orange and red in a tulip design, a primitive spinning wheel, a Topsy Turvy Doll, and two vintage hatboxes.

Finally it was time for my beloved dollhouse. My pulse was racing hard and I fanned myself quickly with the bidder card. Once the bidding started, you had to be careful with any sudden movements.

Patsy wiggled her fingers in a "come to me"–type motion, and I started the bidding. The woman I had been butting heads with all night called out seventy-five; I took a deep

breath and went to a hundred. She topped me at one hundred
and twenty-five. My absolute limit was one-fifty, and that
might be too much.

Damn it, I really wanted this dollhouse.

"Two hundred!" someone yelled from the back of the
room, and I spun around in my seat to see Fiona Adams
raise her bidder card.

I gritted my teeth. "Two-ten!"

"Two-twenty!" Fiona's smile was triumphant.

I ignored Joe's murmur to let it go.

"Two-thirty!" I yelled.

Patsy stood helplessly, her hammer hanging in her hand.

As Fiona opened her mouth to make another bid, Martha
sailed down the aisle, carrying a drink pitcher. Suddenly
she stumbled, her ankle twisting in her high-heeled sandal,
and the plastic jug flew out of her hand, splashing red Kool-
Aid all down Fiona's expensive white suit.

Patsy grabbed the microphone, and spoke faster than she
ever had in her life. "Two-thirty, any other bids, all done, all
through, at two-thirty. *Sold!* To bidder number 21!"

The crash of the hammer snapped Fiona Adams out of
her shock.

"Goddamn it, I wanted it, I wanted it, *I* wanted it!" She
stamped her foot, screaming like a two-year-old having a
meltdown. "You stupid, clumsy *bitch!*"

Martha backed away, making apologetic sounds to no
avail.

"Look what you've done, you idiot!" she cried, gesturing
to her ruined outfit, where the red drink stain was a bloody
gash across the snowy white. She looked like something out
of a 1980s horror movie. *"Jesus Christ!"*

There was a sudden hush over the crowd. There were
plenty of good God-fearing people in attendance tonight—a
lot of them Mennonites—and they were aghast at the Lord's
name being used in vain.

Or maybe they were wondering what their own native

titan would do. But Martha was strangely silent, staring in fascination at this train wreck of a seemingly sophisticated woman.

I knew the suit was ruined beyond repair. Kool-Aid had a food dye in it, which meant the designer outfit was toast, but Fiona was beyond caring, lost in a world of her own as her fury exploded to a nuclear level. As I watched her snarling, almost unrecognizable face, ranting and raving, and using language fit for a sailors' convention, I wondered if this was how Angus acted when he said he saw red.

Could this rabid woman have seen Jimmy stealing the pens that were rightfully hers, and killed him in her rage?

But still, how could a woman, however crazy, have the strength to swing a heavy barn beam?

Chapter Nine

✦

Finally Cyril Mackey had evidently had enough. He marched over to Fiona and stood with his arms crossed, so close to her that she backed up a step.

"Ay up, that's enough out o' you," he barked.

He handed Martha a piece of paper and a pen. "Write tha name and address down, lass."

Martha instantly complied, and Cyril shoved it into Fiona's hand.

"Send her t' bill. She'll pay you for them glad rags," he said. "Now then, be off wi' ye."

Fiona glared at him, crushing the piece of paper between her long fingers, and even from this distance, I could see a green vein swelling on her high forehead. There was a moment when time seemed to stand still and everyone held their collective breath, before she spun on her heel and stalked out toward the lobby.

"Holy *crap*," Patsy whispered down to me from the stage. Luckily the dollhouse had been the last item up for bid, because the auction house was in complete pandemonium now. Released from the spell that had kept us frozen in place, everyone milled around, chattering excitedly. Joe and I rushed over to where Martha and Cyril stood.

Joe clapped him on the shoulder. "Cyril. Good job, my man."

Cyril chuckled. I couldn't remember ever seeing him smile before as he nodded toward the entrance where Fiona Adams had just marched out. "Good riddance t'bad rubbish."

"Daisy, I see what you mean," Martha gasped. "That woman is absolutely *crazy*."

"Certifiable," I agreed. "Now, was that really an accident with your pitcher?"

She winked at me. "I'll never tell."

Patsy jumped down from the stage, her curly dark hair damp from exertion and frizzing around her forehead. "Who *was* that insane chick? I'm so glad you got the dollhouse, Daisy. Wow! Tonight was incredible. Did you see how much stuff I sold?"

"Uh-oh." I smiled at Betty and Sarah, who came over to join us. "I think she's been bitten by the auction bug."

"She did a real good job." Betty's face was smiling, free of the usual worried creases. "You all did."

"Mom, you were awesome!" Claire rushed up and flung her arms around her mother's waist.

"Thanks, sweet pea," Patsy said, bending to wrap her in a hug. "How'd you make out in the snack bar?"

"It was *so* much fun! We sold out of all the popcorn and the ice cream. And I made seven dollars in tips."

"Nice!" Patsy ruffled her hair. "Chip off the old block."

"How about going back to my house for cocktails, everyone?" Martha called to the crowd. There was a chorus of cheers and high fives.

Sarah's face lit up. "Sure!"

Joe looked at me inquiringly. "What do you say, Daisy? After moving all that stuff for days, a cold beer would really hit the spot."

I nodded. "We'd love to."

"Don't worry, Eleanor," Martha said. "I have the good gin on hand."

"Then I'll be there." Eleanor twirled a wedding veil tiara around her finger.

Martha rolled her eyes at me. "Don't do us any favors."

Cyril was standing at the outer edge of the group, and he turned away as if he was about to leave. My heart constricted.

Martha hesitated for a second and then sniffed in his general direction. "You're welcome to come, too, Mr. Mackey, if you'd like."

Cyril smiled again, for the second time in years. "Aye, I would. I fancy a drink meself."

"You'll need to take that cap off before you enter my house, though." Martha gestured to the tweed cap he always wore.

"Yes, missus." Cyril whipped his cap off.

I was sure I was right about the fact that he'd been in the military at one time from the way he snapped to it when Martha gave an order. He recognized a commander-in-chief when he saw one.

I turned to Betty. "Are you coming? Would you like to ride with Joe and me?"

"No, thank you, Daisy. I'm tuckered out. I'm going to lock up here and go on home. You enjoy yourselves. Thank you again." She gestured for Patsy to follow her to the office so she could pay her.

"Pick up your skirt, Henry," Patsy called to a man I recognized as one of the diner regulars who was huffing as he helped maneuver the grandfather clock onto a dolly for transport. Joe, Sarah, and I made a couple of trips back and forth to the car with my loot, including the precious dollhouse.

Once back in Millbury, we parked the car outside our house, and walked a block off Main Street toward Hemlock Lane.

Martha's house was a huge fanciful Victorian painted a deep rose, dusty pink, and cream. Red coral bells, oriental poppies, pink and red impatiens, and pale pink astilbe bloomed along the path that led up to the house. Near the porch, peonies nodded their heavy heads, almost done now for the season, and dianthus smelled like an open bottle of perfume in the still humidity of the evening.

The front door opened into an expansive foyer. In front of us, a wide staircase with dark oak steps and intricately carved banisters swept upstairs in a gorgeous arc. To the left, a hallway with an oriental runner led to the study, piano room, parlor, and powder room, and to the right was the grand living room, dining room, and finally the kitchen in the back with its French doors out to the garden.

Inside was cool blessed relief after the sweltering atmosphere of the auction building. Martha must have had the air-conditioning cranked up full blast. It had cost a fortune to retrofit into the old house with its steam-powered radiators, but to easily overheated Martha, it wasn't an option, but a necessity.

People were already milling around and tropical salsa music was playing. We followed the sound of laughter and found Martha at one end of the long mahogany-paneled living room, struggling to open a bottle of Veuve Cliquot champagne.

Joe grinned as he surveyed the vast array of top-shelf liquors. "I swear, Martha, your bar is better stocked than the Bridgewater Inn. There's anything you could want to drink here."

"Except absinthe," Eleanor said.

"*What?* What are you talking about?" Martha's cheeks were still pink; she was obviously not quite cooled down, and therefore more than a tad irritable. "Who the hell drinks absinthe?"

"I do. But only when I'm entertaining special visitors at home."

Martha and I looked at each other. Who was she entertaining with hallucinogenic alcohol?

Cyril smoothly extracted the champagne bottle out of
Martha's hands.

"Good God. My back is killing me," she moaned, leaning
against the bar and lifting one foot, like a voluptuous
flamingo.

I glanced down at her high-heeled gold sandals. Not
exactly typical chef's footwear.

"And I'm *starving*. I had a small bowl of cereal this morning, and that's all I've had to eat all day." She gave an anxious look in the direction of the kitchen. "Oh, the appetizers!
I almost forgot about them."

"I can handle this," Cyril said, gesturing to the bar. "Go
see about yer food now."

She fixed him with a hard stare. "Are you sure you know
what you're doing?"

"G'oer, lass. I know how to make a bloody drink."

Joe and I sucked in a quiet breath at this show of insub-
ordination, but Martha merely gave him one last pointed
look and hobbled off to the kitchen.

"Personally I saw her consume two hot dogs, a glazed
donut, *and* share a bowl of popcorn with Claire, but who's
counting?" Eleanor flipped an olive into her mouth.

Cyril opened the champagne with barely a hiss, served
three people standing with champagne flutes at the ready,
and quickly filled drink requests for a chardonnay for me,
pinot grigio for Sarah, and a bottle of beer for Joe.

"Dry martini, darling," Eleanor said to Cyril. "Gin. None
of this vodka business. And just show it the vermouth."

He made her drink and obediently waved the vermouth
bottle near the V-shaped glass of chilled gin.

"Cheers." Eleanor took a sip out of the brimming edge
of her cocktail. "Well, I'm off to mingle." She made a bee-
line for Chris Paxson and a group of his young friends.

Debby Millerton, the librarian, rushed over to take Sarah

by the arm, while Cyril poured himself a shot of whiskey as he settled into a conversation with Joe about the latest Phillies game.

"Um, I think I'd better help Martha in the kitchen," I said. Joe nodded absently as I drifted away.

Across the room, Chris Paxson and his friends were laughing at a story Eleanor was telling, and giving her appreciative looks. She had a drier sense of humor than her martini, and as I looked back at my dark horse of a friend, I wondered again how well we really knew anyone.

I made my way through the dining room to the expansive kitchen with its mahogany cabinets and granite countertops. The deep double sink was set into the pink and gray granite, and ornate gold faucets gleamed in the soft recessed lighting.

Martha was pulling a tray of hors d'oeuvres out of the oven as I walked in. I wondered how she'd had time to get them ready, until I spotted the telltale black and silver bags stuffed in the corner from Magic Plate Catering.

This party wasn't as impromptu as she'd made it seem.

She followed my gaze and sighed. "You've found me out, Daisy. I was hoping people would come over after the auction, but I didn't want to make a big deal about it. I haven't had a get-together since Teddy died, and I didn't know if I could pull it off by myself. I mean, what if no one came? That would be too embarrassing."

"Martha, look at your house!" From the kitchen we could hear the laughter, music, and buzz of conversation. "It's packed!"

A slow grin spread across her face. "It is, isn't it?"

The affable Teddy Bristol had been a great host, loud and cheerful, like a party in a box all by himself. He'd adored Martha, spoiled her outrageously, and jokingly called her his trophy wife, even though she was only ten years younger. He had two sons from his first marriage, and Martha was like a doting aunt to them. They adored her, too, but they were both in the military, and so their limited time off was usually spent with their mother.

Her expression sobered again. "I miss Teddy so much. And the boys. I miss having someone to cook for, talk about the day with, and share the good times. And the bad." She finished sliding the mini quiches and stuffed mushrooms onto a serving platter. "It gets lonely in this old house by myself sometimes."

I put an arm around her shoulders. "I know."

Martha was incredibly generous, and involved in lots of charity work, plus the Historical Society, but I decided she needed something more.

Some kind of big project to occupy her energy.

I added a mental note to my to-do list, which was getting longer by the minute.

I hugged her. "Well, I, for one, am grateful you decided to have a party. It was very brave of you. Besides, we *should* celebrate. We helped Betty hold a great auction, and to keep things going until Angus gets back."

My words hung in the air. Martha didn't comment, but I knew she thought I was on a fool's errand trying to prove Angus's innocence.

I carried a tray of hors d'oeuvres into the living room. As people helped themselves to the tidbits on my platter, I watched Cyril expertly wiping down the bar and filling a shaker with ice. From his fluid motions, I could see it wasn't the first time he'd done this. What else had he done in the years between moving from Yorkshire, England, to winding up in our sleepy village?

Some of Martha's neighbors called her over, and I couldn't see Joe, so I wandered around with the hors d'oeuvres, catching snippets of conversation. Warren Zeigler was standing in the corner with his wife and another couple.

"Warren! Just the person I wanted to bump into."

"Oh, yes?"

"Yes. What's happening with Angus's case? Any idea who

the judge will be?" As I peppered him with questions, Warren waited patiently, his eyes calm behind his round-rimmed eyeglasses. I'm not a tall woman, but I was taller than him by a few inches. He looked a bit like a baby owl sporting a bow tie.

"The preliminary hearing is on Thursday. We'll know more after that."

He told me what he knew about the judge, and I felt marginally better. Warren was well-spoken, competent, with an old-fashioned charm, and sounded like he knew what he was doing. Although with the way the deck was stacked against Angus, he had his work cut out for him.

Warren's wife laid a hand on his arm. "All right. Enough work talk for tonight. This is supposed to be a party." She smiled at me, but the message in her eyes was clear. *Knock it off.*

I smiled back and moved away until I was standing in the center of the long room.

My tray was empty. I should have gone back to the kitchen for more, but I lingered for a moment, taking it all in.

Angus was always the life and soul of any occasion. But no one had even mentioned his name tonight. None of these so-called friends seemed to remember where he was. Alone, in prison, with only his jumbled thoughts for company.

"Hey, Mom, you okay?" Sarah came up beside me.

"Yes, fine, just thinking about Angus, that's all."

"Well, he would be proud of the way we pulled it off tonight."

"Yes. You were fantastic, Sarah. Thanks for everything you did."

"Oh, no problem. This is the most fun I've ever had in Millbury!"

Chris Paxson waved at her from across the room, and Sarah wandered over to chat with him and his friends.

Why was I the only one with a sense of urgency about Angus?

Because he always seemed so capable, so well equipped

to breeze through any complications that came his way, that's why, I told myself. They all assumed he could get himself out of this mess, too.

Eleanor came up, nudged me, and took a slurp of her martini. "Hmm. Inquiring minds want to know." She cocked her head toward the bar. "What's going on over there?"

Cyril Mackey was pouring champagne into Martha's glass, his face animated. She was laughing, her hair loose, and sandals kicked off to one side.

I smiled. "He's a man of many talents, I gather."

"I must say, he's come in handy tonight."

"How's your drink?" I asked.

"Probably the best martini I've ever had. And yours?"

I sighed. "Oh, I must have left my wine in the kitchen."

"Now, Daisy. You don't seem too cheerful. What's the matter?"

"What's the matter? Everyone seems to have forgotten about Angus, that's *what's the matter!*" I realized my voice was rising and I took a deep breath.

Eleanor's dark gray gaze zeroed in on me. "We haven't forgotten, but what can we do?"

"Well, I don't know what *I* can do either, but I'm still trying." I set the platter down on a nearby table with shaking hands. "Oh hell, what makes me think I can solve a murder case? I'm not a real detective."

"Yes, but you're smart, and the thing is, you never give up. When you want something, you're like a pit bull with a pork chop."

I chuckled. In a way, she was right. I never gave up. Not even on the worst student.

Eleanor drained her glass and pointed it at me. "Remember when I needed those hand-carved mother-of-pearl buttons for that antique wedding dress? I'd searched everywhere. I was about to use a poor substitute in desperation. You wouldn't stop searching until you found them for me."

I nodded. "It needed to be authentic."

"And you're not afraid of confrontation. Well, except with Sarah . . ."

I grinned ruefully at Eleanor as my daughter came over to us, accompanied by Debby and Debby's sister, Cecilia. Cee Cee was an ex-schoolteacher like me. She'd quit the profession because she was trying to get pregnant, and her husband, Tom, a doctor, suggested that the stress of teaching might be a factor. I could attest to that.

She had beautiful penmanship, and she'd recently started a calligraphy business from home for wedding and party invitations.

Thinking of penmanship reminded me of the pens again, and a new avenue I hadn't explored. "Hey, does anyone know of any famous writers who live around here?" I asked the group.

Eleanor fished the last olive out of the bottom of her glass. "Abigail Weller is writing her memoirs, not that anyone will want to read them. She's had a pretty boring life if you ask me."

"Meow." Sarah nudged Eleanor playfully. "Would you like a bowl of milk instead of that martini, E?"

"Speaking of ICBM's, I need another one," Eleanor announced.

"An intercontinental ballistic missile?" Cee Cee asked, confused.

"No, darling, an ice-cold Beefeater Martini."

We followed her over to the bar as Debby chatted to Sarah about life in New York with stars in her eyes. Sometimes I wanted to put my arm around Debby and encourage her to look at the here and now and make that work. So many people spent their lives wishing them away.

"Are you staying for a while, Eleanor?" Martha asked, taking the empty glass.

"Until the gin runs out. Nice party, by the way."

"Thanks."

Eleanor drank the way she ate. Far be it from me to monitor anyone's drinking, and none of us were driving anyway, but I guessed this had to be her fourth martini, and she showed no sign of it.

Cyril poured me a glass of chardonnay.

"I'm so glad you got the dollhouse, Daisy," Cee Cee said. "I was worried that crazy woman would outbid you. Who is she anyway?"

"Her name's Fiona Adams. She's from New York. Supposedly it was her father's fountain pens that were stolen on the night of Jimmy Kratz's murder."

"But why is she still here?"

"No idea. But I think I need to figure it out. All I know is that she's someone right on the edge."

"Of a nervous breakdown?"

"Of something."

Debby and Sarah were making plans to see Robin Tague, a world-class violinist and composer who was visiting Philadelphia on tour.

"You know I've heard that musicians also cherish fountain pens as the perfect instrument for writing musical scores," Cee Cee said to me.

"Really? That's interesting."

After I finally finished my glass of wine, Joe, Sarah, and I decided to call it a night.

When we got home, we discovered that Jasper had taken the magazines off the coffee table in the living room and reduced them to a pile of chewed-up damp pieces of paper.

Again, I reminded myself that he wasn't my dog. He was Sarah's responsibility, and I turned to her now. "Didn't you put him in his crate before we went out?"

"I must not have latched it tight. It's no big deal. I'll buy you some new magazines, Mom. Don't get all agitated."

It had been a long day, she'd been a fantastic help with the auction, and so I let it go.

For now.

Chapter Ten

⁕

The next morning, Sunday, was visiting day at the prison. Joe and Sarah were still lingering over breakfast when I left the house. I'd gotten a late start, but I couldn't wait to tell Angus what a success the auction had been. It would be a weight off his mind.

When I got there, however, the officer on duty told me that Angus was not available for a visit, because he was undergoing some kind of medical evaluation. I pressed him for details, but he couldn't, or wouldn't, elaborate.

All the way home, I alternated between annoyance over the wasted trip and worry about Angus. Had the infection in his hand from the splinters worsened? Had he gotten in a fight in the prison and was being treated for his injuries? Had his mind finally snapped, and it was some kind of psychiatric testing?

I tried to talk to Joe about it when I got home, but he just sighed and pulled me into his arms.

"I'm concerned about Angus, too, but can't we have a

day to ourselves? Seems like you're always working, or helping Betty, or doing your investigations. I miss my wife."

"I miss you, too." I hugged him back, the comfort slowly
flowing through me as our bodies melded. God, I was tired.
Maybe I could take one day off.

We checked the local paper and, for the rest of the morning, drove around to yard sales. I bought a baby gate for
three dollars so Jasper could have the run of the kitchen and
not be shut up in his crate, and also some toys to keep him
busy. Joe picked up a cookbook published by the Sheepville
Women's Club. He also grabbed a vacuum cleaner with a
FREE sign on it from the side of the road, saying he was sure
he could fix it. Sarah found a pretty wooden tray with
pressed flowers under glass for the store and a box of
assorted costume jewelry that she bundled together and paid
five dollars for both.

It was a perfect June day, the brutal humidity of the day
before swept away by the gentle breeze that rustled through
the butterfly bush in our back garden and swayed the orange
heads of daylilies turned up toward the sun.

We ate a long, lazy lunch on the patio. A simple feast of
a French baguette, cheese, salad, and white wine. Joe flipped
through his new cookbook and read some of the more inviting recipes out loud to us. It was also typical of a French
déjeuner in that we were talking about what to have for
dinner while still eating lunch. We finally decided on a
Chicken Saltimbocca with spinach and prosciutto.

While we relaxed, Jasper occupied himself by digging
up one of the flower beds behind the shed. He trotted back
with a yellow Matchbox car. By the end of lunch, he'd found
a rusty pair of pliers, two marbles, a gold cufflink, and a
heart-shaped cookie cutter.

"I can't believe he found all this stuff in our own backyard!" Sarah exclaimed.

Joe was delighted with his finds. "We should give him
his own box in the store, Daisy."

Jasper's paws were filthy, so I hosed his feet down and dried him with an old towel, while Joe cleared away the lunch and Sarah checked the messages on her phone.

On Monday, I stopped by the diner, picked up some coffee for Cyril, and headed over to the salvage yard. He was in a particularly recalcitrant mood. His good humor from Saturday night had vanished, and he was back to the cantankerous old man I knew.

He basically ignored me, so I sat and watched him work on his crossword puzzle as I drank my own coffee. My attempts to inquire about his past were met with frosty resistance, although I did manage to glean the fact that his family had owned a farm back in Yorkshire, England. He commented that a farmer's life was a hard one, with the farm chores never done.

Such as milking cows early in the morning.

Before I left, I amused myself by telling him the solution to 14 across. I chuckled as I peeked in my rearview mirror and saw him glaring after me and muttering to himself. I could just imagine the epithets hurled in my wake.

I drove back to the store, deep in thought, picturing the Kratzes' farm on the morning of the murder. When Sarah showed up, half an hour later, I decided to ask her a few questions to see if my misgivings were correct.

"Okay, Sarah, picture this scene. Like it's from one of your film scripts. Early morning. Our house. You come downstairs to the living room and you find Dad dead on the couch. What do you do?"

"*Jeez*, Mom."

"Come on, humor me."

"Well, I guess I'd scream, I'd yell for you. I'd see if I could help him. Make sure he was really dead."

"Good. What else?"

Sarah sighed. "I don't know. Call 911?"

"What else?"

"I don't *know,* Mom."

Usually I would back off when she inserted that note of irritation in her voice, but not today.

She threw up her hands in exasperation. "Cry, freak out, scream for help again? I don't know what you want me to say."

"Would you milk five cows before the police got there?"

"I guess not." She chewed on her bottom lip.

I picked up the phone and dialed Ramsbottom. "Were the cows distressed when you got to the Kratz farm on that Saturday morning after Jimmy was murdered?"

"Huh?" He exhaled loudly. "No, they seemed okay to me. They were all out in the field. Is there a point to this, Mrs. Daly?"

"Buchanan. Daisy Buchanan," I corrected him. "And yes, there is a point. How long does it take to milk a cow?"

"What do I look like? A flipping dictionary?"

I refrained from pointing out he meant an encyclopedia. "Look, Reenie Kratz went out to the barn that morning, found Jimmy murdered, called the police, and then calmly milked five cows—and probably fed the pigs, too—while the body of her dead husband was lying on the floor of the barn beside her. Don't you think that's a little cold?"

I heard the sound of chewing on the other end of the phone line and grimaced. Probably a breakfast sandwich of sausage, egg, and cheese.

"Heck, I don't know. People can do strange things when they're in shock. Look, Mrs.—um—you need to stop calling here. I've got work to do, cases to solve. I suggest you concentrate on your nice little store and don't interfere anymore. As far as I'm concerned, we have our killer and he can rot in jail. End of story."

"I could agree with you, but then we'd both be wrong." I slammed the phone down as the door opened and Martha,

Eleanor, and some of the neighborhood ladies, Liz Galla-gher, Ruth Bornstein, and Dottie Brown, walked in.

"Let me ask you guys something." I ignored Sarah, who rolled her eyes as if to say, *Here we go again.* "Ramsbottom says the cows were already out in the field when he showed up. Don't you think that's odd?"

Martha held up a hand. "Hold the phone, *what* cows?"

"Sorry. At the Kratz farm. I'm trying to picture myself in Reenie's place. I'm trying to imagine finding my own husband murdered, and I don't think I could sit next to his corpse, milking cows, while waiting for help to arrive."

Everyone mulled this over as I poured coffee into as many mugs as I could until the pot was empty. I was coming out of the kitchen with another carafe of water for a new pot when the front door banged open again and Patsy strode in.

"Yo! Wazzup, Daisy? Ladies?"

"No diner this morning?" I asked, prepping a fresh filter.

"Took the day off. Figured I earned it. Damn, it's hotter than a three-balled tomcat out there."

I repeated my cow story to get her up to speed.

"Oh well, that's no big surprise. Jimmy used to get liquored up, go home, and beat the bejeezus out of his wife on a regular basis. I don't suppose Reenie was too sorry to see he'd cashed in his chips."

"No big surprise?" I gasped. "I had no idea. And I'm sure Angus wouldn't have been friendly with a guy like that if he'd known."

Martha placed her hands on her hips and glared at Patsy. "And how come I never heard a word about this?"

I couldn't decide if Martha was more shocked that Jimmy beat his wife, or by the fact that she hadn't known about it.

Patsy shrugged. "Not many people knew. Nobody saw her in town much. At least not until the bruises faded."

Nothing seemed to faze Patsy, who'd been a waitress her whole working life. She didn't exactly expect the worst, but close to it. She told me it was better that way because you never got disappointed.

"Reenie and I were friends in high school. We used to keep in touch, but not lately."

I unwrapped Martha's platter. "Well, I suppose that would explain Reenie's dispassionate attitude and ability to get on with chores as usual."

I offered the diamond-shaped pieces of lemon crunch cake to the eager group.

"Did the police know about the abuse?" Liz Gallagher asked.

Patsy shook her head. "Reenie never called the cops. She never pressed charges."

Again, I felt fury toward Ramsbottom. I bet he'd known about it, but had chosen to do nothing. Yet another example of his lackadaisical attitude. "Well, it gives her a good motive, but we're back to the same problem as thinking Fiona Adams was the killer. There's no way a woman could lift a barn beam that weighs well over a hundred pounds."

Particularly not frail, skinny Reenie. I sipped my coffee, frowning. I'd seen Jimmy Kratz at auction all the time. He was medium height, with medium-length shaggy hair, and had dark brown eyes that were always scanning the room. Hard eyes that I'd attributed to the tough way he'd earned a living. I hadn't exactly trusted him, as he seemed like someone always out to make a buck, but he didn't strike me as dangerous exactly.

Although I guess I'd never seen him at the end of a long night of shots and beers.

And would the fact that Angus saw red at the abuse of women mean that he could have done the same thing to Jimmy Kratz that he'd done to Hank Ramsbottom if he'd found out?

Patsy poured a cup of coffee from the fresh pot and drank it black. "That's not all. Jimmy was cheating on Reenie, too. With Carla, one of the diner waitresses. It's a wonder he wasn't as big as a house. He'd eat lunch at home and then come to the diner to see her and eat another one."

A picture of Reenie crying and holding a suitcase flashed into my mind. "Oh my God, was *that* why he packed a suitcase? Because he was planning on leaving his wife?"

"Don't sound so surprised, Daisy," Eleanor said. "You and Joe—you're a living romance novel—but the rest of the world is not that lucky. I read somewhere that fifty percent of spouses cheat on their significant other."

Martha bit daintily into a piece of lemon cake. "Well, I know my Teddy never did."

"How can you be so sure?" Eleanor demanded.

"Because I kept him so busy he didn't have the time. Or the energy."

"Oh, jeez. Too much information." Sarah groaned and put her hands to her ears. "La-la-la!"

I could count on the fingers of one hand the number of times Joe had ever lost his temper in all our years of marriage. I felt an even deeper sympathy for Reenie.

"And what about those poor Kratz children?" Dottie Brown said. "What kind of horrors must they have seen in their young lives so far?" Dottie had a large family and several grandchildren, and the thought of their lack of welfare made her press her lips together into a narrow line.

Suddenly I saw the solution to two problems in one.

"Hey, I have an idea. How about we organize a country fair or flea market, something like that, with the proceeds going towards a fund for the Kratz family?"

Martha's eyes gleamed. "Yes! I'll be in charge. We could have tractor pulls, and a baking contest and—"

"We'll need a place to hold it." Eleanor was ever practical.

"Maybe our farm?" Liz Gallagher said. "No, wait a minute, we really don't have enough open space, and my hubby wouldn't want people tramping through his crops right now."

"What about the auction grounds?" I suggested.

"Don't you think that's a bit awkward?" Dottie said. "I mean, with Angus in prison for Jimmy's murder and all . . ."

Her voice trailed off. Dottie Brown was also a friend of Betty's. She owned a yarn and fabric store in Sheepville, and held knitting classes at night.

"Betty won't mind. I'll ask her," I said firmly. "Besides, it's for the children."

As if sensing she'd made a faux pas, Dottie rushed to put matters to right. "Of course. For the children. Let's see. My knitting-class ladies can make something to sell—socks, scarves, mittens, baby blankets—and I'll donate the wool for them to use."

"That would be great," I told her warmly.

Sarah glanced up momentarily from her phone. "I can organize the parking situation."

"Thanks, Sarah." I guessed that meant she was planning on staying for a while longer.

"I'll spread the word and see who wants to donate goods for the flea market," Liz said. She had five children, all under high school age. She was the president of the Home & School Association, taught a fitness class three times a week, and where she found the energy, I never knew. "The kids can help, too. They can sell tickets for admission and set up a lemonade stand. Some of our farm animals could be used for a petting zoo."

Ruth Bornstein nodded. "Good idea. I have a friend who owns some stables. We could bring in a pony and sell rides."

Tall and elegant Ruth was involved in the Historical Society with Martha and Eleanor. She had some wealthy connections who always seemed to come through with donations or other assistance when needed to save a historic building. I'd bet she'd tap into that network now.

Seeing as this looked like it was turning into a lengthy discussion, I made another pot of coffee.

About twenty minutes later, Martha invited everyone to go to lunch so they could discuss things further. I knew that meant giving everyone a job to do. I smiled as I watched them leave.

I could cross another item off *my* to-do list. I'd given Martha something to keep her busy and excited—a legitimate reason to boss people around.

And speaking of crossing things off my list, Angus's preliminary hearing was coming up in a couple of days, and I needed to buckle down and do some serious sleuthing.

Thanks to Martha, I knew that Fiona Adams was staying at the Four Foxes, a gorgeous bed-and-breakfast owned by my friend Joy David. It was situated south of Sheepville, near the lavender farm, and was more than just a bed-and-breakfast. More like a retreat. Peaceful, romantic, inspiring, with a highly rated gourmet restaurant and spa.

"Sarah, could you watch the store for a while? I have a couple of errands to run."

"Sure, Mom. Leave me here with the dusty old sewing things. That's just *perfect*."

I tried to ignore her sigh of annoyance as she folded her finely sculpted arms and crossed one long tanned leg over the other. I hurried out the door, fighting a ridiculous sense of guilt.

After all I'd done for Sarah, was it really too much to ask? I blew out an irritated breath, in a faint echo of hers.

I opened the doors to the Subaru to let the blazing heat that had built up inside escape, but the steering wheel still scorched my hands. I took the familiar route up to River Road, down Sheepville Pike, and then past the town of Sheepville to turn right on Forty Acre Road. This road was less densely populated than most, and that was saying something in these parts.

A split rail fence was the rustic marker between the narrow road and acres and acres of open fields and gently rolling hills. Sometimes the only hint of a house anywhere near was a mailbox, or a homemade sign saying, HONEY or FIREWOOD FOR SALE.

Through the trees, I spotted the ruins of an old building. A corner of a fieldstone wall and the blackened remains of a fireplace were all that was left of someone's long-ago home.

The entrance to the Four Foxes was marked only by two fieldstone pillars. The Subaru trundled over a short Belgian block entranceway, and then the road smoothed out as it wound through the cherry trees toward the lovely stone and stucco colonial house that had been added on to extensively to make it a luxury getaway destination. I pulled onto the white gravel of the courtyard and parked in front of the garage doors of what had once been a horse barn.

I didn't have much of a plan in mind, other than trying to convince Joy to let me poke around Fiona Adams's room if she was out. I winced at the thought. Joy was a professional innkeeper, and I knew it would take a vast amount of fast talking to get her to agree to this harebrained scheme.

I stepped out of the car and also sidestepped a couple of the free-ranging chickens who provided fresh eggs for the guests' breakfasts every morning. Joy raised sheep, cattle, and turkeys on an adjoining organic farm, which supplied the Michelin three-star restaurant.

As I walked through the brick archway that led to the back gardens, patio, and pool, my heart skipped a beat as I saw the familiar hawk-like figure of Fiona Adams bearing down upon me.

Chapter Eleven

"**Y**ou!" She pointed one long finger in my direction, holding an even longer cigarette, and looking a bit like the Grim Reaper, except one that was dressed in summer sandals and shorts. She was so thin that her knees looked too big for her bony legs.

I looked around desperately for Joy, or the gardener, or anyone for that matter, but the beautiful landscaped grounds were deserted.

"Come with me," Fiona said. "I want to show you something."

With no other viable options, I trailed after her, following a cloud of smoke, past the PLEASE, NO SMOKING sign on the patio wall toward the Rosemary Suite, which overlooked the pool and herb gardens. The intense heat bore down, relentless, sapping my resistance.

At first I was glad to duck into the air-conditioning of the expansive guest quarters. But once inside, Fiona locked the door behind us, and the dreaded sweat started prickling up my back. How had I gotten myself into this?

In the living area, two cotton twill armchairs sat in front of the unlit wood-burning fireplace, where a vase of fresh yellow daylilies stood in place of the flames of winter. A Persian hand-knotted silk rug softened the green and gray slate floor.

In the small kitchen area, I knew the mini refrigerator held a bottle of champagne, wine, some beer, bottled water, and local artisan cheeses to welcome guests.

Upstairs in the bedroom would be a king-sized high feather bed, with luxurious linens, facing a fieldstone wall with a fireplace and flat-screen television. A stunning marble and travertine bathroom, complete with whirlpool tub, two-person shower, heated towel racks, and complimentary bathrobes provided the ultimate pampering experience.

The spacious two-level suite was an inviting paradise for world-weary travelers looking for an escape, but not wanting to get too far from civilization. High-speed Internet access and a state-of-the-art fitness facility were also included. There were only four rooms and two suites here, but all were lavishly appointed.

Rustic done upscale, as Joy liked to call it.

I jumped when Fiona gestured toward the round table in the alcove near the window. A tray was set out with a pitcher of iced tea, some glasses, and tiny dishes of sugared lemon slices and fresh mint leaves.

"Please. Sit down."

We sat down on the upholstered high-backed chairs, surrounded by ficus trees and bromeliads. She carefully poured and garnished two glasses of tea for us, and I stared across the table at her, wondering what the heck she wanted.

"Your klutzy friend must help you win a lot of merchandise," she said, but there was a twinkle in her eye.

I cleared my throat. "Oh, I'm sorry about that, but don't worry, Martha will pay you for the dry cleaning." Or the replacement, I thought.

Fiona waved a hand impatiently. "It doesn't matter." She bent down and pulled a photo album out of a tote bag on the floor and put it on the table. "Look, this is what I wanted to show you." She swiveled the album toward me and started flipping pages. There were beautiful color photographs of a variety of fountain pens, in close-up detail.

The missing collection.

She went rapidly through each page, explaining to me why they were all so valuable. "This is a vintage Parker Duofold Lucky Curve in mandarin yellow. It's a first edition from the 1920s, has a solid fourteen-carat gold nib. Yellow is the most rare and therefore the most sought after." She flipped a page. "Here's a duo pen set by Krone called the Forbidden City. Highly detailed hand-painted pens."

I leaned closer and peered at the photograph. The pens looked like a tiny emperor and empress with exquisite faces and detail.

She showed me a lapis blue Pelikan 101, a Waterman safety pen with gold filigree overlay from the 1920s, and a Montblanc sterling silver Lorenzo de Medici pen, with its octagonal hand-engraved sterling silver body.

"They're incredible," I murmured, and I meant it.

Fiona's diction was perfect, as if she had undergone years of speech training. And in spite of the harsh persona she liked to project, there was also an air of fragility about her, especially when her voice softened as she described the history of the pens.

She traced a finger across the photos of her treasures, lingering over her favorites. It made me think of that gorgeous peacock fabric I'd sacrificed to pay my bills and keep the store afloat in the early days. As a lover of vintage things, I could see why these beautiful pens were so collectible, and suddenly I felt an unexpected connection to this odd woman.

I took a sip of my iced tea. "Fiona, let me ask you something. There was—um—a rumor about an estate liquidation company that contacted Jimmy Kratz."

I'd protected Reenie long enough. Now I needed some answers. "Let's say there was a crooked deal going on whereby Jimmy was supposed to bid on the pens, buy them for a low price, and then this company would get them back to resell them in a bigger market and—"

Fiona waved her hand again. "I already checked into the company the bimbo used. They seem legitimate, and all recent transactions have fetched a fair market price. Completely clueless, though, just like her. They hadn't even known the pens were stolen or filed the insurance claim until I contacted them."

"But why send them to this auction house? Why not one in New York or Philadelphia?"

Fiona blew out a breath. "She *says* it was for sentimental reasons. As if that gold-digging bitch has a sentimental bone in her whole body. Her grandfather was born in Sheepville, so supposedly that's why she sent them here."

I chewed on a piece of sugared lemon. *Damn it.* The estate company theory sounded like a dead end, and the clock was still ticking for Angus. And the police were doing nothing to search for the pens or Jimmy's killer. So now what?

Fiona tapped the current page of the album to bring my attention back. "Here's a Conklin Durograph pen. They were only made for about a year in 1923, so again, very collectible."

Next came a Maniflex pen with a gorgeous tigereye casing, two Parker pens, a Sheaffer, and a Wahl pen with a Greek key pattern.

"These pens must be kept out of sunlight under climate-controlled conditions. If someone else uses them, they can be ruined for the owner because of the way the nib adapts to their particular writing style. I hate to think of how they might be being treated as we speak." Fiona shuddered. "They're easily damaged by heat and can fade or discolor. That's why I cringe when I see them in glass cases at outdoor markets. They're completely compromised by then."

"Did it bother you that your father left all his money to his new wife?" I asked.

It was a blunt question, but what did I have to lose?

Fiona narrowed her gaze at me. "No. I'm a very wealthy woman in my own right. I didn't need any money from the estate, but my father did promise me the pens."

"But he didn't specify in his will?"

"I guess he expected his wife to honor his wishes. Ha! We know how that worked out."

I suddenly knew who Fiona was. She was one of those lost souls walking the earth. I saw them all the time. Oh, they looked like successful, professional people, but inside was a sad, neglected child. The pens signified a link to the past, her only connection to her father, and I understood now why she was so desperate to get them back.

"I think I like this one the best." I pointed to the last page of the album.

Fiona grinned at me, showing her slight overbite. "You have good taste. That's a rare Montblanc Magical Black Widow Skeleton pen."

I marveled at the exquisite pen encased in a web of white gold, with its filigree spider and black diamonds on the clip.

"It's a limited edition," she said. "The last one sold at auction for well over twenty thousand dollars."

"Wow. Thanks for showing these to me, Fiona. I can see now why the fountain pens are so important to you. They're truly magnificent."

I thought I detected a slight pinkening of her cheeks, but maybe it was only from the sun beating through the windows.

"Trust me, I'll do everything I can to get them back." As I stood up and saw the time on the clock in the kitchen, I was surprised to find that almost an hour had gone by. Even more surprised to find that I'd thoroughly enjoyed myself.

After I took my leave of Fiona, I walked back the way I had come in, past the koi pond with the sounds of frogs calling like out-of-tune plastic guitar strings, toward the dramatic two-level patio. Joy was at the poolside bar area, where overflowing mossy flower-filled baskets hung overhead. She was serving frozen margaritas to two bikini-clad guests.

"Daisy! What are you doing here?"

"I was—um—visiting a friend. Fiona Adams," I said, suddenly glad I was sure now Fiona hadn't had anything to do with the murder of Jimmy Kratz. She was a strange bird, but she'd been given the short end of the stick as far as I could see, and I hoped the pens would be recovered, not only for Angus's sake, but for hers.

"Would you like something to drink?" Joy asked.

"Thanks, but I can't stay. I have to get back to the store. Although that pool does look very inviting." It was so hot, I was tempted to throw myself in, clothes and all.

"Guess who else we have staying here?"

I smiled and shook my head.

"Robin Tague! The famous violinist and composer! He's playing some concerts in Philadelphia, but he picked the Four Foxes because he wanted the peace and quiet to compose."

"I can't wait to tell Debby Millerton. She's a huge fan." I nodded toward a deeply tanned guy with an impressive athletic physique lying on one of the chaise longues by the pool. "Is that him?" I whispered.

"Oh, no!" Joy laughed. "That's the driver for your friend, Fiona Adams."

Damn. Just as I was ready to discount Fiona as a suspect.

This guy wasn't big, but he was solidly muscled, and he could certainly have done the dirty deed on Jimmy.

On the way home, I decided to stop at the Perkins Feed Supply Store. Sarah was already pissed off at having to watch Sometimes a Great Notion. What difference would another half an hour make?

The business was right on Sheepville Pike, which was zoned commercial. Down a long driveway behind it was their house and surrounding farmland.

I'd heard Patsy's dire warnings about the Perkins boys, but this was a retail business on a main thoroughfare where they served the public. I'd be perfectly safe. Hey, I'd faced up to Fiona Adams today and survived. Besides, I needed to check them out for myself.

But what excuse would I give for being here? I know, I could say I'd come to buy dog food for Jasper. In addition to cattle feed, a sign outside said they also sold bags of dog, cat, and rabbit food.

When I got out of the car, the oppressive heat was like a hand shoving me in the chest.

God, it was hot today.

The store was deserted except for one bored-looking girl at the register, who didn't look up when I opened the glass and chrome door. The place smelled of fertilizer and sawdust inside. I stepped out into the heat again and wandered around to the back parking lot, past a forklift truck, and over to a huge shed.

I peeked into the shadowed interior. A young man stripped to the waist was perched atop a pile of feed sacks, throwing them up onto a shelf near the rafters. They must have weighed at least fifty pounds each, but he tossed them around like packets of potato chips.

He gave no sign of noticing me in the doorway. His tanned back gleamed with sweat, and I stood transfixed for a moment, watching the smooth muscles work together in perfect unison.

Another man sauntered across the lot toward me, holding a plastic cup. He looked to be slightly older than the first one by a couple of years. He was also bare-chested, furry-chested actually, with a pelt that narrowed to a dark brown line that disappeared under the edge of his belt. Like his sibling, he was all finely toned flesh, the ridged stomach evidence of a life spent outside doing physical labor.

"Can we help you, Mrs. Buchanan?"

"Oh!" My laugh sounded nervous, even to me. "I'm afraid you have me at a disadvantage. You know my name, but I don't know yours."

He didn't answer, but tipped the cup up to his lips, took a mouthful of whatever was inside, and chewed. His dark eyes regarded me, sullen and angry. If he'd been a dog, he wasn't wagging his tail.

The younger, blonder brother slid down off the pallet of feed sacks and came over to us. "I'm Bobby Perkins and this here's Tom. What can we do for you?"

"Well, the reason I'm here is—"

Tom Perkins spat a few hulls onto the ground, one by one. Sunflower seeds. "You're the lady who's friends with Angus Backstead, right?"

I nodded, wary.

"He's the bastard who bought our grandmother's estate."

A bead of sweat trickled down between my breasts. "I heard you got a fair price and—"

"Fair price, my asshole."

I stiffened my spine. He had no business speaking like that to anyone, particularly to a woman old enough to be his mother. "Look, Tom, you decided to sell the whole house. No one forced you into it. You could have consigned the merchandise at auction."

"Yeah, well, I seen you making out pretty good at that there auction, too, scarfing up a lot of our grandmother's stuff. Like that quilt she made for us. Grave robbers, all of ya." He spat a couple more hulls for emphasis.

"Hey, I didn't know what the arrangements were." My jeans were sticking to my legs, and the available oxygen in the air was nearly obliterated by the burning dust. "I simply went to an auction."

"Leave it, Tommy. It ain't her fault." Bobby frowned at his brother as he raked his hair back with both hands against the sweat running down his forehead, making it stick up.

His hair was light brown, bleached to blond in places by the sun. As he lifted his arms, the muscles in his chest tightened, and I had to force my gaze away from all that golden skin and taut, youthful six-pack.

An image sprang unbidden into my head of tangled bed-sheets on a hot summer night, feverish caresses, and the frantic urgency of rough, screaming-out-loud sex. How long had it been since it was like that for me?

A flush spread across my body that had nothing to do with the ninety-degree weather.

"Was there something you wanted, Mrs. Buchanan?" Bobby asked.

I exhaled as evenly as I could. "Um, you know, I was going to get some food for my daughter's dog, but silly me, all of a sudden I can't remember what brand, and I don't want to buy a thirty-pound bag of the wrong one."

I wasn't fibbing. I didn't know what kind Jasper ate.

Tom Perkins took a step closer to me. Too close. The ripe man smell of him was overpowering. If he'd used deodorant this morning, it had stopped working a while ago. I had to steel myself not to take a step backward.

"It's not a good idea to change food suddenly on puppies," he said softly. "You have to introduce a new food slowly and mix it in with the old."

I nodded, heart pounding, staring deep into his cold, dark eyes. "I'll keep that in mind."

"And in my opinion, Angus Backstead should rot in jail. Keep that in mind, too."

A white cat came around the side of the shed, and Tom Perkins knelt, picked up a stone, and in one graceful motion hurled it at the animal. The stone clanged against the metal siding and the cat darted away. Unharmed, I hoped.

I decided to do the same. I walked as fast as I could to the Subaru without breaking into a run. The car was an inferno inside, but I wasn't about to wait for it to cool down. I gunned it out of the parking lot, and as soon as I hit

Sheepville Pike, I stomped on the gas and opened the windows. I scraped my damp hair off my neck up into a haphazard ponytail with one shaking hand, and blasted the air-conditioning.

Suddenly frantic to get home, I stepped harder on the accelerator.

Angus Backstead should rot in jail. Tom Perkins's words sounded eerily similar to Ramsbottom's. My intuition had stood me in good stead as a teacher and I was relying on it now. If I gave Ramsbottom the credit that he was too smart to perform the act himself, then he'd gotten the Perkins brothers to handle the murder and locked down the crime scene evidence with all fingers pointing to Angus.

They certainly had the powerful physiques necessary to whack someone with a barn beam. Even more so than Fiona's driver. And while they hadn't exactly threatened me, they didn't welcome my presence on their property either.

The air-conditioning was blowing cooler now, so I closed the windows.

I was driving through a wooded section before the turnoff to River Road, seeing the scene back at the feed store in my mind's eye, until suddenly a deer loped out in front of me. I braked to avoid it, but then another one followed, and I jammed harder on brakes that were slippery in the blistering heat, until the last one, the baby, froze.

Oh, no.

I wrenched the wheel hard to the right and barely managed to steer the car between two trees until it finally came to a crashing halt in a pile of leaves and undergrowth.

I blew out a long breath, and watched the family of deer trot farther into the dark recesses of the forest.

Pay attention, Daisy.

I threw the car into reverse and steadily powered it back up onto the main road. The Subaru didn't seem any worse for wear, and I carried on, more slowly this time.

I breathed a sigh of relief when I finally saw the sign for

the village of Millbury. My nerves were completely shot. I couldn't wait to get home. Safe. And I couldn't wait to see Joe.

Hunger clawed at my stomach and I realized I'd forgotten to eat lunch.

As I passed Sometimes a Great Notion, I noticed there was still a light on. I banged on the steering wheel in frustration. Did I have to do *everything* myself? Why couldn't Sarah be more careful? I stopped at the store, stomped inside, and checked around to make sure the coffeepot was turned off and the computer properly shut down, too. I ended up spending more time going over the day's receipts.

Another half hour later, I walked in the front door of the house, calling *hello*. There was no answer. Maybe Joe and Sarah were in the garden.

The old house felt cool in spite of the heat because its walls were so thick. We didn't need air-conditioning downstairs, only window units in the bedrooms.

I hurried toward the kitchen, but stopped still as the total and utter devastation gradually registered. "Oh my God! What happened here?"

Sarah and Joe glanced guiltily at each other. Sarah was the first to speak. "Well, I left Jasper gated in the kitchen all day, and I guess he found an interesting rip in the floor."

Extremely interesting, apparently, because he had proceeded to methodically chew up the rest of it, leaving an impressive heap of shredded vinyl. The corners of the cabinets had been chewed, too. Ruined. Completely ruined.

Joe held up a hand. "Now, Daisy, don't freak out—"

I sucked in as much air as I could muster. "Well, why don't you tell me when I *can* freak out, Joe, because God knows I never can around here!"

Joe's lips thinned and he turned and walked out of the room.

I turned on Sarah. "Why the hell didn't you come home at lunchtime and let the dog out?"

"I got busy at the store. *Your* store, which you left me to watch!"

"Couldn't you call Dad and let him know what was going on?"

"Daddy went to play golf. He didn't know."

I ground my teeth out of a combination of frustration and guilt. "You need to pay more attention to that dog."

"Mom, you said you were going to redo the kitchen anyway."

I thought my head might explode. "Yes, but not right now. Not right this *minute!*" I noticed that the legs on our precious butcher block table had also suffered from Jasper's boredom. "*Damn* it!"

The phone on the kitchen wall rang.

"Don't answer it," Sarah begged.

I glared at her and picked up the phone anyway. "Yes?" I snapped.

A pleasant-sounding male voice asked, "Is Sarah there, please?"

"Yes, hold on." I thrust the receiver at her. "It's for you."

Sarah hissed, "I told you not to answer it. Thanks a lot, Mom." She pushed past me and ran up the stairs.

"I'll take it in my room," she yelled. "And by the way, I'm leaving in the morning."

Hallelujah.

"I've got it. Hang up the phone!"

I slammed the phone back into its receiver on the wall.

Joe came into the kitchen at that moment, with Jasper at his heels.

I pointed at him, on a roll now. "You know what? This is all your fault."

"What is?"

"This!" I flung my arms wide to encompass the annihilation of the room. "All of it. You spoil her to death. You always have."

"Oh, *I* spoil her, do I?"

Jasper slunk closer to Joe, wagging his tail ingratiatingly.

"Yes, and I'm sick of it. Sick of always being the one to have to lay down the law with Sarah."

I turned on the canine kitchen destroyer. "And as for you, mister . . ."

The dog moaned and slid under the table.

Joe stared at me. A long, hard stare. "Well done. You've frightened the pup. Are you happy now, Daisy?"

I gasped. Joe never looked at me like that.

He spun on his heel and pushed hard on the back kitchen door, letting it slam behind him as he headed outside.

Chapter Twelve

I stormed upstairs, taking the steps two at a time, ready to give the cause of our angst a piece of my mind. I adored Sarah, but I'd been the unfortunate brunt of her foul moods and dramatic temper tantrums over the years. She could be funny, inspiring, creative, and quite sweet sometimes, but there were other times when she could be a bitch on wheels.

As I reached her room, ramping myself up to finally tell her what I thought after years of stuffing down my feelings, I heard the sound of violent sobbing from behind the door.

Crying as if her heart was broken.

I sagged against the wall.

Jeez, what a day this had been. I trailed back downstairs, almost light-headed with hunger. In the kitchen, Jasper was still hiding underneath the table. Overcome with remorse, I knelt down and met his mournful gaze.

"I'm sorry, baby, I shouldn't have yelled like that." I reached out and he gave my hand a small lick, but he was hesitant about approaching me. "Come on out, it's okay."

Bridge to Engine Room. Urgent need for more patience.

I sat down on the rough exposed wooden floor and sighed. I'd wait. Wait until he was ready. For as long as it took. "I'm sorry, Jasper," I repeated. "It won't happen again."

His tail wagged slowly from side to side.

"It's not your fault. Come here." When he finally bear-crawled out from underneath and into my lap, I bent over and hugged him, burying my face in his soft fur.

Jasper licked my arm as if to say, *Don't worry about it, I forgive you.*

What had happened to my former happy, peaceful existence? My best friend was incarcerated, a killer was running around on the loose, and the house was a complete mess. Like its owner.

"Hey, Jasper, want to get out of here for a while?" I whispered. "Go for a walk?"

He jumped to his feet, panting and dancing around me in excitement.

I stood up and looked out of the open window to see Joe tinkering with a bicycle basket.

"I'm taking the dog for a walk," I called.

"What about dinner?" Joe didn't even bother to look up from his repairs.

"I'm not hungry anymore." I wanted to apologize for my earlier snappishness, but somehow the words stuck in my throat.

I hurried toward the front door, desperate to get out of the place that had once been my sanctuary. Jasper took the lead and I simply followed, stumbling after him down the street, hanging on to his leash like a lifeline.

Thoughts jumbled around in my head like so many angry bees buzzing around the hole in the siding when we'd first bought the house.

We'd called an exterminator, who plugged the opening, but warned us about the bees being irate when they tried to get back inside come late afternoon.

Around four o'clock, I had stood there watching in amazement at how many bees had showed up. Hundreds upon hundreds of them had swarmed around, confused and agitated, until they had finally figured out their home was no longer a place they could come back to.

What the hell was I going to do? About Sarah, and her lack of canine responsibility and, to be honest, lack of responsibility in general. About Joe, and his lack of support with the parental duties. About Angus, and the lack of community interest to help set him free. I was a one-man band where that was concerned.

Jasper and I walked and walked, me trailing along behind him in a daze, until it finally occurred to me it was getting dark and I hadn't been paying attention to where we were going.

"Hey, Jasper, we should head back."

I stopped for a moment to get my bearings until I realized I was right in front of Eleanor's house. A red Vespa was parked outside.

Her house was a Victorian, but much smaller than Martha's. It was painted the palest shade of Wedgewood blue, with white shutters, a white front door, and white rosette and ribbon detailing on the gable. In the tiny front garden, Eleanor had planted only flowers that were white, or a very pale shade of the lightest blue. Sweet alyssum, white verbena, snapdragons, and delphiniums.

Suddenly a light went on over the porch and the front door opened.

"Come on in, Daisy." I recognized her husky voice even though I couldn't make out her face in the twilight.

I gasped. "How did you know it was me? Are you psychic?"

Eleanor laughed. "Not exactly. I just had the feeling you would be coming by one of these nights."

"God, Eleanor, it's been a hell of a day. I'm ready to jump out of my skin."

"Prescription: dry martini. Stat."

"But I have the dog with me."

"So? Bring him in. I like dogs. Better than most people, as a matter of fact."

I opened the garden gate and Jasper and I headed her way. Instead of the usual black attire, she wore a simple white T-shirt and gray yoga pants. Jasper needed no further encouragement as he eagerly pulled me through the front door, sniffing like a bloodhound on a mission.

I was a little eager myself. I'd never been in Eleanor's house before.

In the foyer, a ladies writing desk was softly illuminated by an Art Deco lamp featuring a nude female bronze. I dropped Jasper's leash, and Eleanor and I followed him down the hallway.

In the dining room on the left, a vase of fragrant white phlox stood on a round tiger oak dining table. The house had a faint hint of lemon, of fresh laundry, of newly cut wood.

To our right, we passed a remodeled kitchen with cream-colored French country-style cabinets, marble countertops, and stainless steel appliances.

At the end of the hall facing us was a giant circular clock on a pale gray wall that jutted out slightly as if it housed a back staircase behind it. Instead of Martha's living room crammed with family photos, Eleanor had one gorgeous painting of a barn at sunrise hanging above the slate fireplace. A man walked with his dog toward the barn across snow-covered fields.

The rest of the gray walls were unadorned. There was no television. The sofa and love seat were slipcovered in white cotton duck fabric and arranged in an L-shape. One armchair near the fireplace was upholstered in a blue ticking stripe, like an old-fashioned bedspread. The wood floors gleamed under exquisite wool rugs, and the wide window-sills were big enough to sit on to look out into the garden.

"Glass of wine?" she asked.

"Actually that martini sounds pretty good right about now. Could you make it a vodka one, though?"

Eleanor raised an eyebrow but made no comment. She went over to an antique dresser that had been repurposed into a bar. Jasper followed and flopped to the floor behind her while she made the drinks.

I sank into the striped armchair and tried to breathe.

A few moments later, she handed me a fishbowl of vodka. I watched the pungent oils from a twisted lemon peel smoke their way through the chilled liquor before I took a deep swallow.

The raw power of the drink burned my throat, cleared my sinuses, and raged through every quivering synapse of my system, torching any remnants of rational thought from my mind.

My God.

Eleanor perched herself on the sofa and took a sip of her own martini.

I sucked down another body-cleansing gulp and shuddered.

"Well, Eleanor, I came home today to find the house in a complete uproar. The kitchen floor is ruined, and some of the cabinets and our precious butcher block table, too. All chewed to absolute smithereens by this guy because he was left shut up in the kitchen."

Jasper lay down at her feet and Eleanor stroked his forehead. He swiveled his eyes up to her as if to say, *See, I can be good if I try.*

"But you know what?" I said as I pointed the glass holding the last inch of vodka at the dog, "I don't blame him. Not one bit. No, sir. I blame Sarah."

I blew out a long breath. "Everything is crap, Eleanor. Everything is falling apart. Joe isn't even talking to me anymore."

I drained the glass, smacked my lips, and set it down on the coffee table. "There's something else. Something I've never told you before. Visiting the Perkins brothers today kind of brought it all back."

I pinched the skin between my eyebrows and wondered where the hell to start.

"At the beginning is usually the best place," she said, even though I hadn't spoken out loud. I blew out the rest of the breath I'd been holding. Was she really psychic?

Although with Eleanor I didn't have to spell things out. She understood pain and suffering. If nothing else, from her years of experience as a high school nerd. I knew I could tell her the unvarnished truth and it would go no farther than these four walls. I loved Martha—she was my best friend— but you have different friends for different reasons.

Eleanor slid gracefully over to the bar and began mixing another batch of martinis.

I suppose I should have called Joe to let him know where I was, but I didn't have my cell phone with me, and he hadn't acted as if he cared that much anyway.

She came back quickly with a tray holding two martinis, a bowl of mixed nuts, and another one of green olives. The cocktail napkins said, "What's a nice girl like me doing without a drink in her hand?"

Eleanor slid one of the nuts to Jasper. I pretended I didn't notice. I was certainly a tad more relaxed. Maybe this prescription was working.

I took a sip of the fresh martini, more conservatively now, and looked back into the dark recesses of my memory bank, a place that I avoided whenever possible.

"I was teaching in Harlem. It was my first teaching job. Joe and I had been married for a couple of years by this time, and we were trying to start a family." I glanced over at Eleanor and saw the spark in her dark gray eyes. "Yeah, yeah, I know. The trying was the fun part. Well, I'd just found out I was pregnant."

Jasper let out a heavy sigh and sprawled out across Eleanor's feet.

"There was this one kid—there's always one—that you want to save. That you root for more than the others. Julio Lopez was his name. Always in trouble, always late to class.

"The breakthrough moment with him came when I was teaching my history class about the Bayeux tapestry. Something about it appealed to his sense of design. I saw the interest in his eyes for the first time, and I knew that, visually anyway, I had him."

I paused for a moment, enjoying the memory.

"He talked to me for a couple of minutes after that class. He was fascinated with the idea of telling a story through art. From that day on, I encouraged him to think about a career in graphic design. After all, I'd seen his doodling when he was supposed to be taking notes. And he'd been busted for graffiti a few months prior. Even though it was wrong to desecrate school property, it was still good stuff, Eleanor. He was really talented."

"I'll bet you were a great teacher." Eleanor slid her feet gently out from underneath Jasper's snoring body and lay against the arm of the sofa, her chin propped in her hand.

I smiled. "I don't know about that. But that *was* the best part of teaching, you know. Finding the key with each kid that unlocked their interest and passion for what you were trying to convey. Seeing them make that connection was tangible, wonderful, and made it all worthwhile."

I'd always enjoyed showing students new ways to think about things. That sense of adventure and of curiosity was perhaps why playing detective held appeal. Come to think of it, history teachers *were* like detectives in a way. We spent a lot of time researching unexplained things in history to make them relate to today. It also meant I noticed the small details that might tell me a kid was in trouble.

I took another slug of the icy vodka. There was a photographic volume about historic homes in Philadelphia on Eleanor's coffee table.

"I gave Julio a book on art and design. Quite an expensive

book. The next day his eyes were puffy, and he didn't stay after class the way he usually did. I hurried after him and made him talk to me. Turns out his mother's latest boyfriend had ripped the book apart in a drunken rage, just because he knew it meant something to the boy."

I glanced at Eleanor. She was clutching her glass, not drinking, like she hardly dared to breathe. Silence reigned except for the gentle snoring of the one who had caused all the fuss in the first place.

As if sensing my appraisal, Jasper opened his eyes slightly, gave his tail a lazy wave, and went back to sleep.

"That was the worst part. The stuff you heard, that you couldn't do much to change. The abuse, the neglect. But I was determined to help Julio. To help him get financial aid and go to college, if that's what he wanted. To me, teaching was also about making a difference in students' lives by showing them other options. A way out of the cesspool they were born into."

I drained the last of my second martini.

"After that he fell in with the wrong crowd. Ignored his old friends, which was a big red flag. One day after school, I went to the convenience store where he worked. He used to be tired in class because he worked nights, but the kid behind the counter said he'd quit.

"I finally tracked him down at the basketball court. 'Are you okay, Julio?' I asked him. 'What's going on with you?'

"He threw a rock against the fence and it pinged against one of the metal posts.

"'Nothing,' he said.

"'Come on,' I replied. 'You're not talking to the kids at McDonald's now, you know. This is the all-seeing, all-knowing Mrs. B.'

"That brought a small smile, but it quickly disappeared. 'My mother's knocked up again.'

"'By the same guy who trashed the book?' I asked, but he wouldn't look at me. Said he didn't know. Then I told him I'd heard he wasn't working at Mo's anymore, and asked if he was doing okay for money.'

" 'Don't you worry about me, Mrs. B,' he said. Then he pushed up to his feet. 'Gotta go. See ya.'

"But I did worry about him. And that afternoon I followed him. To a pretty bad section of town where there was an abandoned movie theater.

"He turned down an alleyway and slipped inside. I waited a minute, and then swallowing my misgivings, I followed. I caught a glimpse of him heading up a stairway next to the old concession area.

"There was no electricity, and no lights were on because the place had been abandoned for years. I could hardly see where I was going as I crept up the stairs after him. Turns out I'd walked into a drug deal gone bad. Even now I don't know the details except that all of a sudden one of the guys pulled out a gun. I looked into his eyes and knew I was going to die. I knew he was going to pull the trigger and he wouldn't care."

Eleanor sucked in a breath, but I didn't look at her now. I stared at the plain gray wall behind her until the elegant living room faded away and I was back in that red-carpeted hallway that stank of cat urine and mold and fear.

"Julio was there, at the top of the stairs, but so was a group of other guys, and they didn't look happy with him. Something about selling them some bad shit.

"Julio saw me and whispered, 'What the hell are you doing here, Mrs. B?'

" 'What are you doing here?' I touched his arm.

"Suddenly one of them stepped forward out of the dark, turning a gun that had been pointed in Julio's direction toward me.

"I froze, heart thudding in my chest, as I stared into that dark, expressionless face. 'Who's this, Julio? What's going on?' I knew we were in serious trouble, but I wasn't giving up. I wasn't leaving there without him.

" 'Go! For God's sake, go.' Julio gave me a desperate push. Startled, I stumbled backward toward the stairs, losing my footing on the first step. Shots and laughter ricocheted off the walls as I crashed and tumbled down the whole long endless flight.

"At the bottom I lay there, barely breathing, sure that I'd broken my back. I looked up and watched Julio get shot, point blank, and there wasn't a thing I could do about it. I saw the blood spread across his stomach, and felt mine, and knew that I'd lost the baby. I couldn't save either one of them."

I wiped at my face, surprised to find it soaked with tears.

Wordlessly, Eleanor handed me a cocktail napkin. Her eyes were fixed on me, full of compassion. Jasper scrambled to his feet, planted his paws on my knees, and stretched up to lick the salty tears from my face.

"Okay, okay, boy." I petted his head and encouraged him to sit. "Someone must have heard the shots and called 911. It's a bit fuzzy after that until I woke up in the hospital."

"And the baby?"

I closed my eyes for a second. "I didn't lose her right away. Not until a few days later. The doctors couldn't be sure the experience and resulting shock are what caused it, but Joe was convinced."

Every time I tried to bring up the subject, Joe's face would harden. *Daisy, don't defend that son of a bitch who killed our baby.*

"I tried to explain that Julio never meant to hurt me. He didn't exactly push me down the steps. I tripped and fell. He was trying to save me. Joe didn't look at it that way, though. He refused to ever talk about it again. And so I never did. With anyone."

Eleanor cleared her throat. "Daisy, thank you for sharing your story with me."

"I'm not sure why I suddenly did tonight."

"Vodka. It's the great truth serum. Next lesson is absinthe, but not now."

I managed a watery chuckle. "Oh, jeez, Eleanor."

"Did they ever catch the guys who did it?"

I shook my head. "I tried to give them a description, but I guess I was focused more on the gun than the guy who was holding it. And after Julio was killed, I shut my eyes and lay as still as possible so they would think I was dead, too."

Eleanor poured the last of the contents of the shaker into my glass.

"It was funny—I'd faced down the gun and survived—but afterwards I fell apart. I started having nightmares, waking up in the middle of the night screaming, jumping at shadows. I got a new job in a better school district, but it took me years to stop looking over my shoulder. And could I have done more to save Julio? The lack of an adequate answer to that question has haunted me ever since."

I blessed the fact that Eleanor didn't try to come up with a reassuring response. She looked years younger in the soft light from the table lamps, her body lithe and trim in her casual yoga wear.

I took another tart, fiery swallow of vodka to give me the fuel to finish the story. "It took years to get pregnant again. I was thirty-two when I had Sarah and it was a difficult birth. After that, Joe and I considered adoption, but we were both busy with our jobs, and I had my 'kids' in my classes to take care of. I guess you can see now why I spoil Sarah. I've always been so afraid of losing her, too."

Eleanor shook her head. "We all have pain in our lives, Daisy. There's nothing to be done about the past, but we can fix the present. How old is Sarah now?"

"Twenty-six." I felt the warm weight of Jasper's head on my knee.

"Exactly. Time to start dealing with her own bumps in the road. Sarah *acts* laid-back, but she worries, too, you know. Everybody does. Her nonchalance is her way of trying to show that things don't bother her. But she's going to be fine. You can let go a little. And she'll still love you."

"Okay," I sighed.

I knew Eleanor had her own demons. Not only the brutal high school years, but rumors of an engagement that ended when her beau was killed at the very end of the Vietnam War. She deserved her own three-martini session, but I was too far gone to handle it tonight.

I put Jasper's leash back on and we both said a fond farewell to Eleanor. Me with a hug, and Jasper with a long, wet kiss on the mouth.

Eleanor laughed as she wiped her lips. "You know, dogs live in the moment, Daisy. We can all learn a lesson from that."

Moonlight illuminated her garden as we walked outside, and now it was revealed in all its magical, romantic glory— the bright white mounds of the impatiens, the gray of the hostas, the silver of the velvety lamb's ears. As I closed the gate behind me and the dog, I brushed against some heliotrope, and its fragrant vanilla scent was a sweet finale.

Jasper seemed to know the way home and pulled me all the way there. Thank God I had his leash to hold on to, to keep me upright.

I'd always known that Eleanor was the right one to hear my story. Martha would have enfolded me in a huge hug after the first sentence, unable to bear my pain. Eleanor had let me walk through a tunnel of fire and waited patiently for me to come out on the other side.

I was drunk, tired, and my makeup was no doubt a complete mess, but I felt better than I had in a long time.

When I stumbled in the front door of our house, Joe was there in an instant, his arms crossed. "Where the hell have you been, Daisy? I was just about to send out a search party."

"I stopped at Eleanor's. We had a drink together and—"

"Are there no phones at Eleanor's house?"

I opened my mouth and closed it again.

"Next time, please do me the courtesy of calling to let me know. *Try* to be more considerate in the future."

And with that stiff declaration, he stalked off upstairs,

leaving me standing open-mouthed. Wasn't I always the considerate one? The one who always worried about everyone else except myself? I would have gone after him to give him a piece of my mind, except the wide flight of stairs wavered in front of me and I thought better of it.

I went into the library, collapsed on the couch, and covered myself with an afghan. Jasper flopped down on the rug by my side.

For the first time in my married life, I didn't sleep with Joe.

Chapter Thirteen

The next morning, a pack of elves were standing inside my head, apparently trying to carve my brain into some kind of modern sculpture with a thousand tiny ice picks. I groaned, but didn't dare turn over. Jasper's tail banged against the floor, but he didn't get up either.

I didn't want to go to the store. I didn't want to worry about Angus or Sarah or anyone else for that matter. I didn't want to do a damn thing except lie there and moan.

After about ten minutes of this, I finally hauled myself upright and headed for the bathroom.

Joe was walking out of the steam-filled room in his shorts, all freshly showered and shaved. "Everything okay, Daisy?"

"Yes, fine," I mumbled.

"I thought I'd go and pick out some new hardwood for the kitchen today. That old wood floor is in such bad shape, it's not worth refinishing."

"Okay." I leaned against the door frame.

"And while I'm at it, I may as well replace the cabinets, too."

Oh, God. I can't deal with this right now.

"Fine."

And that was it. He walked past me and jogged downstairs.

It wasn't fine, of course. Not by a long shot. I had a sudden urge to take Jasper and just jump in the car and drive. Maybe we'd end up in Maine, in a tiny cottage on a deserted beach somewhere, with only the seagulls for company. I'd throw sticks for him into the water, and we'd walk for miles with no one to bother us.

Even in my wild imaginings, though, my practical brain wouldn't let me be. Where would I get coffee in the morning? Would there be a supermarket nearby? Would Jasper get lonely without other dogs or people to play with?

Oh, for God's sake, Daisy. You may as well get ready for work.

At the Last Stop Diner, I ran in to get coffee for Cyril. It was becoming a habit to stop and see him each morning before I went to the store. People tended to ignore him because of his grubby appearance and off-putting manner, but he had a quirky way of looking at the world that I appreciated.

The diner was housed in an old trolley car that sat askew on the grass at the corner of Main Street and Grist Mill Road, as if it had simply run out of track. It was painted red on the bottom, with a cream-colored top half and a chrome roof. Inside, the black and white checkered floor, fat round stools, and red leather booths were classic diner décor. A small green building constructed behind the trolley car held the kitchen, storage area, and bathrooms, but it was still tight quarters inside.

The waitress on duty was Carla, who, in addition to being Jimmy's girlfriend, according to Patsy, was a bit of an alley cat, a party girl who often showed up for her shift late or hungover. She wore thick dark blue eyeliner all the way around her eyes, and her overly bleached hair looked as though she'd thrown it up into a ponytail without combing it first.

"Patsy's not here today?" I asked.

"She went on a field trip with her kid's school or something." Carla leaned against the counter next to a cake stand, her skin a strange off-white, making the heavy eye makeup seem even more garish.

"Are you okay?"

She held up a finger. "Be right back," she mumbled before dashing off, a hand over her mouth.

Five minutes later, when she hadn't come back, I wondered if I could pour some coffee for myself and leave a couple of dollars on the counter.

Some of the other customers were getting restless, too.

I sighed. I'd better go see if she was all right.

I walked down to the end of the old trolley car and through the swinging door. I grimaced at the sound of someone throwing up in the bathroom. I took a few deep breaths to steady my own undulating stomach. The one thing I couldn't deal with at school was kids getting sick, and I certainly wasn't in the best shape to handle it today.

"Carla?"

There was no response so I finally pushed the door open. She was sitting on the floor of the ladies' room, leaning back against the wall. I wet a paper towel in cold water and pressed it against her forehead.

"Rough night?" I could certainly sympathize. In fact, it was quite possible I was still drunk.

"No. Worse than that."

I stared at her. "You're pregnant?"

Oh, God. And this was the waitress Jimmy had been cheating with. I felt nauseous myself as the truth hit me. "With Jimmy's baby?" I whispered.

She glanced at me in surprise. "Yes. At least I think so . . ."

I sank into a crouched position next to her. "You can't be

sort of pregnant—either you are, or you aren't. Let's get you tested."

"No, wait, I mean I know I'm having a baby, just not exactly sure whose it is."

"Sweet Jesus," I murmured.

"It could be my crazy ex who's the father. I split up with him, though. Couldn't take his jealousy." She laughed rue-fully. "He had good reason, as it turns out."

When I couldn't take the squatting anymore, I straight-ened up, my knees cracking in protest.

What a mess.

I left Carla in the bathroom freshening her makeup, and drove the short distance to the salvage yard, pondering the situation.

Did Carla's crazy ex know she was pregnant? Did *he* kill Jimmy in a jealous rage?

A new pile of hubcaps teetered next to the main gate and there was a Sinclair Dino gasoline pump that I hadn't seen before. It scared me that I was able to pick out anything new in the mess of tools, bicycles, chairs, sinks, gas and oil signs, and tires.

"You!" Cyril pointed at me as I got out of the car. "Yer late."

I kicked at a rusty oil drum. "It couldn't be helped. Oh, and you need to make tea for us this morning. Problem at the diner. Ran out of coffee."

Cyril rolled his eyes. "I got summat to show you any-ways. Come here, you."

I trudged after him into his office.

"See it?" He nodded toward something in the room.

All I could see was a gray metal desk, a filing cabinet, a Hamm's Beer motion clock, a sign that said, CASH OR CHECKS ONLY, and a colorful array of battered license plates on the back paneled wall.

Why did one filthy, crusty old man make me feel so stupid?

I shook my head. *"What?"*

He gestured impatiently toward a five-gallon glass jar in the corner. It was almost full. "That's what ah've collected walking around town. A penny here, a dime there. It adds up. You need to keep yer eyes open for the things that most people miss."

Cyril, the born scavenger. But he had a point. How many people bothered to stop and pick up a penny these days?

"Ah'll go make the bloody tea." He stomped off into the back room.

I stared at the jar of change, which must have been worth a few hundred dollars. What would a scavenger notice that other people wouldn't?

Things on the ground, things out of place, things hidden from the casual observer.

I wandered over to the wall with the license plates. It seemed as though he had one from every state. The rolling motion beer clock was mesmerizing, and I watched the sun set over the lake scene a few times before I finally sat down in one of the chairs in front of the desk. There was a rectangular tin with a picture of Queen Elizabeth II on the lid.

I lifted it an inch and gasped. *Chocolate toffee bars.* My most favorite of Martha's treats.

I jumped as Cyril suddenly reappeared. "Um—I was admiring your biscuit tin here. Don't suppose you'd consider selling it?"

He slammed a mug down on the desk in front of me.

I gritted my teeth. If anyone had the right to an attitude, it was me. Those *were* my favorite treats after all. "What's the problem, Cyril? You seem out of sorts today."

He didn't answer, but glanced at his crossword puzzle. I grinned as realization sunk in. He was crabby because he hadn't been able to finish it before I arrived. There was even a thesaurus sitting next to the newspaper. I took a sip of the tea. It was as full-bodied and sweet as I remembered. "Thanks. This is delicious."

His lips turned up slightly. "It's what we call builder's grade tea in England. Strong enough to put hair on yer chest."

A black shadow flew past my shoulder and landed on the desk.

"Hey!" I ducked too late and liquid splashed over the side of my mug. I shook the drips off my hand onto the floor. "What the—"

"This is His Nibs, or Nibs for short." Cyril had a real smile now as he petted the cat that nudged up against its owner and regarded me with dark yellow eyes.

Somehow I'd never pictured Cyril taking care of anything or anyone else.

There you go, jumping to conclusions again, Daisy Buchanan. A real detective would look at all the facts . . .

With that, my thoughts spun back to Angus. "Damn, I just wish I could figure this whole murder thing out and get Angus off the hook. I have the feeling that the answer is right in front of me, but I can't see it."

"If wishes were hosses, beggars 'ud ride." Cyril gave the cat a rub between its ears. "Now, whatever happened with that narky woman with the bee in her bonnet?"

"Who? Oh, you mean Fiona Adams. She's not so bad. She taught me a lot about the pens. I got an inkling of why they're so valuable." I realized what I'd just said and snickered. "Inkling. Pardon the pun."

Cyril shook his head mournfully as if doubting my ability to size up people. "If I were you, I'd go back to the scene of the crime. Where Jimmy popped his clogs. Keep yer eyes open, but more importantly, your mind."

"Okay. Want some help with that puzzle?"

He shoved the newspaper toward me so violently that the paper smushed together like a concertina.

I smiled, smoothed out the pages, and selected the largest chocolate toffee bar I could find out of the tin.

* * *

It was a busy day at the store, and I did a lot of prep for the open house, which was quite a feat with a head that felt about three times its size and equally heavy. Determination was another good quality for a teacher, in a profession that was not for the weak of spirit. God knows teachers didn't do it for the accolades—or the money.

During a break in the action, I called Betty and asked her if she'd be willing to let us use the auction grounds for the country fair.

"Of course, Daisy. There's no auction scheduled for July Fourth weekend, so you could hold it then if you like."

"Sounds great. And that would be a month before the 4-H fair, so it's perfect. Thanks so much, Betty. Hey, I'm going to visit Angus tomorrow. Do you want me to pick you up?"

"Oh, no, that's okay. You go on without me."

"How about a ride to the hearing on Thursday? You *are* going to that, aren't you?"

There was a slight pause while I felt my blood pressure ratcheting up. She'd better damn well be going.

"Warren said he'd bring me."

"Okay, I'll see you then. Thanks again for the use of the land."

I called Martha and gave her the good news and then had to listen to a complete rundown of the preparations so far, which left my ear sore and tingling when I finally hung up the phone almost an hour later.

I didn't rush home that night, and when I walked in the door, horror dawned as I saw the dining table set for a special dinner. Was it too late to run out and get a card?

Joe came out of the kitchen and smiled at me. "Guess you forgot what day it is?"

"June twenty-first. Oh, Joe, I'm so sorry. There's been so much going on and—"

"Never mind. Happy anniversary. Come and have some champagne."

Sarah was in the kitchen, filling three champagne flutes. My heart sank. Apparently she'd forgotten her announcement from the night before that she was leaving.

What kind of mother isn't happy to see her own daughter?

I forced myself to toast with them. The pale, sparkling wine was dry against my tongue, almost not like a liquid at all, and did nothing to loosen the tightness in my throat.

Joe proudly showed me the flooring he'd picked out. Brazilian cherry in seven-inch-wide planks. The cabinets were a raw cherry wood, which was beautiful, but not to my taste. I'd always pictured something lighter, more modern.

"It's very nice."

"You don't like it?" His face fell.

"I do, it's just that . . ." I thought with a pang of the pictures I'd cut out of magazines in anticipation of the fun we'd have planning the remodel. The hours spent sitting around the butcher block table, talking, laughing, dreaming, mixing and matching, until we both decided on the perfect combination. Together.

Life was so ironic. Finishing the kitchen was something I'd wanted for a long time. But not right now. And now it was all being done in a rush.

Jasper, ignored in the excitement, lifted his leg and peed on a scrap of what was left of the vinyl floor.

Thanks to years of teaching, I knew the serenity prayer by heart. I carefully set down my champagne glass. "Come on, Jasper, let's go outside."

Even though it was shutting the barn door after the horse had escaped, I had to start somewhere. I didn't even ask when was the last time anyone had thought to let him out.

I followed the puppy into the yard and sat for a moment in the metal glider on the back porch. We'd bought it at auction, wobbly, rusted, and missing screws. Joe had painstakingly sanded it down, made it sturdy again, and painted it with several coats of aqua paint until it gleamed.

Jasper peed up against the corner of the shed, and then again on the pedestal of the birdbath, and finally he produced one long stream against a clump of emerging daylilies.

I leaned my head against the glider, feeling like I'd been falling apart a little more and more every day since Sarah had come home. Now my emotions were so close to the surface I was a walking raw wound. Had I really been that peaceful and happy before, or was I just kidding myself?

I took a deep breath, stood up and went back inside.

"I'm sure the kitchen will look great when it's done, Joe. Now, let's celebrate."

Joe grinned and we hugged, and Sarah topped up everyone's glasses. I poured some water for myself.

We chatted about the preparations for the country fair over dinner.

"Hey, Mom, I asked one of my PA friends to lend us some walkie-talkies for the parking attendants to use. She's going to ship them to me here."

"What's a PA?" Joe asked. "A pain in the—"

"Daddy! No, it's a production assistant!"

Sarah laughed, the sound as light and joyous as the bubbles in the champagne. How beautiful she was. How precious to me.

She made no mention of leaving again, nor of any work on the horizon. I knew she expected me to ask, but the new Daisy would let her make her own way. She'd either pay her mortgage or lose the condo. Simple as that. It was out of my hands now.

There was a slight lull in the conversation.

"I wonder what will happen at the preliminary hearing for Angus," I said.

Joe dropped his fork onto his plate with a clang. "Could we please stop talking about Angus for one night? You're depressing everyone. Ruining the mood."

I fixed my smile in place. "Sorry, *everyone*."

Sarah looked down at her plate, not meeting my eyes.

Joe sighed. "I admire your desire to help people, Daisy, I really do, but I'm worried about what this is doing to you—and to us."

"Okay, okay." I smiled harder. "This Veal Marsala is delicious, Joe. However did you make it?"

Somehow we got through the rest of the evening, and managed to convince ourselves that everything was fine.

They say God only gives you what you can handle. I was guessing He'd gotten me mixed up with someone else.

The next morning I awoke to the sound of rain lashing against the windows of our old house. It was Wednesday, which meant visiting day at the prison.

I slipped out of bed, so as not to disturb Joe, dressed quickly, and left a note in the kitchen.

River Road was flooded over in places, and water rushed by in a vicious brown torrent. My wipers barely kept up against the driving rain, which clattered against the roof of the car. I gripped the steering wheel, hoping the Subaru would make it through some of the deeper puddles. Many streams and creeks flowed downhill and under River Road, which made it about ten degrees cooler and pleasant on summer days, but today the terrifying power of water swept all along before it. Some of these cottages at the river's edge would be flooded out if this kept up.

I passed the quarry, with gigantic blocks of rock and a towering cliff above me, and raced alongside the river, where a flotsam of logs, branches, a Styrofoam cooler, and a wooden pallet whipped along, marking the pace of the thunderous current.

"What's up, Daisy Duke?" Angus greeted me with a flash of his former exuberance when he walked into the visiting room.

"What's up, Burger Boy?"

He surveyed my attire—a hastily thrown together combination of long-sleeved cotton top and khakis. "How come you didn't dress up to come see me?"

"Ha! And this from the guy who was always telling me to wear jeans." I wiggled my fingers through my rain-dampened hair to release some of the moisture.

We smiled at each other briefly, and then he lapsed into what was becoming his habitually morose expression.

"Why doesn't Betty ever visit?"

"She had hip surgery, Angus." I could feel my smile fading in disappointment. I'd thought for a moment he was back to his old self. "I *told* you that before."

"But she doesn't even call."

I bit my lip. "Look, don't worry about that right now. She'll see you at the hearing tomorrow."

He rubbed at his forehead.

"Are you all right? I came to see you on Sunday, but they said you were undergoing a medical evaluation."

"Don't know what you're talking about," he mumbled. "Will you give me twenty dollars for the lot?"

I skipped over that for the moment. I needed to get my questions in. "I want to know about this estate company that consigned the pens. Had you dealt with them before?"

He shrugged as if I were speaking a foreign language.

"The *pens*, Angus. The valuable pens that were stolen?" I doggedly recited every detail of what I'd found out so far, hoping that perhaps something I said would resonate.

"Don't wanna talk about this. No point." He seemed more despondent, more confused than ever. "You get a line, I'll get a pole, we'll go fishing in the crawfish hole."

"Okay." Struggling for a lighter note, I told him about the successful auction with Patsy's bid calling and Martha's party afterward.

He leaned forward, a spark in his faded blue eyes that crinkled up like check marks in the corners.

"That Martha, I tell you, Daisy, she was a firecracker in her day. She was something else. She still dresses up like she's going to the prom."

He went off on a tangent about some of the friends he remembered from high school. At least he was coherent when talking about the past.

Could Alzheimer's come and go like that? And if it came to a jury trial, how the heck would Angus hold up? If he fell apart when questioned about the murder or recent events and started talking nonsense in the courtroom, he'd lose his case right then and there.

"Yeah, Grandma Perkins was a real ol' witch," he said. "Shot Sammy Jones with a BB gun when he wandered onto her pumpkin patch by accident."

At the mention of the Perkins name, I snapped to attention. "What happened?"

"Kid got a glass eye, that's what happened." His lip curled up. "Screw that whole Perkins family. They're pure evil. Including the grandsons."

"What do you mean?" I whispered, so as not to break the fragile train of his erratic thoughts.

"There was a girl, a friend of Patsy's, that one of them Perkins boys took an interest in. She wanted nothing to do with him. Think it was the older one, Tom. Well, one night, he went over to her house and stole her cat."

I swallowed. This was going to be the story that Patsy couldn't tell me in front of Claire. I flashed on a scene from *Fatal Attraction* and the pet rabbit . . .

I couldn't deal with this right now. I didn't want to pass out like I almost did in Ramsbottom's office. I held up a hand. "Angus, stop. Please."

"Okay." He lapsed into silence.

I blew out a breath. A minute passed and then my curiosity got the better of me.

"Oh, hell. Just tell me—was the cat dead or not when all was said and done?"

Angus shook his head.

"Then give me the PG version."

"They played what they called 'Bowling with Kitty' at their house with some friends. Set up a stack of pins at the end of the wooden hallway upstairs and threw the cat down the length of it, skidding head over arse along the varnished floor until it knocked over the pins. Finally, when they got tired of the game, they tossed it out of a second-floor window."

I gasped. "But I thought you said the cat didn't die."

Angus chuckled. "He didn't. He came back inside, went upstairs, and took a massive dump on the old lady's bed."

I snorted with laughter.

"That cat was never the same after that, though. Had a real attitude problem."

I raised an eyebrow. "I can see why."

"Finally bit and scratched one of the girl's neighbors really bad. Enough to send them to the hospital. The parents had to put it down."

"I thought you said the Perkins boys didn't kill the cat!"

"They didn't."

I shook my head. Men could be so annoyingly literal at times.

The lights flickered. "Look, I'll see you tomorrow, Angus. Keep the faith, okay?"

"You're an amazing woman, Daisy Buchanan. I love you."

I swallowed against the sting of tears in my eyes and gave him the biggest hug I could muster. "I love you, too. Don't worry, Angus. Everything is going to be fine."

In the prison parking lot afterward, I sat in my car for a while, leaning back in my seat, fighting a spirit-stealing wave of depression. Maybe the situation *was* hopeless after all.

When I got to Sheepville, the rain had eased, so I decided to stop at The Marmalade Cat, a wonderful independent bookstore in the middle of town. I'd look for a nice anniversary gift for Joe. If nothing else, being around books always cheered me up.

As I walked up the street, I saw Reenie coming toward me. She was wearing a clean T-shirt and jeans, her hair was shiny, and I smiled at the peach color in her cheeks, glad to see her looking so much better than the last time I'd seen her.

Amazing what losing an abusive husband can do for your appearance.

"Reenie! I'm so happy I ran into you. You look great."

"Thanks." She smiled back, a faint dimple appearing.

"How's it going?"

"Okay. Me and the kids are fine. But one of the cows had milk fever. Second one this month. The vet came out, so same old story. Never enough money to go round. He said I could pay him off in eggs, though, which was nice."

"Reenie, you're not going to believe this. I have great news for you!" I was almost jumping up and down with excitement.

Her smile was quizzical, inquiring. "Yeah?"

"Yes. The ladies in Millbury are planning a country fair and flea market. On the Saturday before July Fourth. You don't have to do a thing, but all the profits will go towards a fund for your kids. To pay for their college or whatever else they might need."

Reenie stared at me for a few seconds. She opened her mouth, but no words came out.

I grinned, feeling as if I'd just handed the lottery check to this week's winner. Whatever it took to pull the event off, I'd do it ten times over to see that look of wonder on her face.

"Daisy, I can't believe you're doing this for us. It's too much."

"Shh. No, it's not."

"Thank you." She squeezed her eyes shut, and then wiped at them roughly. "I guess you haven't found out any more about what happened to Jimmy? Anything about that estate company?"

"I'm afraid not. That seems like a bit of a dead end." I winced. *Pardon the pun.* "But don't worry, Reenie, I won't stop until I figure it out. And I'm going to make sure that you and your kids are well taken care of."

She stared at me again, as if she could hardly comprehend what I was saying.

Suddenly she gave me a quick, hard hug. "I wish I'd had a mom like you growing up. Maybe things would have been different," she whispered into my ear before she hurried off.

I stumbled into the bookstore, swallowing against the lump in my throat. It had been a watery morning, all things considered.

I almost lost track of time inside the tantalizing shop, but eventually I found a book on vintage bicycle restoration for Joe, the latest paranormal by Sarah's favorite author, and for me, Sunday's New York newspapers. They were a few days old, but I'd still enjoy reading them.

As I drove home along River Road, the grass was completely flattened and sullied brown along the edges, showing how far the water had risen over its banks. I had to use the wipers every now and then to clear the mud-splattered windshield.

When I arrived in Millbury, I parked outside the house and hurried toward the store. As I passed Tony Z's barber shop, I did a double take.

Cyril Mackey was sitting stiff-backed in one of the red vinyl chairs.

I couldn't help it. I stopped dead in my tracks and watched open-mouthed as wet pieces of his long gray locks fell to the mottled vinyl flooring.

Cyril glared at me, hard enough to crack the hand-lettered glass.

I waved and chuckled as I walked on.

Hey, wait a minute. I took a surreptitious step back and checked out his attire. Was Cyril wearing a new jacket, too?

It hung on him somewhat, but it was a definite improvement on the old one.

It wasn't until I'd unlocked the door of Sometimes a Great Notion and started the coffee brewing that I realized where I'd seen that particular green tweed jacket before.

Chapter Fourteen

I willed Eleanor to appear so I could share that tidbit with her, but the universe wasn't listening. She must have actually decided to open her own place and do some work for a change. Martha didn't show up with any baked goods either, so I dug into my emergency supply and poured a bag of M&M's into a glass bowl.

I treated myself by admiring the dollhouse for a few minutes, which I hadn't had a chance to do before, and then spent the next several hours printing out and filling orders received through the website. I'd make a run down the street to our tiny historic post office before it closed at 5 p.m. with my stack of neatly wrapped packages.

Later that afternoon, when the sun was shining once more through the front windows, I was greeted by a welcome "Yo!"

"Patsy!" I threw my eyeglasses down on the sorting table and rushed to meet her. "Congratulations on doing such a great job at the auction on Saturday. I know I told you at the time, but I'm saying it again for good measure."

She grinned. "Thanks again for recommending me. I couldn't believe how much money I made. Sure beats waitressing."

"No one else could have pulled it off the way you did. Although I'm sorry you missed Martha's party."

"Ah, it's okay. The kid and I had one all by ourselves. We built a fort in the basement with chairs and blankets, made popcorn, and crawled in there and talked for hours. I wouldn't have missed that for the world."

I smiled, thinking about Claire, and put on a pot of coffee. I'd better get ready. Visitors usually seemed to come in waves.

Patsy leaned on the ten-drawer seed counter and watched me work. "Daisy, I heard something that I think you ought to know. Whispers that Jimmy Kratz was involved in some serious gambling. And that he got in over his head."

"Really?" I stared at her, the coffee filter dangling from my fingers.

Did Jimmy make up the whole crooked estate company story for his wife because he didn't want her to know how deeply in trouble he really was?

Martha burst in, barely shutting the door behind her. "You are not going to *believe* this. I was just in Sheepville and saw Reenie Kratz and Betty Backstead chatting on the street. Chatting! I must say, I'm not sure I'd be so chummy with the wife of the person who supposedly murdered my husband."

I gritted my teeth. "Okay, for one thing, Angus didn't kill Jimmy, which Reenie knows as well as you or me, and for another, it wouldn't be Betty's fault even if he did."

Martha sniffed. "I know. Just think it's weird, that's all."

I took a deep breath and said the serenity prayer. The smell of roasted coffee beans percolated through the store as the machine dripped hot liquid into the pot. The doorbell jangled as Eleanor arrived. The universe must have told her the coffee was ready.

I leaned on the counter facing Patsy. "So maybe his plan was to sell the pens, pay his debts, and get himself off the hook, but the gambling ring took him out first."

"Back up the truck!" Martha held up a plump hand. "Whose plan? What ring? What are you going on about now?"

"Jimmy Kratz," I explained to her. "Sounds like he had a gambling problem. That may have been why he was killed."

"Yeah? And you think there's some big scary Mafia-type syndicate running an operation around *here?*"

We all looked out of the front windows at the sleepy, bucolic village basking in the golden afternoon sunshine. Apart from the paved road, it could have been a scene from the early 1900s. The quiet street mocked me in its innocence.

"Too much late-night television, Daisy?" Eleanor drew her fingers idly through the candy, making the hard pieces clink against the cut glass. She glanced at the bowl in disdain. "Is it my imagination, or do we get less treats than we used to?"

"Funny you should mention that," I said as I poured four cups of coffee, the memory of the coveted toffee bars at Cyril's fresh in my mind. "I saw Cyril Mackey in the barber shop this morning, getting a *haircut.*"

I waited a moment for the collective gasp. "He was wearing a jacket that I'm sure I've seen somewhere before." It wasn't long before I saw the comprehension dawn on Eleanor's face.

She turned on Martha. "You gave Teddy's clothes away to the church rummage sale at the beginning of June, right?"

Martha looked flushed. "Hell's bells. It's so damn hot in here. Don't you have the air-conditioning on, Daisy?"

I was wearing a cardigan over my T-shirt and I could clearly see the goose bumps on Eleanor's slender arms.

We all waited.

Martha slammed a hand down on the counter. "All right, give me a break. The man needed something better to wear than those awful old rags."

Eleanor wasn't afraid of a little confrontation. "No one's arguing about that. I'm talking about the *treats*."

Martha glared at her. "I have a perfect right to distribute my treats as I see fit."

Things got kind of tense until Patsy spoke up. "Hey, yeah, so like Betty said, she's going to use me for all the auctions from now on. Maybe I'll be able to afford to buy a place for me and Claire someday instead of living down in my sister's basement. And if Betty hires me full-time, I could quit the diner."

"That's great!" Martha beamed at her.

I chose my words carefully. "Yes, it's wonderful to have plans, Patsy, but what about when Angus comes back? He'll want to take over the bid calling again, I'm sure."

I didn't miss the shared glances.

Pity mixed with kindness.

"Anyone else going to the preliminary hearing tomorrow?" I asked.

Patsy cleared her throat. "Daisy, sweetheart, mostly everyone in town has accepted the fact by now that Angus could be the murderer."

Everyone except you, that is. Her unspoken words hung in the air.

"You don't have to tell me that," I snapped. "Even his wife doesn't go to visit him or call him anymore." I turned on Eleanor. "Are you in this majority, too?"

Eleanor shrugged. "I'm sorry, Daisy, but he *was* the last person to see Jimmy alive. He has a history of fighting, he was drunk, and his fingerprints are all over the murder weapon. And no other hard facts have come to light."

Martha squeezed my hand. "Something else you might not know yet. One of the Backsteads' neighbors saw a strange car pull up in front of the auction house that Saturday morning. People are saying that Angus quickly got rid of the pens to lose the evidence."

"Sometimes youse just gots to face facts." Patsy brushed her palms together briskly as if to beat off any crumbs from our nonexistent treats.

"What does Joe say?" Eleanor asked.

I gripped the counter. "Joe is usually supportive of anything I do, but he wants me to let it go, too. But I don't see how you can desert someone who was a good friend to all of us. How can you be so ready to think the worst of him?"

"I'll go with you to the hearing, Daisy," Martha said loyally.

Eleanor drained the last of her coffee. "I *would*, but I have a reporter from *Philadelphia Magazine* coming out here tomorrow morning. They want to do a feature piece on me and my store."

"That's awesome!" Patsy exclaimed.

And with that, the conversation veered away from any further mention of Angus.

I didn't sleep well that night. A particularly gruesome nightmare woke me at 3 a.m. Someone had skewered Fiona Adams through the throat with a stainless steel fountain pen as big as a hunting spear. As her blood spurted over a length of vintage Irish linen, Ramsbottom grabbed Jasper, put the dog in the back of his patrol car, and drove away down River Road. I ran alongside the car screaming at him to stop until I couldn't keep up anymore and watched in despair as the taillights disappeared into the darkness.

I opened my eyes, gasping for breath until the familiar shapes of the bedroom furniture materialized and I heard Joe's sleepy sigh at being disturbed. I fell back against the pillows, trying to calm my galloping heartbeat. It must have been because of everything that had happened lately that those feelings of terror and helplessness I'd thought were buried long ago had crawled back up to the surface.

After two more hours of watching the red digital numbers on the alarm clock tick away one by one, I finally dozed off again around 5 a.m. When the alarm went off at 7 a.m., I dragged myself out of bed feeling as though I'd been run over by that same police cruiser.

A long shower and several cups of coffee later, I was sitting in my car outside Martha's house, drumming my fingers on the steering wheel. The sweltering humidity was back and my hair was still slightly damp because I'd only been able to stand so much additional heat from the blow dryer in the already steamy bathroom. I leaned forward and ruffled it in front of the air-conditioning vent in the car.

Martha finally appeared, perfectly made up, wearing a lime green sundress, orange sandals, and a fantastic vintage necklace of tangerine ceramic flowers on a gold chain with wrapped orange glass pearls. We headed toward downtown Doylestown and the Bucks County Courthouse.

To my surprise, we found a parking spot right on the street. I hurried through one of the brick archways looping along the sidewalk and up onto the wide promenade in front of the imposing circular glass building. Martha followed, panting for breath, and I waited impatiently at the top of a set of shallow steps.

"Come on, Martha, I don't want to miss anything."

"If you don't slow down, you'll be missing *me*. Permanently."

I rolled my eyes. "Come *on*." I grabbed her hand and half towed her into the building.

A small group of people had gathered outside the courtroom on the first floor where the hearing was scheduled to take place. There were a few older men who were auction regulars, a couple of Angus's drinking buddies, and someone I barely recognized.

Cyril Mackey.

He looked years younger with the stylish haircut. He'd shaved, too, and the new clothes were a big improvement. He didn't look half bad, come to think of it. The gray hair was cut to collar length, but now it was aging rock star rather than scruffy homeless person, and the tailored clothes enhanced what I was sure was an ex-military bearing.

He sensed my appraisal and smirked at me, his eyes a dark green in the muted light of the hallway. "Look right posh, don't I?"

"Nice jacket." I grinned at him.

Martha gave him a regal nod, her chest still rising and falling with her efforts to keep up with me.

"Mornin'," Cyril muttered.

If I wasn't so anxious about Angus, it would have been cute, the way these two pretended to be so indifferent to each other.

"Where *is* everybody?" I glanced at my watch. In spite of having to wait for Martha, it was still fifteen minutes before 9 a.m., the scheduled time for the hearing.

"I thought Angus had lots of friends," I whispered to her.

Martha looked at me, her eyes full of compassion. "Oh, Daisy, you're always so willing to believe the best in people."

She twisted the flowers on her necklace for a moment before she spoke again. "You see, country folk are bred to accept the hard parts of life along with the good. The deaths of animals, the loss of a farm, they expect the worst and hope for the best. The reality of human nature doesn't shock them as much. And for the ones who are old enough to remember the Hank Ramsbottom story . . . well, it's the nail in the coffin for Angus."

I blew out a breath. "But where's Betty? I can't *believe* she's not here! And I can't believe Ramsbottom isn't here to gloat either."

Cyril frowned as he looked around. "Summat's wrong."

I spied a clerk hurrying by and stepped in his way to halt him in his tracks.

"Excuse me, is this the right room for the hearing for Angus Backstead?"

He consulted a clipboard full of papers. "Backstead? Oh, it was canceled. His attorney waived the hearing."

"What?" I barely restrained myself from grabbing the front of his shirt. "Are you sure?"

"Yes, sorry, please excuse me." He scurried off down the hallway as I struggled to suck in enough air.

Dimly I heard the murmurs of those behind me.

I blinked to clear the black spots in front of my eyes. "Damn it. I knew I should have found a good criminal attorney for Angus." My throat was so constricted I could hardly grind the words out.

Cyril shook his head in dismay. "Aye up. Thought Angus were in trouble before. He's really buggered now."

"Thank *you*, Mr. Mackey." Martha glared at him. "Good God, man. There are ladies present."

"Oh, Martha, he's right!" I ran my hands through my hair. "Is Warren out of his tiny mind? What the hell was he thinking?"

She squeezed her fingers together in a choking motion. "Let's go see that boll weevil and shake some sense into him."

I ran out of the building, Martha hard on my heels. Down the hill from the courthouse on North Broad Street was a collection of Federal-style buildings called Lawyers Row. Warren Ziegler's offices were located in an ornate brick-fronted building with an elegant black and gold carved sign hanging on the wall outside.

"Good morning," his receptionist greeted us. She sat at the far end of the room behind a mahogany desk and an expanse of oriental carpet.

"Good morning," I replied politely as we hurtled past, ignoring her squawks of protest, and straight into Warren's bookshelf-lined office.

He didn't seem inordinately surprised to see us.

"Just give me one good reason why," I said, gasping for breath.

Warren sighed softly and templed his small pale hands together. "It was not in Angus's best interest to go through a hearing at this time."

"What in the hell kind of answer is that?" Martha demanded, striding up to his desk and towering over him.

He blinked calmly behind his round spectacles. "I deemed it best to eliminate the rehashing of allegations without any new evidence to clear the defendant."

"Huh?" She turned to me, breathing heavily. "Daisy, what's this bow-tied worm talking about?"

Warren took his glasses off and rubbed his eyes, showing a hint of weariness, or maybe he was just trying to block the blinding view of Martha's décolletage.

He looked directly at me, almost pleading. "We have nothing to refute with. It would simply be more bad publicity in the court of public opinion. If this goes to a jury trial, we're going to need all the sympathetic jury members and character witnesses we can get."

Damn it, he was right. The number of people who still believed Angus was innocent was growing alarmingly small.

"And to warn you both, I might waive the arraignment, too. Perhaps a bench trial is our best hope in a case that offers little hope."

I nodded glumly. He didn't have to spell it out. Obviously Warren had also talked to Angus lately and seen his fragile, confused state of mind.

I'd been so sure that Warren had made some huge blunder. Now in his calm, measured way, he actually made some sense.

"Perhaps by the time this comes to trial, you'll have cracked the case, Ms. Buchanan."

I smiled wanly back at him.

He straightened his bow tie a fraction. "At least we might get some concessions. Reduced jail time and the like."

I nodded to Martha, calling off my rabid dog, and we trailed out of his office and onto the street.

"Now what?" I asked.

"You can leave me here. I need a mani and pedi after all that drama. They have the best salon up on East State Street. I'll grab a cab back to Millbury."

"Are you sure?"

"Yes, yes." She waved her fingers at me. "I don't plan on doing any more strenuous physical activity today, other than taking out my credit card."

Jeez. Martha seemed in a hurry to get rid of me. Maybe I'd pushed her a little too hard.

Doylestown was a beautiful town, full of great stores and restaurants. It had become the county seat in 1813 and the resulting buildings clustered together along the walkable Main Street were an interesting mix of styles from late Federal to Colonial, Italianate, and Victorian. Residences with wooden decorative porches were set back from the street with mature trees shading the wide sidewalks. Black gas lamps held overflowing flower baskets.

The courthouse was the only odd man out in the historic district, but it was set apart on its own triangular block at the top of the hill.

There were the typical art galleries, antique and gift shops, but also contemporary high-end apparel and home furnishings stores. Quirky used bookshops and cafés snuggled in between only added to the charm. Even the Starbucks was tastefully housed in an old tavern.

If I didn't have to work, I'd have loved to stay and spend the day with Martha. I'd hung a sign on the door that Sometimes a Great Notion would open late today, but I needed to get back.

Once in Millbury, I was heading for the store when Joe called and asked me to come and take Jasper off his hands. He sounded rattled.

Hey, join the club.

I had my second shock of the day when I saw the state of our kitchen.

All the cabinets had been pulled off the walls. Countless haphazard piles of dishes and pots and pans were crammed together on the tiled floor of the adjoining sunporch, blocking the entrance to the room. Joe was sanding the uneven patches on the old kitchen floor and a fine dust lay over everything.

It wasn't how I would have organized it, of course. I'd have put the contents of the cabinets in covered boxes—labeled—with neat walkways in between. I'd need to rewash every single one of these dishes when he was done.

God, what a disaster! How long was it going to be a mess like this?

I mustered all the goodwill I could find. Joe was bare-chested and sweating from his hard work, and I could see he was on his last nerve, too.

He'd hung some plastic sheeting at the kitchen doorway to stop dust traveling throughout the rest of the house. Guess I should be grateful for small mercies.

Jasper was snuffling around, his paws and nose covered in sawdust, as he checked out the power tools lying on the floor.

Joe grabbed the sander. "You can see why I need you to keep him out of my hair."

I deliberately kept my voice light. "Where's Sarah this morning?"

"She's gone with Debby to Philadelphia to see that famous violinist—what's his name?"

"Robin Tague."

"That's right. I guess he's performing at the Kimmel Center, and there's some kind of private reception afterwards. Sarah pulled some strings to get them an invitation, so Debby's over the moon."

"Oh, that's wonderful." I clipped the leash on the dog. "Okay, come on, Jasper."

It was all so very pleasant and polite. I wanted to cry.

The puppy trotted behind me, peeing on every tree from the house to the store. He peed on the geranium-filled cauldron on the porch for good luck.

What the hell was I supposed to do with a rambunctious dog inside a sewing notions store filled with valuable antiques and precious fabrics?

Calm down, Daisy.

If there was one thing I'd learned from being around Jasper, it was that he was hypersensitive to my moods. If I was happy, he was ecstatic. If I was down, he was miserable. He was like some kind of canine empath.

I brought him into the store, grabbed a bottle of water from the fridge, and took a long, cooling swig.

As he casually sniffed at the dollhouse, I decided he needed some kind of toy. I stuffed an old sack with scraps of fabric and tied a tight double knot at the end. He grabbed it and happily lay down next to me as I went on-line and checked out the latest web orders. I updated the site by removing the sold items, and made a list of the new items I needed to photograph and upload.

On a whim, I typed *Robin Tague* into my browser. His official website popped up, a Wikipedia listing, several newspaper articles, a fan site, and an interview he'd done a couple of years ago with *BBC Music* magazine.

I took another deep swallow of my water and settled down to read. Mr. Tague was fairly cagey. He didn't give the juicy uninhibited answers that celebrities usually did in these interviews. If he decided to change careers, he could be a politician.

I was skimming through toward the end when I found one answer that made me grip the water bottle and lean closer to the screen.

They'd asked about his creative process and how he set

about composing some of the wonderful, haunting pieces for violin that were fast becoming classics.

First, he said he needed a room where there was no color. Everything had to be in shades of gray or black. Not even a red flower or a blue coffee mug.

I rolled my eyes. Sounded like a bit of a nut to me. Second, he had to have absolute quiet. He'd added soundproofing and a second interior wall to his home so no outside noise could penetrate. Third, he fasted for three days before working on a new piece.

And fourth, it turned out he was very superstitious and only ever used one particular type of writing instrument to compose—a rare Magical Black Widow fountain pen.

Around 4 p.m., the weather reports were calling for another thunderstorm, and since I hadn't had a customer in over an hour, I decided to close early.

Cyril's words about going back to the scene of the crime still resonated inside my head. Knowing that Ramsbottom would not have been thorough in his search, to say the least, was it too much to hope I'd spot something the police had missed?

I gently pulled the soggy sack from Jasper's mouth, took him outside, and let him water all the trees on Main Street between the store and the house.

"Jasper, you can come with me to Reenie's, but I'm begging you, please don't pee in the car?"

He looked up at me panting, his mouth split open in a wide grin.

I opened the passenger-side door to the Subaru and he hopped in. I walked around to the driver's side, only to find him sitting in my seat.

"Come on, buddy, move over." I opened the door a crack and slid in, not giving him room to escape, and nudged him over to the passenger side.

When I started the engine, I watched him carefully for any reaction to the unfamiliar noise, but he sat up, his ruffled chest held high, gazing out the window as I eased away from the curb.

When we got to the Kratz farm, Jimmy's pickup truck was gone. The cornflower blue sky darkened as somber clouds swept in, passing over the sun. I'd need to make this fast.

I stepped out of the car and Jasper jumped out after me. I grabbed hold of his leash and knocked on the kitchen door, but there was no answer.

Jasper pulled hard, going crazy from the barnyard scents. He was straining to explore, wrenching at my shoulder, so I let him have his head, zigzagging across the farmyard, which still hadn't dried out from the torrential rain the day before. I grimaced as his oversized paws made deep prints in the mud. I tried to step on the drier patches, glad that I was wearing boots with my jeans, not sandals. Hopefully I still had an old blanket in the trunk.

I wanted to take another look inside the barn and was trying to steer him in that direction, but he seemed determined to head for the henhouse. The chickens protested, squawking at the sight of the enthusiastic golden puppy. I stopped him a couple of feet away so he could look and smell but not get pecked.

The chickens were immaculate and healthy looking. White leghorns with red coxcombs, black cochins with their gorgeous plumage, Rhode Island Reds and pretty gray-speckled Sussex chickens all milled around inside the wooden structure.

Reenie took better care of these guys than she did her own kids.

Suddenly Jasper starting digging furiously at the ground, mud flying up behind him in a high spray. I stepped to one side to avoid the gritty shower.

"Jasper, stop it!" In a few seconds of scrabbling, he'd turned up an impressive pile of dirt.

I was kicking it back into the hole he'd made and smoothing it down with the sole of my boot when a dot of yellow caught my eye. I bent over and picked up a slim, dirt-encrusted object.

With shaking fingers, I brushed the muck off as best as I could. Fresh in my memory from the visit with Fiona was her description of a Parker Duofold Lucky Curve mandarin yellow pen.

The killer must have dropped it in his haste, and it had been squished down unnoticed into the mud. Until now.

I grinned at my dog. *"Good boy!"*

Jasper wagged his tail so hard his whole gangly body swayed back and forth.

I stood there for a moment staring at this new development. A crack of thunder sounded in the distance. "Jeez. I guess we'd better get going."

I wrapped the pen in my handkerchief and stuck it in the back pocket of my jeans. I opened the trunk of the car and thankfully there was a blanket stuffed in between the reusable grocery bags, flashlight, and umbrellas. I laid it on the passenger seat and installed the panting puppy with his mud-caked paws carefully on top. This time he stayed put as I got in on the driver's side.

As I was turning the car to head back down the driveway, Reenie raced up in the pickup truck, not slowing down, as if she hadn't even seen me.

I swerved to avoid her and crashed into a recycle container at the end of the row of garbage cans outside the barn. It fell over, spilling its contents onto the ground. I jammed the car in park and got out to start picking up the empty milk jugs, beer bottles, empty peanut butter container, and soda cans.

"Oh my God! Look what you've done! Oh my *God!*"

Reenie jumped out of the truck and ran her fingers through her baby fine hair, skewing it into short tufts.

"I'm sorry, Reenie, I'll put everything back. It's okay."

Her distress seemed a bit out of proportion to the situation, seeing as it was only a few recyclables that spilled, but who could blame her? She'd had a lot to deal with lately.

"Why are you poking around here?"

I cringed inside at my arrogant interference. She was right. Why *was* I trespassing on someone's private property? I'd definitely gone too far this time.

"I just thought that maybe I could find some kind of clue or—"

She flung her hands out in front of her. "Oh, Daisy, Jimmy's *dead*. Nothing will bring him back. I'm trying to forget he was murdered and put it behind me, but you keep bringing it up again!"

The two kids were sitting in the front seat of the truck, their eyes wide. Neither was wearing a seat belt.

She took a deep breath. "I'm sorry, I know you're trying to help us with the country fair and all and I appreciate it—I really do—but I can't take much more. I want to move on with my life."

"I'm sorry, too, Reenie. The last thing I want to do is upset you."

She sniffed and stared past me for a moment at the barn. "You know, I didn't say nothing to the police, and I didn't want to tell you this before, seeing as you and Angus are good friends, but I *did* hear a car pulling up outside our house early that morning. I can't be sure, but I think what happened is Angus slept off his drunk, found the pens missing, and then came back here and whacked Jimmy."

"No, you see, I checked the odometer and—"

The little boy started wailing inside the truck.

Reenie turned around. "Please. No more, Daisy. Just go. Please."

She seemed so upset that I hurriedly got back in the

Subaru and bumped back out to the main road as fast as I could over the potholes.

Fat raindrops splattered the windshield, and a bright finger of lightning raked the sky.

Jasper slumped down on his seat, his eyes fixed on me. I reached over and stroked his narrow back with one hand as I drove, the thunk of the wipers an uneasy rhythm punctuated by distant rumbles of thunder.

I wondered if there were any fingerprints left on the pen, although between the wet mud, Jasper's slobber, and me wiping the dirt off, I seriously doubted it. I should take it to the police, but I didn't trust Ramsbottom. I was getting to be like Reenie with my mistrust of authority.

I could go over Ramsbottom's head and contact his supervisor, but I didn't want to make things worse for Angus. And if I *did* give it to the police, it didn't prove anything anyway. It wouldn't get Angus out of jail.

Jasper fell asleep before we got to River Road and I kept stroking his back in a gentle massage, the skin loose on his skinny body.

I'd ask Joe and see what he thought I should do. Although then I'd have to admit I'd been on Reenie's property without her permission. *Crap.*

But when Jasper and I arrived home, the house was deserted. There was a note on the table in the ripped-apart kitchen that said Joe and Sarah had gone to the movies and would catch dinner in Sheepville afterward.

I glanced at my cell phone. No messages. Guess no one had bothered to see if I'd wanted to go.

What a darkly serious day.

"Oh, stop being such a baby, Daisy Buchanan. You should be able to make dinner for yourself once in a while," I said out loud.

Jasper's tail instantly began wagging at the sound of my voice.

"Guess they abandoned you, too, huh? Never mind, we'll

manage." I fed him a scoop of his dry puppy food, and then opened the fridge and stared inside, not knowing what I wanted.

I shut the door again and then, in defiance, went down into the wine cellar and picked out a very nice bottle of Shiraz. It was another of those special-occasion wines that Joe and I had purchased in the wine store in Lambertville.

Maybe I'd give the pen to Fiona, I mused as I cut the foil seal around the top of the bottle. Or maybe I'd do nothing with it until I figured things out.

I spied some juice glasses teetering at the top of a nearby pile of dishes. I grabbed one, rinsed the dust out of it, and poured in a couple of inches of the crimson elixir. I took a fortifying swallow and sighed in satisfaction as the essence of crushed raspberries swirled over my tongue.

"I know. A grilled cheese sandwich. *If* I can find a frying pan," I said to Jasper. "How does that sound?"

Thunder boomed outside, getting closer now. He rolled his eyes anxiously toward the window.

"It's okay, buddy." I set the bottle down and smoothed out the worried wrinkles on his forehead.

I maneuvered a few feet into the sunporch, through the stacks of new hardwood flooring and kitchen paraphernalia, and was searching for a pan when the phone rang. I hurried back out to the kitchen and grabbed the cordless receiver. "Hello?"

"Mrs. Buchanan?"

I recognized the same pleasant-sounding voice from the other evening. "Yes," I said, gratified he got my name right. Obviously the type who paid attention. "You must be Peter."

"I hope you don't mind me calling this number again but I've been trying Sarah's cell all day and she doesn't answer."

I retraced my steps into the sunporch, stepping over a mound of dinner plates and cereal bowls. "She went out with her father to the movies."

"Oh." The disappointment in his voice was evident in that one simple syllable.

I wedged the phone between my ear and shoulder and, balancing on my left leg, took a huge stride with my right toward an open space. I thought I saw the edge of my red frying pan in a heap against the back wall.

"I'll tell her you called." I knew Sarah would be pissed off that I was talking to him, but I wasn't going to live in fear of her reactions anymore. Sarah was obviously in pain, too. She needed to face up to reality and try to work things out with this guy. Or if they couldn't, at least they'd both be able to move on.

"Um—I don't want to put you in the middle of anything," he said, "but I'd really appreciate it. I need to talk to her."

I was tempted to encourage him to spill the beans, but I'd overstepped enough.

And then he bared his soul to me anyway.

While I listened patiently, I stretched as far as I could and hooked my finger in the hole at the end of the pan's handle. My heart went out to him. I knew how hard Sarah could be to deal with at times. I murmured that I hoped they'd be able to connect soon.

Peter cleared his throat. "I'm sorry to unload on you like this. Could you give me your address there, please?"

"It's 327 Main Street, Millbury, Pennsylvania." I eased the pan slowly close enough to grab, hoping the pile didn't collapse with an almighty crash. He was probably planning to send Sarah flowers or something.

"Well, I'd better let you go," he said. "I'm sure you're busy."

"Nice talking to you, Peter."

"You, too."

Clutching the prized pan, I hung up the phone and made my way back into the kitchen that had no cabinets, or countertops, or floor.

I poured some more wine and filled the dog's water bowl. A few minutes later, the smell of bread frying in butter went a long way toward soothing my frazzled nerves.

As the storm pounded the windows outside, I curled up on the couch, gave Jasper a corner of my sandwich, and discovered that a forty-five-dollar 2006 Sonoma Valley Syrah actually went quite well with grilled cheese.

Chapter Fifteen

⚙

I got up early the next morning and took Jasper for a walk. It was a clear, sunny morning, as if the storm had washed the world and left it fresh and clean again.

At the intersection of Main Street and Grist Mill Road, next to the Historical Society in its one-room schoolhouse, Jasper sniffed intently at the massive oak tree. Sort of like a message board for dogs.

I couldn't bear the thought of him shut up in a New York apartment all day. Would Sarah make the proper arrangements for him while she worked late, or would he be sitting there in the dark, patiently waiting while his bladder was fit to burst?

Damn it.

Sarah and Joe had come in last night around 10 p.m., full of tales about the movie and the neighbors they'd seen having dinner at the Bridgewater Inn. Sounded like she and Debby had had fun at the concert, too. They'd met Robin Tague at the reception afterward and he'd signed autographs for them. I'd asked if he had used a fountain pen, but it was only a regular ballpoint.

Two kids were throwing a football to each other in the middle of the street. As I waited for Jasper to finish his business, I remembered the old photos of Ramsbottom in his football uniform standing proudly next to his father. Had Angus's actions ruined his character? How would he have turned out otherwise?

You'd like to think life would get clearer as you got older, but it never did.

Friday was another busy day at the store. I'd definitely decided to give the dollhouse to Claire for her birthday at the end of October. It was rather an expensive present for a child, but Patsy couldn't afford to buy her much, and I knew Claire would treasure it. It would be a fun project to fix up, and I made a list of the items I'd need to keep an eye out for. There was some furniture already inside, but it needed a dining table and chairs and accessories for the bedrooms, such as bedspreads and lamps.

I scanned the local paper for upcoming auctions. The ads often listed the types of items that would be up for bid, and even specific descriptions of particularly nice pieces. There were a couple that looked promising. There should be plenty of yard sales going on tomorrow, too.

Patsy came flying in around 3 p.m.

"Hey, Daisy, I have a huge favor to ask you! Sarah and I want to go to the pub tonight, and I thought my sister could babysit, but it turns out she has plans. Would you mind watching Claire for a couple of hours?"

Sarah certainly has an active social life all of a sudden.

"Sure, no problem. I'll come over to your sister's house, though. Our place is a disaster right now with the kitchen remodel."

Patsy's sister lived in a nice end-unit townhome in a development called Quarry Ridge. She was the one who watched Claire in the mornings before school when Patsy had to be at the diner by 6 a.m.

"Thanks, Daisy. And guess what? Betty asked me to do an auction with her on Sunday at a house on Swamp Pike."

I raised an eyebrow. Betty hadn't even asked for my help this time. She must really be taking over the reins of the business.

I'd been to a few whole house auctions with Angus. I liked them, often more so than the regular ones. The auctioneer would bring everything necessary with him to the house—tables to display the items, a microphone, cash register, and even a snack trailer and Porta-Potties for the larger auctions. Some had quite the party atmosphere going on.

After Patsy left, I called Joe to let him know about the babysitting.

"That's okay," he said. "I'll be busy working on the kitchen anyway."

"I didn't think you'd mind."

"You know I don't, but . . ."

"Yes?"

"Well, you always do whatever you want to do anyway, Daisy. See you later."

And he hung up.

I sucked in a breath as I stared at the phone, the dial tone humming. I'd thought Joe was always so easygoing, proud of my independence, and content to let me have my moments in the sun. It never occurred to me he might resent it.

Claire was sitting coloring at the farmhouse table in the dining room when I arrived. The townhouse had a great open plan kitchen, dining and living room with vaulted ceilings, and a fireplace. The spacious kitchen had pickled oak cabinets and a tile backsplash dotted with pictures of herbs. Some of Claire's framed artwork hung on the khaki-painted walls, and the refrigerator was covered in magnets and notes. A tabby cat lounged near the sliding doors leading out to the wooded backyard. Patsy had picked Sarah up and they were doing their makeup together in the powder room. I'd said I'd give her a ride home with me later, so she could enjoy herself and not worry about drinking and driving.

"Look at this!" I said to Claire. "A real kitchen with cabinets and a countertop and everything!"

She giggled. "Daisy, you're funny."

Patsy had wanted her to call me Mrs. Buchanan when we first met, but I preferred plain old Daisy. I set a paper bag on the table. I'd bought cheese curls, Swedish Fish candy, and lemonade at the convenience store attached to the post office.

"Ooh, what's in there?" Claire grinned at me, dark eyes flashing. She knew what was in the bag. I got her same favorites every time.

I sat in one of the white Windsor dining chairs as she pushed a coloring book toward me. "Pick a page for you to color."

Obediently, I selected an ocean scene and a variety of blue crayons.

The brick townhouse had a finished basement that ran the whole length of the house, where Patsy and Claire spent most of their time. It was carpeted with a big-screen TV, a huge sectional sofa, and a desk for Claire to do her homework. There were two beds at one end behind a screen, a second bathroom, and built-in closets under the stairs. It was close to a thousand square feet, and quite a nice space, but still, I knew what Patsy meant about wanting her own place someday.

Patsy came out of the powder room and sat next to her daughter. She never talked about Claire's father. It was as if he'd never existed. All I knew was that when Patsy's mother died in a car crash, she went a little wild and crazy, got pregnant, and had to drop out of school. Her older sister had taken her in and basically raised her.

Patsy didn't have a high opinion of men, to say the least, and I wondered how that would influence Claire. I still wanted her to be a kid, to dream and be innocent for as long as possible, but unsentimental Patsy with her hard-core common sense was determined to teach her about the ugly side of human nature. I myself was an innocent compared to Patsy. When I was teaching in the early days, a kid brought in a bag of weed that he'd found in his dad's sock drawer. I thought it was parsley.

After Patsy and Sarah left, Claire and I went downstairs with our snacks. She lay on her stomach on the floor, watching a fashion designer reality show on television. The tabby cat sat at her side, on guard for any dropped cheese curl crumbs.

My cell rang. It was Martha, in full commander-in-chief mode. "I've planned an organizational meeting for the country fair," she announced. "Tomorrow at my house. It's a working lunch." She said it like we would be at a Fortune 500 company boardroom meeting.

"Aye, aye, Cap'n."

"Oh, and Betty's volunteered to be on the committee, too."

There was a slight pause.

I smiled to myself. "You want me to give her a ride to your house, right?"

I could almost feel Martha smile back at the other end of the phone. She loved it when a plan came together.

"No problem," I said. "Betty's being nice enough to let us use the auction grounds. It's the least I can do."

Claire was shuffling around now in a pair of Patsy's shoes, hands out at her sides, acting like a model sashaying down the runway.

"It's okay, Daisy," Claire whispered as she caught me

watching her. "Mommy's giving this stuff to the Salvation Army anyway." Her little feet slipped around in the high-heeled pumps.

Jeez. Patsy must have really big feet. Just like Angus.

A tiny bell dinged in the back of my mind, but with the angst on television and Martha's monologue, I couldn't concentrate.

"Don't trip on the carpet," I whispered back, seeing the slight indentations she made in the smooth pile as she paraded around.

After I hung up with Martha, I called Betty to offer her a ride. I also made a few calls to some other store owners I knew in Millbury and Sheepville to ask for their help with the country fair.

After the show ended, we played games for a while until Claire yawned and rubbed her eyes, so I told her to put on her pajamas and brush her teeth. I lay down on the twin bed with its purple butterfly comforter next to her and read our favorite stories until I almost fell asleep myself. I glanced over at the other twin bed, Patsy's, and again thought how much she would appreciate having her own bedroom some-day. I hoped the Backsteads could find a way to keep her on at the auction house, even when Angus came home.

As Claire's breathing evened, I crept upstairs and took a mystery novel out of my tote bag and settled down to read.

Around 11:30 p.m., Patsy and Sarah returned, pink-cheeked and laughing.

"So I gather you guys had a good time?" I asked them.

"Hell, yeah!" They both said it at the same time and col-lapsed in laughter again. It was a good thing Claire was sound asleep in the basement.

On the way home in the car, Sarah chatted to me nonstop. "Wow. I haven't danced that much in a long time. It was a great band, Mom. I couldn't believe it."

I smiled. She sounded like a teenager again, full of bub-bling enthusiasm.

"But, man, that other diner waitress that Patsy works with—Carla? She's going to get herself in trouble one day with the way she carries on. Patsy's no angel either, but I mean, this girl's *really* crazy."

I gripped the wheel. Pregnant and drinking? I'd need to have a little chat with Carla.

"Her jealous ex-boyfriend showed up while she was literally dancing on the bar. He was freaking out. It was like free entertainment in addition to the band."

My cell rang.

"Hi, babe." It was Joe. He hadn't called me that in a while.

"What's going on?"

"Well, let's see, there's a nice young man here who showed up looking for Sarah. Says you gave him the address?"

Oh, boy.

Here we go again. One step forward, two steps back in my relationship with my daughter.

"Okay," I said as casually as I could, "thanks for letting me know."

"What's the matter, Mom?"

"Nothing," I said as we pulled up in front of the house. She jumped out and I trailed after her toward the front door. Toward my doom.

At the end of the wide entry hallway, behind the plastic sheet hanging over the kitchen archway, came the unmistakable murmur of male voices.

"Do you know anything about cabinet installation, young man?"

"Not really, sir."

"Well, get ready for a lesson."

"What the—" Sarah ran toward the sound and whipped back the plastic to reveal Joe standing next to an extremely good-looking man with dark hair and blue eyes.

"Hi, Sarah," he said.

"Hi," she said softly.

"I'm sorry, Sarah," I managed to choke out. I hadn't taken a full breath since I'd walked into the house and my chest was on fire. "I just thought he needed our address to send flowers."

She turned and stared at me. I turned and glared at Peter, who spread his hands wide.

"I apologize, Mrs. Buchanan, but I *had* to see her. I couldn't take it anymore."

There was a moment of silence where we held our collective breath.

Suddenly Sarah burst out laughing. "This is so surreal."

I exhaled slowly.

Joe stepped forward. "How about you take this nice young fella down to the basement and pick out a bottle of wine, daughter? Think we could all use a drink."

"Okay, Daddy." She led a willing Peter downstairs.

Joe grinned at me. "Come here, Judas." He put an arm around my shoulders and I leaned into the embrace, grateful for his calm strength.

"There's also an open bottle of a rather nice Shiraz on the counter," I said, and felt Joe's chuckle rumble through his body.

"Don't think I didn't notice that, wife."

Sarah and Peter reappeared after a few minutes, and I hunted around for wineglasses and rinsed them out. Joe motioned for us to sit down at the butcher block table. Jasper picked a spot on the floor next to me and I stroked his head.

"He looks a lot calmer," Peter commented. "I mean, I heard he ate the linoleum and all, but still . . ."

"He's a good dog," I said.

"Looks like you have quite the project going on here, sir," Peter said, clearing his throat.

Joe's dark eyes were full of his familiar good humor. "Call me Joe, please. And yes, it's one of those mushroom endeavors."

"Mushroom?"

"It starts off with, while I'm at it, I might as well . . ." He gestured to the bare walls. "And before you know it, *this* is where you end up."

We all laughed.

"You didn't want to restore the old floor?" Peter asked.

"I would have, but it was in such bad shape. And you know, it wasn't original to the house anyway. In the days when these houses were built, the kitchens weren't attached to the house for safety reasons. If the kitchen caught on fire, as they often did, it meant that the whole place didn't go up. Where we're sitting now used to be the walkway to the summer kitchen, which is long gone."

I glanced down at the floor. It was lined with new plywood and dust-free. Joe had done a lot of work in a short period of time. Maybe there was a hint of light at the end of the tunnel that wasn't an oncoming train.

And the fact that Peter was concerned about the historical preservation of the house made me like him all the more.

Joe leaned back in his chair, sipping appreciatively at his wine. "The cabinets were from the fifties. They weren't worth refinishing either, although I saved what I could to use in the toolshed."

I'd never liked the cabinets. I stroked Jasper's head again. We even had room for an island in here, come to think of it, and perhaps some new lighting.

As Peter asked about the history of the house and Joe started on the long list of renovations we'd accomplished over the years, I watched Sarah as she listened to the conversation, never taking her eyes off Peter. He was almost a younger version of Joe, although I had to admit, even better looking. And I'd never seen her content not to be the star of the show with any guy she was dating. It couldn't have been easy for him, coming here and facing all of us, but he was handling himself well and I gave him points for courage.

I murmured to her, "Should I ask Peter if he'd like to stay

here tonight?" It was an offer I'd have naturally made to a guest, but I wasn't about to put another foot wrong without checking first.

"Thanks, Mom," she whispered back, "but he's staying at the Four Foxes."

I raised my eyebrows a fraction. The Four Foxes was not cheap, by any means. This young director must be doing all right for himself.

Peter whistled softly. "Sounds like you've done a lot of work here. But I warn you, sir—I mean, Joe—I'm no handyman."

"Just an extra pair of hands is all I'm asking for." Joe nodded at Sarah. "You can help, too, young lady."

"Okay, Daddy." Sarah smiled.

We chatted about the techniques of installing hardwood floors for a couple of minutes more before Joe finished the last of his wine and stood up. "Come on, Daisy. Time we left these young folks to talk."

Joe and I went up to bed, hand in hand. We didn't make love that night, but we slept together, and that was a start in the right direction.

Peter evidently wasn't getting his money's worth out of his suite at the Four Foxes, because he was already back at our house again early the next morning. When I came downstairs, he was sitting with Sarah in the library, and they were deep in conversation.

I said "hello" quickly before I hurried out on my way to pick up Betty.

As I walked down the hallway, I overhead Peter say, "Your mom works on a Saturday?"

"She works all the time," Sarah replied.

"I thought they were retired."

"That's what Daddy thought, too."

I shut the front door quietly behind me. Sometimes a

Great Notion wasn't open to customers on Saturdays, only by appointment, but I often went in to catch up on prep work. I hadn't told Sarah about going to Martha's today, but the end result was the same. I was leaving the house.

The store was mine to do with as I wished—without the constraints of a school system dictating lesson plans or schedules. Joe let me have free rein, of course, as he had done for all of our married life.

Like teaching, each day was full of surprises. The store usually energized me and I never minded the hours I put in. But did Joe? Had I mistaken calm acceptance for underlying dissatisfaction?

I stopped at the diner for coffee. The early breakfast rush was over and the trolley car was almost empty. Carla waited on me, and as I paid her, I wrestled with myself as to whether I should say something or not. I tried not to judge people anymore. I always figured you needed to walk a few miles in their shoes first. But I couldn't help myself.

"Carla, I heard you were out partying last night. You shouldn't be carrying on like that in your condition."

"I know, Mrs. B."

I shivered. It was a nickname from the past, and it spurred me into grabbing her shoulders. "I'm not kidding." I resisted the urge to shake her. "You need to get it together now, today, Carla. Not tomorrow, not next week, not when the baby is born, but *now*, do you hear me?"

Carla stared at me, her kohled eyes wide. At least I had her attention. Some of my desperation must have gotten through to her.

"Okay, okay." She glanced around the diner. Only one old man sat at the end of the counter, engrossed in his newspaper.

"Sorry," I murmured, aware that I'd blurted out the fact that she was pregnant. I let go of her and stepped back.

"Actually I was drinking tonic water all night," she said in a low voice. "I told the bartender when I got there that whenever I said 'vodka tonic' to skip the vodka part.'' Carla glanced over at the lone customer again and leaned closer, talking under her breath.

"You're the only person who knows right now. I'm not ready to tell everyone until I've figured things out. Me not drinking would have definitely tipped them off.''

I nodded, understanding. "Just take care of yourself, okay? Please?''

"I will.''

Deep in thought, I headed over to Sheepville to pick up Betty. At The Paddocks, several young girls were trotting around the ring, learning how to ride.

Here we were planning a charity event for the Kratz children, but what if Carla was carrying another one of Jimmy's offspring?

I shook my head. We'd better raise a lot of money with this country fair.

Betty was walking much easier now and seemed excited at the prospect of an outing. She got into the Subaru without my help and chatted all the way to Millbury. When we pulled up outside Martha's house, there were already a couple of cars in the driveway, in addition to the Lincoln. In my rearview mirror I saw Eleanor pull up behind me on her red Vespa.

Martha opened the wide front door and came out onto the porch to greet us. She brought us through to the dining room, where Liz Gallagher and Dottie Brown were already assembled.

Detailed leaded glass doors led into the room with its coffered ceiling and three arched stained glass windows. Bradbury and Bradbury wallpaper in a classic Victorian design decorated the walls between the cherry-paneled wainscoting and crown molding. A rosewood and walnut burl Edwardian sideboard stood along one wall.

The dining table was fourteen feet long and made of solid mahogany with carved, turned legs. A six-arm chandelier with etched swirl glass shades hung overhead. The table was laden now with thermal carafes of coffee, pitchers of iced water and juice, and towering plates of cranberry orange scones and date nut bread.

An easel was set up in one corner, with a rough sketch of the auction grounds.

As soon as the rest of the ladies arrived, and everyone was fed and watered, Martha called the meeting to order.

"Right. We have a lot to do today. Let's get started." She thrust a pad of paper and a pen at Betty. "You take the minutes." Martha pointed a black marker at Liz Gallagher. "Liz, how are you making out?"

"Well, my neighbor is going to help run the lemonade stand with her kids and mine. Hubby offered to bring his prize antique tractors and put them on display. And I'll set up the petting zoo with some of our farm animals. We have a couple of baby goats right now. Arthur the donkey will enjoy it, and the pigs won't care what junk the kids feed them."

"Sounds good." Martha was busy at the easel, sketching out the location of everything Liz had mentioned.

"I asked the school nurse to run the first aid booth. I thought we'd have a Lost and Found there, too, including for lost children!"

"Good idea," I said.

"Oh, and Henry Moyer said he could run the tractor pulls." Liz frowned. "I still have to organize the flea market, though. I've asked the PTA moms to give me stuff, but I need more."

"I can help you with that," I said. "I have lots of stuff to get rid of in my basement. Sarah can help me clean it out."

Half of it was hers anyway. Too bad Sarah's shoes were too big for me. Most of them were barely worn.

There was that feeling again—like déjà vu—or a ghost of a dream that you struggle to remember when you wake up but it drifts away.

Dottie Brown choked down a bite of date nut bread as Martha swung around to her. "I've asked the sheep farm where I get my handspun yarn to do a sheep-shearing demonstration. And my knitting class ladies have made three baby blankets and four scarves so far."

Across the table from me, I watched in fascination as Eleanor slathered two hefty slices of bread with a half-inch layer of butter and took a cranberry orange scone, which she wedged onto the side of her plate.

"Ruth, you're up!" I think we all jumped as Martha rapped on the easel with her marker.

Unperturbed, Ruth consulted some notes in a cream leather binder she'd brought with her. "Let's see, my friend who owns the stables will be providing two ponies for pony rides. I have a roster of judges lined up, and some angel sponsors will provide the prizes for the flower, fruit, vegetable, baking, needlework, and junior art competitions. I've convinced Precision Rentals to supply tents, tables, and an admission booth." She frowned as she peered at her notes. "Oh, and Tony Z will provide haircuts for free, but we'll ask people to make a donation."

"Excellent, excellent!" Martha beamed at her as she strode back and forth. Her gaze landed on me. "Daisy?"

"Um, I thought we could do a farm stand." I was improvising as I'd only come up with this idea last night. I hadn't had much time to devote to the fair preparations until now. "Ellen at the lavender farm has promised to donate honey, and Annie from the herb shop will give us soaps and candles. Flutter Gifts in Sheepville is donating ten homemade birdhouses, and Fresh and Fancy will give us fruit butter, chutney, pickles, and homemade jellies. Joe and I have lots of fresh vegetables in our garden, too, and I bet I can find others willing to spare some extra produce."

"Very nice. Good idea." Martha blocked out a farm stand not far from the entrance to the auction grounds.

"Sarah has some walkie-talkies for the parking

attendants to use, and it turns out that Chris Paxson knows the band that played at the Sheepville Pub on Friday night. They've offered to play for free."

"Wow! That should bring in some people," Patsy said. "They were awesome!"

"And Chris offered to help with parking or wherever we need him."

Patsy waved a hand in the air. "I'm here to volunteer, too. Use me and abuse me as you need."

Debby and Cee Cee nodded. "Us, too," Debby said. "We're not on a committee, but we'd like to help."

Martha smiled. "We're going to need lots of publicity for this thing. Feet on the street, handing out flyers, and asking merchants to post a notice in their windows."

Patsy raised her hand as if she were still in school.

Martha pointed the marker at her.

"I know the deejay on WSEP. I bet I can get him to do an announcement on the air."

"Fabulous."

Betty cleared her throat. "I can open the auction building so people can use the restrooms. We can also use the snack bar for water and ice and to store food."

"That's great," Eleanor said. "Although it brings up another question. What about insurance?" Eleanor had volunteered to be treasurer. "I'll look into that. And how about an admission fee of five dollars per person?"

"That sounds good," Martha said.

"And what are you doing, madam?"

"I'm *organizing*. Plus I'll be running the baking competition."

"Of course." Eleanor gathered up the last crumbs of her scone with her pale pink painted fingernails.

We hashed over names of volunteers and got into more specifics of each job until it was time for lunch. Martha had hired Magic Plate Catering, and the servers went around the table now with a first course of strawberry spinach salad.

My heart warmed at watching Martha in her element, seeing the sparkle in her eyes. Her house was full of people, with lots of good food and good conversation. Just the way she liked it.

Betty was eating salad with one hand and writing with the other as fast as she could.

The second course was a Monte Cristo sandwich. I bit into the smoked ham and melted Gruyère and closed my eyes in delight. There were tiny containers of maple syrup and blackberry jam on the plate for dipping as well as home-made potato chips and thin slices of melon.

Heaven.

"Now, what else?" Martha said. "There has to be something we're forgetting." She crunched on a potato chip. "Ooh, I know. We'll need a cleanup crew afterwards, so that we leave the auction grounds exactly as we found them."

"And trash and recycling containers," Liz Gallagher added.

"Do you have anyone to create the flyer for the event?" Cee Cee asked.

We all stared at her. How could we have forgotten her exquisite penmanship and access to commercial printing companies?

"We do now," Eleanor said, to the sound of laughter from around the table.

"Seriously, that would be great if you'd handle that." Martha beamed at Cee Cee.

"No problem."

It was amazing how my one simple idea had grown into such a grand event. There were so many things to think of. Ruth had a huge binder already, and Betty was writing nonstop.

I pushed my plate away, leaving half a sandwich. I had a notion in the back of my mind to ask Joe if he'd like to go to the Bridgewater Inn for a romantic dinner tonight. I knew he would be toiling away on the kitchen all day, and Sarah's comment about me working too much still rankled.

Betty set her pen down and flexed her fingers. "I think I'm getting carpal tunnel. You know I'd love to help out with the flea market, but I donated a whole bunch of stuff to the church rummage sale at the beginning of June. It felt so good to clean out my closets."

Among the answering murmurs of agreement, I heard that tiny bell again.

"What kind of stuff?" I demanded. "Any shoes? Boots?"

"Oh, I'm sure there were. But why on earth do you want to know, Daisy?"

"Just humor me. What kind of footwear?"

"Let's see. Some sandals I didn't like anymore, a pair of blue velvet shoes that were dyed to match a dress for a wedding that I'll never wear again, and several pairs of Angus's old boots. Although who would want those, I don't know."

A chill ran down my spine. What if the killer had bought some of Angus's boots at the rummage sale? What if he wore them to walk around the barn and commit the murder, leaving the only footprints visible those of big-footed Angus?

"Did you see who bought them? Angus's boots?"

"Why?"

"Because I think it's possible that if someone got hold of a pair, they could have worn them to cover their tracks and put the blame squarely on Angus."

Across the table I saw Eleanor watching me closely. Even though she was convinced, like everyone else, that Angus was guilty, I could tell she was intrigued by my reasoning.

"No, I didn't even go to the rummage sale," Betty said. "It was right before my hip surgery. I called the church and they sent someone round to pick up the boxes off the porch."

"Who?"

She frowned, thinking back, while I held my breath.

"Little Frankie. Frank Ramsbottom's kid."

Chapter Sixteen

I had a sudden wild urge to talk to Cyril. He would understand the monumental importance of this discovery,
whereas around me talk scattered in all directions like it
does when a bunch of women get together. How much
money the church raised at the sale, how hard it was to clean
out a house when a parent died, how much clutter one could
accumulate over the years.

No one else seemed to see the significance of this latest
piece of information. I wasn't sure what I could do with it
either, apart from being absolutely sure that I wasn't going
to give the precious pen I'd found to Ramsbottom.

As the conversation veered toward the best method to
make margaritas, I realized the meeting was about to turn
into a full-fledged party.

I'd planned to leave here by early afternoon so I could
get home in time to freshen up. After all this time spent with
Angus and Ramsbottom and especially the Perkins boys, I
suddenly craved a night alone with my husband.

Speaking of the aggrieved brothers, I did have one piece of unfinished business.

"Betty, are you ready to go?" I asked.

Her face fell. I could see she was intrigued by the thought of fruity frozen cocktails.

"Look, you can stay here for a few minutes longer if you like. I need to stop at the store and pick up something anyway before I bring you home."

I left Betty being treated to her first ever strawberry daiquiri.

Outside Martha's house, the Subaru turned over once and then faded. I tried a couple more times, praying I wasn't flooding the engine, before it finally coughed into life. I gave it a good rev and took off.

When I got to the store, I headed straight up to the second floor. There were three bedrooms upstairs—two to hold sold items and new merchandise, and one room for cleaning supplies, repairs, and ironing.

I'd gone through my records of early purchases and knew exactly which auction item Tom Perkins had referred to. I'd never sold the quilt his grandmother made because I liked it so much, and appreciated how much hard work had gone into its creation. It was an extremely difficult, but beautiful Amish pattern called "Robbing Peter to Save Paul," the irony of which was not lost on me.

I stood on a step stool and took it down off the wall, smoothing the soft fabric, and admiring the curved patterns of purple, pink, blue, and orange and the intricate interplay of light and dark for the last time.

I folded it carefully and found a large shopping bag to place it in. If life was all about maintaining good karma, then I was going to try to fix mine. No matter what Angus said about the Perkins family getting a fair price, I wanted to absolve my part in the whole thing as much as I could. If nothing else, it would ease my conscience if I gave the quilt back to them. Money could do strange things to families after someone died, and I was prepared to give them the benefit of the doubt.

I went back to Martha's to get Betty, but getting her out of there was like dragging a fifteen-year-old away from the school dance. I waited impatiently as she slowly sipped her drink. Why the hell did Martha have to give her such a tall hurricane glass? This was going to take forever.

When we were finally in the car, I called Joe and asked if he'd like to go to dinner. He said he still had about another hour's worth of work in the kitchen before he wrapped things up. I told him I had one more errand to run anyway.

As I hung up, I reflected that he'd sounded pleasant enough, but not particularly interested. What was that magazine article about half of married couples cheating on each other? How superior I'd felt that it could never happen to Daisy and Joe, the fairytale romantic couple.

I swallowed against a quiver of panic. I'd make it up to him tonight.

Once in Sheepville, Betty decided she needed to stop at the grocery store, and I didn't have the heart to refuse. The daiquiri had made her slightly loopy, and each purchase was an event to be discussed and ruminated over until I thought chewing on broken glass might be less painful. Finally we reached the checkout, and I stood as much of the friendly conversation between Betty and the girl on the register as I could until I grabbed some bags and started stuffing produce into them before she'd barely rung them up.

Back at her house, I helped Betty carry the groceries inside and put them away. "Okay, Betty, that's everything. I'd better get going. Thanks again for taking the notes today and for letting us use your place for the fair." I headed for the front door.

"Oh, it's no problem at all. I'll type up the notes and send them around to everyone. There is one more little thing while you're here, Daisy, if you wouldn't mind?"

I sucked down a deep breath, and smiled as brightly as I could.

"What is it?" *Let's hope it's a quick little thing.*

"Well, Angus never had time to put the window unit in the bedroom and it's so hot up there. I haven't been able to sleep."

It was on the tip of my tongue to tell her that I'd get Joe to come and install the heavy air conditioner for her, but with all that he had going on, who knew when he'd get to it?

Resigned, I followed her up the stairs and into her bedroom, which was certainly god-awful hot. The setting sun blazed orange fire against my eyeballs as I struggled to lift the air-conditioning unit up onto the windowsill. Betty wasn't much help, and I bore the brunt of its weight. She disappeared downstairs for several minutes searching for a screwdriver to secure the side panels, while I held it steady, my arms quivering. I counted to one thousand and started over again, feeling the sweat prickling across my forehead.

The sun was touching the horizon now.

Time was slipping away, I thought in desperation. Joe would have stopped work on the kitchen by this time and be waiting for me. I'd have to rush in the door with yet another excuse.

It was like one of those dreams I used to have when I was teaching, where I was trying to get ready in the morning, but everything was moving in slow motion, everything was going wrong, and when I finally made it to the school building, I couldn't remember which class I was teaching, or which room.

Betty came back with a manual screwdriver, and we finally got the unit situated in the window. I screwed the panels in on either side. When I finally satisfied myself that it was safe, I blasted the setting to max cool and stood there for a moment gasping for breath.

Now I'd need to take a shower when I got home, too. Joe

and I would have to have one of those late European dinners.

I jumped in the car and took a left out of the auction grounds. I should have taken a right and headed straight home, but the quilt sitting in a large bag on the front seat reminded me how much I wanted closure. Joe used to laugh that there was no stopping me once I got the bit between my teeth. Besides, it would only take a few more minutes.

Back past the pub, the bank, and the supermarket, through the center of Sheepville, past the intersection with Burning Barn Road and Hildebrand's garage, I drove until I came to the outskirts of town and Perkins Feed Supply.

Not surprisingly, the store was already closed for the day. I got out of the car and looked around, but the huge shed was locked up, too, and the parking lot deserted.

Damn. I'd have to venture down to their house.

The driveway seemed endless as I drove down a slight slope toward the substantial sprawling brick ranch. The grass in the front yard had been cut with a mower blade set too low, and had burned out in scorched patches. No landscaping or summer flowers softened the austerity of the house's façade. It looked as though someone had created a flower bed under the living room window at one time, but now it was just a rectangle of bare earth spotted with weeds.

There were no lights on inside the house. I knocked on the front door, but there was no answer. I peered in the living room window. Typical minimalist bachelor décor. Black vinyl couch, massive flat-screen TV, a coffee table littered with last night's pizza box and other debris, a pair of sneakers on the floor, and not much else. I walked around the house, past two forlorn bushes, looking for any sign of life. There was an extensive deck built across the back that looked fairly new and an industrial-sized barbeque grill.

At this time on a Saturday night, the Perkins boys were probably already down at the Sheepville Pub, tying one on.

The house was set in a dip in the land and the ground

that gradually sloped up behind it held a white barn, a silo, and several clusters of outbuildings. I looked over at the hay barn, pig stable, and smokehouse up on the first rise to the left, but all seemed still and quiet there, too.

To the right of the house and set back about a hundred feet was another large building, most likely for farm equipment. Past that, and directly in line with the house, was a smaller structure, hidden from view of the main road. A dim light was on inside.

I shifted the heavy bag holding the quilt to my other hand. This would be my last try. If I couldn't find anyone there, I'd leave the bag on the front step with a note.

I headed across the grass toward the weak pinpoint of light, but after only a few feet I skidded on something slimy.
Crap.

Literally. I'd stepped in a cowpat about six inches in diameter. I lifted my foot up to take a look at the sole of my shoe, grateful that I wasn't wearing open-toed sandals. I kept going, trying to wipe my shoe off against the dry grass as much as I could.

There was one windowless door in the front of the dilapidated wooden building, but instead of knocking, I decided to take a tour around. I'd rather meet up with one of the Perkins boys out in the open than in a confined area.

When I walked around the back, I gasped in surprise. There had to be at least twenty cars parked in the field in long vertical rows.

What were all these cars doing here? And why not park in the front? One of the pickup trucks looked like Jimmy's, but it couldn't be. As I got closer, I saw there were no stickers on the bumper.

I took a quick look at the rest of the cars. Why the heck was there a patrol car in the last row? Had the police come to arrest Tom Perkins for something?

There was one window in the back of the outbuilding, but it was too high up for me to see inside. Against the wall was a jumble of construction-type garbage almost grown over with grass, so I set the bag down and hauled a five-gallon paint bucket out of the debris. I turned it upside down against the side of the building. Teetering on top, I stretched up inch by inch until I could peek inside.

A group of men were sitting at what looked like four folding banquet tables pushed together in a square. Across from me I recognized Smitty, one of the bartenders from the pub; Arnie Holder, Sheepville's tax collector; Henry Moyer, president of the 4-H Club; a bunch of the auction regulars; and Tom Perkins, who was smoking a cigar.

I tried to control my breathing even as my pulse accelerated.

Four men had their backs to me. I was sure one of them was Ramsbottom. That looked like his bull head and those familiar love handles swelling over his belt. In the center of the table was a pile of cash, and Henry was busy dealing cards. Assorted beer bottles and glasses of liquor sat next to each player.

I suddenly flashed back to the scene in Ramsbottom's office when he'd been talking to someone about a top-secret event going down on Saturday night. This must be it.

And here I was, spying on illegal gambling activities attended not only by an officer of the law, but also by several prominent members of the local community.

Get the hell out of here, Daisy.

Tom Perkins glanced up toward the window and I immediately ducked down. I didn't think he'd seen me, but I stepped off the bucket as silently as I could and set it carefully back in the garbage pile. Something told me these guys wouldn't be too happy to know their little secret had been discovered. I should listen to myself and get a move on.

Humping the quilt bag against my side, I hurried toward the front of the building, watching my step this time in the dusk.

As I rounded the corner, I almost crashed into Bobby Perkins coming from the other direction.

I stumbled back, my whole body one wildly pounding heartbeat.

"What the hell are you doing here?" He towered above me, his face in shadow. He wore denim overalls, and nothing else, showing a bare chest and muscular arms.

"Um—I came to give this quilt back to you," I stammered, holding the bag in front of me like a shield. A light near the top of the building suddenly came on from some kind of motion detector.

"We don't need your guilty presents," he said, barely glancing at the quilt, his voice as cold as his older brother's. His somewhat respectful attitude from the other day had completely vanished. Why on earth had I ever thought him attractive?

I took a step past him, edging in the direction of the house and open space.

As he followed me under the halo of light, I sucked in a sharp breath as I saw that his overalls were covered in blood. His arms and face were splattered red, too.

He must have seen my stricken look, because he said, "We was butchering a pig earlier."

Oh, right. Regular Saturday night entertainment.

He wiped his hands down his pants, leaving a bloody smear, his hands still stained. He gestured impatiently at the bag. "You may as well keep it."

He glanced toward the building as if nervous that Tom might come out and see him consorting with the enemy. "Look, you're probably a nice lady, but you need to go home now. And if you know what's good for you, you'll forget whatever you think you saw here tonight."

I nodded. I didn't need any further encouragement.

I took off running as hard as I could until I reached the car, threw the bag in, and sped off down Sheepville Pike.

It wasn't until I reached Millbury that my breathing finally returned to normal. I'd make one last stop to put the quilt back in the store. I didn't want to leave it folded up to develop creases. I'd have called Joe, but I was afraid my voice would reveal how shaken up I was.

When I got to Sometimes a Great Notion, I hung the quilt back on the wall in the upstairs bedroom with the last of my strength. At least *I* appreciated it. It was a beautiful piece and would be wasted in the midst of all that mess of blood and guts with the Perkins boys. I trailed back downstairs and, suddenly light-headed, sat down on the stool behind the register.

What the heck should I do about what I had just seen? Go to the police would be the logical answer. But was I ready to be the whistle-blower on half this town?

I took a deep breath of the familiar lavender smell of the store. I'd stay here for a few minutes. I needed to get my act together before I faced my neglected husband. I peered in the mirror next to the register. Exhausted, scared, and pale. "Look like hell, don't I, Alice?"

Alice, diplomatic as usual, kept her mouth shut.

"Have I been ignoring you, too?"

She didn't answer, but her expression was faintly reproachful.

"Hey, how about a new outfit?" I went over and picked her up and brought her back to my stool behind the register. I stripped off her Christian Dior suit.

Suddenly excited that I could accomplish at least one useful thing tonight, I ran into the prep room and came back with a Jean Paul Gaultier summer dress. I helped Alice into the knee-length silk chiffon with a deep sexy plunge in the front, and fastened the halter tie. The design reminded me of a profusion of flowers—yellow, magenta, pink, lavender, and green.

"Hold on, Alice. Now for some bling."

I left her propped up against the stool and wandered over

to the jewelry trunk against the right-hand wall of the store and rummaged through it. It was overflowing, thanks to one of the box lots that I'd bought during Patsy's stint as auctioneer.

There was a lot of costume jewelry here, but some nice pieces, too. I should be able to find something appropriate to match Alice's outfit and mollify her. I'd just decided on a retro green Bakelite polka-dot bracelet and a three-strand amber necklace when one of the plate glass windows of Sometimes a Great Notion was shattered by gunfire.

Chapter Seventeen

I dove to the floor, covering my head, until I heard the screech of tires outside. I scrambled to my feet and, through the gaping hole in the store window, glimpsed a truck that looked like Jimmy's, or the one I'd seen at the Perkins farm, careening off down Main Street.

What just happened?

Glass lay everywhere, all over the floor, sparkling in the light from the lamp on the Welsh dresser. I glanced over toward the register, which was directly in the line of fire.

"Alice?"

I rushed over to the ten-drawer seed counter. Alice lay sprawled on the floor behind it, an ugly hole blown straight through one of her impossibly high and pointed fiberglass breasts.

I should call 911. I should call Joe. That expensive Jean Paul Gaultier summer dress is completely ruined now.

That bullet could have gone straight through my own flesh-and-blood body.

I cupped a shaking hand around my left breast, at which moment Eleanor opened the door and picked her way over the broken glass.

"Am I interrupting something?"

"Oh God, Eleanor." I couldn't say any more.

She came over and put her arm around me. "It's okay, Daisy. I already called the police."

"What are you doing here?" I shook my head, frozen in place, barely able to think, let alone talk.

"I was working late in my shop. On a dress for a bridezilla's wedding at the end of the month. Heard the gunshots and here I am."

"Did you see anything?" I whispered. "Did you see the truck?"

She shook her head. "Nope. Just saw your car outside and the damage to the window."

She must have called Joe and Martha, too, because they came rushing in the door next. Joe managed to get in a quick hug before Martha grabbed me and enfolded me against her pillowy chest. "Good God. Thank *God* it was just the doll that got shot, and not you. Now sit down."

"Martha, I'm not hurt." I dug up a smile for Joe, but I could read the worry in his eyes. And all the unanswered questions.

"Yes, but what a shock it must have been." She pushed me gently down onto the stool. "Sit, sit."

"Poor Alice," I murmured. "She's the one's who's injured."

Martha kindly ignored the fact that I was talking about Alice as if she were human. She kept hovering, feeling my forehead and patting my back, but I let her. It was kind of nice to be fussed over for once.

"Why the hell would someone do this?" Eleanor asked.

"That's what I'd like to know," Joe said with a grim set to his mouth.

A few moments later, the whine of sirens split the air.

A tall stranger strode in, dressed in a light gray tropical-blend suit that fit him as if it had been custom-made for his lean, muscular body. His hair was salt and pepper like Joe's, but his face was a lot younger. I'd guess this guy had to be in his mid-forties.

"Detective Tony Serrano." He flashed his badge and slid it back inside his jacket in one smooth motion. "Who's the owner here?"

"I am. I'm Daisy Buchanan." I slid off the stool and stood up on legs that were still trembling.

A couple more police officers followed him in, already moving over to the window, and snapping pictures.

"Is there another room we can use while my guys do their inspection, Ms. Buchanan?"

From the way he said *there* and *here*, I detected a distinct New York accent. What was this sharply dressed guy doing out in the sticks of Millbury?

Martha, springing on point at the sight of a fine-looking male, took charge of the situation. "No problem, Officer, sir. Follow me."

"Are you new in town, Detective?" Joe asked as we all followed Martha to the prep room.

"Yes," he said, but he didn't elaborate.

I swallowed. "Um—look—Detective Serrano—before we get into what happened in the store tonight, there's something else I need to tell you."

I quickly gave him the rundown of my outing to the Perkins place, avoiding any eye contact with Joe, especially when I got to the part about spying on the illegal card game through the window, bumping into bloodstained Bobby Perkins, and running like hell for my car.

Detective Serrano stared at me for a split second before he said, "Excuse me," and whipped out of the room, barking commands into his phone as he went.

A couple of minutes later he was back, and sat down at the head of the table. "Well, I can tell you that little card party on the farm is about to break up. The guys are picking them up as we speak."

He looked thoughtfully around the room. His eyes were a brilliant blue, striking against the pale suit and gray hair. I had the impression that he was taking a quick snapshot of each of us for his memory bank.

"Oh, yeah, Martha," I said wearily. "We'll need to find someone else for the tractor pull at the fair. Henry Moyer was there."

"Dear little Henry Moyer!" Martha placed a manicured hand over her chest. "I can't believe it!"

Serrano fixed his gaze on me, shifting slightly in his seat. I picked up on his impatience.

"Martha, I could really use a cup of coffee," I said. "Would you mind very much making some for us?"

"No problem. I'm on it. Good job I brought refreshments, too. Those young officers are going to need some sustenance." She lifted a tote bag from the floor and swept out of the room.

Eleanor gave her statement first, and then me, although apart from my fleeting sight of a truck speeding away, but no license plate number, I'm not sure how much useful information we provided.

"Normally I'd have asked if you could think of anyone who might harbor a grudge against you, but I guess we have a whole building full of candidates now." Detective Serrano set down his pen and leaned back in his chair. "We'll be checking the bullets we find against any firearms owned by those guys we nailed tonight."

There was a pause in the conversation. I pictured Ramsbottom being taken into custody at that moment. It was odd. I should have been triumphant, but all I felt was vaguely depressed. He had a wife and son, too. How would they cope?

"So you're from New York?" Joe asked.

Serrano nodded. "Originally."

Jeez. It was like trying to pull personal information out of Cyril.

Martha came into the prep room with a tray. "They found a bullet lodged in the Walker seed counter!" she announced breathlessly. She set five mugs down on the table, plus sugar, cream, and a plate of her maple pecan tarts.

Eleanor took two tarts. One for safety, I guessed.

I sipped my coffee black, sighing as the bracing taste steadied my nerves. "Detective, I don't know if you're familiar with the Jimmy Kratz murder, but there were rumors that Jimmy was also involved in the gambling ring. I don't know whether there's any connection between that and his death."

Detective Serrano jotted a note on his pad. "I've been assigned to the Kratz case, so I'll check into it. It definitely makes more sense than killing him over some old fountain pens."

"They're not just some old pens," I blurted out. I sounded like Fiona now. I took a deep breath. "I've seen photos of them. I know it might sound crazy, but they are truly beautiful. Works of art, in fact."

"I'll take your word for it." Detective Serrano finished his maple pecan tart with relish. "I'll tell you what *is* a work of art. This fricking pastry."

Martha winked at me.

"So what's new with the case?" I asked as casually as I could. And why had *he* been assigned to it?

"Well, for one thing, I'm pissed off at the way things have been handled with this whole fricking murder investigation. Sorry, ladies, excuse my language."

"It's okay." I liked this guy. He was plainspoken, but I appreciated his candor. He looked elegant and conservative, but he spoke like a true New Yorker.

He leaned forward and took another tart. "First off, they should never have lifted prints from the barn beam on-site. Prints from a rough surface like unfinished wood need to be done in the lab. Second, I've speeded up the results from the autopsy. They should have been back by now. Ridiculous. Third, I'm going over every inch of this case. Every interview, every step of crime scene procedure, and all the way along the chain of custody."

I grinned as I set down my coffee mug. I *really* liked this guy. Maybe Angus would stand a chance now with a new detective on the scene.

"Mom! Mom!" Sarah rushed into the room with Peter close behind. "Oh my God! I just got Daddy's message. Are you okay?"

"I'm fine. Poor Alice is a little worse for wear, though."

Detective Serrano stood up. "Well, I think we're done here. I'll leave you folks to it." He handed me his card. "Call me if you think of anything else."

"Thank you." *Oh, I will. Don't you worry about that.*

There was so much I hadn't told him yet. About the oil change and proof that Angus didn't drive back to Jimmy's. About Ramsbottom's vendetta. About Carla and her crazy ex-boyfriend. And of course, there was the pen, wrapped in my handkerchief at the bottom of my pocketbook. Explaining how I came to be in possession of it would have been beyond the limits of my energy tonight.

"Do me a favor, Ms. Buchanan. I'll place an extra patrol along the street, but don't be here by yourself late at night. Maybe shorten the store hours for a while until we figure this thing out."

Joe smiled at the detective and shook his hand.

After the police left, Martha grabbed a broom and started sweeping up the broken glass. Joe took the tarp that Peter had brought along and tacked it up over the shattered window. Eleanor picked up Alice and set her back in her familiar corner.

The sight of the bullet hole in the mannequin that some-one obviously mistook for me suddenly made my head swim. I grabbed hold of Sarah for support.

"Mom, are you okay?"

Who could possibly hate me enough to try to kill me?

Eleanor glanced at me, took off her own cardigan, and put it on Alice, buttoning it up to the neck.

"I'm fine." I blew out a breath, patting Sarah's arm. "Now, how was your day?"

Peter smiled at me. "Well, not as eventful as yours, obviously. Although I thought I was useless with home repair, but Joe's a good teacher."

"Joe's good at a lot of things." I slanted a glance at my husband, who grinned at me.

"Now, Daisy, no flirting in front of the kids."

Peter looked around. "This store is incredible, too. I love all the antiques. What a fantastic atmosphere."

Sarah made a mock scornful face. "He's just trying to suck up to you."

The first thing I noticed when Joe and I walked into our house was that the plastic was gone from the end of the hallway, and I caught a glimpse of a real kitchen floor.

I hurried to the doorway and then walked slowly into the room, lost in wonder.

"I installed a couple of the base cabinets so you can see what it'll look like when it's all finished," Joe said.

The Brazilian cherry hardwood floor gleamed under the glow from the new light fixtures hanging overhead. The warm tones in the floor and the cabinets were a perfect complement to the rustic charm of the brick wall, one of my favorite features.

"Oh, Joe, it's perfect. Absolutely perfect."

The lighter wood I'd had in mind would have been much too modern.

Joe opened the dog crate and Jasper bounded out to greet me. As I bent and ruffled his ears, I glanced up at Joe. "You think we can trust this guy in the new kitchen?"

"Oh, Jasper and I had a long talk. He assured me he won't do it again."

I must have looked doubtful, as Joe paused for a moment and then burst out laughing. "I picked up some stuff at the hardware store that's supposed to taste bitter to puppies. It's all over the bottom corners of the cabinets."

"I love the schoolhouse light fixtures, too." The domed lights hanging down over the butcher block table were another welcoming touch.

Typical of Joe's thoughtfulness that he'd chosen something to honor my past career.

"Did you see the sink?" Joe asked, almost hopping from one foot to another like a kid on Christmas morning. "I found it at Cyril's salvage yard."

"It's amazing." I admired the burnished copper apron front sink propped up against one wall, waiting to be installed.

"Sarah cleaned it while Peter and I hung the lights. She did a real good job." He rubbed a hand across one of the cabinets. "See this raw cherry wood? It'll deepen in color over time. The cabinets will only get more beautiful as they age. Kind of like you."

"Aw, jeez. Flattery will get you everywhere, mister."

We laughed.

Joe pulled me into his arms and I willingly leaned into him. As his mouth met mine, my eyes closed, and the years spun away. I was back in the arms of that hot young guy with the hard body I'd fallen for so long ago. The kiss deepened and my pulse raced, my hands sliding up his back, touching him eagerly.

"I'm sorry I've been such a brat lately," I murmured against his mouth. "I wanted to do the kitchen together, I suppose, like we've done everything else around here."

I remembered the countless hours of scraping paint, steaming off wallpaper, refinishing woodwork with me acting as Joe's assistant. I'd missed the whole process this time.

"Well, I still need to pick out some knobs for the cabinets. Maybe we could do that together?"

"That would be great." I smiled at him.

"And here's a sample of the granite countertop. But you

can pick out something else if you don't like it." He held out
a piece of the black and beige speckled stone.

"No, I love it. Really. And I'm sorry about the dinner, too."

"I don't care about dinner, but I *do* care about you." He
pulled back a fraction and looked deep into my eyes. "Now,
Daisy . . ."

Uh-oh, here it comes.

"I held back from giving you a hard time at the store, but
tonight was a warning. It might not even be from the guys
who were gambling. It might be from whoever was involved
in Jimmy's murder who feels like you're becoming a threat
with your snooping around. You need to let the police handle
things from now on."

I sucked in a breath. I wasn't sure I liked being referred
to as a snoop.

"Daisy! I'm serious." Joe gave my shoulders a tiny shake.
"You need to let this go. Angus was a good friend to us, I
know, but there's nothing more you can do for him now."

I winced as I buried my face in his shoulder. Joe smelled
of paint and wood shavings, and maybe faintly of dog. Like
the scent of home.

"You could have been killed tonight," he whispered into
my hair. "That scared the hell out of me."

Me, too.

"I'll be fine." I looked up and forced a smile for him.
"You know what, Joe, you worry too much."

"Very funny, Daisy. But I'm not kidding. Enough is
enough."

Joe never insisted on anything, usually letting me have
my own way, so I knew when he was rattled or angry, it was
time to pay attention. When Sarah was a child, I could
scream and yell at her all day long, but if Joe so much as
raised his voice one iota above its usual calm level, she'd
burst into tears.

"Promise me?"

I took a deep breath, feeling my heart twist at the thought

of abandoning Angus to his fate. The only bright spot was that Detective Serrano seemed as though he was capable of taking care of things the right way.

"Promise," I mumbled.

"Good. Now let's celebrate the fact that you're still in one piece." Joe's voice was a tad husky. He pulled a bottle of champagne out of the refrigerator, and as I watched him open the top carefully, I looked around the kitchen again, admiring all he had done.

"Hey, Joe. Do you think we have room for an island in here?"

"Sure. I was thinking that myself. Easy enough if we don't add any plumbing. Some more prep space would be nice, and maybe some shelves at the ends for cookbooks?"

The champagne popped open, fizzed over the top, and a couple of drops landed on the floor. Jasper licked them up before either of us could move.

"Clean up on aisle three." I shook my head in despair. I hoped a small amount of champagne wouldn't hurt him. Jasper caught my eye and waved his tail slowly. He looked beat. He must have been charging around the whole day, getting in everyone's way.

"I suppose I should thank you, you little monster," I said to him. "I wanted new hardwood floors forever and never got them, but now I have."

I clinked glasses with my husband. "And thank *you*, Joe. Everything you've picked is just right for our kitchen and the house. I can't believe you got so much done already."

"Peter was a big help. Sarah, too."

"I like him so much, Joe. I think he might be The One."

"Don't go jumping the gun now."

We both winced at the same time.

"Sorry," Joe said. "Speaking of Peter and Sarah, where are they?"

"They were going to grab a late dinner, and then Sarah's staying at the Four Foxes with him tonight."

Joe frowned. "Overnight? I'm not sure I like the sound of that."

"Joe!" I chuckled. "She's twenty-six! Besides, it means we have the house to ourselves."

I slid my arms around his neck. I watched his eyes darken as I pressed closer to fit even more intimately against his body. "I need to take a shower first," I whispered.

"I'll help," he offered.

A few minutes later, I was standing under warm, healing water, the stress and anxiety of the night washing away, feeling Joe's hands slowly caress my wet skin.

Suddenly I wasn't tired at all.

The next morning, after a lazy hour in bed talking and reading the paper, we took Jasper for a walk and then decided to go for a bike ride and stop by the house auction on Swamp Pike. I'd have to skip going to the prison today. Joe and I were finally connecting again, and I knew there was no way I could suggest it without him going ballistic.

I'd have to see Angus on Wednesday, the next visiting day. I sighed as I buckled my helmet. He'd think I'd deserted him, just like everyone else.

We rode down to the end of Main Street, past the bicycle shop, which was already doing a booming business. I waved to Chris Paxson, who was outside adjusting the seat on a new mountain bike for a prospective customer. Sweet Mabel's, the ice cream shop housed in a Victorian confection with gingerbread trim painted a happy teal, purple, and yellow, was also packed. People were sitting at the tables outside or wandering up Main Street licking at overflowing cones. It was going to be another hot one today. The temperature already felt like it was in the high eighties.

We took a left up Grist Mill Road, past the little bridge, and then pedaled off the road, bumping over a well-worn trail that led to the old canal towpath. We rode for a couple of miles, enjoying the cool shade of the trees and the silence only inter-spersed by the gurgling splash of the water over brown gleam-ing rocks, the rapping of a woodpecker against the trunk of a tree, or the call of a yellow warbler. *Sweet, sweet, I'm so sweet.* The canal path veered away from River Road, and we'd passed the point where it would intersect with Sheepville Pike.

Finally we rode back onto River Road at the Bridgewater Inn, where the veranda was full of people enjoying brunch. We took a right to head south on Swamp Pike, bounded by acres of golden corn shimmering in the heat.

Once in a while, there was a clearing between the corn-fields with a brick Cape Cod and a wishing well on the front lawn, or a farmhouse where somehow the owner had man-aged to find the time to plant a few marigolds as well as attend to all their farm chores. A red and gold painted sign adver-tising custom furniture, millwork, and cabinetry stood at the end of a winding drive. Outside an old hotel that was now a bar, a sign hung saying, BIKERS WELCOME. From the Harleys and Schwinns outside, it obviously catered to both the motorized and the manpowered varieties.

Here and there I saw signs for the country fair tacked to a telephone pole or a building. Cee Cee had done a great job on the design, and Martha's marketing committee had been busy. When we passed a nursery displaying a bounty of summer vegetables and flowers, I finally remembered to tell Joe about our part in the fair.

"Oh, by the way, Joe, I volunteered you to supply vege-tables for a farm stand at the benefit for the Kratz children. Sorry I didn't mention it before."

"That's okay," Joe gasped as we headed up a slight hill. "I've got more rhubarb than I have recipes for, and there's plenty of spinach, cabbage, and scallions coming up. Think there's still some snap beans, peas, and strawberries, too."

I didn't know the exact address of the auction, but it was easy enough to spot. Cars were parked along both sides of the road, and a crowd had gathered on the grass in front of the white ranch house on its large corner lot. Also it would have been tough to miss Patsy's voice coming over loud and clear on the microphone. It was a sure bet that no one in this neighborhood was sleeping in.

I grinned at Joe, and he smiled back, in the tender way of men and women who have just spent a passion-filled night together. I got off my bike slowly. *Ow.* Whose idea was it to ride bikes today?

Patsy and Betty looked like they were working well as a team. There was a break in the action as a couple of guys brought a mahogany tilt-top pedestal table up to the front. Patsy leaned down and gave me a high five. She clicked the off switch on the microphone. "Glad you're okay, Daisy. Heard about what happened at the store."

"Thanks." I turned to Betty. "Hey, Betty, did you hear there's a new detective on the case now? Maybe it's good news for Angus?"

Betty made some sort of murmured agreement and then turned away to direct the men where to put the table. I couldn't decide if she was distracted or simply not interested.

Seeing as the auction had started at 10 a.m., Joe and I had missed the preview, so we took a quick walk through the rows of tables set up under the attached carport to check out the remaining merchandise. Betty had lucked out with this house by not having to bring in tents to provide relief from the sun blazing overhead.

It was obviously an estate sale by the age of the furniture and the kitchen utensils, which must have been purchased when the person got married in the fifties. A hint of mothballs still clung to some of the fabrics, even out in the fresh air. Items were displayed on trays with a number attached to each one. Joe was intrigued with an antique coffee grinder from Brussels, until I reminded him we were riding our bikes.

The relatives were chatting with one another, and helping out with the auction by carrying sold furniture to people's trucks. Even in their grief, you could sense the love, the connection, the great joy they'd shared with the person who had died. I knew there was a good foundation that would see them through the dark days ahead. That was the legacy the loved one left behind.

Not so with the Perkins boys.

Eleanor was right. That grandmother must have been a real harridan, no matter how accomplished a quilt maker.

Suddenly I became aware that people were staring at us, in particular a group of elderly women in the next row. We didn't look that bad, did we? A little sweaty, and our hair might be messed up from the helmets, but bicyclists weren't that unusual a sight around here.

Joe moved on to another table, but one woman was still staring at me, as if she could bore holes right through my cycling tank top. She looked vaguely familiar. I caught snatches of their voices under Patsy's chanting. Not that they were bothering to keep their conversation private.

There's that busybody teacher who trespasses on people's private property.

She should mind her own business, instead of poking her nose where it's not wanted.

I was ready to grab Joe and leave when I saw Liz Gallagher walking across the grass with two of her five children in tow.

"Liz!"

"Hi, Daisy. I heard about the shooting. Are you okay?"

News traveled fast in a small town.

"Yes, I'm fine."

"I heard all those guys made bail except Frank. They're investigating the funds of the 4-H Club now to make sure there were no misappropriations."

I leaned closer. "Liz, don't look now, but do you know those women at the next table? In particular the one in the middle who's staring at me?"

Liz bent down and pretended to button up her toddler's shirt as she answered. "Oh, that's Edna Ramsbottom. Hank Ramsbottom's widow."

Now it made sense. Not only was I the friend of the guy responsible for her husband's brain damage and eventual death, but I'd played an instrumental part in putting her son behind bars. No wonder she was giving me the evil eye.

I ignored them and bid on a pack of postcards of famous actresses from the 1920s and 1930s and an Art Deco beaded steel evening bag. Joe picked up a box lot of early leather wallets.

"What were those women saying?" He looked worried. "Daisy, do you think this could hurt your business?"

"People who are upset that an illegal gambling ring was shut down are not the people I want as clients of Sometimes a Great Notion anyway!" I snapped as I struggled to fit everything into the carrier bags on the backs of the bicycles.

"Don't let it bother you, Daisy," Liz said. "You did the right thing. Screw those people."

In spite of her reassurances, the whole encounter bothered me and I didn't sleep well that night.

On Monday morning, I was sitting at the kitchen table, still thinking about it. Was I really too pushy? Should I mind my business and get on with my own life, and stop trying to fix everyone else's? Now everyone around here resented me for my interference, and Angus was still in jail.

I was dragging my spoon through my bowl of granola and nonfat milk when Sarah came bouncing into the room.

"Hi, Mom! How's it going?"

"Okay." I let the spoon fall into the milk. "You know, Sarah, I haven't had a chance to apologize to you for giving Peter our address when he called that night. I'm sorry if I overstepped my bounds. Seems like I've been doing that a lot lately."

She sat down next to me at the table.

I sighed. "There was just something in his voice that got

to me. Something . . . so yearning, so sweet, so *in love*, that I couldn't help myself."

"Mom, it's okay. You did good actually."

"Yes?"

"Yeah. We've talked about a lot of things lately. And it feels good to be completely honest with someone."

"Do you love him?"

I waited, and now it was her turn to sigh. Sarah had learned long ago not to lie to me. She complained it was worse than being put under an X-ray machine.

"I think so."

I smiled at her. "Well, that's good. I really like him."

"Me, too." She looked at my barely touched bowl of cereal. "So how are you doing, after the shooting at the store and everything?"

"Fine." I rubbed at my throbbing temples. "Well, not that fine. Turns out I'm not very popular with some of the people in this town. Your father wants me to give up on Angus's case, too. I don't want to defy his wishes, but it feels like I'm deserting my best friend. It's killing me."

"Relax, Mom. I think you did the right thing."

I looked up to see Sarah smiling at me, her face soft with compassion, and it was like stepping out of the woods on a cold winter's morning into sunlight and feeling the warmth on your face.

"And you don't give up on friends just because they go through a rough patch. Do *you* think Angus did it?"

"No, of course not," I said.

"Well, then. Do what you think is right, and Daddy will have to adjust."

And to her, it was as simple as that.

"Hey, why don't I make us a real breakfast?" She didn't wait for my answer, but rummaged through the fridge, and a couple of minutes later, the kitchen was filled with the scent of frying bacon.

I shook my head in wonder as I watched her cook. Who

would have thought that Sarah of all people would turn out to be an ally?

For the first time I saw how she could keep her cool in the craziness of a film set. How that laid-back quality and way of thinking that had always seemed so scattered to me was probably a good way of following various threads at the same time, which in film continuity would serve her well.

A couple of minutes later, she plunked a toasted kaiser roll stuffed with gobs of cheese, crispy bacon, and a fried egg in front of me. Sarah didn't even comment when I squeezed ketchup inside the heavenly mess. I took a huge bite of salty bacon and gooey cheese and refused to think about the calorie count.

"Ohmigod, Mom, look at Jasper." The dog was sitting, one leg askew, gazing at the sandwich she held, his fuzzy ears pricked. "You know how they say people look like their dogs? I'm so glad a cute dog picked me to rescue him." She slipped him a piece of bacon.

I sucked in a deep breath. I'd miss Jasper terribly when she left, but I didn't want to think about that right now.

"Oh, and by the way, I landed a new film gig. Filming starts the second week of August."

I had to laugh at myself again. I'd been so worried about her getting a job. She hadn't worried at all, and it had fallen into her lap. "That's great, Sarah. I'm glad something turned up."

"Mom, I had to work *hard* to get it, you know. What do you think I've been doing all this time?" She gestured with her phone. "Networking."

Just as I took another bite of the sloppy sandwich, Joe came into the kitchen with Peter.

"We're going to install more cabinets in here today," Joe announced. "Then I thought we'd take this young man out for a farewell dinner."

I gulped down my mouthful with an effort. "Oh, you're leaving, Peter?"

"Yes, unfortunately I have to get back to New York for meetings."

"I'm staying until after the country fair this weekend and then I'll be heading back, too," Sarah said, smiling at him.

"I thought we'd go to the Bridgewater Inn tonight," Joe said. "That okay with everyone?"

"I don't know. I might still be full after this sandwich." I grinned at Sarah.

Peter bent down to pet Jasper. "I've heard the food there is delicious, although I have to admit I've been spoiled at the Four Foxes. There's nothing like tasting vegetables the day they're picked. The chef is fantastic."

I wiped a smear of ketchup from the corner of my mouth. "Joy lured him away from a spa in California."

"Robin Tague likes it, too, apparently," Peter said. "He's staying for another couple of weeks even though his concerts are over in Philadelphia. Says the vibe there inspires him."

Guess he learned how to write with color around.

"You talked to him?" Sarah asked.

"Yeah, we were hanging out at the pool together and we started chatting. Poor guy. His apartment building burned down to the ground last month. He lost everything."

"Everything?" My ears perked up. *Including his Magical Black Widow pen?*

I had to remind myself that I wasn't supposed to be getting involved in this investigation anymore. Although I might mention it to Serrano if I happened to run into him.

I stood up and stretched. "Now that I'm in a food coma, I'm going to work. Thanks for breakfast, Sarah."

She rose and gave me a hard tight hug. Sometimes actions spoke louder than words.

Joe waggled his finger at me. "Come straight home after work, Daisy."

I steeled myself against rolling my eyes.

As I walked out of the house, I couldn't explain why his comment irritated me so much, except that demands like that were almost guaranteed to make me want to rebel.

Well, now I'd go see the biggest rebel of them all. I couldn't wait to get Cyril's take on the latest development in Angus's case.

Part of what looked like an old carnival ride had been dumped in the middle of the salvage yard, and I inspected one of the rocket ships with interest. The battered stainless steel ride car would make a neat addition to a kid's playroom, or even provide fun décor at a restaurant or nightclub.

"'Bout time." Cyril flung the trailer door open. He spun on his heel and marched back inside.

I walked in, holding my two cups of coffee, nudged the door shut with my elbow, and sat down opposite him at the kitchen table. Cyril quickly folded the newspaper and set it aside.

"What the heck *is* that?" I asked, pointing at the orange mass on his plate. "What are you eating?"

"Wazzit look like?" Cyril glared at me. "Baked beans on toast."

I watched in fascination as he ate his odd breakfast. "Did you meet the new detective in town yet?"

"Aye up. Nice chap. Brought me coffee without being asked, too."

I shoved one of the cups toward him.

"A real wick copper, that one. Nowt like Ramsbottom, who were as thick as two short planks."

I wasn't sure what he meant, but I thought the gist of it was that Serrano was smarter than the detective currently sitting in jail.

"Heard yer store was like summat out of the Wild Wild West on Saturday night."

I told him about visiting the Perkinses' house, discovering the gambling ring, and the gunshots fired through the store window. I also confided how upset I was at not being able to visit Angus on Sunday.

"Oh, it's all right. I went to see 'im."

"You did?" Relief flooded through me. "I didn't know you were on the visiting list."

"It weren't none of yer beeswax."

I closed my eyes briefly and exhaled. "How was he?"

"He's not right in t'head no more." Cyril shoveled a square of toast laden with beans into his mouth.

I bit my lip. "Look, there's something I want to show you, but please don't tell anyone about it."

He waved at me impatiently with his fork, so I dug down into my pocketbook and pulled out the Parker Duofold Lucky Curve mandarin yellow pen.

"I found this in the Kratzes' farmyard. The killer must have dropped it when he ran off. I kept it because I didn't trust Ramsbottom, and now I don't know what to do with it."

"Sometimes when you don't know what to do, it's best to do nowt." Cyril took the pen from me and held it up to the light. "Have you taken it apart yet?"

"No! Why on earth would I do that?"

"To see if there's anything inside."

I gasped. As an aspiring detective, I was completely useless. What if the real value of the pens, beyond the obvious worth, was because they were being used to smuggle something? Like diamonds or drugs? Something that someone would kill to own?

Cyril was wrestling with the nib, which didn't seem to want to unscrew.

"Be careful," I said, wincing. "Don't break it. Are you sure you can put it back together?"

"Lass, that's how I got started in this business. Because I liked to take things apart and see how they worked."

He grabbed a pair of rubber-tipped pliers out of the kitchen drawer.

"Um, perhaps we should leave it alone and—"

Cyril made a rocking action to pull the nib section from the barrel and finally the sections loosened. He spread the pieces out on the table and shook them one by one, but there was nothing inside.

"The Lucky Curve feed is still intact, though," he said. "That's good."

"The Lucky Curve feed," I repeated. "See, how do you *know* that? How do you have all these random skills? What did you do before you owned this junkyard?"

He sighed. "I were a miner in Western Pennsylvania, Armstrong County. After I'd had enough of living like a mole and seeing men die young, I hitchhiked out this way. Met a guy in Reading who had a scrap yard. Repaired an old outboard motor for him and he gave me a job, fixing the broken stuff so he could sell it. Let me sleep in an abandoned trailer in back of the yard for free. Guess that's why this place feels like home."

This had to be the longest speech Cyril Mackey had ever given. And now he was living here in Millbury and somehow involved with my best friend.

I sipped my coffee and wondered how to bring up Martha, the pink elephant in the room.

"A gentleman never discusses his affairs," Cyril said primly, handing the rebuilt pen back to me.

I could add *mind reader* to his list of talents.

"Oh, so it's an affair now, is it?" I smirked at him as I stood up to leave.

He grimaced, and then his expression turned serious. "Watch tha step, lass. You didn't make any friends busting up that poker game."

For some reason, Cyril's warning frightened me more than anything.

Chapter Eighteen

Joe had contacted the owner of the plate glass shop where we'd originally purchased the windows, and soon after I opened the store, they called to say they would be coming by in the afternoon with a new piece of glass.

I spent the next hour pulling everything out of the left front window, shaking it all out and vacuuming every inch of the store. I assembled some items in a convenient box to make a fresh display. It was Monday, after all. Time to change things up. Some vintage purses, a baby cradle made of mahogany, some loops of velvet and lace trim, and a floral uncut fabric panel all sat waiting for their moment onstage.

Every five minutes I glanced at the phone. I really wanted to call Detective Serrano. Would that count as breaking my promise to Joe not to get involved anymore?

The bell jangled over the door and Mary Willis came in, holding another large white bag.

I'd sold the last collection she'd brought in for five

hundred and fifty dollars. In spite of Patsy's mockery of my
charitable gesture, I'd still made fifty bucks on the deal.

The linens she pulled out of the bag were even more
exquisite than last time, including a pair of tambour lace
curtains and several yards of Victorian velvet that made my
mouth water. There was also an antique child's christening
gown that she said had been used for her late husband and
all three of her children.

"Don't you want to keep this?" I swallowed against the
lump in my throat.

Mary shook her head firmly. "No. It actually feels good
to clean out the house. To simplify my life. I've realized that
I don't need all this *stuff*. And if my kids don't want it, it'll
be less for them to get rid of when I'm gone."

I looked into her eyes and saw the determination there,
but also the peace.

As I tallied up the value, I thought about "things" and
what they could do for you. For some people, they provided
comfort and memories, to others, they represented financial
security, to a collector, they gave satisfaction, but in some
cases, they caused anxiety by creating too much clutter.

At the bottom of the bag was the best part. A shirt box
filled with doll's clothes and dollhouse furniture. I gave her
a very fair price. Not the sympathy price of before, but I
could tell it was still much more than she'd expected.

"There you go, Mary," I said as I counted out seven crisp
one-hundred-dollar bills from the register. "Pleasure doing
business with you again."

"Thank *you*, Daisy," she said, her cheeks pink. "You
know, I'm going to spend part of this money paying off some
of my debts, and then I've already decided I'm going to
spend a little on a bus trip to visit my sister in Lancaster. I
haven't seen her in three years."

I smiled. "Sounds like you have it planned out well."

As she headed for the door, I had a brain wave. "Hey,
Mary, if you come across anything in your house that you

would donate to charity anyway, bring it to the country fair on Saturday. It's for a good cause. A fund for the Kratz children."

"Oh yes, I heard about that. I'll see what I can find."

After she left, I put a pot of coffee on. I couldn't believe Martha and Eleanor hadn't made an appearance yet.

As the coffee finished brewing, Detective Serrano strode in. "Morning, Ms. Buchanan."

The man moved like a predatory cat, full of tightly coiled energy, sizzling and ready to explode. Today he wore a black leather jacket over a white shirt and jeans, and was even more devastatingly good-looking than I remembered. He glanced briefly at the displays, scanning everything like he'd done with our little group the other night, but he paused at the Welsh dresser. He ran his tanned hand across the top, tracing the grain of the wood. "You know, I remember seeing my grandfather chopping up a dresser like this for firewood once."

"Don't tell me!" I stuck my fingers in my ears. I had no idea why some people couldn't see the value of old things. It broke my heart to hear that kind of story. "Look, Detective Serrano—"

"Call me Tony. Please. I stopped in because I sensed there was more you wanted to tell me on Saturday night, but perhaps were reluctant in front of the others."

Was I that easy to read? First Cyril, now the detective.

I bit my lip. It was okay to give the police information, right? And it wasn't as if I'd been *looking* for trouble. "Um— Tony—how about some coffee? This might take a while."

"Sounds great."

I filled two mugs and we sat at the bistro table.

"So I gather you're acquainted with the accused, Angus Backstead?" he said.

"Yes. We're good friends." I took a deep breath and told him first about the oil change and proof that Angus didn't drive back to Jimmy's the next morning. Then about Ramsbottom's vendetta against Angus and the long-ago fight with Hank Ramsbottom. About the rummage sale and the boots. And finally the story of the Perkins brothers and their resentment over their grandmother's house sale.

Serrano listened carefully, making notes from time to time.

"Oh, and Reenie Kratz thought her husband had some kind of deal going on with a crooked estate company that sent the pens out here to auction for below market price."

Even though it seemed as though the estate company was a dead end, I was determined to tell him everything I could think of. "They'd pay a guy like Jimmy Kratz to place a bid, and then resell them afterwards for a much higher price."

"Sounds kinda kooky, but I'll check it out. I went back to the crime scene yesterday and spoke to that Kratz woman. She seemed a little on edge. Couldn't get much out of her."

Reenie had had enough of me poking around her place. I'm sure she didn't appreciate the police coming back again either.

"She's had a lot to deal with lately," I said. "Jimmy was abusive when he drank, and now he's left her with nothing but debt." I cleared my throat. "He was also cheating on her."

Serrano looked up at me. In the daylight his eyes were an even more intoxicating pale blue. Like a Siberian Husky, perhaps.

I cleared my throat, trying not to stare. "Jimmy's girlfriend is pregnant and doesn't know who the father is. It *could* be Jimmy's baby. Word is that she has an extremely jealous ex-boyfriend. I've never met him, but if he knew she was pregnant, or at least having an affair, it might have been a reason for him to bash Jimmy's head in with a barn beam."

I sank back in the chair, exhausted.

"A very thorough investigation. If I ever need an assistant, I know where to go." He smiled at me. "And I owe you one. You've made me look pretty good with being able to shut down that gambling ring practically the minute I got into town."

I smiled back. Actually I was grinning from ear to ear. He was the first person to take me seriously with my findings, and for that, I could kiss him.

Thinking about kissing the detective's firm, masculine mouth made my internal temperature zoom to a dangerous level and I shifted in my chair.

"Actually, the main reason I was brought down here, Ms. Buchanan, and this goes no further than this room, mind you, is that Frank Ramsbottom was under investigation anyway due to some questionable activities on his part."

I gasped.

"He's had lots of money to flash around recently. Too much. A new addition on his house, new cars, expensive jewelry for the wife. We weren't sure what it was—extortion, gambling, selling drugs, what? Guess now we know."

Serrano tapped the pad with his pen. "And Ms. Buchanan—"

"Oh, you can call me Daisy."

"Okay. Daisy. Now I've got some news for *you*. Good and bad. As I mentioned, I fast-tracked the results from the autopsy. It shows that Jimmy Kratz was killed around midnight, at which point your friend Angus was still passed out on his glider, in full view of numerous witnesses passing by on Sheepville Pike."

I stared at him for a moment, hardly daring to breathe. "Wait a minute. Does that mean Angus is off the hook?"

He nodded.

I bounced in my seat. "That's *fantastic* news!" Now I really did want to kiss him.

The detective held up a hand. "Hold on, there's more. Don't celebrate just yet. The bad news is that Angus Backstead finally had a physical for the first time in years, and the docs discovered a brain tumor, a meningioma, I believe it's called."

"Oh, God. How bad is it? Will he be okay?"

"Tough to say, but they think it's benign and he should make a full recovery."

"I guess that would explain how confused Angus has been lately, and the bad headaches. He hardly knew what he'd eaten for breakfast, yet he could remember things from years past." I was talking faster and faster in my excitement. "I know it's serious, but it's sort of a relief to finally find out what was wrong. Can I see him now?"

Serrano shook his head. "He's already at the hospital, undergoing prep. Surgery is first thing tomorrow."

There was a sudden commotion at the front door. Martha came in carrying a round cake tray, with Eleanor close behind. "Why, hello, Detective sir. What a pleasure to see you again." She took the lid off with a flourish. "How about a piece of pineapple passion cake?"

Eleanor winked at me. "Try saying that ten times fast."

Serrano accepted a plate with a huge piece of cake and dug in with relish. The man must work out like a fiend to keep that trim body with the amount of food he could pack away. Martha beamed at him.

I gave them the good news about Angus.

"I knew he was innocent all along," Martha declared.

I rolled my eyes. If I kept this up, I'd look like one of those vintage Kit-Cat Clocks.

"What about the strange car that pulled up outside the auction house that morning?" Eleanor asked. "Everyone thought Angus had made some kind of handoff with the pens."

"Oh, we canvassed the neighbors again," Serrano said. "Turns out it was Fiona Adams in her Mercedes, asking about the auction and for directions to the bed-and-breakfast. She's in the clear, too. She was at some charity event in New York the night before, and the driver took her there and back. They were nowhere near the crime scene."

He licked a clump of butter cream frosting off his fork while we all watched in rapt attention.

"Well, I'll keep you posted," he said, standing up. "Let me know if you think of anything else. That cake was spectacular. Thanks, ladies." He winked at Martha and walked out of the store.

Martha stared after him, open-mouthed. "Good God," she murmured. "I think my heart just stopped."

"Talk about encouraging stray cats," Eleanor said in her best Mae West impression. She turned to Martha. "What do you put in those treats anyway—some kind of catnip for men?"

"Like I said, I know what men like." Martha's gaze was still fixed on Serrano through the unbroken window as he got into his car. "And he's a *fine*-looking specimen."

"I certainly wouldn't kick him out of bed." Eleanor's gaze was more speculative.

I suddenly realized I'd forgotten to give him the pen. Maybe it was some kind of mental block on my part. Maybe I was holding on to it so I'd have something to give to Fiona after all was said and done, assuming the other pens were never found. It would be nice if she had some small reminder of her father. I'd rather give it to her than have it collecting dust in some evidence room at the police station.

Later on that afternoon, the plate glass company came to fix the window. After they left, I stepped up onto the display area with the new items. I placed the baby cradle in first, then an arrangement of the vintage purses. A truck went by on Main Street, and standing exposed and a potential target in the front window suddenly spooked me so much I dropped the fabric panel and velvet trim and hopped down, leaving them where they fell.

I called Betty, but she wasn't home. I left a message saying what a relief it was to hear Angus was cleared of Jimmy's murder. She must be at the hospital. At least she'd have no

excuse not to go *there*, I thought bitterly, trying to let go of
my resentment that she'd basically abandoned her husband
throughout this whole ordeal.

At 5 p.m., I dutifully closed the store and went straight
home.

The next day, after a tearful good-bye to Peter, Sarah
accompanied me to Sometimes a Great Notion. I had to
admit I'd been a little misty-eyed to see him go, too. I didn't
know what the future held, but if Peter ended up being my
son-in-law, I'd have no complaints.

Martha and Eleanor burst into the shop a few minutes
after we opened.

"Good God, did you hear the news?" Martha was waving
a copy of one of the New York newspapers over her head.
"That crazy Fiona Adams? The one who had the meltdown
at the auction? Her father's new wife has just been found
dead in her New York penthouse!"

"What?" I grabbed the paper from her. "Let me see that.
Do they know what happened yet?"

Sarah was already scanning her phone. Before I'd had a
chance to turn a page in the newspaper, she answered me. "Says
here there seems to be no sign of foul play, as if she died in her
sleep, but a toxicology report and autopsy are under way."

My mind was racing as Martha, Eleanor, and I stared at
one another.

"Do you think Wacky Fiona knocked off the trophy
wife?" Martha asked in a hushed voice.

Eleanor shrugged. "Well, I'm no lawyer, but if Fiona did
it to get her hands on her father's estate, I don't know that
she'd automatically inherit anyway. I think it would go to
whoever is mentioned in the wife's will. But if she didn't
have one, I'm not sure how that works."

Sarah frowned as she read further. "It must be weird to
have a stepmother who's younger than you."

"Heads up! Speak of the devil," Eleanor hissed as Fiona Adams strode into the store.

Martha took a step backward and landed on my foot. I winced and pushed her off with an effort, and we marshaled ourselves into a straggling line.

"Good morning, good morning, everyone!" Fiona sang out. "How are we today?"

She pointed a long finger at the newspaper I held. "I see you've read the wonderful news. Ding dong, the witch is dead!" she sang out. Then she laughed, but it wasn't a normal laugh, more like a horrible hyena-like hacking sound.

I shuddered involuntarily and glanced at my compatriots. Sarah was wide-eyed, Eleanor open-mouthed, and Martha looked frankly panicked.

"Um—Ms. Adams," she stammered, "you never sent me the bill for that white outfit."

"Oh, please, don't worry about it." Fiona laughed again, waving her hand in dismissal. "All water under the proverbial bridge now. I'm heading back to New York soon, but I wanted to say good-bye to *you*, Daisy. I didn't expect to meet someone so cosmopolitan in this podunk town."

I could feel Eleanor's thoughts stabbing me like a pack of embroidery needles. *Who does this bitch think she is?*

Fiona took a quick glance around the store, making a grunt of approval. "Very nice. You have excellent taste. Just as I expected."

She paused, and the giddiness vanished for a moment. "I don't suppose you ever found the stolen pens, did you?" She asked the question in an offhand way, but as I looked into Fiona's eyes, I saw the chronic pain and deep-rooted sadness there, despite the surface merriment.

That's when I knew for sure she didn't do it.

Money didn't mean that much to Fiona. She could afford to buy herself a duplicate set of the pens, with or without her father's estate. She might have all the money in the world, but she could never buy his love or attention. I had one small memento that would mean the world to her hidden in the bottom of my pocketbook. I decided then and there to give her the pen. But not now. Not in front of everyone. If I was doing something vaguely illegal, I wasn't going to involve my daughter and friends.

After Fiona left, Sarah was the first to recover. "Jeez, that woman seems too happy for her own good."

Martha blew out a long breath. "It's like she had a personality transplant or something. She's as violently happy as she was violently angry before."

We didn't have much time to recover from Fiona's visit before the doorbell jangled again and Cyril marched in.

"Ah found that part tha needed for yon car." He gestured toward Martha's Lincoln parked outside. I knew she had a tough time getting it serviced because it was so old. "Ah could come by later to put it in, if tha like."

It seemed as though he walked a little taller, his shoulders a little straighter these days.

"That would be wonderful, thank you." Martha's cheeks were as pink as the rose-colored linen dress she wore.

I ignored Eleanor's dig in my ribs and refused to look at Sarah. I took pity on Martha and ransacked my mind for a conversation starter. "So, Martha, how's everything coming along with preparations for the fair on Saturday?"

She took a deep breath, gathering her composure around her like one of her fur stoles.

"Well, all seems to be under control. The flyers are posted, the exhibits are lined up, and the volunteers procured. The only snag is that Ruth isn't sure how many more tables she can get for the flea market. She's pushing Precision Rentals as hard as she can to donate more, but they say they need to keep some on hand for their business."

"How about a boot sale like they have in England?" Cyril said.

I don't know why everyone looked to me for a translation. "For selling boots?" I asked faintly.

"No, no," he said impatiently, "you know, the boot—the trunk of the car. Everyone pulls their cars up in a big circle, opens the trunks with the stuff inside to sell, and Bob's yer uncle."

"Oh. I see." I glanced at Eleanor and she raised her eyebrows in approval.

"Actually, that's a pretty good idea. Sounds like the solution to all our problems," she said dryly.

"Well, I'd best be off." Cyril hurried out the door.

Under her breath, Eleanor murmured, "What have you *done* to that man, Martha?"

"He looks like one of the lost members of the Rolling Stones or something," Sarah said. "Sort of sexy in a way. For an older guy."

Eleanor grinned. "She's an absolute miracle worker."

"Knock it off, you two," I said.

Sarah giggled. "I just have one question. Who's Uncle Bob?"

Chapter Nineteen

※

It wasn't until Friday that I was allowed to visit Angus. The surgery had taken over fourteen hours, and then he'd been in ICU for a while. But he'd made it through, and for that I was truly grateful.

It was around 4 p.m. I closed the store early. I'd have asked Sarah to stay, but I didn't want her closing up by herself. The shooting had bothered me more than I'd realized.

Hospitals freaked me out, too, but I'd make the effort for Angus's sake. I walked for what felt like about a mile down the polished tile hallway at Doylestown Hospital until I found the right room.

A tiny old man was sleeping in the first bed, his mouth hanging open. Around the blue curtain that didn't go all the way to the floor was Angus in his bed. Even though his head was totally wrapped in bandages, his color was good, and one look into his eyes made me feel like cheering.

Angus was back!

"Hullo, Brat."

"What did you do? Climb over the wall or something?" I teased as I gave him a hug.

"Something like that. I sure am glad to be out of that prison. Hell of a way to get sprung, though."

I dragged a chair closer to the high bed, careful not to bump the IV stand. I laid some collectible and antiques magazines on the blanket, plus the local auction listing newspaper. "Here you go. To bring you up to speed."

"Thanks, Daisy. You know, there's some things going to change when I get home. I did a lot of thinking when I was sitting in that prison cell. No more drinking. Even without the brain tumor, I was a mess and I know it. I've not been a very good husband to poor Betty either. She's had a lot to put up with."

I didn't see any sign of Betty, and I didn't ask if she'd been to see him.

He grabbed my hand and squeezed it. "Thanks for sticking by me, kid. I know I was out of it for a while. At least that's what they tell me. But you always believed in me. I remember that part, and I'll never forget it."

"Sometimes a good friendship is like a good marriage," I said. *Sometimes more enduring.* I'd come so close to losing him—either to a murder conviction or a meningioma.

My eyes welled up and I plucked a couple of tissues out of the box on his bedside table. "Jeez, my allergies are so bad today." Although in a climate-controlled hospital, who was I kidding?

Angus leaned back against the starched white pillows with a sigh. "I'm going to be in physical rehab for a couple of weeks. They tell me I'll be real tired for a while when I go home and not allowed to lift anything heavy. Might be a couple of months until I'm fully recovered. Sounds like Patsy's been doing a good job. We're thinking about hiring her part-time to help out. What do you think?"

I smiled at him. "I think that's a great idea. She seems to have a knack for this business. And more importantly, the passion."

"Even when I'm back on my feet, I don't want to work all the time like I did before. I want to enjoy what's left of my life. The doctor said the five-year survival rate is pretty good for the type of tumor I had."

I blinked rapidly. I wasn't going to cry. But thinking about the rest of his life in terms of a handful of years? I was determined to make the most of every minute with him in the future. I'd never complain about getting up early to go picking again.

His eyes misted over, too. "The doctor said I can expect to go through all kinds of emotions in my recovery." He blew his nose loudly. "And I still wanna know who killed my friend Jimmy. I know he wasn't perfect, Daisy, but he didn't deserve to die."

I wanted to tell him about Jimmy's abuse of his wife, and the gambling, but in the unforgiving light from the fluorescent bar over the bed, Angus still looked fragile, so I kept quiet.

A comfortably plump nurse came in with a tray full of pills and a syringe.

Angus groaned. "Here's Ms. Misery. Probably here to stick more needles up my ass."

"Now, now, Mr. Backstead," she said in a thick Jamaican accent as she grinned at me. "Try to be a good patient."

I slipped out of the chair. "I'll leave you to it."

"See you. Love you, Brat."

"Love you more."

In the hospital parking lot, the Subaru hesitated before it started, and then sputtered out again. I pumped the gas and turned the key, holding my breath until it fired up. I raced the engine, kept one foot on the brake, and quickly threw the car into drive.

Once I was back out on the main road, I called Joe to tell him I had a couple of errands to run before I came home.

There was one last piece of the puzzle to slot into place before I could truly let this whole thing go. Joe wouldn't be pleased if he ever found out, but it was something I had to do.

Hey, perhaps I could star in a new reality show on TV, I thought as I turned off Sheepville Pike onto Forty Acre Road. *Ex-Schoolteachers Behaving Badly.*

Fiona's driver was loading luggage into the trunk of the Mercedes roadster as I pulled onto the graveled driveway of the Four Foxes. Just in the nick of time.

I got out of the car and was about to ask him where she was when I heard a rhythmic clatter and Fiona appeared at the brick archway, the wheels of her rolling suitcase bumping over the flagstones on the patio.

"Daisy! What are you doing here? Any news about the pens?"

"Not exactly. I do have something for you, though, but you must promise me you'll never tell anyone where you got it."

"How intriguing." She handed the suitcase to the driver. "Do I need some kind of code word? Like Rosebud?"

I rolled my eyes. Again. "Just promise, okay?"

"Yes, yes." Fiona waved her arms impatiently.

I dug into the recesses of my pocketbook and handed over the precious Parker Duofold Lucky Curve pen.

"Oh my God. Is this what I think it is?" She grabbed the pen and held it up to the light.

"Yes." My smile was so big it stretched the skin on my face.

Suddenly Fiona's eyes narrowed. "How much do you want for it? Where's the rest of them?"

The driver moved closer.

"Oh, no, Fiona, you've got it all wrong," I said hurriedly. "I found this at the Kratzes' farm when I was looking around on my own. I think the killer dropped it when he was fleeing the crime scene."

I didn't tell her about Jasper digging it up and slobbering all over it, knowing how fastidious she was. "I should hand it over to the police, but as I know how much it means to you, I wanted you to have it."

Fiona took a deep breath. "Thank you, Daisy, and you're right. It does mean the world to me."

At that moment, Detective Serrano and Joy came strolling around the other side of the garage.

Oh, boy.

Fiona clapped a hand to her mouth.

Joy came up and hugged me. "Daisy! What a nice surprise!"

Serrano looked at me and raised an inquiring eyebrow.

"Oh, um, hi, Joy, and um, Tony, I was saying good-bye to my friend Fiona here. She's going back to New York."

I risked a glance back at Fiona, who smiled tightly and nodded, but didn't say anything. She was wearing a sleeveless top, and a tight linen miniskirt with no pockets. Where the heck had she put the pen? She had no sleeves to shove it inside, and if she'd stuck it down her skirt, well, it should have made some kind of outline.

However, Detective Serrano was currently focused on one person. "Daisy, I've been checking the marketplace for those pens, but there's not a whisper of them for sale anywhere. They seem to have vanished into thin air."

He frowned as he did his scanning thing of the courtyard, the Mercedes, a stray wandering duck, Fiona, the driver, and then back to me. "There's something very odd about this whole affair. I bet they're right in front of us and we just can't see them."

I made a sound that I hoped sounded like agreement. After a few moments, Joy and Serrano moved on, with Joy leading the way to the main house.

Once the coast was clear, I turned to Fiona. "What did you do with it?" I hissed.

She didn't answer, but simply opened her mouth and

slowly pulled the pen out of her throat, like a snake regurgitating a thin mouse.

"Holy moly!" And here I had worried about her being squeamish because Jasper had picked it up.

Fiona shrugged. "What can I say? I dated a sword swallower in college."

I shook my head as I gave her my handkerchief. "Why don't you keep this to wrap it in?"

If Fiona were anyone else, we would have hugged. As it was, we shook hands, but the unexpected warmth of her touch and the sparkle in her eyes made me grin like a fool all over again.

"I'll never forget what you've done for me, Daisy. If there's ever anything I can do to repay the favor . . ."

"Don't mention it. Have a safe trip. And a good life."

I watched the Mercedes ease down the driveway and waved until she was out of sight.

As pleased as I was with myself, I needed to get a move on and get the heck out of there before the detective came back. I was the world's worst liar, and I knew I couldn't fool him for long.

I jumped in the Subaru and turned the key. *Click*. Nothing.

Damn it. I pounded a hand on the steering wheel of the old car. I felt like pounding my head on it, too. I was going to be so late.

A shadow appeared at the driver's side window.

"Car trouble?" Serrano inquired politely.

"Yes, it appears so." I suddenly realized there was no police car parked in the courtyard. "Hey, where's your car?"

He nodded in the direction of the organic farm. "I came in that way and walked up to the main house, so as not to alarm the guests. This was a social call."

Social call? Joy was an attractive woman in her early forties. Guess the detective was a fast worker once he arrived in a new town.

"I was hoping I might run into Robin Tague," he said, doing the mind-reading thing again. "See if I could get a handle on the guy. It's a long shot that he's involved with the fountain pen murder, but you never know." He pointed at me. "Hold on, I'll be right back."

In a few minutes, the cruiser rolled into the courtyard and Serrano parked nose to nose with the Subaru. But once he'd attached the jumper cables and told me to try to start it, the Subaru's engine refused to turn over, even with a powerful V-8 attached.

"There's probably something wrong with the alternator or starter motor," he called to me. "Do you need a ride home?"

I knew that George Hildebrand would have closed the garage by now. I should leave the car here, get home at a reasonable hour to appease Joe, and deal with this tomorrow.

"Fine. Thanks."

I'd never ridden in a police car before, and I always wore a seat belt anyway, but I was glad I'd buckled mine now because Serrano drove the way he moved, fast and fluid. The scenery whipped by, and he cut lines through the twisting corners like a downhill skier.

I breathed in a whisper of intoxicating aftershave. It was silly, but being alone with this devastatingly attractive man in a high-performance vehicle made me suddenly tongue-tied.

"You miss the New York delis, Daisy?"

"Oh, yes," I said, grateful for the opening gambit. "Although there's a deli in Doylestown that's pretty good." We chatted for the next few minutes about wonderfully safe topics such as smoked salmon and what constituted the best pastrami sandwich.

We passed the Kratz farm as we headed up Sheepville Pike, and I tried to breathe as evenly as possible and not look too guilty about giving the one piece of evidence away.

"Um, Tony, did you ever check into that estate company that contacted Jimmy?"

Serrano's tanned fingers flexed on the steering wheel. "I searched for other items they've sold, for anything that would stand out as an unusual item better handled with the bigger auction houses. There *was* one table that Angus sold for them a few months ago, and I thought I was on to something, but I checked with Christie's, and it reached close to what they estimated it should bring. I've checked with other police departments, and no one has any wind of anything like this in the area. If it exists, it's a very small operation."

"And what about the gambling ring? Did Jimmy owe anybody money?"

Serrano shook his head. "Not according to the guys who were there at the game that night. They all swear they had nothing to do with Jimmy's death. And no reason to kill him."

"Any of them own guns? Do you have any idea who might have tried to shoot *me?*"

"Well, Ramsbottom, of course. And the Perkins boys go hunting all the time. Sounds like even the old lady was packing."

I remembered Angus's story about the grandmother shooting one of his friends in her pumpkin patch.

"The thing is, the guys you saw inside that building were all still sitting there when we picked them up. They say that no one left at any time. And it's not like they had a chance to coordinate their stories."

I gasped. "Except for Bobby. He was outside. No one would have known when he came and went."

The one who had seemed so much nicer than his brother.

Serrano glanced at me. "And Bobby doesn't have an alibi for the night of Jimmy's murder either. He dropped Tom Perkins off after the pub and went home alone. Apparently there's some woman Tom sees in Sheepville."

I resisted the urge to say *eeuw*.

"She's married. They get together when her old man's out of town. She was reluctant to admit it at first, but our boy Tom drove the bus over her as fast as you like to save himself."

"But what's Bobby's motivation?"

Serrano grinned. "Hey, I'm supposed to ask those kinds of questions."

I smiled back. In the waning sunlight, his eyes were deep blue smoke.

"In a small town like this, everything's connected. It's like a big fricking spiderweb touching everyone, and it's easy to get on each other's nerves."

"True enough."

The cruiser swung onto Grist Mill Road. "Wonder if there's some long-ago feud we don't know about," Serrano said. "Know of any kind of connection with Jimmy and Bobby, or Bobby to Reenie?"

"No. But I have my sources." I'd ask Martha.

He frowned. "This case strikes me as a crime of passion."

"Passion for a woman, passion for the arts, what?"

"You're thinking about Tague. He's a little off, but I don't get the killer vibe from him. He probably doesn't weigh much more than you, Daisy, no offense. No way could he have handled a murder weapon like that barn beam."

As we drove up to the house, Joe was standing on the front step, his arms crossed. Like a father waiting for his errant teenager to come home after a date.

"Good luck. Talk to you later," Serrano murmured as I got out of the police car.

I waved as he pulled away, and then I walked past Joe into the house. I refused to get into a screaming match out on the street.

"You promised, Daisy! You promised not to get involved anymore." The disappointment in Joe's eyes was worse than his anger.

"You know what," I said, keeping my voice as calm as possible, "this has nothing to do with Angus and the murder investigation. I wasn't in any danger. I was just giving the pen to Fiona before she went back to New York."

"What pen?"

Oops.

"Well, I sort of found one buried in the farmyard. Actually Jasper dug it up. I think the killer must have dropped it, and I didn't know what to do with it. I didn't trust Ramsbottom."

"And you don't trust *me?* Why the hell couldn't you talk to me about it?" Joe exhaled, as if summoning up the last of his patience. "I'm your husband. We're supposed to share everything. The good and the bad."

"Oh, well, in that case, there *is* one more thing . . ."

"Yes?"

"I think the car needs a new alternator."

"*That* I can fix. The rest of it? Who knows?" Joe shook his head at me. "I guess I've always been a bit jealous of Angus, truth be told, and now it looks as though you have a new boyfriend."

"Don't be ridiculous." I gasped in disbelief at this insanely jealous remark until I saw the teasing glint in his eye.

"Come on upstairs with me, Daisy Buchanan." Joe took my hand and pulled me with him toward the stairs. "Obviously I need to remind you why you married me. *Again.*"

Chapter Twenty

❋

The next morning, Saturday, Joe called George Hildebrand and asked him to pick up our car and take it to his garage.

I stuffed the trunk of Sarah's Volkswagen Beetle and most of the backseat with the produce for the farm stand, and the items she and I had cleaned out of our basement. I'd have to sit with a box on my lap, and Sarah would somehow have to squeeze into the back.

No dogs were allowed at the fair, so I'd taken Jasper for a good walk earlier and he would have the run of the kitchen today. Fingers crossed. He was in his favorite spot, sprawled out on the cool tiled floor in the pantry. At this time of the morning, the temperature was still in the low sixties, but the day promised to be a hot one.

We drove up to the auction grounds. White tents were spread out across the grass, and with the sun rising over the horizon, it looked like some kind of magical encampment.

Precision Rentals had dropped off the tables, tents, and

chairs yesterday. The entrants for the various contests were also required to bring in their items for judging the day before.

Martha came over to my side of the car and gave me a map of the fairgrounds. I recognized Cee Cee's penmanship and talent for design.

"This looks amazing already," I told her, reaching up and giving her as much of a hug as I could around her gigantic straw hat. Martha was wearing sensible flats today, and a flowing summer dress.

She smiled in weary satisfaction. "We have a long day ahead of us, but it should come together nicely."

From the map, Joe quickly found the farm stand, dropped Sarah and me off with the produce, and then drove to the flea market area to unload the rest of our stuff.

Some trucks with trailers were already arriving, holding the ponies for the kiddie rides and the animals for the petting zoo. Sarah grabbed her tote bag of walkie-talkies and headed over to the admission booth to direct them where to park. The plan was to fill the paved lot first and then an area to the right, which had already been roped off and designated for extra parking. From Sheepville Pike came the unmistakable rumble of a fire engine, and soon it pulled slowly onto the grass near the auction house. Martha must have made arrangements for the kids to have their pictures taken on it. She'd thought of everything.

My farm stand was made up of three trestle tables arranged in a U-shape with a canopy overhead. I arranged our fruits and vegetables on one table, and the soaps, candles, and pots of honey from the lavender farm on another. Debby and Cee Cee walked up with a cart laden with the donated birdhouses, jams, jellies, and chutney.

"Wherever did you get that cart? It's a brilliant idea!" I exclaimed.

"It's from the library. I asked if I could borrow it for the weekend," Debby said. "I'm going to help you today, and Cee Cee is doing face painting for the kids."

"Another great idea. I can't get over how fantastic everything looks."

Cee Cee nodded. "Martha's incredible. It's like she was destined for this."

By 8:30 a.m., we were set up, and the fair wasn't scheduled to open until 10 a.m., so Debby stayed at the farm stand while I took a walk to see where I could help out.

Liz Gallagher's kids were already bouncing around at the lemonade stand. I passed the antique John Deere tractors on display, and the area where the sheep-shearing demonstration would take place. Dottie's knitting ladies had a table set up with their handmade baby blankets and scarves for sale. I knew we'd make money there.

At the flea market, there were a few tables full of bric-a-brac, but the cars were the star of the show, all backed in with trunk lids open, making a huge semicircle. Patsy was in charge, and as soon as she saw me, Claire rushed over and grabbed my hand.

"Daisy, I won first prize for my painting. Come see!"

I let myself be dragged over to the exhibit tents. As we walked toward the corner where the junior artwork was displayed, we passed the baking contest entries, with a mouthwatering selection of apple, peach, cherry, rhubarb, strawberry, and blackberry pies. The winner was a double-crust nectarine raspberry.

Claire's painting was also adorned with the coveted blue ribbon.

"Congratulations." I put my arm around her.

She beamed up at me. "*And* I won ten dollars!"

The painting showed a magnificent house out in the country, with horses grazing peacefully nearby, three apple trees in the orchard, and a dog running up to the front door.

"This is the house I want Mommy to buy for us someday."

"It's beautiful, Claire." The house also looked like it cost the best part of a million dollars, but I didn't point that out.

"The second place ribbon is red, third is yellow, and honorable mentions are white. You also get seven dollars for second place and five dollars for third," she informed me. "Guess honorable mention means you only get the ribbon." Claire wrinkled her nose.

"*And* the satisfaction of knowing you tried and you did your best." The teacher in me couldn't resist a life lesson whenever I could impart one.

"I know, Daisy," she said, but I could tell she was glad she'd earned her first place ribbon.

After we had sufficiently admired her painting, we walked around hand in hand, and marveled at the gorgeous mixed flower arrangements and perfect specimens of strawberries, carrots, fresh eggs, and corn arranged on white paper plates.

I was especially interested in the needlework contest with the quilt wall hangings and exquisite embroidery. It was comforting to know that the ancient arts were still surviving, even in this digital age. I often thought that the reason knitting and crocheting were suddenly popular again was because they were a welcome escape for busy professionals from the constant buzz of instant communication.

Chickens and rabbits in cages that had been brought in that morning were being judged as we walked by. I waved to Ruth, who was accompanying the judges and taking notes.

As we came out of the tents, Cyril was driving around with trash and recycling containers on his truck, dropping them at strategic places, together with large drums of water for the animals. The petting zoo and pony ride with two docile-looking ponies were in place and waiting for youthful customers. I guessed that patch of grass on the auction grounds would be well fertilized by the time this was all over.

I brought Claire back to her mom, where the flea marketers were ready for action. On my way to the farm stand, I passed the band members setting up. Chris Paxson was helping them hook up the sound equipment.

"Dude, this is so early for us," one of them moaned to Chris. "Actually I'm not sure if it's like really early or really late."

"I'll get you some coffee," I promised. Near the auction building, they were testing the microphone for announcements at the first aid booth. Inside, Betty was working full speed in the snack bar to keep up with the demand for caffeine from the vendors.

I came out with a paper tray holding six cups of steaming coffee. Even though it was well before 10 a.m., people were already arriving, some of them bringing their own lawn chairs, ready for a big day out. I could just about see Sarah at the entrance, and even from this distance, the confidence in her movements and her command over the situation were apparent.

I handed the coffee to a grateful band and hurried back to Debby at the farm stand. People were picking up produce and jams and handing over money.

Martha's voice boomed over the sound system. "Good morning, everyone! I'd like to welcome you to the First Annual Sheepville Country Fair! As you know, proceeds from today's activities will go towards a fund for the Kratz children. Enjoy yourselves today. Let the festivities commence!"

The whine of an electric guitar tuning up split the air.

I glanced over to where Reenie, eyes bright, stood with her kids, each clutching one of her hands.

I thought back to that first Sunday when I'd gone to visit her, and Reenie had insisted on giving me fresh eggs, even though she was so desperately poor. I'd sworn to myself that day that I'd find a way to help. My scalp tingled with the realization of how I'd made good on that promise. And then some, with the assistance of my amazing friends and neighbors.

The band roared into action, and soon there were kids dancing in the grass. Teenage girls hung out in front of the stage, giggling and making eyes at the lead singer.

Debby and I packaged up candles and birdhouses and stuffed cash into our shoe box as fast as we could go. As the day wore on, the tantalizing smell of barbecue wafted through the air, not to mention that of cinnamon rolls, spicy fries, funnel cake, and apple fritters.

My stomach growled. There was a plethora of fresh healthy fruits and vegetables in front of us, but what I really craved was a succulent rib that had been stewing in marinade overnight and was now slowly basting on the grill.

Martha came up with a plate covered in aluminum foil.

"And what to my wondering eyes doth appear?" Debby murmured. "Is that what I think it is?" She peeled back the foil to reveal a rack of crusty barbecued ribs.

"Martha, did I ever tell you I love you?" I said.

"Yes, now hand over the cash." Not only was Martha keeping us fed, but she was making one of her periodic trips around to collect the money and make change if we needed it. "Eleanor says that we're well over twenty thousand dollars at this point."

"Oh my God, that's fantastic," Debby said.

"Mmmf," I agreed through a mouthful of juicy, savory meat.

Martha handed me a pile of napkins out of the pocket of her dress. "It's such a success, there's talk about making this an annual event. We could pick a different charity each year."

I saw that she'd appropriated one of Sarah's walkie-talkies. It buzzed now with some indecipherable babble.

Martha pressed the talk button. "Roger, copy that, over and out."

"Do you know what they just said?" I demanded.

"Not a clue, but this is so much fun."

Later in the afternoon, Sarah strolled over to the farm stand. "How's it going, Mom?"

"Great. We're almost sold out here."

"Daddy is having the time of his life at the tractor pull. Did you see that guy with the llamas?"

I shook my head. "No, he must have set up after I got here."

"He has some kind of exotic farm off Grist Mill Road with ostriches, llamas, and peacocks, stuff like that. Says he often rents out his place for modeling shoots. One of them took a dislike to Martha, though."

Sarah shook her head, puffed up her small chest, and cleared her throat. " '*Good God*. That beast just spit at me!' " she declared in a wicked imitation of Martha.

I laughed, even though I shouldn't have.

Sarah grinned. "Speaking of shooting, I sent those photos I took of the Kratz kids and the farm to a friend who has a stock photography business. He loved them and wants more." Her walkie-talkie buzzed again. "See ya later."

So now Sarah had also found a way to help Jimmy's family out with a little extra income.

I glanced up at the powder blue sky. Not a cloud on the horizon.

"Debby, would you be okay here for a few minutes by yourself?"

"Sure, Daisy."

I found Reenie and her kids at the face-painting table. Cee Cee was putting the finishing touches to a bumblebee on the girl's cheek, while her brother hid behind Cee Cee.

Reenie smiled. It seemed like she looked younger and more beautiful every time I saw her. "This is all so amazing, Daisy," she said, shaking her head. "Thank you again for everything you're doing for us. I'll never, ever be able to tell you how grateful I am."

I smiled. "My pleasure."

Martha sailed over to us. "Hey, kids, don't forget the ice cream–eating contest. Do you want to give it a go?"

Cee Cee glanced over her shoulder at the little boy, who shook his head but mustered a shy smile. "Maybe we could just get a cone?" she suggested. He nodded, and a dimple appeared in his soft cheek.

"Walk with me?" Martha offered, and I nodded and fell into step beside her.

Tony Z was busy cutting hair and belting out "*La donna è mobile*" from Verdi's opera *Rigoletto*. He was an inch or so shorter than me, but the voice that came out of him was gigantic, with no need for a microphone. Farther on, a woodworking demonstration was under way, and then we came to Sweet Mabel's ice cream booth.

Martha ordered a waffle cone with butter pecan, and I selected a sugar cone laden with mint chocolate chip.

"So how come you didn't enter the baking contest, Martha? I would have thought you were a shoo-in."

She sniffed. "Well, I *would* have won, but I didn't want people to say it was rigged."

We stopped to watch the goat races, which was where I decided to pump her for the lowdown on what the heck was going on with Cyril.

She shrugged. "He's an interesting man and I'm enjoying getting to know him."

"Okay." I licked my ice cream cone and waited.

She flipped up the brim of her straw hat. "Oh, Daisy, I don't know. It's kind of like looking at a deep lagoon and being intrigued by it, but you don't want to dive right in. There might be something lurking underneath that you'd hit your head on. Better to slide slowly into that cool water."

Martha was called over to one of the booths, and it looked like she'd be tied up for a while, so I kept walking.

Detective Serrano was hanging out by the fire engine, wearing a T-shirt and jeans, and also licking at a cone.

"What kind of ice cream did you get?" I asked him.

"Coffee mocha."

Of course. What had Sarah said about people looking like their dogs? Did they also resemble their ice cream choices?

He took another long, loving lick at the cone. Too bad Martha and Eleanor were missing this.

"By the way, I checked with my pals in New York," he said. "They're still waiting for the autopsy results on Fiona's stepmother, but seems as though there's nothing suspicious. It looks like she died of natural causes—a preexisting heart condition. Fiona's father was a heart surgeon, and that's how they met."

"Thanks for letting me know." Obviously the detective was one of those people who never took a day off.

"And speaking of autopsies, I'm also ordering a more in-depth review of the one for Jimmy Kratz. He had some kind of allergic reaction right before he died. Perhaps from the mold, pesticides, or other hazardous substances he came into contact with as he cleaned out houses."

I appreciated how thorough this guy was. The fact that Jimmy's head was completely bashed in would be reason enough for most people as the cause of death.

Serrano licked all the way around the top of his cone, swirling the ice cream into a sharp point. Martha would have been in the first aid booth by now. "I also noticed our boy Jimmy was snipped a couple of years back."

"Snipped? You mean he had a vasectomy?" I gasped.

"Yup."

I stared at him. "So he couldn't possibly be the father of Carla's baby? Oh, wow, that's a huge relief!"

Serrano made a slight inclination with his head, and I turned to see Carla heading toward us, hand in hand with a tall guy that I assumed was the crazy boyfriend. They stopped to chat with the firefighters, and I could feel Serrano giving the guy the once-over just as I was doing. He didn't look that homicidal to me. Freckle-faced, and possibly hot-tempered, but not crazy.

I moved closer and managed to maneuver Carla to one side and whisper the good news that her baby wasn't Jimmy's.

She nodded. "Yeah, once I calmed down, I did the math

and I didn't think it could be his. But thanks for letting me know for sure."

Carla had on about a quarter of the makeup she usually wore. Like Reenie, she looked much healthier and prettier.

"My boyfriend's actually really happy about the baby. He said it's time for both of us to grow up."

I gave her a quick hug. "I'm glad."

Serrano had disappeared by this time, so I thought I'd go find Joe and see what he was up to. On the way, I passed a cow lift in demonstration and stopped to watch. It was an apparatus that rolls a cow that is down on the ground with post-calving paralysis or some other ailment onto a fabric sling, which was then attached with hooks to a front end loader to gently lift the animal.

The old farmer demonstrated how there was an open area for the udder to hang through, to reduce stress and pressure. "This here cow lift can lift up to twenty-two hundred pounds."

My phone chimed with a text message. It was Sarah. *Gone to Kratz farm to take more pix. Lite perfect now. Rain tmrw.*

I sighed. I'd better tell Reenie that Sarah was over at her place. I didn't want her to freak out again.

It was almost 3 p.m. We'd planned a brief ceremony at 3:30 p.m. to present Reenie with a symbolic check. The actual money would be donated once any fixed expenses for things like the insurance were deducted and the accounting finalized.

Cee Cee was still at the face-painting table. Reenie's son was sitting in her lap and the little girl was wiping the table with a wet paper towel.

"Have you seen Reenie?" I asked.

"She asked me to watch these two for a bit." Cee Cee smiled at them. "Said she was going home to change before the presentation, but she'd be back in half an hour."

Oh, crap. That meant she'd bump into Sarah. I hoped she wasn't as mad as when I stopped over unannounced.

Suddenly there was a commotion at the admissions booth, and I thought I heard someone screaming.

I ran, my feet flying across the grass of their own accord, and as I got closer, I saw Liz Gallagher weeping uncontrollably, surrounded by several of her friends.

"The cash box with the money is missing!" Eleanor's face was white as she rushed up to me. "I asked Liz to watch it while I went to the bathroom. She got distracted when two of the kids started fighting, and when she looked back, it was gone. Jesus, Daisy. There was about twenty-five thousand dollars in that damn box."

As I stared at Eleanor in shock, I suddenly realized where I'd seen one of those cow lifts before. At Jimmy's place, for the cows that were down with milk fever. You could probably lift quite a few barn beams with one of those devices.

My heart started racing. Reenie had mentioned a dozen pens, but as I forced my frantic brain to do a quick mental calculation, there were actually thirteen in Fiona's photos. Who would know to describe them as a dozen other than someone who had seen them firsthand?

Minus the one that I'd found.

I looked around, panic-stricken. I didn't know where Joe was and Serrano was nowhere to be seen. Sarah had taken the car, and even if I could get someone to give me a ride in a hurry, the fair was winding down and a long line of cars were sitting at the exit, waiting to pull onto Sheepville Pike.

I didn't have that kind of time.

I sprinted back to the flea market, praying that the bicycle I'd seen for sale was still there. The price tag said ten dollars.

I thrust a twenty at the owner and rode faster than I ever had in my life.

Chapter Twenty-one

When I got to the Kratz farm, heaving for breath, there was no sign of Sarah or Reenie.

I dropped the bicycle on the ground and ran into the barn, praying I was wrong, but I felt around inside the cow lift and my hand came out with a small pile of wood shreds.

I looked up and my world ground to a sickening halt as Reenie walked Sarah into the barn at gunpoint.

"I'm so tired of you two sneaking around, checking up on me," Reenie snapped. "I tried to warn you off once. Why the hell didn't you listen?"

"She stole the money we collected at the fair, Mom."

"I know."

Sarah's eyes were hot with anger. "The cash box is on the front seat of her truck."

"Shut it." Reenie shoved the end of the barrel of the gun into Sarah's back.

My mouth was dry and I took shallow breaths. Now was not the time to pass out.

"You know, you people crack me up. When I saw you in town that day, talking about a fund for the kids' *college*, for Christ's sake. College! You have no idea. I need the money now!"

My mind was racing. I couldn't rush Reenie. She might pull that trigger and Sarah wouldn't stand a chance. I fingered a seam ripper in my pocket and edged closer.

"Yeah, I always wanted to go to Florida. It's cheaper there. I figured I may as well wait until after the fair and get the cash, too. There's my gas and rent money until I can sell the pens."

"What did you do with them?" I knew the police had searched this barn and the house.

Reenie smirked. "Wouldn't you like to know?"

Sarah frowned. "You were planning on leaving your kids behind?"

Reenie shrugged. "They'll be better off with Cee Cee and her fancy doctor husband than me. I need to start a new life. I deserve it! After all I've been through."

I swallowed, never taking my eyes off Reenie. I was praying that someone at the fair would put two and two together. I had to keep us alive until I figured something out.

"I know you used the cow lift, Reenie, but how did you manage to keep Jimmy still long enough to hit him with the beam? After all, he drove Angus home, so he wasn't *that* drunk."

She chuckled. "I left cookies in the barn that night for when he came back and got the munchies. Jimmy only ate a certain brand, because he had a real bad peanut allergy. I made some that looked the same, except with a trace of peanut butter."

A picture flashed into my mind of backing into the recycling container. That's why she had been so upset. I remembered now, too late, the empty peanut butter jar on the ground.

"After he had an allergic reaction, I waited until he was

unconscious. It was easier to hit him with the beam when he was passed out."

Even with a gun poking her in the back, Sarah rolled her eyes at this.

"When I was sure he was dead, I took the keys and went to the auction house and stole the pens."

In spite of the fact that Reenie had committed a greater crime with no compunction, I was shocked as another fact hit me. "Hey, wait a minute, did you really leave two young children home alone?"

"They were fine. Why don't you shut the hell up?"

She swung the gun in my direction.

It felt like my heart had crawled up and was now beating in my throat instead of my chest. I swallowed again, struggling for the right words.

"Reenie, you're not a murderer. Killing Jimmy was a crime of passion after all you'd been through. You don't really want to hurt us."

Sarah moved ever so slightly to her right.

This was the opening I'd been waiting for and I hurled myself at Reenie. If she shot me, so be it. I'd lost one child to a maniac with a gun, and I'd be damned if I'd let it happen again.

Reenie whipped it around and cracked me on the side of the head with the butt end. My brain exploded and I crashed to the floor. She pointed it at Sarah now and I looked up at them as I desperately tried to make my stunned body move, hearing the screaming inside my head.

But Reenie was slightly off balance, and one of Sarah's long legs swung in a roundhouse kick, sending the gun into a nearby pile of hay.

I fought a wave of dizziness, struggling to all fours to the sounds of grunts and heavy breathing as the two fought.

They were unevenly matched. My taller, athletic daughter with slight, shorter Reenie, but with the desperation of a cornered animal, Reenie scrabbled for the weapon again in the hay. As she came out with it, I saw by the glint in her eyes that this time she'd take the shot.

I pulled the seam ripper from my pocket and lunged at Reenie, gashing her calf with a nasty slice. She screamed in pain, and with that split-second advantage, Sarah grabbed the gun, twisting it in Reenie's hand to break her grip.

For good measure, Sarah whacked Reenie on the side of the head, too, the same way she'd hit me. She fell to the ground, unconscious, blood already oozing through her baby fine hair.

A car pulled up outside, and Serrano and two other police officers came rushing in.

"Daisy! Are you guys all right?"

"We're fine. Nice of you to show up," I said, heaving for breath.

He grimaced. "Finally figured this one out when I saw that cow lift at the fair. Told you it was a crime of passion."

One of the officers handcuffed Reenie, and the other radioed for an ambulance.

"Oh, Sarah." I scrambled to my feet, held out my arms, and my daughter fell into them.

"Guess all that fight-scene training on film sets paid off, huh?" she whispered.

"You were amazing," I said. She squeezed me tight, and I felt the lithe strength of her.

Serrano coughed. "So this just leaves one question. Where are those damn pens? We've already searched this fricking place. Maybe we need to go over it again, all the nooks and crannies. There's acres of farmland as well." He ran a hand wearily over his cropped hair.

"Hold on, I have an idea." I let go of Sarah and hurried over to the henhouse, remembering how well Reenie had cared for the chickens. Better than her own children.

I felt under the straw, and smiled when I felt the shapes beneath my fingers. With a flourish, I pulled out a clutch of valuable fountain pens.

Serrano grinned at me. "I'm no country boy, but them's some funny-looking eggs, ma'am."

I caught my breath as I held up the Magical Black Widow pen, the beautiful silver web gleaming in the sun.

After Reenie was driven off in the ambulance, and the police had taken our statements, Sarah and I walked over to the car and my bicycle.

"You know what, Mom, you're so brave. I never realized it before. You fought for Angus when no one else believed he was innocent, and now you risked your life fighting for me. You did good."

"Thanks."

"Um, Mom? There is one more thing . . ."

"Yes?"

"Would you be willing to look after Jasper while I'm on location? I know he'd be happier here at home with you than with a sitter. What do you think?"

I grinned at my daughter. "I think that sometimes you come up with a really great notion," I said as I got on my flea market bicycle. "Race you home."

The Millbury Ladies' Home Companion

Daisy's Yard Sale Tips

Whether you call them yard sales, tag sales, garage sales, or rummage sales, they're a lot of fun, and there are bargains to be found!

- The early bird catches the worm, but don't get there so early as to be obnoxious.

- Plan your route to save gas. Block or neighborhood sales are great because you can park and walk from house to house.

- Bring plenty of single dollar bills and quarters. It's harder to haggle when you need change for a twenty.

- Speaking of haggling, don't be afraid to ask for a better deal. Experienced sellers expect it.

- Bundle! If there are several items you have your eye on, add up the prices and make an offer on the lot. For example, if your items total eight dollars, ask the seller if she'll take five. Chances are she'll agree in order to move the merchandise.

- If you're the seller, price everything to move. You're better off selling ten books at two dollars each than one book at five dollars.

- Put a few grocery bags in your pocket so you can carry your small items to the car. Not all sellers have them, or they run out.

- If you see something that you're interested in, pick it up and carry it around so someone else doesn't buy it out from under you. Finders, keepers!

- Be friendly and chat with the seller. Building a rapport can often get you a better deal. I've had sellers throw in "extra" things for free just because we hit it off.

- It's okay not to buy. It can be strange to be the only buyer in the yard, but don't feel obligated. Just say, "Thanks very much," or "Good luck with the sale," and move on.

- And finally, my favorite tip. Go back to the yard sales that you attended on Saturday late in the day on Sunday or on Monday morning before trash pickup. Chances are that the remainder of the stuff is now out by the side of the road with a FREE sign next to it. Can I tell you how many books I've collected that way? Really nice hardcover cookbooks and novels. Hey, I'm not too proud to pick through. As they say, one man's trash is another's treasure.

- Happy yard saling!

Martha's Awesome Oatmeal Cookies

Martha often brings these oatmeal and dried cherry cookies into Sometimes a Great Notion for the customers. We tell ourselves that the oatmeal and fruit make them healthy. One thing's for sure—these delicious treats don't last long!

MAKES ABOUT 4 DOZEN

1½ cups all-purpose flour
1 teaspoon ground cinnamon
½ teaspoon salt
½ teaspoon baking soda
½ teaspoon baking powder
1 cup (2 sticks) unsalted butter, room temperature
1 cup dark brown sugar
½ cup granulated sugar
2 large eggs
1 teaspoon pure vanilla extract
2 cups old-fashioned rolled oats
2 cups dried sour cherries

Preheat oven to 350°F. Line baking sheets with parchment paper. In a medium bowl, mix the flour, cinnamon, salt, baking soda, and baking powder. Set the flour mixture aside.

Beat the butter and sugars together for a couple of minutes until light and fluffy. Add the eggs and vanilla, and beat to incorporate. Add the flour mixture to the butter mixture, beating on low speed until all is combined. Stir in the oats and dried cherries.

Using a small scoop, drop the dough onto prepared baking sheets, leaving 6 inches between cookies. (The cookies will be rather large when baked.)

Bake until the edges are just turning brown, about 20 minutes.

Cool for a few minutes on the baking sheet, and then remove to wire racks to cool completely.

Crème Brûlée Cheesecake Bars

I have yet to meet the person who doesn't drool over these cheesecake bars. Evil, but so good!

MAKES 36 BARS

1 pouch (1 pound 1.5 ounces) Betty Crocker sugar cookie mix
1 box (4-serving size) French vanilla instant pudding and pie filling mix
2 tablespoons packed brown sugar
½ cup melted butter
2½ teaspoons vanilla
2 eggs plus 3 egg yolks
2 (8-ounce) packages cream cheese, softened
½ cup sour cream
½ cup sugar
⅔ cup toffee bits, finely crushed

Heat oven to 350°F. Lightly spray the bottom and sides of a 13-by-9-inch pan with cooking spray. In a large bowl, stir together the dry ingredients—cookie mix, pudding mix, and brown sugar. Add the melted butter, 1 teaspoon of the vanilla, and 1 whole egg until a soft dough forms. Press the dough to cover the bottom and slightly up the sides of the pan (with your spotlessly clean fingers!).

In a separate bowl, beat the cream cheese, sour cream, and sugar with an electric mixer on medium speed until smooth. Add the remaining whole egg, 3 egg yolks, and remaining 1½ teaspoons vanilla; beat until smooth. Spread over the crust in the pan.

Bake 30–35 minutes or until set in the center. Depending on the temperature of your oven, it may take a little longer. Keep checking at 5-minute intervals until the center is no longer wobbly and a knife comes out relatively clean.

Immediately sprinkle the top with the crushed toffee bits. If you can't find toffee bits, use Heath bars. Crush them inside a plastic bag with a rolling pin.

Cool 30 minutes. Refrigerate about 3 hours or until chilled. For bars, cut into 9 rows by 4 rows. Store covered in the refrigerator.

How to Make a Lavender Sachet

I have lots of these in my store, providing a calming aroma for the customers!

Lavender has been used for centuries as a natural moth deterrent and sleep aid.

- Cut the lavender before the purple flowers reach full bloom, which is when the fragrance is strongest. Cut just above the leaves, getting the longest stem possible on the flower.

- Use bunches of no more than six stalks, or they won't dry properly.

- Gather together at the cut ends with a rubber band. A rubber band holds the stems tight while they dry. If you use anything else, the stems will fall out as they shrink.

- Hang upside down in a warm, dry, dark area to preserve the delicate purple color. (If the color doesn't matter, you can set outside in the sun for a day to dry. In the dark, it will take about a week to ten days.) When the bunch feels almost brittle, it's done.

- Remove the dried lavender from the stems. To separate the flowers, place the lavender in a bag or pillowcase and roll over gently with a rolling pin. Pull out the stems and pour the buds into a container. (You can use the stems on a wood fire for a great scent as they burn.)

- Cut some 4-inch fabric squares—two for each sachet. Glue three of the outer edges together, pattern sides facing. Let the glue dry.

- Turn right side out and fill with lavender flowers. Turn the raw edges under and sew closed.

- You can also buy premade organza or drawstring bags from the craft store.

- Place the sachets in closets, drawers, inside your pillowcase, or even in your car.

They also make great gifts!

- Dried lavender will retain its scent for up to one year.

New Uses for Old Sweaters

- Find a nice selection of old wool sweaters at a thrift store or yard sale (at least 80% wool). Try to find ones with interesting patterns or designs.

- Toss them in the washing machine to felt them.

- You have to "shock" the wool, so wash on hot, with cold rinse, on a heavy wash cycle, so there's lots of agitation. Add a few lint-free items such as jeans to help with the agitation and felting.

- Put them in the dryer on high heat. The fibers will shrink into a tight weave. Repeat if necessary to get the desired feel.

- Make a cozy throw pillow. Add 1 inch for seam allowance. Seams can be on the outside, if you like, sewn with a serger, for additional texture and detail.

- Make pocketbooks and mittens from the felted remains. The mittens can have fronts and backs from different colored sweaters. Add a little buttoned flap on top of the hands for a cute, useful touch, and line with polar fleece.

- Or how about a colorful patchwork blanket from all the scraps? Recycle an old bedsheet for the lining. Long-wearing and warm!

- A sweater bag is easy. Make the handles by cutting the neckline out and the sleeves off. Sew up the bottom of the sweater. Turn inside out and fill with stuff.

- Making wine bottle covers out of the sleeves is easy peasy. Simply sew up the cut end, and the cuff end goes around the neck of the bottle, and voilà! Cable sweaters work well for this one.

- The sleeves can be used as leg warmers. Because the wool is felted, it doesn't unravel.

- Or take the sleeves and make a cozy plant cover. Cut the sleeve about two inches higher than the pot and either tuck outside the pot rim or inside and cover with small stones.

- With the leftover pieces, I'll make a stuffed dog toy for Jasper!

Repurposing an Old Sewing Machine Cabinet

I see old sewing machine cabinets priced for a song at yard sales, or even discarded by the side of the road on trash day. They were often made to fit one type of machine, so they don't work for an updated model, but it's a shame to throw them out, because many of them were well-constructed, attractive pieces of furniture made from quality wood.

Why not repurpose and give them a fresh new lease on life? They make great desks or craft tables. Or how about a gift wrap station, a nightstand, a vanity, or a side table?

- First, remove the vintage sewing machine from the cabinet. It may have wing nuts attaching it, or you may need to get to work with a screwdriver.

- Take off the flip-top panel of the cabinet and save the hinges and screws. (Once the weight of the machine is gone, the cabinet may tip over when the panel is in the open position.) Set aside the top panel.

* Measure across the rear edge of the top of the cabinet and replace the hinges so the top panel opens with a front-lift motion. Install a toy chest prop lock.

* Make the hollow interior usable for storage by adding a shelf. Cut a piece of wood to fit and screw to the underside of the cabinet. Now it's a great place to store magazines, a laptop, sewing supplies, or desk accessories.

* Prime and paint.

Some old sewing cabinets already have wheels attached, which makes them great candidates for a rolling bar cart or serving station. For a bar cart, take the top panel off completely and repurpose it into a serving tray. Use the space inside for glasses or plates and utensils. Some cabinets have a metal storage container already installed on the door for machine attachments, or you can install small hooks for bar accessories. A glossy finish on the top is a good idea so it's easy to wipe down and clean.

A vintage treadle sewing machine base makes a great decorative base for any table with its gorgeous detailed iron-work. I've even seen them repurposed for a small kitchen island or bathroom vanity, with space to hold towels under-neath. If you do reuse a treadle machine cabinet, immobilize the pedal as a safety measure. Bolt the pedal to the iron frame, or install a wooden bar across the pedal mechanism to block any movement.

About the Author

Going Through the Notions is Cate Price's debut mystery, the first in a series featuring the proprietor of a small-town vintage notions shop. Cate is hard at work on her second novel. Visit her online at www.cateprice.com.

SUSAN WITTIG ALBERT

WIDOW'S TEARS

After losing her husband, five children, housekeeper, and beautiful home in the Galveston Hurricane of 1900, Rachel Blackwood rebuilt her home, and later died there, having been driven mad with grief.

In present-day Texas, Claire, the grandniece of Rachel's caretaker, has inherited the house and wants to turn it into a bed-and-breakfast. But she is concerned that it's haunted, so she calls in her friend Ruby—who has the gift of extrasensory perception—to check it out.

While Ruby is ghost hunting, China Bayles walks into a storm of trouble in nearby Pecan Springs. A half hour before she is to make her nightly deposit, the Pecan Springs bank is robbed and a teller is shot and killed.

Before she can discover the identity of the killers, China follows Ruby to the Blackwood house to discuss urgent business. As she is drawn into the mystery of the haunted house, China opens the door on some very real danger . . .

susanalbert.com
penguin.com